STRAIGHT GIRLS INITIATED INTO THE LESBIAN HAREM

10 Books of First Time
Lesbian Stories

<u>A.S. Harper</u>

CONTENTS PAGE

SUBMITTING TO KENDRA

Allison

I had no reason to suspect that the hot tub party at my friend's house one night would be anything different to the dozens of other hot tub parties we'd had there before.

Brooke had messaged the group chat and Taylor and I were quick to accept her invitation. To be clear, it's not so much a party as it is my two best friends and I sitting in Brooke's hot tub on her porch, drinking refreshments and gossiping. It may sound like a low-key way to spend a Saturday night in your wild college years, but honestly, it was one of my favorite things to do, especially on a frigidly cold winter's night. We'd normally get into our bikinis, get into the warm water, sit in the bubbles and get a little tipsy. We'd talk about the latest boy that was driving us insane, chat about our favorite reality TV shows and once the water had turned us into human prunes, we'd all go to sleep in Brooke's bed.

After we'd already accepted the invite, Brooke announced she was having a new friend join us. Her name was Kendra and they'd met at the gym a few weeks ago. Taylor apparently had already met Kendra and responded that she was excited to see her again, which vexed me a little as I'd never heard about her before.

Why was Brooke and Taylor hanging out with this new girl without me? Brooke, Taylor and I always did everything together. We'd known each other since high school and all went to the same college, all lost our virginities around the same time, and always went to parties together. Still, I didn't want to come off as rude so I simply said I was looking forward to meeting Kendra and couldn't wait for the night.

Well, night rolled around pretty quickly and I knocked on Brooke's door dead on seven o'clock. Brooke's parents were loaded and they'd bought this cute little house near the campus for Brooke to live in when we came to college. Taylor and I had the opportunity to live there as well but we opted for a more traditional college life, choosing to stay in the dorms instead. Still, we ended up back at Brooke's after most nights anyway, if we weren't off with a guy.

"Allison!" Brooke cheered as she opened the door and gave me a big hug hello. She looked great, although it struck me that she was done up a little much for a hot tub party; she had eyeliner and mascara on, as well as some smokey eye-shadow, really making her green eyes pop. Was she trying to impress Kendra? I felt an irrational pang of jealousy that my friend was so interested in hanging out with someone else. She never tended to care what people thought of her, why was this Kendra woman different?

Brooke led me through to the kitchen where the presumed Kendra was standing at the counter to meet me. Immediately I was taken aback. She was strikingly beautiful. She had big brown, animated princess looking eyes that looked at me from beneath her long lashes. Her cheekbones were high, at either side of an adorable button nose. Her lips were full and luscious and her skin was the most gorgeous shade of light olive. Her long, flowing brown hair cascaded down her shoulders.

She must have had Eastern-European heritage, she looked like she'd come straight to Brooke's house from the shore of some Croatian beach. She was dressed for comfort, with a loose fitting t-shirt and white jeans. Still, she had some knee-high leather boots that added a flair of sexiness to her ensemble. I found myself wondering if she had a body underneath that matched the attractiveness of her facial features.

I'd always been able to admire the beauty of a

woman. We have a poise and gracefulness about us that men lack, and I find it quite enchanting. I only say this because of how secure I am, or was, in my heterosexuality. I'd never felt the urge to date or sleep with a woman before, and in fact while I'd seen Brooke and Taylor make out with girls at parties for attention, I found it a little pathetic, and never partook. It's crazy to think what desires the night ahead would unlock in me, and how they must have always been there, on some level.

Kendra's full lips parted into a smile as Brooke introduced us, her pearly white teeth beaming at me, her face truly was flawless. We exchanged hellos and she shook my hand, her skin as soft as it looked. Brooke poured me a glass and we stood around the kitchen counter while we waited for Taylor to arrive. We made small talk for a few minutes before Taylor's knock was heard. Brooke went to answer the door, leaving me alone in the kitchen with Kendra.

"Brooke never told me she had such beautiful friends! I've met Taylor before and I have to say, you're just as much of a knockout!" Kendra exclaimed.

I thought it was pretty rich coming from her, considering the beauty she exuded. "Oh, you should talk!" I said back. Her comment didn't really strike me as flirtatious, more just polite banter between girls.

"No really, if I had to choose three girls I'd rather spend a night with, wearing little bikinis in a hot tub... I couldn't think of a sexier threesome."

Okay, that comment seemed a bit out there. The way she said it too was kind of sultry and a little pervy. My brow furrowed at the remark and I wasn't sure what I was meant to say in reply. Fortunately I didn't have to figure it out as Taylor burst into the room, a bottle in one hand and her other up in the air.

"C'mon ladies, let's go!" she proclaimed excitedly. "I want to get into the hot tub, it's fucking freezing!"

I had come prepared, with my bathing suit on under my clothes. Brooke and Taylor were similarly prepared but Kendra was not, and Brooke showed her to a nearby bedroom so she could change, leaving the three of us in the living room as we undressed down to our bikinis.

"So, you like her right?" Brooke asked me.

"Kendra? Yeah she seems nice," I half-lied, unsure of what to make about the comment earlier. I made a mental note to tell Brooke and Taylor about it the next day.

"She's really excited to meet you, Allison," Taylor said.

"How do you know her again, Taylor?"

"Oh, we have a class together. She's minoring in history."

That didn't sound right to me. The way Taylor had phrased her message in the group chat implied that her and Brooke had been together with Kendra at some point. And I noticed that Taylor had a similar amount of makeup on as Brooke did, especially around her eyes. Still, she was one of my best friends, and I couldn't think of a reason that she'd lie to me about something that trivial, so I told myself I must have misinterpreted the message and let it go.

Kendra reappeared, now in only her bikini. And well, I had my answer; her body was as stunning as her face. She wore a black bikini with tiny pink flowers patterned across it. The top held her heavy boobs up and pressed against her chest, making her breasts look perfectly round and causing her cleavage to have this seductive, curvy Y shape. Her stomach was taut and I could see the outline of her abdominal muscles. I could see how Brooke met her at the gym because she clearly worked on her body a lot. She wasn't overly muscly by any means, but her arms, stomach and legs were perfectly toned in a very feminine way. Her hips were a little wider than the average woman's and added to her curvaceous but toned physique. Coupled with her flawless olive skin she reminded me of the Greek goddess, Aphrodite.

"This way, ladies," Brooke said as she guided us to the back door.

Kendra walked ahead of me and without meaning to, I immediately looked down at her butt. It was exactly as I had expected. Big and plump, hanging out the sides of her bikini bottoms, which were wedged in between her juicy cheeks. Still, it looked firm and she definitely did as many squats as she did crunches. It was a great ass, but as soon as I realized what I was doing I looked away ashamedly. Not two minutes ago I was thinking she was the pervert and now there I was staring at her ass.

Brooke and Taylor were not lacking in the looks department either, I should make clear. Brooke had blonde hair that was cut short to just above her shoulders. She looked after herself too and rarely a day went by that she wasn't at the gym, so her tight stomach and round butt were on display also. But she lacked the genetic predisposition Kendra had, and her frame was a lot straighter, her boobs a bit smaller in a B-cup and her butt not as large as Kendras. Still, she looked great in her light pink bikini that was held together more by strings than straps, as her body didn't really need much support. Two pink triangles covered her breasts that stayed up on their own, and her bottoms were so thin that they rode up the crack of her ass completely, more of a thong than a bikini.

Taylor was smaller than the rest of us girls, being almost a whole foot shorter than myself. She was always the partying woo-girl who would do what she wanted and eat what she wanted and still magically maintain her petite body. Still, she was graced with a bigger set of tits than her body would dictate, and tonight she housed them in her favourite bikini, which was bright blue with white polka dots all over it and little ruffles at the edges. Her short, thin legs jutted out below her cute little bum as she scurried excitedly towards the hot tub.

We giggled as we scurried across the porch towards the warm water of the tub, seeking refuge from the freezing cold evening air. Mercifully, Brooke had it hot already, and the steam coming off it was visible in the overhead porch lights. Brooke turned on the bubbles and we all refilled our glasses. Brooke and Taylor immediately ducked below the water level, getting their hair wet straight away. They reappeared and slicked their hair behind their ears, their somewhat gratuitous makeup now slightly smudged, which only drew the attention to it more. I did my hair up in a bun, not wanting it to get wet.

It wasn't long before my earlier inhibitions about Kendra were washed away, which was at least in part due to her lively conversation, and I was enchanted by her sultry voice which had just the tiniest hint of a European accent. We each sat against a wall of the hot tub, frequently topping up our glasses and laughing a lot, becoming fast friends. The jets massaged my lower back and shoulders and I was really relaxed, having a great night.

About an hour later the conversation had turned to boys, and Kendra was talking about this guy she'd met at the gym.

"It was late at night, and it was only the two of us still there working out. I was over near the mirrors and doing my squats, with a barbell across the back of my shoulders. I don't know what it was but I felt these eyes watching me, you know that feeling? I looked in the mirror and saw the only other person in the gym, sitting on the leg press, staring directly at my ass."

"Oh that's so creepy, guys can be so gross." I said, fearing where the story was going. Brooke and Taylor stayed silent but looked engrossed in the story, sitting next to each other on the other side of the hot tub.

"Oh, I dunno," Kendra continued, "For some reason it just really turned me on. I found myself putting on a bit of a show for them. I made little grunts with each squat, I stuck my ass out a little more, I was kind of getting off on the attention, controlling their gaze."

"Did he say anything?" I inquired.

"No, just continued to stare for a while until I finished my set and then they got up and went into the shower room."

"So what did you do?" I asked, apparently the only one inquisitive about the story, although certainly not the only one invested, as Brooke and Taylor looked on with wide eyes, completely rapt.

"I followed. I went into the shower room and saw them stark naked under the water and vigorously masturbating to the thought of me."

"Holy shit. Did you run?"

"Hell no, I announced myself and asked what was going on. The awkwardness was hilarious to me," she giggled, remembering fondly her sexual exploits. "I loved having the upper hand on someone and we fucked hard against the wall of the shower. I knew I had control in the situation and that was so hot to me. Any sexual desire I wanted I could have gratified by them. They would completely bend to my will, not only because they were attracted to me, but because I'd caught them, I had leverage against them. I could have any dirty thing I wanted."

This was a lot hotter than our usual boy stories in the hot tub. I was starting to flush red a little. I was feeling flustered but really wanted to know what depraved thing Kendra had made him do to her.

"It turns out, the thing I wanted was to have my breasts pressed against the cold tiled wall, spread my ass cheeks and have them rim me until I came."

Holy shit. This definitely was steamier than our usual conversations. Now I felt the warmth that was in my cheeks flush down to my groin, and a little bit of the sexual excitement made its way to my ass. I'd always been turned on by the thought of rimjobs and butt play. I'd even asked a couple of guys to go down there but they didn't really know what they were doing, and left me more disappointed than satisfied. But the image of the voluptuous Kendra pressed against the shower wall while some guy ate her asshole was extremely sexy to me.

No one said anything for a second, and the silence felt even more deafening as the bubbles turned off. I looked down at the water and thought I saw something weird. I could have sworn I saw Taylor's hand in between Brooke's legs, and she pulled it away as soon as the bubbles dissipated. But I couldn't have. Those were my two best friends, it must have been a trick of the light distorted by the rippling water.

I dismissed the thought and remembered the climax of Kendra's story. "Fuck," I sighed as Brooke stood, turned and bent over to turn the bubbles back on, her bikini still completely ridden up her crack, giving us a full eyeful of her bottom. Another act that struck me as strange, as she could have easily just turned her body and reached the button, instead of pointing her ass at me and Kendra. The night was full of oddities I was struggling to make sense of. It wasn't just the presence of a new person in the group. My friend's were behaving strangely.

"Wow," said Taylor, who had been uncharacteristically quiet throughout the story.

"Yeah I'm pretty sure that is the hottest story I've ever heard," I declared honestly to the group. "I don't have anything that can come close to that."

"Oh, I don't know about that, Allison," Kendra said with her warm, wet voice. "You're a very sexy girl, you must have guys fawning over you and willing to do anything to sleep with you."

"I guess a little, but all of my stories with guys would take place in a bedroom, nothing like a gym shower room."

"What about girls?" she asked.

"What?"

"You don't have any stories with girls? That would certainly qualify as something hot."

"Oh, no. Never actually. I've haven't ever really felt that particular inclination." My eyes were locked onto hers as she questioned me, unable to look away, like she had me in some kind of tractor beam.

"Oh, you should!" Kendra said, seemingly in disbelief that I didn't have any lesbian tendencies. "No man makes you cum quite like a girl can."

"I don't know, I just don't find the idea of it that sexy really."

"You don't find *that* sexy?"

I didn't know what the hell she was talking about, but she raised an eyebrow and cocked her head towards the opposite side of the hot tub. I followed it and my mouth fell open in shock at what I was witnessing. Brooke and Taylor had their tongues down each other's throats! My two best friends were making out, hard. They were both holding each other's heads and devouring each other's faces.

Kendra glided through the water and sat herself directly next to me so that our legs touched. "Tell me you don't find that enticing."

Strangely, a small part of me did. I couldn't quite feel it properly in the moment due to the overriding confusion, but there was something deliciously naughty about seeing my two childhood friends kiss each other so deeply and hungrily. The sight fanned the flame that was already in my crotch from Kendra's steamy story.

Kendra placed a hand on the inside of my thigh and lent over so that her succulent lips were less than an inch away from my ear and she half-whispered, "What if I told you that guy in the gym shower wasn't a guy at all, and it was in fact was your naughty blonde lesbian friend over there who tongued my ass."

The image of Kendra getting her ass eaten in the shower again popped into my head, except now the guy was replaced with Brooke; on her knees in the shower, her short blonde hair wet and slicked back as it was in the hot tub, her hands holding onto Kenda's hips as she forced her tongue up her asshole. The confusion subsided immediately, and the flames in my pussy were now a bonfire of horniness. I don't know if it was more the rimming, or the fact that it was two women, but that was sexy to me. That was *really* sexy to me.

"Well, what do you have to say to that? Does it

turn you on?"

"Yes," I whimpered, barely audible.

"What was that?"

"Yes, that turns me on!"

Kendra turned my head towards her and covered my mouth with her own. My first kiss with a woman. Her lips interlocked with mine and she kissed me tenderly. They were the softest, most luscious lips I'd ever kissed, and I wondered why I had been so opposed to this for so long. Kendra's tongue ran over my lips and I opened my mouth, granting her entry. We kissed as deeply and as passionately as Brooke and Taylor were, our tongues dancing with each other between our mouths.

"Watch your friends," Kendra instructed as she broke the kiss and turned my head back towards my best friends. Brooke had undone Taylors bra at some point, and was now burying her face between Taylor's big tits, who seemed to be enjoying it, as she threw her head back with her eyes closed. Brooke took one of Taylor's breasts in her hand and began flicking at her nipple with her tongue. Brooke's glistening tongue darted up and down against it, causing it to harden, and I felt my own do the same sympathetically, pressing against the inside of my bikini top. Kendra began kissing my neck and shoulders, her arm wrapped around my waist as if to prevent me from escaping.

The thought did cross my mind to push her off me and get the hell out of there. The whole situation was insane. I had a woman kissing my neck while my best friend played with the tits of my other best friend. I had a feeling the lesbian antics weren't going to stop at breast-kissing either. But for some reason that was precisely that feeling that prevented me from leaving. I felt a previously unknown curiosity to see what path the night would take exactly. And I admit the thought of Kendra with my best friends, doing something I wasn't involved in, did give me that pang of irrational jealousy, even when that something was lesbian sex.

The mixture of sexual curiosity and fear of missing out proved too strong. I decided to roll with it and enjoy the exotic woman kissing my neck and two beauties pleasuring each other in front of me.

"Brooke, my dear," Kendra said. "Why don't you eat Taylor's snatch, and make sure your curious friend here can see."

Brooke said nothing but simply obliged. Taylor stood up on the seat of the hot tub, now only dressed in her bikini bottoms, which she promptly slid down her short legs to reveal her smooth, hairless pussy, her little slit visible. This was the first time I'd seen Taylor completely naked. I guess I'd never stopped to admire her body but seeing her like this I realized she was a complete knockout. Her small stature, small butt and yet large breasts earned a lot of attention around campus, and now it earned mine.

She sat down on the edge of the tub, removed her bikini over her feet and spread her legs as wide as she could, her labia peeling open to reveal her pussy inside for me to see. Brooke moved through the water and placed her head at Taylor's opening, pressing her face against the leg farthest from me, ensuring I had an unobstructed view as she started licking up and down Taylor's vagina.

The reaction from Taylor was immediate, moaning in pleasure at the touch of Brooke's tongue against her pussy. The reaction in me was pretty immediate too. I found it really hot, and I could tell that even under the water, my own pussy was wet with arousal. Taylor's pleasure moans seemed to be a cue for Kendra, whose hand I felt delve into my bikini bottoms and straight to my pussy, sliding a finger up and down my moist slit.

It felt amazing. There was something about being touched by another woman that made the act way hotter than the countless times I'd had my pussy rubbed before, like I was rediscovering the joy of it. Of course watching my best friend eat out my other best friend in front of me also helped; this was by far the naughtiest thing I'd ever been a part of.

Brooke continued to eagerly devour Taylor's cunt, focusing her licking and sucking on her clit. Taylor's heavy breasts heaved up and down rhythmically with the deep breaths she was taking in, as she whimpered softly in ecstasy. Kendra focused her attention also, and used her index and ring fingers to spread my lips, her middle finger finding my clitoris with ease. She began to circle it and apply pressure while her mouth made its way to my ear, sucking my lobe and rolling it around in her mouth.

The fire in my groin was about to explode, and I felt the pressure of an orgasm swirling around inside me. I locked eyes with Taylor as her face contorted and I could tell that she too was close. Her tits started heaving a little more uncontrollably and randomly as her stomach muscles contracted over and over, Brooke's short wet blonde hair slicked back against her neck as it must have been when she did this very thing to Kendra's ass.

Taylor's mouth opened and her brow furrowed, her eyes intently on mine while she orgasmed. A deep, primal moan reverberated out of her mouth and the sound of her unrestrained pleasure sent me over the edge. I braced one hand against the side of the tub and the other around Kendra's shoulders as I felt my ass push back against the wall, my leg muscles tensed and I rose out of the water a bit as my own orgasm rocked me. Kendra's finger ground into my clit in circles, eliciting wave after wave of pleasure as I rode the climax in unison with Taylor, still looking into each other's eyes.

My orgasm subsided and I relaxed back down into the hot tub, Kendra removed her hand from my bikini and started planting soft kisses on my cheek while I caught my breath. Opposite me, Taylor had sunk back down into the water, and she started kissing Brooke passionately again, their heads being the only thing above the water, hair wet and makeup running just a little.

"Oh my God," I exclaimed after a minute. "That was crazy, I can't believe that just happened."

"Oh it's far from over, darling," Kendra said. "Two people have cum and only one of us is naked. That hardly seems fair, does it?"

I realized she was right, Taylor was the only one nude, the rest of us still had our bikinis on.

"Do you think that's fair, Brooke?" Kendra asked.

"I don't," Brooke stated in a deadpan sort of way, as if she was being scolded by a superior.

"Why don't you even things up a little then?"

Brooke stood up without hesitation, her groin sitting just above the water's surface. Taylor giggled and kissed at her waist while Brooke undid the string of her light pink bikini top, allowing it to fall away and exposing her lovely, round globes, which of course held perfectly in place even without the aid of the bikini. She tossed the top aside and Taylor undid the string at the side of her bottoms with her mouth, tugging on it and letting it fall a little. She undid the other string and then with her hand reached underneath Brooke from behind, threading between her legs and upwards, gripping the waistline of the bikini as she pulled it down, back through Brooke's legs and then upwards, prying it from it's home between Brooke's ass cheeks. And just like that, I was seeing my other best friend completely nude. Her pussy was also clean shaven, which struck me as odd because I thought Brooke typically liked to keep a trimmed patch of pubes like me, she'd said as much to me in the past.

Brooke looked at me hungrily but when she spoke I knew she was addressing Kendra. "What do you want me to do?"

"Turn around and bend over the side of the hot tub, show us your supple ass," the mysterious Kendra commanded, her voice dripping with arousal.

Brooke once again did as she was instructed, as if she was under some kind of spell, desperate to please Kendra in whatever way she desired. She bent over the side of the tub and poked her butt up, showing her neat, small pucker sitting atop her perfectly shaven, perfectly pink pussy.

Kendra once again spoke to me, "Do you like what you see?"

I nodded my head. I shouldn't have liked what I saw, I was straight after all and this was my best friend of many years, but the sight was undeniably inviting. Seeing Brooke bent over and presenting herself to us so willingly and submissively was incredibly hot.

"Do you think her adorable little asshole deserves to be licked?"

I nodded again. I kind of wanted to be the one doing the licking. I'd never felt that urge before, I guess the thought of doing that to a man was unappealing, but to do it to a woman sounded right to me. I wanted to shove my face in between her firm cheeks and not come out until she was satisfied.

"I'm going to do to your friend as she did to me in the shower of that gym. I'm going to eat her cunt and rim her asshole, just like she was so eager to do to me, and then you'll get your turn. Taylor, why don't you come over here and tell your friend why she should do as I say, just like you two good girls."

Taylor and Kendra swapped sides of the hot tub, and Taylor sat her naked self sideways on my lap, wrapping her arms around my neck and giving me an excited hug. I could feel her bare pussy touching my leg, still slick with cum. Again, the sensation was so naughtily erotic with it being my best friend of so many years. She seemed so casual, as if we'd done this a million times, but it was all wonderfully new for me. Kendra positioned herself at Brooke's rear and seemed to be taking a moment to admire it.

"Oh Allison, I'm so excited we're here," Taylor said to me as I watched Kendra in anticipation. "You *have* to do whatever Kendra tells you to. That's really all there is to it. She will open your eyes to a whole new world of sex you didn't even know existed," she spoke with glee.

Kendra decided it was time for her to lick Brooke. Her tongue started at Brooke's clit, made its way through her slit and continued over her asshole to the top of her crevice. Brooke squealed in delight, arching her back as the olive-skinned beauty used her mouth to please her.

"Brooke only introduced me to her first because she thought I would be more open to it than you, and that the two of us doing it would convince you to join in," Taylor continued as I half-listened, my eyes glued to the sight in front of me. Kendra had her face buried in Brooke's vagina, who was looking out over the side of the hot tub and breathing heavily. "I had no idea the kind of orgasms I could have from my ass being played with, but Kendra's tongue and fingers will certainly get you there. If you give yourself over to her control, she will make you cum harder than you ever have before. She only asks that you follow her commands and look pretty for her at all times, so makeup is a must."

"Uh-huh" I replied.

"Oh and you'll have to wax your pussy."

"What? Wax my pussy?"

"Yeah, I know you like to keep a bit down there but it's her first command. She's the only one who's allowed pubic hair, if you want to join me and Brooke and be one of her good girls, you have to wax. Shaving isn't enough, it's got to be perfectly smooth. No stubble."

I might need a little convincing on that, I thought. But a strong case was certainly being made in front of me. Kendra's face had gone from being buried in Brooke's snatch to being buried in her ass. Her tongue worked around the hole and her saliva ran down the crack, where it joined with the wetness of Brooke's pussy and dripped below into the steamy water. I thought it was the single sexiest sight I'd ever seen. I loved the thought of anal play and watching it being done to my friend by Kendra's expert tongue was intensely arousing.

"You're going to find out soon enough how good that feels," Taylor giggled in my ear.

"I've had my ass licked before," I retorted, I wasn't a prude like she was suggesting.

"I meant doing the licking," Taylor corrected. "It's so hot giving someone pleasure in such a naughty way, especially when the ass you're doing it to is as juicy as Kendra's or as round and firm as Brooke's."

"So you've eaten both?"

"Oh yeah, like I said, Brooke introduced me to Kendra. It was when you had gone back home to visit your parents. Brooke invited me over to hang out and when I got there Kendra was waiting for me. They turned the conversation to lesbian sex and I admitted I'd always been curious. It didn't take much to get me to agree to cumming over and over at the mouths and hands of two women that look like that. I masturbate to the thought of Kendra seducing Brooke in the shower just about every other day... Kendra spreading her juicy ass cheeks for Brooke to sink her tongue into."

I felt the warm feeling shoot to my bottom

again. The image certainly was hot. As was the one of Brooke starting to move her rump back and forth against Kendra's face before my eyes.

Abruptly, Kendra stopped, denying Brooke her orgasm. She floated through the water away from Brooke's posterior, and traced around the bottom of her mouth with a finger, collecting all of Brooke's valuable cum off her chin before sucking it off her finger.

"Allison, darling," she said softly but authoritatively, "It's time for you to become one of my good girls and eat your friend's ass until she cums."

Taylor squealed excitedly and squeezed my shoulders. She was giddy at the thought of my initiation, and to see me lick Brooke's butt. She climbed off my lap and whispered in my ear, "Just go with it. You'll love it, I promise."

I made my way through the water to the other side of the hot tub where Brooke's firm derriere was waiting. The short swim across the small hot tub seemed like a lap in an olympic sized pool, as adrenaline flushed my brain, my neurons firing rapidly as I tried to figure out if this was something I really wanted to do. Brooke made some stepping motions with her feet, causing her ass to wiggle a little bit for me, her wet butthole in the centre of her glistening, round butt cheeks as they raised and lowered like a seesaw.

"Please, Allison," she begged, "The only way I can cum is with your tongue in my ass."

That did it. I felt the familiar tingling shoot to my own butthole and my loins were on fire again. Brooke looked so fucking sexy and submissive in front of me with her ass presented for my consumption. I wanted to do this, I wanted to do this really badly. Kendra placed a gentle hand on my back and with a light push, guided me to Brooke's back door. I placed a hand on each of her cheeks, and gave them a squeeze. Brooke moaned approvingly. I stared at her asshole for one last moment before I put my mouth up to it and extended my tongue, laying it flat against her pucker and licking up. Brooke moaned louder this time, apparently I did something right.

"Good girl," Kendra said softly from behind me as she stroked the back of my neck. "Keep going."

I did as I was told, not that I needed the instruction. I eagerly licked Brooke's asshole again and again with my wet tongue. Brooke's groaning continued with every lick, encouraging me to do more. I started moving my tongue around in circles, rimming her ring of muscle. The feeling of having my face between her ass cheeks and causing her this amount of pleasure was absolutely intoxicating to me, I was getting really wet just by giving it to her. I grabbed her by the cheeks with my hands again, spreading them apart as far as I could, and I sunk my tongue into her hole. Brooke just about screamed in ecstasy and her asshole relaxed to let my tongue in, pushing as hard as I could.

I heard the familiar sounds of Taylor's orgasm from behind me. She must have been receiving some pleasure of her own from Kendra, I knew she would be loving the sight of me tonguing Brooke's ass. I wanted to turn around and see what Kendra was doing to her, but I couldn't bring myself to take my face out of Brooke's delectable butt. I withdrew my tongue from Brooke's bottom and rammed it back in again easily, using my neck muscles to rock my head back and forth, allowing me to truly tongue-fuck her.

"Oh fuck!" Brooke cried out as her orgasm arrived. Her head dropped down and her back curved, pushing her ass higher up and into me. I grabbed her by the hips and with one last insertion drove my tongue as deep as it could reach inside her. Her legs quivered as she came, and the muscles of her asshole pulsed rapidly around my tongue. It felt fucking amazing to be doing this to someone, to be completely smothered by a girl's ass, licking her most private area. I got excited at the thought that my anal desires for myself would soon be finally realized. I'd just imagined that they'd be at the tongue of another woman.

Brooke collapsed to her knees on the seat of the hot tub, causing my tongue to slide out of her ass. She didn't turn around, but rested her head on her folded arms, collecting herself and enjoying the afterglow of her climax, not ready to address anyone yet.

I turned around and saw Taylor sitting in Kendra's lap, both of them facing us. Taylor's head was pushed back and flushed red, a blank affect on her face, her heavy tits bobbing just above the surface of the water as she sucked in lungfuls of air. Kendra's hand was reaching around her waist and presumably playing with her pussy beneath the surface, my view obstructed by the bubbles. Like our blonde friend, Taylor was trying to collect herself after her climax. Kendra just looked at me with a knowing, satisfied grin on her face. I guess this meant I was one of her good girls now.

"I think it's only fair that you get your ass eaten too, darling. Which one of your friends would you like to do that?"

I really wanted her to do it, but that didn't seem like an option right now. "Well, I think Brooke is a little indisposed right now," I answered, as I wasn't sure Brooke hadn't passed out from pleasure.

"Your friend will do anything I tell her to do. If

that means shaking herself out of her post-cum haze and face-fucking your ass, then that's what she'll do."

Wow, Kendra really did have control over them. I could see why though, in my so far brief foray into being one of her good girls I had experienced the naughtiest, sexiest acts of my life, and I was loving it. "I think I'd like to start with Taylor," I said, taking mercy on Brooke.

Taylor's face looked giddy again. "Yay," she said, "I've been wanting to go down on you for weeks now!"

"What should I do?" I asked, unsure of the best way to please Kendra.

"First, you're going to need to take that bikini off."

I was the one obliging now, standing up out of the water and untying my bathing suit, tossing them aside. I instinctively wrapped my arms around my breasts to shield them from Kendra and Taylor's gaze.

"No, put your arms to your sides," Kendra commanded, her expression remained the same but Taylor had gone from looking giddy to hungry.

Again, I obliged and put my arms to my sides, showing off my generous bosom and trimmed pubes hovering above the water.

"Those will have to go," Kendra said, motioning towards my pubes. "I like my girls smooth."

I nodded hesitantly. I did like to keep some pubic hair down there, it made me feel like my own woman, but I guess stripping me of that was kind of the point. Still, I wasn't sure if I'd do it.

"Taylor, honey, why don't you go and sit in that seat over there and put your head back on the edge of the hot tub, looking up at the ceiling." Taylor did so happily. "Now Allison, you climb up on top of her and straddle her face with your pussy."

Wow, that was not what I expected. But I probably should have. I decided I was game, it was a night of new experiences after all. There was no way Taylor could get to my asshole from that position but I trusted in Kendra and knew we'd get there eventually. I placed one knee to the side of Taylor's eager face, and pushed off the floor of the hot tub to place my other knee on the other side. Mercifully there was a porch post within reaching distance so I could steady myself, and I thought our position must have been by Kendra's design, she definitely had a plan. I looked down at Taylor's sweet face, who met my gaze, her eyes pleading with me to let her eat me out. I granted her wish and lowered my muff onto her open mouth.

Taylor wasted no time getting to work on my pussy, and it felt amazing. Her head rocked back and forth as her protruded tongue licked my slit from base to top, messily licking every inch she could. Her face looked angelic as I watched her, my trimmed pubes sitting above her nose while I grinded my snatch harder against her mouth. My heavy breaths were visible in the night air and my nipples were hard enough to cut glass from the combination of the cold night and the pure eroticism of face-fucking one of my best friends. Taylor was moaning in appreciation of my pussy as she continued to lick up and down, my juices already spilling down her chin and cheeks.

I was not sure what Kendra was doing throughout all of this, with my back turned to the rest of the tub. I'm sure she was enjoying the show though, from her angle she would have seen my tight backside tensing as I ground it against Taylor's face, Taylor's hands holding onto my thighs and her gorgeous tits bobbing up and down in the water in synchronization with the movements of her head.

The bubbles stopped. The hum of the hot tub ceased and I suddenly realized how loud I was moaning in the silent air. I became a little self-conscious and stopped, taking me out of the moment briefly. I could hear Kendra talking softly behind me, presumably to Brooke, unable to hear what she was saying. Taylor was not dissuaded by the sudden quietness and kept devouring my pussy. I heard the movement of water and Kendra knelt on the bench next to Taylor. She placed her hand on the back of my neck and whispered into my ear.

"Lean forward and hold onto the pole in front of you for support. Bend all the way down."

I did as I was told without saying a word, making myself almost horizontal, sure to fall over if not for the post. The action meant I could no longer get a good grinding motion on Taylor's face, nor even see her face. It also meant my ass was raised a little into the air, and my bottom spread apart unassisted as I bent, exposing my asshole to the night. Not three seconds later I felt a tongue on my back door. The reaction was instantaneous. It felt incredible and I almost lost my balance and fell over the side from the unexpected bliss I was feeling in my ass. I wondered if it was Kendra's tongue or Brooke's, either way it knew what it was doing.

"Oh that's so fucking sexy seeing my girls please each other like this," Kendra said, confirming that it was in fact Brooke who had come out of her sex coma to give me the rimjob I was so desperate for. The crisp winter air was cold on my whole body, but the warm tongues in my pussy and ass had lit a fire inside me that made me sexually charged and hotter than the sun.

Brooke's soft, slippery tongue slithered inside my butthole in between long licks around it. Taylor focused her efforts on my clit, putting pressure on it and swirling her tongue around. Kendra watched the scene unfold before her. The heavenly feeling caused my concerns about noise to dissipate, and I returned to moaning deeply, not that I could stop myself if I wanted to. I once again imagined how it looked from behind, with me bent over, Brooke straddling Taylor and burying her tongue in my ass while the petite girl below her nibbled at my clit, their nipples brushing against each other with their movements. The thought of Kendra watching us made something snap and I felt my climax begin.

I came with the most spectacular orgasm I'd ever experienced. I let out a long cry of pleasure and my muscles flexed against the post, pushing my ass further back against Brooke's tongue, I felt my hole automatically relax for a brief moment, sucking the pink tongue further into it, before the sexual energy smashed into the front wall of my pussy, and I came all over Taylor's face. The two of them made muffled groans of appreciation into me which paled in comparison to my own scream of nirvana. My abdominal muscles spasmed and my back arched uncontrollably as if an electric shock was running through my spine. The fantasies I'd had of cumming while being rimmed had finally come true, and the fact that someone was sucking on my clit at the same time was just icing on the previously unimaginable cake.

We all untangled from one another and I slid back into the warmth of the hot tub. My pussy tingled as it hit the heated water and sent a little aftershock up to my head, my hips quivering. I leaned back and sighed in approval at what had just happened. Brooke and Taylor sat to either side of me with big smiles on their faces, happy to have me in their little club. And I was happy to be there. Following Kendra's commands and playing out whatever sexual ideas came to her mind only made the whole night all the hotter. Although it occurred to me that she was still sitting on the opposite side of the hot tub, the only one not naked and the only one not to cum yet.

"I believe that makes it my turn, girls," she said, and she submerged herself completely in the water, only to reappear in the middle of the hot tub, standing up in front of us, her black bikini with pink flowers still on, her long hair now wet and pushed behind her ears. She reached around behind her and unclasped her bikini top, letting it fall away into the water below. Her breasts were larger than any of ours, and they hung just a little lower without the support of the bikini. They adorned the full breadth of her chest and two lovely, erect nipples pointed at us.

She bent down and pulled her bottoms down, stepping out of them beneath the water, revealing her gorgeous snatch which sat below a thick tuft of dark pubic hair, which covered everything north of her clitoris, but was completely absent below. It was trimmed but long enough for there to be some curls, and it looked absolutely divine and womanly.

She really was the image of Aphrodite, the most feminine woman I'd ever laid eyes on. Brooke and Taylor came off the seat, kneeling down on the floor of the tub, glaring at Kendra adoringly. I felt compelled to do the same and the three of us knelt there, our shoulders poking out above the water, looking up at our goddess.

Kendra stepped forward and bent down to kiss Brooke to one side of me, holding her chin in her hand. She did the same to Taylor on the other side of me before it was my turn. She took my chin and we kissed. I felt compelled to please her and give her an orgasm like she had just done for all of us. That was the power Kendra had. We wanted to serve her.

She broke the kiss and straightened, and the hand on my chin moved to the hair on the back of my head. Kendra parted her legs a little and pulled my head forward towards her groin. I didn't have to be told what to do. My mouth was open and tongue out before she'd guided my head the full way, and I took her pussy into my salivating mouth with great enthusiasm. Her sex tasted magnificent, and I lapped up every drop of cum that I could get off of her cunt. I lovingly licked up and down and sucked gently on her clit. I heard the sounds of Brooke and Taylor rising to each side of me and I looked up, through her womanly pubes, to see Brooke passionately kissing her and Taylor flicking one of her nipples with her tongue.

I reached around and held Kendra's bountiful butt cheeks in my hands, using them to pull her groin forward and giving me better access to her pussy. Her hand came down and grabbed one of mine by the wrist, where she guided it between her ass cheeks, she took my middle finger and placed it on her asshole, pushing it around in circles to stimulate her opening. Her hand moved away and I continued, applying light pressure to her hole with the pad of my finger while I circled it around and around. I couldn't stop looking up at the way her body sensually gyrated to the movements of me in her groin, Taylor on her chest and Brooke on her face and neck.

Even when Kendra came, she did it with grace. Her orgasm wasn't the vigorous spasming of muscles as mine had been, but her knees bent, willing my face to go harder into her sex, and I inserted just the very tip of my finger into her ass. I saw her bite Brooke's bottom lip and her brow crease in ecstasy. As she shuddered preciously in the arms of her loyal concubines, her cum dripped down the side of my face and into my thirsty mouth. I loved giving this heavenly creature pleasure, and I loved submitting to her sexual will in whatever way she desired.

After drying each other off and giggling with glee at each other's naked bodies, I was still in disbelief that what had just happened, had in fact happened. The night ended much the same way our other hot tub party nights did, with us curled up in Brooke's bed. Only this time there were four of us, and we were all naked and cuddling each other.

I woke up the next morning and Kendra was already gone. Brooke and Taylor were still fast asleep and I didn't want to wake them just yet. I put on my pyjamas that were as yet unworn and made my way out to the kitchen in search of coffee or Kendra. She was nowhere to be found, but there was a folded note on the kitchen counter. It read:

Allison, my darling. You were such a good girl last night and I had a fantastic time watching you and your friends pleasure one another. Rest assured, I will see you again soon. Make sure next time you look the part of one of my girls. Brooke and Taylor can fill you in, should you need. I have big plans for us, and there will be plenty more curious girls to taste. Until next time my darling, Kendra.

I smiled to myself in the kitchen, a warm, fuzzy feeling in my tummy at the thought of serving Kendra more. I was going to have to book a waxing appointment.

THE END

THE LESBIAN THEORY

Aubrey

"I think my roommate might be a lesbian," I said to my friend, Laura.

She almost spat out her sip of coffee at the statement, which had admittedly come out of nowhere. She looked around the cafe to see if anyone had heard me. "No way!" she replied, "She's too pretty, too feminine. There's no way she's not with a new gorgeous hunk of a man every other night."

"You can fuck girls and still be feminine, Laura."

"Would you keep it down? Someone's gonna hear you."

"So what, we're in a college cafe, most of the people here have probably fucked a girl in the last week, and I'm including all the women in here."

"Oh yeah, that includes you, does it?" Laura

retorted.

"I guess not. But that's not to say I haven't thought about it."

"Really?" Laura scrunched up her face in excited disbelief, "You want to... you know... with a girl?"

"I mean it is college, right? We're already a year in and it's meant to be one of the defining moments of the whole experience. Experimenting with girls, copious amounts of partying, an education somewhere in between that. What, you've never wanted to?"

"Aubrey! Never!" Laura always was something of a prude. She'd sleep with guys she went on a few dates with, but never hook up at a party, and never tell me any details. I suppose I didn't really expect a different answer. "What makes you think she's a lesbian anyway? Have you seen her making out with a girl or something?"

"Well, no... not exactly. But she's always going out; she says with her girlfriends. And she often has this one girl over at night, but I go to bed before she does, so I'm not sure if the friend leaves or stays the night."

"That's your evidence? That she spends time with her friends?"

"It doesn't sound like much when I say it out

loud, but I don't know, it's just a feeling when I'm around the two of them."

"There's no way."

"There's not *no* way!" Just then my phone buzzed. I looked down and saw a message from her! My heart skipped a beat. Could she have heard me somehow? Had someone in the cafe overheard us and texted her? I read the message and relaxed.

"Well someone's ears must have been burning," I said to Laura. "She just texted me, she says her friend is coming over tonight and they want to watch a movie."

"*The* friend?"

"One and the same. I bet they're going to have hot lesbian sex afterwards!" I said a touch too loud, trying to embarrass Laura.

"Jesus, Aubrey!" It worked. "Maybe you should hide in the closet to see if you're right and then join them if it'll get this apparent lesbian obsession out of your head."

She meant it teasingly, but the idea didn't sound so bad. Of course, I didn't know how kindly they'd take to me watching them. And this was all pure speculation; what if I was wrong, how would I get out of there or explain myself? Still, I wanted to keep mocking Laura's timidness.

"Maybe I will, and maybe it'll be the best sex I've ever had!"

Laura looked at me with an unamused look. "I have to go," she announced. It was a little earlier than I knew she had to but she'd had enough of my lesbian talk.

"All right, I'll message you later?"

"Yeah sure. Have fun having sex with Kendra and her friend!" Again, she meant it teasingly, but part of me hoped that with some fantastic sequence of events my night would somehow end up exactly there.

+++

After a few hours studying in the library, I headed home to mine and Kendra's apartment just off of campus. We'd been living together for a few months now. I'd initially been staying in the dorms, but I had issues adjusting to a lot less space than I was used to. Coupled with the fact that I didn't get along with my roommate very well, I wasn't having a good time. So I decided to look for a room in the surrounding areas, and found an ad online posted by Kendra. The apartment was spacious and after meeting Kendra and getting along with her great, I jumped on it. Kendra was also stunningly beautiful and I had hoped she would bring in a parade of good looking guys through the apartment, but so far there was only the occasional girlfriend coming over to hang out.

I opened the door and found Kendra standing in the kitchen, chewing on a peach. She swallowed and beamed a big grin at me. God, she really was stunning. Her full, pouty lips were her best feature in my opinion, although most guys would probably say her plump, juicy ass. Her wavy hair fell down just below her shoulders and it was the same shade of light brown as her eyes. I thought if I ever was to sleep with a woman, I would be lucky for it to be her.

"Oh, hi Kendra. Nice peach?"

"Oh yeah, the best. Hey it's still all right to have a friend over to watch a movie tonight, yeah?"

"Of course, I'm out tonight anyway."

"Party on campus?"

"No, a date actually."

"Really? Are you excited?"

"Not really, just some guy from class who asked me out and I was horny enough to say yes."

Kendra's lips formed the cutest little grin as she giggled, "It's a sure thing then?"

"I wouldn't say a sure thing, but I think so. I'll make it so I'm irresistible," I said with sarcastic confidence.

"Oh, I don't doubt it. If you want to absolutely drive him wild though, you should shave your pussy completely, that really would be irresistible for him."

Kendra and I often talked freely about slightly risque subjects, one of the many things I couldn't do with my previous roommate. "I haven't done that in a while, but maybe I will. Although I should think if we get to that point then sex is already most certainly happening."

"You just tell him half way through the date that you're bare down there, then it's all he'll think about for the rest of the night."

"That's a little forward, but brilliant."

"Well, feel free to bring him back here. Just keep it down," she said as she winked at me.

I took myself off to my wing of the apartment and climbed in the shower to prepare myself for the evening's promised relief of my horniness. It occurred to me that that was why I kept talking about the lesbian theory, I was just horny and needed any kind of release. I decided to take Kendra's advice and shaved my pubes completely. It had been a couple of years since I'd seen my pussy as smooth as it was, and it did give me a certain confidence, knowing that I had this little secret in my panties that only I, and Kendra, knew about. I washed myself from top to toe and paid good attention to cleaning my asshole. I definitely wanted to get my pussy eaten and I always worried any smell might turn the guy off, or give him an excuse not to go down on me. I finished up and put on my makeup in the mirror, taking care to do it right and make myself look as hot as possible. I dressed in a short denim skirt and a tight red top with ample cleavage to show off my breasts.

I went into the living room and found Kendra in a new outfit, sitting on the couch on her phone. She wore an orange blouse that showed off her own cleavage, which was much more impressive than mine. I'd think she was trying to look good for someone except that she just had an ordinary pair of jeans to go with it. She saw me emerge from my bedroom and wolf whistled, "Wow, you really do look irresistible!"

I blushed a little at the comment, "I hope so! I've been needing a good dick for a couple of weeks now."

"Well I'm sure tonight you could get whatever you wanted." she said as her phone buzzed. "Brooke's here! I gotta go let her in."

"You can't just buzz her in?"

"Oh no, she always uses the back door. It's just easier from the parking lot."

"Fair enough. Actually, would you mind if I joined you guys for a little while, I'm a bit early for my date."

"Of course, no problem, we're just going to watch a movie and maybe go grab some dinner."

"Sounds good to me," I said as she left the apartment to go and collect Brooke. I realized they were no ordinary pair of jeans as she walked out the door. Her ass looked absolutely incredible in them. Her big round cheeks filled them out so nicely and reminded me of my unshakeable horniness.

I felt a bit peckish and still had a while before dinner so I looked around the apartment for a snack. I found a peach in the fruit bowl and having seen Kendra enjoying one earlier made me want it. I sunk my teeth into it and sucked at it's flesh. Kendra was right, it was really good. I'm not normally one for eating peaches but I found myself really enjoying it.

The door swung open and Kendra and Brooke made their way in. Brooke was looking gorgeous as always. No matter what the occasion, whenever I saw her she was made up perfectly with eyeliner and smokey eyeshadow. Tonight was no exception as I hugged her hello and told her how pretty she looked. It was girly politeness but I did mean it, she looked good in a tight, shiny white top that was almost see through and equally as tight black, faux leather pants. I could tell she wasn't wearing a bra underneath her top as the straps would definitely be visible if she were. Not that she needed it, Brooke had smallish breasts and kept her body tight, I had no doubt that her boobs would be pert without anything supporting them.

"You look amazing," she said back to me as she looked me up and down.

"Aubrey's going on a date tonight and she's hoping to get laid," Kendra interjected.

"Well I'm sure you won't have any problems with that!" Brooke said politely.

"Did you do that thing I said to make it a certainty, Aubrey?" Kendra winked at me.

I shot her a friendly look as if to say *not in front of Brooke*, and Kendra just giggled at me, I think she'd gotten her answer.

"Shall we watch the movie?" Brooke asked the group.

"Let's," Kendra said.

While we sat and watched the film together, the lesbian theory ran through my head again. I tried to look for clues, seeing if they would touch each other, seeing how they would look at each other. But there was nothing that suggested anything sexual between them. One thing I did notice though was Kendra being a little bossy. She wouldn't ask, but rather tell Brooke to go and get her a drink from the fridge, and Brooke gladly would, despite it not even being her home. It struck me as odd, but certainly not sexual.

I had resigned myself to the fact that I must have been wrong, which strangely made me feel disappointed. Then, as the climax of the movie was going on, Kendra got up to go to the bathroom, and Brooke's head followed. Instead of watching the end of the movie she was staring directly at Kendra's butt swaying in those fantastic jeans as she walked off. It was definitely what she was doing. It wasn't just a quick glance in Kendra's direction, she stared for the whole distance between the couch and the door. My suspicions reignited, and I smiled a little at the thought that maybe there was something going on after all.

The movie ended and we all talked about how disappointing it was, thankfully it was relatively short.

"Well, Brooke and I are gonna head out for some dinner I think," Kendra announced.

"I should probably be going too," I said, contemplating following them covertly to see how they acted without my presence. "I just have to touch up my makeup and get a jacket. I'll see you guys later though!"

"Have fun on your date," Brooke said with a cheeky grin, "I hope you get some."

On their way out Kendra turned to me and said, "You'll thank me later, trust me," referring to my newly hairless pussy. She shut the door behind her before I could retort.

I went back into my bathroom and looked at the mirror when all of a sudden the thought popped into my head. What Laura said before, about hiding in the closet to prove once and for all if they were fucking. She'd said it in jest, and I'd dismissed it as impossible, but here I was with the perfect opportunity. They were out to dinner, and when they returned to an empty house they'd just think I was on my date. They would have no idea I was in the closet watching them.

No. It was crazy. Brooke just stared at her ass, that doesn't mean anything, Kendra has a great ass! I stared at it earlier and I'm not a lesbian! I wasn't going to stand in my roommate's closet for some untold number of hours in the hope that they'd come home, make love and then wait for them to fall asleep so I could make my escape. Still, I was really curious. Not only to put the lesbian theory to the test, but to see if I liked what I saw.

I stood there for a good few minutes contemplating the notion. It was either guaranteed dick, or the slim chance that I got to watch two women fuck each other, and maybe finger myself to the thought of it later if it turned me on. "Fuck it", I thought. I had to know. I texted my date to cancel and made my way into Kendra's room, hiding myself in her closet and surveying the room from between the slats of the doors, which fortunately gave me an excellent view of the bed.

I sat in the dark closet and waited, trying not to talk myself out of it. This was crazy, this was wrong. I was spying on my roommate in the hope of catching her fucking another woman. Still, that was exactly the reason I wanted to stay; I wanted to see for myself, I wanted to know if I liked it. My indecision was soon made irrelevant by the sound of the front door opening, and I heard Kendra and Brooke talking in the living room. There was no turning back now, I was here, and I wasn't getting out of it. I silently prayed that I would somehow get away with the wild scheme.

Their voices were slightly muffled outside of Kendra's bedroom, but I could still mostly make out what they were saying.

"Aubrey?" Kendra called. My heart just about skipped a beat. How the fuck had she known I was still here, she wasn't even in the room!

"Aubrey, are you still here?" she continued. Oh thank God, I hadn't been found out, she was just seeing if I was still home.

"She must have gone," Brooke said.

"I guess. I wonder if she'll bring that guy home. She did look hot as fuck in that red top," Kendra said.

"Yeah, her tits looked delicious."

I sat in the closet, admittedly a little flattered that they were talking about my looks so nicely. Although I thought delicious was a little bit of a strange word to use, not the kind of word you'd use in the usual girly politeness.

They fell silent. I wondered why they weren't talking and then heard the faint sounds of whispering, impossible to hear from my vantage point in the closet. Silence again. This was weird.

"I'm going to the bathroom," Brooke said. She entered Kendra's bedroom and walked straight past the door I was hiding behind. My heart pounded as I hoped she wouldn't see me, or think to look in the closet for whatever reason. As she walked past I could see her tight, white top again, hugging her slim figure and showing the outline of her breasts and drawing my attention to something unexpected.

Her nipples were erect! Her little bolt-on nipples were standing to full attention underneath the revealing fabric. I flushed red at the sight of something I shouldn't be privy to, even if it was just Brooke's nipples poking through her top. My voyeurism gave me a pang of guilt, at how wrong it all was, as well as a pang of lust, at how naughty it all was.

I heard water running from Kendra's bathroom and then the door opened as Brooke presumably reemerged, out of my line of sight. Only she didn't walk past the door this time. Was she just standing there? Why wouldn't she go back to the living room?

"Walk to the end of the bed," I heard Kendra's voice from somewhere near the opposite doorway. I was frustrated at not being able to see what was going on as I had a good view of a majority of the room, yet both of them were in blind spots.

Brooke appeared then in my field of vision, stopping at the end of the bed just like Kendra told her to. She just stood there, not moving, her nipples still hard as diamonds. What the hell was going on?

"Your ass looks superb in those pants, honey, but I'm going to have to insist you take them off now. Face the bathroom," Kendra said.

Holy shit. Did I just hear that right? Brooke turned around and bent down as she lowered her faux leather pants. They were so tight she had to peel them down, revealing her bare ass to Kendra and unknowingly, me. She stepped out of her pants and tossed them to the corner as she stood up, naked from the waist down. She really did have a great butt, it was so tight and pert and held exactly in place. She definitely worked on it a lot at the gym. I shook my head as the reality of the situation dawned on me. I was right after all! They were about to fuck. This was all part of their foreplay and they were about to have lesbian sex for my spying eyes to witness.

I felt a little light-headed as I processed the way the evening was turning out. I was looking at a bottomless blonde who was apparently the lesbian sex object of my roommate, and I was stuck in the closet with no choice but to watch it all and wait for them to fall asleep so I could get out without being caught. The series of escalations that were bound to take place seemed especially voyeuristic now that I had my suspicions proven. Right now, Brooke had no pants on. Soon enough, she and Kendra would be naked, kissing, licking each other's vaginas and doing God knows what else while I watched them. I felt a little disgusted with myself that I ever thought this was a good idea, and cursed Laura for putting such an idea in my head in the first place.

"God that ass looks delicious," Kendra said. There's that word again, *delicious*, it's most certainly in a sexual context this time. "Turn around and let me see your cunt."

Wow, Kendra certainly was being commanding. Brooke turned and I saw a neat slit at the bottom of her groin, she was completely clean shaven down there just as I had recently become. With how tight her top was, and her nipples poking through, she may as well have been naked. It was a stunning body. Perfectly toned while still looking very much like a woman. Her thin, narrow frame led all the way up to her pretty face with her short blonde hair bobbing to and fro above her shoulders. If I had to watch two women have sex, I could certainly do a lot worse than Brooke and Kendra.

Kendra appeared in my field of vision for the first time since I hid myself in her closet. She gracefully stalked her way across the floor of her bedroom to meet Brooke at the end of the bed. She held Brooke's pretty little face in her hands and kissed her, passionately, softly. There was no sound apart from the wet sounds of their tongues and mouths intertwining, and I realized that my breathing was getting a little heavier, my eyes a little wider, and my hands a little shakier as I watched the two women embrace. Kendra's hands made their way around to

Brooke's bare bottom and she squeezed, causing Brooke to stand on her tiptoes as they kept kissing. Brooke's feet fell flat again and I saw one of Kendra's hands move to the middle of Brooke's ass. She placed her middle finger between the cheeks and moved it up and down Brooke's crack, her finger snug between her lesbian lover's ass cheeks.

I realized my pussy was a little warm at the sight of the two of them. I could feel a hint of wetness in my lace underwear and I was decidedly liking what I saw. Although at that point I wasn't sure how much could be attributed to the fact that they were women, and how much can be attributed to the fact that I was secretly watching two lovers being intimate with each other.

Kendra broke the kiss and placed her hands on Brooke's hips. She turned her and with a push, forced her hips down onto the edge of the bed. "Spread your legs," she said and Brooke obeyed, spreading them as far as she possibly could and giving me an unobstructed view of her crotch. Her labia peeled open to reveal a neat, inviting, pink pussy; a little hood at the top covering her clitoris, her vulva just the slightest shade of red in excitement and the whole thing glistening a little with wetness.

Kendra got down on all fours in front of

her, blocking my view with her long, wavy hair. Interestingly, I felt a little disappointed at the thought of not being able to see properly, and as I still tried to figure out whether I had any lesbian inclinations, I put that feeling in the plus column. Just then, Kendra flicked her hair over to one shoulder, and moved her head slightly, and I could see! I could see Brooke's pussy on display and Kendra's face right next to it. My disappointment melted away and was replaced with excitement to see exactly how Kendra pleased her lover.

Kendra opened her mouth and placed it over the top of Brooke's pussy, making a gentle sucking motion on Brooke's hood and clit. This elicited a moan from Brooke, who closed her eyes and tilted her head back, pushing her still clothed chest forward. Kendra started licking up Brooke's slit with precision, her strong tongue gathering the wetness from Brooke's vagina and spreading it across her whole pussy. She would periodically stop licking and place gentle little kisses on Brooke's vulva and inner thighs, allowing her a reprieve from the onslaught of pleasure. I could feel myself getting a bit wetter underneath my skirt, another sensation for the plus column.

The sight was so erotic to me from the protection of the closet. Brooke's flushed face and creased forehead as she tried to keep her eyes open and watching Kendra, her heaving tits below her with just a thin layer of fabric separating her chest from my gaze, her legs spread wide apart with Kendra's face between them, whose wavy hair bounced up and down according to what she did with her tongue in Brooke's snatch.

Kendra began to focus her oral efforts exclusively on Brooke's clit, and the redness in Brooke's face deepened a little. I knew what was coming; it was about to be Brooke. It was rare for me to feel my own face flushing red like that when I was with a guy, and in that moment, I felt the inescapable urge to have Kendra's tongue on my own pussy, doing to me everything she did to Brooke. I wanted to have lesbian sex. And I wanted to have it with my beautiful roommate.

Brooke inhaled sharply and held her breath in, her mouth and eyes open wide, suddenly silent. She looked towards the closet and for a moment I thought she was looking at me, but she was just staring into space as the energy of her orgasm was about to break through. I saw her abdominal muscles vibrate beneath her white top as she let out a loud moan, her legs uncontrollably came together and clasped Kendra's head between them like a vice. Her orgasm looked fucking amazing to me. I was really jealous of her then. It continued on for a lot longer than any orgasm I'd ever had, as Kendra kept her head deep between Brooke's legs, with Brooke holding her hair in both hands as she rode out her incredible looking climax.

Eventually, Brooke's legs relaxed and Kendra came up for air, rising to her knees and kissing Brooke from below. Her plump butt mocked me from beneath her tight jeans, as if it was teasing me that I could only masturbate to the memory of it later. As hot as it was watching from the closet, I was trapped by my own unethical plan. Of course, I wanted to leap out and sandwich myself between Brooke and Kendra, but that would mean admitting what I'd done, and there was no way either of them would want to fuck me after that.

"Take off your top, honey," Kendra instructed. Brooke did so, exposing her lovely little B-cups which held up fine without her shirt, just as I expected. Brooke's body really was sexy, she was an amazingly well put together specimen of a woman.

Kendra stood up and took her orange blouse off. I could only see the strap of her bra from behind but I hoped soon she would turn around and I could see her breasts. Brooke unzipped her jeans and tugged them down over Kendra's feminine hips along with her underwear, showing me the true loveliness of Kendra's naked ass. It was bigger than Brooke's, but firm, the result of good genes and a lot of squats. Kendra stepped out of the jeans and kicked them away, turning around to show Brooke her ass and me her front. Her large breasts were housed within a black, lacy bra and looked magnificent, jutting out from her chest and rippling slightly as she moved.

I followed her toned physique past the outline of her abdominal muscles and down to her groin, where I was surprised to see a neat tuft of pubic hair adorning her mound. It suited her though, her whole look was so perfectly feminine; her olive skin, large bosom and trimmed bush had me not only admiring her, but wanting to have sex with her. Brooke leaned forward and sunk her teeth into the flesh of Kendra's rump, who reached behind and undid her bra, allowing it to fall away beneath her and affording me the lovely view of her heavy breasts, complete with small, puffy nipples.

Brooke's hand ran between Kendra's legs, up and down her thighs with the tips of her fingers while she planted kisses on Kendra's butt cheeks. One of her hands reached right between Kendra's legs and up to her belly button, where she made a claw with her hand and ran her nails down from the belly button to Kendra's mound. Kendra sighed and I watched as her nipples hardened right before my eyes. The sight was so fucking hot and I was made painfully aware of my own wet pussy once again.

"Brooke, honey, remember the shower at the gym?"

"Mhmm," Brooke moaned from behind her.

"I want you to fuck me like that."

"Okay."

Brooke rose from the edge of the bed as Kendra climbed on to it, facing the closet. She lay herself on her stomach, her head and shoulders hanging off the end of the bed, steadying herself by placing her hands on the floor. Her legs lay straight behind her and Brooke climbed on top of her calves, looking down at the sultry Goddess below her. I obviously didn't get the gym shower reference, but it occurred to me that Brooke would struggle to lick her pussy from this position though.

Kendra brought her knees up towards her a little bit, pushing her rump up in the air a few inches, I could see the lovely curves of the top of her peach bum from my spot only a few feet from Kendra's head, the slats of the closet being the only thing keeping my presence a secret. Was Brooke about to do what I thought she was? Surely not. Surely such an act wouldn't appeal to someone as feminine as Kendra.

I was proven wrong though, as Brooke's face lowered in between Kendra's juicy cheeks. Her protruded tongue licked up and down the opening of Kendra's ass, and Kendra immediately looked like she was enjoying it.

"Good girl," Kendra moaned, as Brooke continued satisfying her ass.

I'd never thought of ass eating as something particularly enticing. I just didn't see how it could be so pleasurable, and yet there was proof in front of me that it was. I guess I was always self-conscious about anyone going down there, and I certainly had never felt the desire to do it to someone else. Why then was my pussy getting warmer and wetter? My panties were practically soaked, and my horniness was in overdrive at the sight of Brooke's face buried in Kendra's ass. I decided I couldn't take it anymore. The two of them were too caught up in each other to notice me. I had to cum, I'd just have to be quiet about it. I reached beneath my skirt and slipped my panties over my feet. I hoisted my skirt up around my midriff and suddenly I was as bottomless as the two other women in the room, not that they knew it.

I ran my finger up and down my slit and rubbed my clitoris while watching Brooke go to town on Kendra's rear. I could see her hand reach behind as she fingered Kendra's pussy at the same time, her arm moving like a piston, finger-fucking her vagina while tongue-fucking her asshole. I wondered how many fingers she was using as I circled my clit with my forefinger. I was already feeling the sexual energy accumulating in my stomach and groin and knew it wouldn't take much to cum. I'd just have to make sure I didn't scream.

Kendra took her hands off the floor and reached behind herself to pull her ass cheeks apart for Brooke. I could see Brooke's tongue licking up and down and occasionally it would disappear into Kendra's opening, only to re-emerge seconds later and continue rimming. The effect it had on Kendra was the most alluring thing I'd ever seen, as her face contorted with lips quivering while she enjoyed having Brooke behind her in, well... her behind.

I thought about how much I'd like to go out there and shove my own ass in Kendra's face, having her service my asshole, and seeing if I liked it. This certainly was a night of new desires for me. First the confirmation that I did in fact want to fuck a woman, and now the less expected urge to have my ass devoured by one.

Brooke's face came up for a moment of air as she said, "I love being your good girl, Kendra."

Kendra moaned in approval, "You're my best girl, Brooke. Don't stop licking."

Brooke returned to her post in Kendra's butt

and I rubbed my clit more furiously now, slightly worried that they'd hear the noises of my wet-ness but mostly confident I wouldn't be heard over their moaning. My orgasm hit me suddenly and violently. I used my free hand to cover my mouth while I flicked my clit and shuddered in ecstasy, feeling like my legs were going to give out beneath me. I couldn't help it, a tiny moan escaped my mouth. Fuck! I looked up through the slats of the closet to see if they'd heard. Brooke was still busy in Kendra's rear, but Kendra was looking right at me! She was cumming as well! I couldn't tell if she was looking at me or just star-ing into space but her eyes were pointed directly at me!

I stopped rubbing myself in an effort to fin-ish up the orgasm prematurely. Fuck. Had I been caught? Had she seen me or did she just happen to be looking in my direction as she came? Fuck, fuck fuck. How was I going to explain this? *Sorry, I just wanted to know if you were a lesbian so I hid in the closet and fingered myself to the view of your girlfriend eating out your ass.* I took my hand from beneath my skirt and stayed perfectly still, hoping with all my might that I had gotten away with it.

Kendra rode her orgasm to completion and rolled over, allowing Brooke to lay down on top of her as they kissed and nibbled at each other's necks, their naked flesh pressed up against each other. I saw Kendra nibble at Brooke's ear and whisper something into it. What had she said?

Brooke looked up at the closet. Fuck. Oh, God I had been caught. Kendra told her there was a little perve in the closet watching them fuck. Brooke climbed off of the bed. This was it. I better come up with something of an excuse quickly. She walked off towards the bathroom door though, out of sight. Kendra sat up on the edge of the bed. Maybe I was safe after all?

The door swung open.

I was exposed.

Kendra sat on the edge of the bed looking at me with an arched eyebrow. Brooke stood to the side of the open doorway, expressionless and naked.

"Aubrey!" Kendra exclaimed, "Nice of you to join us. I guess your date didn't work out the way you'd hoped."

"Kendra, Brooke, I am so so sorry," I stammered. "I just wanted to see and I thought if I hid in the closet you wouldn't know and… I just wanted to see."

"See what?" Kendra asked.

"See if you and Brooke were fucking. And to see if I liked it."

"Well?"

"Well what?"

"Well, we are fucking. So I suppose my 'well' is in reference to your second statement. Did you like what you saw?"

I stood in silence, petrified with embarrassment.

"Well?" Kendra repeated.

"I don't know," I lied, afraid to say the truth.

"You're standing there in my closet with your skirt hiked up, shaved pussy on display and cum dripping off your fingers because you don't know?"

Oh, God, my pussy was exposed. I immediately tugged my skirt down.

"No," Kendra said, "Pull it back up."

I don't know why I did what she said, but I felt like I should. Kendra had the moral high ground on me and I felt inclined to do whatever she told me to. I pulled my skirt back up around my midriff, my groin bare for the two of them to see.

"So, is it safe to assume that since you were finger-fucking yourself in there, you *did* like what you saw?"

"Yes," I looked up at Brooke, who just stood there expressionless, seemingly not caring about the whole situation, nor bothered by her own nakedness in front of the strange woman in her girlfriend's closet. "But I'm not a lesbian," I added for some reason.

"Oh, of course you're not a lesbian, you just like it in the closet," she chuckled. "Did you see me telling Brooke what to do, and her being a good girl and doing it?"

"Yes."

"Would you like me to tell Brooke to lick your sweet little pussy until you cum?"

I thought about what I should say. I knew what I *wanted* to say, but wasn't sure what I should say. But I was caught, there was nothing left to hide anymore, no worse could the situation get by me telling the truth, so I simply said, "Yes."

Kendra smiled, "Good girl. Come over here."

I obliged and walked over to my nude roommate on the edge of the bed. She took the hand I'd been masturbating with and enveloped my fingers with her mouth. I could feel Brooke move into a position behind me, and she reached around and cupped my breasts through my red top. Kendra's tongue danced between my fingers as she licked the cum off them. It felt good. It felt really good. I couldn't believe the night had actually ended up here. I reminded myself that I was caught though, and Kendra could tell everyone I knew about my voyeuristic exploits. For tonight at least, I would do whatever she told me to do.

"Brooke, honey, why don't you take off our friend's top, as good as she looks in it."

I felt Brooke's hands at my sides, pulling my top off from beneath my skirt. I didn't resist. I raised my arms and allowed her to slide it over my head, making me effectively naked apart from the short denim skirt that was only covering my stomach.

Kendra ran her hands over my breasts, dangling right in front of her face. My nipples had gone a bit soft from all the embarrassment but as soon as she ran her thumb over them, they rose to attention once more. She stood from the bed, her head a good few inches above me. God, she looked attractive and imposing, towering over me and having me completely at her will. She leaned her head down and kissed me, her luscious lips taking mine between them and setting fireworks off in my brain. Behind me, Brooke undid my skirt and nibbled at the back of my neck, having me now nakedly sandwiched between them. I felt Brooke's groin push into my bottom which forced my own groin into Kendra's, who's bush I felt prickling my soft skin. It was the sexiest kiss of my life to say the least.

Kendra's hands reached around the back of me and cupped my ass as she had done earlier to Brooke in the same spot. Brooke's hand's reached around and cupped my bare breasts. I was entangled in their limbs and loving the feeling as Kendra pulled her face away from mine.

"Brooke does as I tell her because she knows that if she submits to me, I'll give her the most incredible orgasms she's ever had. I have my most incredible orgasms by watching curious girls like you do as I say before I fuck the straightness out of you. I make Brooke and her friends do all sorts of things to each other for my own pleasure, and theirs. Brooke's going to eat your cunt now, and I'm going to watch you enjoy her hot mouth while I tell you about the things you're going to do for me."

"Okay," was all I could say, all I wanted to say. I gave myself over to her.

Kendra stepped away from the bed and Brooke pushed me down onto it. I rolled over on my back and crawled my way up to the pillows as she climbed on top of it, locking eyes with me.

"I've always found you very sexy, Aubrey," Brooke said to me as she made her way up my body. "I've been wondering if I'd ever get the chance to eat your snatch, if Kendra would ever give me the order to seduce you with her. When we returned home and saw your purse still on the chair, yet you nowhere to be found, we figured you must have been hiding and waiting to watch us fuck. I'm glad you liked what you saw."

Of course, I left my bag on the couch. How stupid could I be? They'd known from the very start that I was watching them screw each other's brains out. It was all theatre. They were putting on a show and hoping to seduce me just by watching them. It worked.

Brooke leaned down and kissed me. Her mouth was just as soft as Kendra's, but tasted a little different, a little salty. I realized it was probably Kendra's asshole that I was tasting on Brooke's mouth and tongue. It wasn't unpleasant, and the thought of tasting Kendra bottom vicariously through Brooke's mouth made my groin tingle with delight.

Brooke kissed her way down my chest and placed her face between my breasts, kissing my sternum while her hands held both my breasts firmly. She took my left nipple in her sweet little mouth and flicked it with her tongue, rolling it around with her actions. On its own, my pelvis started gyrating into her tight stomach, as her playing with my tits made my pussy burn with desire. She continued down, planting kisses on my stomach and sides as she made her way south. She finally reached my bare mound and kissed that too, lighting up my nervous system every time I felt her wet lips on my hairless skin. I spread myself for her and she looked up and smiled at me. Then she glanced over to Kendra, who was sitting in a chair by her dresser. Kendra gave her a permissive nod and she delved inside my slit.

It felt so much better than I ever thought possible. I'd had curiosities about women for a while now and I cursed myself for not acting on them sooner. Her soft, wet tongue licked up and down the folds of my vagina, and she used her thumb to pull back the hood of my clit so that her tongue could attack it. The sight of her short, blonde hair between my legs was so sensual, and she looked up and made eye contact with me while she ate me out, spurred on by my reactions to her oral.

"Oh, that looks wonderful, ladies," Kendra said from her chair, her legs crossed as she sat there casually watching us. I thought she would be masturbating, but she was just looking on hungrily, perhaps denying herself the satisfaction until later. "So if you want to be one of my good girls, Aubrey, there's a few rules for you to follow," she continued. "First, as you can see, Brooke's pussy is perfectly smooth, waxed clean, that's how I like it and that's how I expect you to be from now on." So, she didn't make me shave for my date, she had my shave for her, somehow she must have known. "Also, Brooke always looks her best for me, with perfectly done makeup and sexy clothes. Living with you, I'll allow you some leeway with that, but when we're fucking or out in public, this is how you should look. Lastly and most importantly, you must do as I say. As you no doubt witnessed from your secret perving hiding spot, Brooke was licking my ass."

"Yes, I saw," I said between moans, loving every second of Brooke's head between my legs.

"In order for me to give you the intense, earth-shattering orgasms I give all of my girls, I need you to be open to the idea of having your ass licked, and returning the favor. Is that something you can do?"

I wasn't sure about that. I liked what I saw from the closet, but I thought that may have just been because I was watching such a lewd act in secret. I was hesitant to have anyone put their tongue on my asshole.

"I don't know," I admitted.

"Brooke, stop," Kendra commanded, and the blonde did so immediately. She brought her face up and wiped my pussy juices off her chin. It pained me to have her stop. "If you want to be one of my good girls, like Brooke," she continued, "you have to be open to new experiences. Now... are you open to new experiences?"

I reconsidered my willingness, really just desperate for Brooke to return to my pussy so that I could cum. I decided I was willing to try it, at least for the night. What's the harm? And if it was being done by women as stunningly sexy as Brooke and Kendra, who was I to turn down that opportunity?

"Okay," I said.

"Okay?" said Kendra.

"Okay, I'll do whatever you want me to do, including eating ass."

"Good. Brooke, you may return to Aubrey's pussy. And if you would, please make her cum, I have something I want to see."

Brooke did return to my pussy, and with careful precision around my clit. With every twinge or groan that her tongue would elicit from me, Brooke would remember it and know how to do it again. I was on the verge of orgasm when she started circling my clit, increasing the pressure. Then I felt two of her fingers go inside me and start moving back and forth. The first thing that came to mind was that these were the fingers that were inside Kendra minutes earlier, while Brooke was eating her ass. My orgasm arrived with this thought, rocking my hips as they moved with the motion of Brooke's fingers. My legs clamped shut around Brooke's soft face and her tongue never stopped. My legs crossed behind her neck and toes curled as my abdominals crunched and I stared at the top of Brooke's blonde hair, which I held on to with both hands.

It was a sensational orgasm, and as I lay down I looked to the ceiling as my body quivered with aftershocks. Brooke kissed her way back up my body and nestled her face in my neck while I lay there motionless, trying to recover.

"Oh girls, that was lovely," Kendra said with approval from her chair. "Aubrey, it's your turn to return the favor now."

"Okay," I said as I willed myself out of my catatonic state.

"How do you want me, Kendra?" Brooke asked of her lover, eager to please her however she saw fit.

"Sit on top of my bed head, honey. Spread your legs wide so that our new girl can get into your snatch easily."

Brooke did as she was told and stood up on the bed, making her way to the front of me and perching herself on the frame of Kendra's bed head. I looked up from below and had an upside down view of her hairless pussy facing out and her cute little pink pucker of an asshole just below it, facing downwards, her cheeks only just being able to fit on the three-inch thick bed head. I rolled over and the image turned the right way up as I made my way onto all fours, still feeling like I was half-catatonic and having something of an out-of-body experience as my face made its way towards Brooke's wanting pussy without my brain telling it to.

I could smell her scent, it was intoxicating. Sweet but stung my nostrils just a little, in exactly the right way. I snapped out of my state and realized where I was, about to lick a woman's cunt for the first time. This is something I'd given a fair amount of thought to in the last few months, and I was grateful that it was Brooke offering herself to me.

I licked up her slit in one long, slow motion, savoring the flavors of her pussy as each drop of her cum hit my taste buds. She exhaled heavily with the motion and I ran my tongue over her clit. It felt right to me, I really liked it and couldn't wait to lick again, and again. So I did. In retrospect, I was probably a little too eager and messy with my technique, but Brooke didn't seem to mind. Her face contorted with every lick, and I tried to look up at her whenever I could. I licked the walls of her labia and inserted my tongue into her vagina while my nose tickled her clitoris. Her juices covered my face and chin and dripped down below, over her taint and collecting around her butthole. I was in heaven watching the effect my tongue was having on another woman.

I didn't even notice Kendra get up, but suddenly her face was to the side of mine. She whispered in my ear to stop, and I begrudgingly followed her command.

"You're doing a splendid job for a first timer, Aubrey. Look at the pleasure you're giving to Brooke. Doesn't it fill you with joy making another woman feel this way?"

"It does," I said honestly.

"Look at the way her ass has spread apart on the frame of the bed head, look at how her wetness has slid down her pussy and moistened her adorable little asshole. Do you think it looks tasty?"

"I do," I said. I actually did. Her asshole did look like it could use some attention, and I found myself wanting to try it.

"Be a good girl and lick her asshole for me, then," Kendra instructed. I was just grateful to be doing something to Brooke again, I didn't mind what I did. I opened my mouth and pressed my pink tongue against her awaiting pucker. I felt it tighten as my tongue lay flat against it and Brooke let out a higher pitched moan. I recognised the taste from Brooke's mouth, the saltiness of her asshole was the same as the taste of Kendra's had been on her tongue. I kind of liked it. And I certainly liked the reaction it elicited from Brooke.

I licked again and again at her little hole, gaining more confidence with every stroke. I felt Kendra's wavy hair on top of my head as she started nuzzling Brooke's clit above me. Brooke's moans became more and more intense and she was definitely going to cum soon, not that I could blame her.

It seemed to be because of her imminent orgasm that Kendra pulled away and made me stop once again. Without saying a word she took my forefinger and ran it between Brooke's labia, coating it in cum and saliva. Then she lowered my hand below the blonde bombshell, and placed the tip of my finger at Brooke's ass.

"Gently," she said, "Brooke cums best when she has a finger in her ass."

I touched Brooke's butthole with the tip of my finger, and she breathed out, relaxing the muscles of her ass as she did so to let me in. I inserted my finger just a little, just to the first knuckle. Unsure, I looked up and saw Brooke smile and moan in appreciation. I felt her ass contract, squeezing my finger and sucking it in a little deeper. Her leg kicked a little at the feeling of it. Still, I forced my finger deeper within her ass. It was warm around it, and so impossibly tight. I could feel her heartbeat through a nearby blood vessel, it was going fast and steady. I couldn't believe I had my finger in a girl's ass, and with one final contraction of her ring, Brooke accepted the full length of my forefinger inside her.

I took a moment to admire the sight with completely rapt eyes; Brooke's pussy was open and glistening, dripping sweet nectar down below, lubricating her asshole which had my entire finger inside it. I was wearing the fit blonde like a ring and it felt naughty as fuck. I loved it. It was then that I noticed that Kendra was no longer next to me, and I suddenly felt her hands holding on to my hips from behind. Not even a second later she was licking my asshole, her warm tongue running up the crevice between my cheeks.

"*Oh!*" I gasped at the unexpected amount of pleasure I felt from it.

Brooke grabbed my head by my hair and thrust it back into her pussy, feeling neglected. It was an overwhelming experience, having one sensual woman eat my ass while I had my finger inside another whose pussy I was feasting on. I continued to lick up and down Brooke's nethers, and withdrew my finger from her ass slowly, almost all the way, before it started its slow journey back inside.

"Fuck yes," she encouraged, "Fuck my asshole faster!"

I did what she wanted and started making the movement's of my finger a little faster, the full length of my finger disappearing into her butt with rhythmic motion, her hole fully accepting it. Kendra's tongue rimmed me, and I felt the familiar swirling of an orgasm, only it wasn't in my groin as I was used to, but it was in my ass, begging to be let out. I hadn't felt anything like that there before, but the alien sensation felt incredible, and I started moaning into Brooke's pussy with anticipation of what was to come.

I licked hungrily up Brooke's slit, and I could feel her heartbeat get faster from the finger I had in her ass, it was really racing now, I knew she must be close. I started swirling my tongue around her clit and applying as much pressure as I could while my finger slid in and out of her with greater speed, my digit being choked by her tightest hole the entire time.

Kendra's slippery tongue wormed its way inside my own butt and she slid it in and out, using her hands to spread apart my cheeks so she could get inside deeper. That was too much for me and the ball of sexual energy I felt in my ass exploded like a fucking nuclear bomb. I'd never felt anything so intense, as an electric shock coursed through every cell in my body, a massive rush of endorphins flooded my head and my hips vibrated violently while I struggled to stay upright. Still, Kendra's tongue did not leave my ass and she followed my gyrating hips with her head, holding on to me as if I was a bucking bull she had to stay on.

The surge of my orgasm forced my finger deep within Brooke's ass and my mouth to suck her clit hard as I stifled my scream with her pussy. This set of a chain reaction and her own orgasm tore through her. I felt her asshole pulse rapidly around my finger, holding it in so tightly I think I lost some blood flow to it. Her hands held on to my head and pushed me further into her groin as her legs quivered and she tried desperately to stay perched on the bed head. I pulled my finger out and that seemed to send another massive wave of climax through her system, and this time she did fall down onto the pillows below. She took my head in her hands and kissed me as I rode out the last waves of the best orgasm of my life, my ass still quivering around Kendra's soft tongue.

At last Kendra removed her tongue and I collapsed down onto the bed, my whole body twitching with the aftershocks of my massive orgasm. Brooke stroked my hair while I lay there, feeling like I was about to pass out, sucking in deep breaths. Kendra made her way up the bed and I could hear her and Brooke kissing above me. That was the most incredible sex I'd ever had, and it was all because I submitted myself to my roommate Kendra, allowing her to have her way with my ass. I was supposed to go on an average date and get some average dick from some average guy; this was *way* more fun.

After a few minutes, I kissed both Brooke and Kendra goodnight, and thanked them for an incredible evening of the best sex I'd ever had. Still naked, I closed the door on them as I made my way across the apartment. The last thing I saw was Kendra pushing Brooke's head down towards her crotch as she told me I was one of her good girls now.

I certainly felt like one of her good girls. I crawled my way into my own bed and thought about the implications for the future, how I wanted more nights like that one and if that meant wearing makeup everyday and keeping my pussy waxed, then that was just fine with me. It occurred to me that Kendra had mentioned how she'd gotten some of Brooke's friends to submit to her too and I found myself really wanting to meet them. I wanted to satisfy as many women as possible, to taste their pussies and rim their lovely butts.

I checked my phone quickly before resigning myself to sleep. One message. It was from Laura:

So did you find out if she was a lesbian?

I thought about what to say for a moment before I replied:

Still not sure. But she's having her friend over again in a couple of nights, why don't you come over so I can get a second opinion.

I smiled wryly as I hit send.

THE END

THE PLEASURE PRINCIPLE

Anita

I sat in my psychology tutorial while Professor Jones droned on about human behaviours exhibited in the animal kingdom, but I wasn't really listening. I couldn't take my mind off of the previous night. I couldn't believe I'd kissed another woman. Not only that, but it was with my best friend, Yasmin, who I'd been best friends with since middle school. We were so close that we'd even chosen the same college just so that we'd still be together. I'd never felt that way about her, but last night… something just came over me.

We'd been studying together in her room, as we often did during the week. There was nothing different from the dozens of other times we'd done it before, except for her new bright ruby red hair color she had debuted earlier that day. It looked amazing, and I was distracted by it the whole study session. It made her look sexy and different and exciting and I felt a strong impulse to kiss her, an impulse that I followed.

We must have kissed for ten seconds before I ran out of her room, suddenly ashamed of my actions and desires. How could I risk our friendship like that? I'd never even been attracted to a woman before and I chose my best friend to try and kiss. Still, she did reciprocate. She didn't pull back in disgust and slap me, she *did* kiss me back before I ran out with my tail between my legs, afraid of the possibility of it going further.

While I was stuck in my own head, replaying the night over and over, I missed the part where Professor Jones told us to split into groups of three for our next assignment. I snapped into the present and noticed the groups were mostly already formed. I scanned the room for my only half-friend in this class and saw she was already at a table with two others. It was rapidly looking like I was going to be alone for the assignment when I felt a tap on my shoulder.

"You look a little lost," the voice said.

I turned around and saw Taylor, a petite brunette I knew from a couple of classes. She was shorter than your average woman and when I turned, I found myself at head height with her generous cleavage. Taylor's bosom was much more ample than her slight frame would otherwise suggest. Flustered by my recent confused feelings, I looked up before I could be accused of staring at her chest. I'd never really noticed her properly before, but she was very pretty, with a cute little button nose and smokey eyeshadow bringing out the light brown of her eyes that matched her straight hair worn just lower than her shoulders.

"Oh, hi Taylor. Yeah I guess I am a couple of members shy of a team."

"Well, you should come and join my friend and I on our team," she beamed back at me with a bubbly excitedness that would suggest she'd had five cups of coffee after never trying it before. But I knew from classes that that was just Taylor.

"Sure, that'd be great," I accepted her invitation. I didn't really know Taylor but I liked her fine, and I hoped the social interaction and assignment planning would keep my mind off of my embarrassing lesbian experience the previous night.

I picked up my books and bag and followed Taylor over to her table where her friend sat, smiling at me as I approached. She was gorgeous. I'd not seen her in class before but she really made an impression. The way she stood up to greet me, her graceful movements and confident body language suggested a woman older than most college girls, someone who was more sure of themselves, yet I was certain she was at least close to the same age as Taylor and I. She extended her hand towards me and I took it in mine as her full lips parted into a smile.

"Hi, I'm Kendra," she said. My mind was at least temporarily taken off Yasmin and was filled with Kendra. I'd known her two seconds and yet I was completely in awe of her. I tried to decide whether I was attracted to her, or just taken aback by her beauty. Two stirrings of sexual feelings for two women within twenty four hours after feeling none for twenty years seemed a bit crazy to me, and I figured I was just crossing wires with my confused feelings for Yasmin.

"I'm Anita," I said after realizing I had taken too long to answer. "I don't think I've seen you in class before, are you new?"

"Yeah, I have history with Taylor and was in need of a new elective."

"So why'd you pick psychology?"

"Taylor said there were a lot more girls," she said with a wry little smile. It made sense, there were a lot of girls in psych, and someone who looked like Kendra would probably get sick of all the guys in class drooling over her constantly.

"Well, you're not wrong," I said. "So what is this assignment about anyway? I was kind of zoned out for a bit there."

"Yeah, Professor Jones can have that effect on

people," Taylor joked as we sat down around the table.

"It's about human behaviours that we can also observe in animals," Kendra explained. "Looking at the wants and needs of the id and identifying any evolutionary purpose for them."

"Okay, that sounds easy enough. What do we have to do?"

"We have to pick a behaviour we see in the animal kingdom and show how that same behaviour exists in a subject. The subject can be one of us or anyone really."

"I'll be the subject if you want, seeing as you were nice enough to bring me into your group."

"Great, shall we brainstorm ideas of different behaviours and get together tonight to figure something out?" Taylor suggested.

"Sure, my roommate is actually not in town at the moment so we can use my dorm room if you'd like," I volunteered.

"You picked a good one, Taylor!" Kendra said as she winked at our mutual friend.

"I'll say," Taylor agreed, bubbly as she always was. "Well, we'll see you tonight then, Anita! It's gonna be so much fun."

I wasn't sure what Taylor's idea of fun was,

but mine's not doing a psychology assignment. Still, I was thankful to have the distraction. The events with Yasmin were something I'd have to deal with at some point, but thanks to Taylor and Kendra, that wouldn't be until at least tomorrow.

✦✦✦

The sun mercifully went down, eventually. While I'd left psych class with a positive mind-set, the afternoon had brought text messages from Yasmin wanting to meet up and talk about the previous night. I was still really ashamed of my actions and not ready to talk to her, plus I had Taylor and Kendra coming over, so I couldn't meet up anyway. I was thankful for the excuse. I had ignored every one of Yasmin's messages and while I felt awful about ghosting my best friend, I had nothing to say yet.

Was I a lesbian? Why was it that my best friend changed her hair color to something a bit adventurous and suddenly I wanted to stick my tongue down her throat? Why had she kissed me back? Did she want to take it further?

The knock on my door thankfully interrupted my overanalyzing brain. I opened the door and let Taylor and Kendra in, hugging them hello. Taylor wore a plain white crop top that, despite showing zero cleavage, accentuated her heavy breasts and exposed her midriff. I could see her two very distinct globes through her top and could tell she wasn't wearing a bra. A simple, high-cut black skirt showed off her thin but short legs. Standing next to Kendra, Taylor looked even more petite than she was, a full head shorter than her confident counterpart. She was still perfectly made up with her smokey eyeshadow and blush. Anticipating this, I'd actually carefully applied some make-up myself. I wasn't sure if I was trying to compete with Taylor's prettiness or if I did it for Kendra's approval, but the thought that it could be both crossed my mind.

"Anita, you look stunning!," Kendra exclaimed. The comment meant more to me than it should have coming from a veritable stranger. "Did you just come from a dinner date or is this all for little ol' us?"

I tried to suppress the blush I could feel in my cheeks, "Oh, well, you ladies looked so lovely earlier today that I thought I should try and be on the same level."

"Oh, please," Taylor said as she almost skipped in like an over-excited mouse, her short skirt bouncing behind her as she made her way into the room and set down her books on my roommate's bed. "I've got nothing on you, you're drop dead gorgeous."

Kendra walked in with the poise I'd expect from her. The black dress she wore swayed with her hips and I could tell she had a bountiful, round ass concealed beneath the thin fabric. I caught myself thinking about it and cursed myself for doing so. I didn't know what it was with women those last couple of days but it was certainly not helping my confused feelings. Perhaps my wires weren't as crossed as I thought earlier on when I was trying to figure out if I was attracted to Kendra. Maybe I did have a bit of a thing for her.

Taylor and Kendra took their place on my roommate's bed and I sat opposite, on mine, as we opened our books. I tried to refocus myself on the task at hand. "So did you guys come up with any interesting animal behaviours we could write about?"

"Well," Taylor leaned forward, her permanent smile still on her face. "Kendra and I were talking, and we thought it would be interesting to write about sexual behaviours that can be observed in animals and humans."

"I guess," I said, hiding my disappointment and wanting to think about anything besides sex. "But all animals have to have sex to reproduce, I don't know if there's that much to write about that everyone doesn't already know."

"Not so much the need for the act itself," Taylor continued, "More the way in which we do it, and why. Dolphins sometimes have sex for pleasure rather than reproductive purposes, for example."

"I suppose," I said, still not wanting to take this route.

"Well, you're our subject," Kendra said, "Purely from a scientific perspective, is there anything about the way you like to have sex that you might say is animalistic?"

"Oh Kendra, I'm not sure I-"

I was interrupted by a knock at the door, the second time tonight that a doorknock had saved me from discomfort. The relief didn't last long however, as I opened the door to find Yasmin standing there, a worried look on her face, dyed red hair flowing down just past her shoulders.

"Yasmin, what are you doing here?"

"We need to talk, Anita."

"Yas... now's not a good time, I have company," I opened the door a little wider to reveal Taylor and Kendra on the bed.

"Well I tried to talk earlier but you've been ignoring me. It's important. It has to happen."

"It can wait until tomorr-"

"It's fine!" Kendra called from the bed. "Honestly, it's okay, come in. We don't mind."

I should have been a little mad at Kendra

giving orders in my apartment, but I wasn't. I was more just nervous about letting Yasmin in and airing our dirty laundry in front of relative strangers. Especially when that dirty laundry was a lesbian kiss we'd had the night before. Yas accepted Kendra's invitation and practically pushed me out of the way to get in.

I sighed as I closed the door behind me and turned to see Yasmin standing there awkwardly, looking down at the floor and rubbing one arm. Curiously, I noticed she was wearing her black pleather pants. This was interesting as these were the pants she always wore when she wanted to show off her legendary ass, which had always been Yasmin's best feature. Large and soft, Yasmin never had to work on it, she just always had plenty of back. I'd often told her with some squats she could tone it and hoist it up a bit more, but she was perfectly happy with how it was, and so she should be. Kendra remained seated on the bed, unperplexed by the whole situation. Taylor besides her, mouth open and staring at the curls at the ends of Yasmin's newly red locks. It seemed now that she was in the room, she was starting to regret her insistence.

"Yasmin, this is Kendra and Taylor. We have psych together," I said, minding the niceties even in the awkwardness.

"I'm sorry Ani, but we have to talk about..." she

glanced over at the audience on the bed. "...you know."

"Yas, I'm sorry I did it but I... I dunno... I'm really uncomfortable right now."

"What happened?" Taylor asked, almost with glee.

"Taylor, would you mind-" I started.

"Anita and I kissed last night," Yasmin announced, apparently unafraid to share the information with strangers.

Taylor's face lit up and I thought I even heard her squeal a little.

"Yas! Do we really have to!?" I protested.

"Girls, it's fine," Kendra said, speaking for the first time. "You guys are obviously close friends, right?"

"Yes, since middle school," Yasmin replied, seemingly fine with talking about it in front of people she'd only just met.

"How do you feel about the kiss, Anita?"

"Kendra, look. I get you're just trying to smooth things out, but I really don't think this is appropriate," I said.

"It's fine, sweetie," she replied. "Girls kissing at college is nothing to get shy about. It's hardly original. Besides, it may help us with our assignment. Lesbian behaviour is exhibited in a handful of species."

"I'm not a lesbian! It was just a dumb, fleeting moment of infatuation!" I almost shouted, and Yasmin made a wounded look.

"I'm not saying you are sweetie," Kendra explained calmly. "But kissing another girl is undeniably a pleasurable experience. There's nothing wrong with it. Why don't the two of you come and take a seat on this empty bed and we'll work this out?"

I was still hesitant about it all, but Yasmin didn't seem to be as she walked over immediately and took a seat on my bed, opposite the other girls. They kind of had me in a box here. Yasmin clearly wasn't going anywhere and neither was Kendra and Taylor. I could either turn around and run out the door myself, or I could sit down and try and work things out with my best friend. I chose the latter and joined Yasmin on the bed, who couldn't bring herself to look up at me.

"May I ask who initiated the kiss?" Kendra asked, Taylor now being the silent one, sitting there in attentive excitement.

"I did," I confessed.

"And what made you choose last night of all nights to kiss your best friend? Was this something you've wanted to do for a while?"

"No, I just... I was overcome with the urge to. We were studying like we always do, and I couldn't take my eyes off of her. She'd just dyed her hair that color yesterday."

"So do you think it was the red hair that caused your attraction to Yasmin?"

Taylor let out another almost inaudible squeal at this for some reason. I guessed she was just loving the gossip.

"I mean I guess so. What else could it have been?"

"Well it's likely that you've always felt some attraction to Yasmin on some level, even if you've not realized it until last night. It's interesting that her red hair is what made you realize it, there are plenty of species of birds that use displays of color in order to find a mate."

I had to refrain from rolling my eyes at Kendra's comment, as she really was seemingly studying us for the assignment.

"To be honest, Ani," Yas spoke for the first time in a while, still looking at the floor. "I've been having some feelings of attraction towards you for a while. I'm not sure if they're anything more than sexual, but they're definitely there, and I think part of the reason I dyed my hair this color was to see if you found it sexy."

My head was spinning at her confession. Yas was attracted to me sexually? I'm sitting on my bed opposite two relative strangers while my best friend tells me she wants to fuck me?

"Yas… I don't know what to say," I said honestly. I had no idea how to process this whole situation, much less respond to her.

"There's clearly some attraction felt both ways," Kendra filled the silence. "There's no need for this to be awkward, girls. This is something that's been on Yasmin's mind for quite a while and something that's been locked away in Anita's subconscious for at least equally as long. Yasmin, you can look up at your friend."

Yasmin decided to take the advice and lifted her head to look at me in the eyes, I could see tears welling up. Her sharp cheeks were almost as ruby red as the hair which cascaded down either side of her face.

"Anita, do you remember what it said in last week's reading about Freud and the concept of the id?" Kendra asked.

"That it's the only part of the personality that's present from birth. It is the source of our bodily needs, wants, desires and impulses. It acts according to the pleasure principle."

"That's right. The pleasure principle is what drives us to seek immediate gratification from our actions and impulses. Do you remember that?"

"Yes."

"And do you feel the pleasure principle driving you when you look at Yasmin?"

"Yes."

"So then kiss her," Kendra instructed firmly.

I should have been taken aback by the way Kendra was talking, but instead I couldn't think to do anything else except for what she told me. Especially when I looked at Yasmin's pretty face and hair, the same impulse I felt last night had once again made its way into my brain. I reached out with a hand and pushed one side of Yasmin's red hair over her shoulder, reaching around to the back of her neck and gently pulling her towards me.

Our lips met halfway between us and we kissed for the second time in twenty-four hours. My heart was beating at a million miles an hour and I felt lighter than air as her soft lips parted to mine. This kiss felt much more right than the short one yesterday. It was as if it was something that had been coming for so long and now could finally be had, I felt the release of a ball of anxiety in my head that until now, I hadn't even realized was there. The ball melted into a cocktail of endorphins and serotonin and washed away all the stress, self-consciousness, overanalyzing and muddiness that I normally felt. I was focused only on Yasmin's mouth and my head was clear of all other thoughts.

"Doesn't that feel good, girls? Doesn't that drive your id wild?" Kendra asked. This time Taylor's squeal of excitement was audible, although I still didn't know what she was getting out of this.

Kendra was right though, the feeling of Yasmin's face on mine was driving me wild. We began to kiss deeper and harder, our tongues flicking each other. Yasmin pulled me closer so that she could up the intensity of our kissing, and placed a hand on my waist.

"Give in to your animalistic desires. They've been wanting to come out for so long," Kendra continued.

Perhaps due to the encouraging words of Kendra, Yasmin's hand moved from my waist to one of my breasts. This snapped me back to reality and my ego retook control from my id. Kissing was one thing, but feeling me up in front of two other girls we barely knew seemed a step too far. I broke our kiss and pushed her hand off my breast.

"Yas! We're in front of company!"

"We don't mind," said the sultry voice of Kendra. Embarrassed, I turned to face her to apologize and instead my jaw immediately dropped. Kendra was leaning back on the bed, propped up by her elbows, with Taylor on the floor in front of her, her head buried between Kendra's legs underneath her dress!

What the fuck was going on? Taylor was eating Kendra out while she watched Yas and I tongue each other? This was all so bizarre but my mouth could only remain wide open, too in shock to say anything.

"Wow," Yasmin said. "I like your new friends." She leaned over and took my ear lobe in her mouth as I tried to take in the sight before me. Taylor was on all fours, causing her short black skirt to ride up, revealing her tight little ass covered by small bubblegum pink panties. Her head was completely beneath Kendra's dress and I could see it bobbing up and down beneath the fabric. Yasmin lightly bit down on my ear lobe and I felt an electric shock shoot down my neck and into my crotch, as the id fought to take over once more. I was suddenly aware of the wet patch that was forming in my panties.

I was usually one to second guess my feelings; I did it when I kissed Yasmin the night before, I did it when I questioned whether I was attracted to Kendra when I met her, but I wasn't doing it now. Perhaps it was because of the kiss with Yasmin that I was seeing things so clearly, but one thing was for certain, I was majorly turned on by the sight of Taylor's firm butt; I was majorly turned on by her bobbing head, veiled by Kendra's dress; and I was definitely majorly turned on by Yasmin flicking my earlobe in her mouth. I had to acknowledge that there was a significant portion of me that had desires for other women, and I decided I was going to follow the pleasure principle for the rest of the night and try to satisfy my id as much as possible.

It was hard to tell whether Yasmin was just horny for me or if Kendra's watchful gaze was making her extra wild. After all, I'd never seen Yas in a sexual light before.. At the very least, she didn't seem to mind the audience, and she pulled away from my earlobe and lifted her top over her head, exposing the small, cute nipples adorning her also small breasts. She looked at me with a shy puppy dog expression, as if awaiting my nod of approval before she proceeded any further. In an almost trance like state, I pulled my top over my own head and undid my bra, tossing it aside so that we were both topless. Neither one of us was alone in this. The shy look was replaced with an excited smile and she leaned over, lowering her head to my chest.

Her mouth took one of my nipples in it completely, her warm tongue darting around the areola for a second before her teeth bit down ever so lightly on the nipple, causing it to harden. It felt fucking great. She balanced the teasing of her tongue with the naughtiness of the biting perfectly, placing kisses all over my chest in between the nipple play.

I could feel the damp patch in my panties getting damper and I bit my bottom lip in pleasure. Eager to do something to return the favor without taking her mouth off of me, I reached underneath her and cupped one of her significantly smaller breasts with ease. The next time she bit down, I pinched her nipple and gave it the gentlest little twist, sharing the erotic pain. It seemed to work and she let out a soft moan of approval into my tits.

I was about to work up the willpower to push Yasmin off my chest and return the favor properly before Kendra interrupted our little chest session.

"I think the two of you need to see each other's bodies completely," she suggested.

It may not seem like that's necessarily sound logic, but in the moment it made a tremendous amount of sense. The desire to kiss Yasmin had been fulfilled, the desire to play with her breasts had been fulfilled, the next desire the pleasure principle dictated was to be naked with her.

"Taylor," Kendra said calmly, as if there wasn't even a girl beneath her dress eating her pussy. "You should come up and see this."

Taylor didn't need to be told twice, and her face emerged from beneath the dress before she re-took her position on my roommate's bed next to Kendra. She wiped her dripping mouth with her forearm and watched on with her big brown eyes.

Yasmin was once again the first to take the plunge and stood from the bed, facing away from us. I took in the lovely arch of her bare back, the movement of her shoulder-blades as her arms moved, her pale white skin contrasting the black pleather pants that housed her plump rear. She slowly peeled the pleather down her legs and stepped out of them, now wearing only her panties. Her ass was that big that her crack ate most of the cotton underwear, and her bountiful cheeks were on show for the three of us, with dark, heart shaped creases below it where it slightly rolled over the backs of her thighs. Yas was always a bit self-conscious about her small tits, but the confidence was largely made up by her fantastic ass.

It certainly seemed to have an effect on Taylor, who instinctively reached out to touch it, before quickly withdrawing her hand just before it completed the journey, as if she'd suddenly remembered she was only permitted to look. She giggled and playfully nudged her head into Kendra's shoulder, unable to take her eyes off of Yasmin.

"Your turn," Yasmin said as she turned around and looked at me.

I stood up and looked at the faces around the room, fighting my instincts to cover my naked breasts. First I looked at Yasmin, who met my gaze with a pleading expression, as if to say *'Please don't back out on me now."* I turned to Kendra, who looked on with hunger in her eyes, which she tried to mask with indifference. Finally at Taylor, whose wide eyes made no cover-ups about what she wanted, and she looked on with anticipation.

I hooked my thumbs into my shorts and with a thought of *"Fuck it"* I made sure they were hooked into my panties too. I pulled them both down in one motion and stepped out of them, kicking them behind me. Yasmin's face lit up and a huge smile burst out. Her gaze started at my feet, made its way up my long legs to my completely shaven vagina, up past my stomach and round breasts until finally she met my eyeline. Without saying a word she pulled her panties down and revealed her thin airstrip of pubes atop her otherwise hairless pussy. It occurred to me that the strip was her natural light brown color, she apparently did not match the carpet to the drapes.

So there we both stood, completely naked in front of my fully clothed psychology partners, who seemed to be really getting off on the situation. It was all so alien to me anyway that I didn't really care that they were there, in fact, I was glad they were. If it wasn't for Kendra I might never have admitted my feelings to myself, and for some reason it felt really good that I was gratifying her in some way. As if I was paying her back by letting her see us nude.

Yasmin and I stood for a moment, drinking in the sight of each other's nakedness before I broke the silence.

"Now what?" I asked.

Yas nervously giggled, "I dunno. I've never done this before."

"Now Yasmin you lay on the bed," Kendra interjected. It seemed as good a suggestion as any, and Yas complied, climbing onto my bed and laying on her back.

"Anita, position yourself at your best friend's crotch and kiss up and down her thighs and stomach."

To tell the truth I was kind of grateful for Kendra's unprompted instructions. If I just did as she said, I didn't have to worry about what to do, and that took a lot of pressure off. I climbed on top of the bed between my best friend's legs, sitting on my knees and bending over so that I was at Yasmin's entryway. I took just a second to admire the pretty package before me, her juicy ass acting as a perfect cushion and propping up her neat, pink slit. A small hood sat atop it and the airstrip pubes seemed to point directly down as if to say *'Lick here!'* I wanted to lick there, but thought I should follow Kendra's instructions since she clearly had more experience in the area.

I planted sweet kisses around Yasmin's thighs, making my way across her midriff and going as far south as her pubic mound. It seemed be doing something for her as she wriggled a little in delight with every kiss, and the smell of her sex began to penetrate my nostrils, filling me with lust and making it harder not to immediately devour her pussy.

The thoughts of disobeying Kendra became greater, as I strongly considered going rogue and going down on Yasmin properly. I wasn't sure what she was waiting for, and I wasn't sure what I was waiting for. Maybe she'd finished giving instructions. She had helped to get things off the ground and now she was leaving it up to us to provide her with a show in return.

Just as I was about to go for it, she gave the order. "Anita, lick your friend's pussy from the base to the top."

Despite my confidence mere seconds earlier, I was mostly relieved that Kendra was still telling us what to do, and obliging her brought me almost as much joy as getting to eat Yasmin's cunt. I dove in and extended my tongue, finding the base of Yasmin's vagina and licking all the way up to her clit. Yasmin wriggled a little more violently this time as my tongue passed over her clit and up her hood. She let out a sharp moan of ecstasy and for a moment I thought she was about to cum on the spot. I let her settle and then did it again, and again, and again. Each lick would cause a little moan to escape her lips, and make her back arch a little higher, and make her small tits bobble just a little bit more.

Her pussy was slightly sweet tasting, and I loved the flavor of it in my mouth. I swallowed and allowed the honey to slide down the back of my throat. I purposefully favored her vagina over her clitoris so that I could taste more of her, probing as far into her as I could with my tongue, she was so delicious. Her velvety lips were soft on my tongue, allowing me to slide over them easily. The act wasn't penetrative like the first blowjob I ever gave. It was sweet, tender, and felt incredibly right, like I was made for it.

I must have only been eating her out for a minute before Kendra interjected again, this time very unwanted.

"Wait stop," she said. "This is wrong."

"What are you talking about?" I protested, "I'm just doing what you told me, and it seems to be working."

"It is," Yasmin said through a heavy breath, her voice suggesting she was dying to be sent over the edge and wanting me to finish the job.

"The two of you have been best friends for years, right?" Kendra asked.

"Yeah..." I answered hesitantly. I'd say I got past that little barrier the moment I put my face in Yasmin's snatch, why would it be a problem for Kendra now?

"You've done everything together, you even made sure you came to the same college. It's not right that Yasmin cums alone while you go down on her."

"I don't think either of us really mind, Kendra," I protested again, this time with a bit of attitude.

"I mind!" Kenda exclaimed, not angrily, but forcefully. "It's a lot more poetic if you cum together."

"What are you suggesting?" Yasmin asked, intrigued by the prospect.

"Anita, climb on top of Yasmin so that you can sixty-nine each other. It will really be worth it if you just do what I say, I promise you."

The thought of Yasmin's mouth on my pussy while mine was on hers was certainly an alluring one. And I would be lying if I said I didn't feel something innate inside me that wanted to please Kendra. If that meant getting my pussy licked, I decided that was just fine with me.

I sat up and moved to the side of Yas, who looked up at me from the bed with a gleeful look in her eyes. More than anything I just wanted to take my post at her pussy again, so without hesitation I swung a leg over her and crawled backwards a little so that my face hovered above her pussy, while my hairless one hovered above her pretty head. Yasmin's arms reached beneath and around my spread legs, grabbing both my ass cheeks firmly as she pulled my groin into her open mouth.

The sensation was incredible. Yasmin placed her entire mouth over my gash and probed the walls of my labia with her tongue. She licked up and down, eagerly feeding on my sex like her life depended on it. Blood rushed into my cheeks and I collapsed in ecstasy, finding my face once again at her pussy.

I bit lightly into her inner thigh before setting my tongue back to work in her snatch. Her wetness coated my mouth and chin the same as mine was no doubt doing to hers. Sufficiently ready to cum, Yasmin's mouth focused on my clit, and so I returned the favor. She nibbled gently on my little button, occasionally sucking it into her mouth and running her tongue over it, applying pressure. I mirrored her actions, figuring she was doing to me what she liked being done to her. I figured right. Her arms were now wrapped around my waist and she pulled me in closer as I circled her clit, her actions became a little more haphazard and I could tell she wasn't far off.

Yasmin let out a terrific moan as she achieved orgasm. Her arms hugged my waist tightly and her hips bucked into my face. Lubrication started dripping out of her and I tried to catch every last drop with my tongue before I came with her. My body shook and I tried to be mindful to not smash my groin too hard into Yasmin's face below it. My abdominal muscles tensed, driving my groin downward onto Yasmin's still open mouth and she pushed hard into it, her tongue entering my vagina. I allowed my tensing muscles and arching back to sit me upright, and I replaced my tongue on Yasmin's clit with my middle finger, trying to prolong the orgasm.

The two of us gyrated and contorted on my bed. Wave after wave of ecstasy washed through me as I sat on my best friend's face, her ruby red hair was all that wasn't being smothered by my ass and cunt. I pushed my head back and opened my mouth to scream but no sound came out, only stifled gasps. I had to guess Yas was having similar feelings as I could feel the vibrations of her moans in my pussy, and could see her toes curling in delight, and her own slit rising into the air repeatedly before lowering back down onto the cushions of her ridiculous ass. Without my mouth to collect it, Yasmin's gratuitous cum was dripping out of her and soaking my bed sheet. I didn't mind, it was fucking hot.

Eventually the orgasm subsided and I thought I better let Yas come up for air, so I swung a leg around and lay myself alongside her before flicking my hair over my shoulder and kissing her deeply. Our tongues rolled around in each other's mouths and I could taste the tartness of my own cum on her, in contrast to the sweeter taste of hers. I used the hand I just fingered her with to play with one of her tits while we made out. Her lubrication coated two of my fingers, which I used to tweak her nipple and make it glisten in the light with her own wetness. My sense of time was compromised, but at some point we were interrupted by Kendra.

"That was lovely, girls. I never tire of seeing two close friends express their feelings for each other sexually," she cooed in a slow, wet, almost orgasmic voice.

I'd almost forgotten that her and Taylor were even in the room. I looked up and saw Taylor sitting in Kendra's lap, thighs spread, her bubblegum panties around her ankles, skirt hoisted up with Kendra's hand playing with her pussy, which I could see was as bare as my own. Taylor had a blank sort of look on her face as if she'd just cum herself, her smile that I thought was permanent was replaced by an open, exhausted mouth as she panted. Kendra raised her hand to Taylor's face and she immediately took two fingers inside it, sucking her own cum off of Kendra. She moaned, apparently enjoying the taste.

"Anita, that was everything I could have hoped for," Yasmin said to me softly as the two of us regained our senses. I just looked at her and smiled.

"Now wasn't that the best sex you've ever had?" asked Kendra.

Yasmin and I made eye contact briefly, before we turned our heads and nodded in agreement. There was no penetration, no penis involved, and yet we both knew without a doubt that we'd just had sex. It was a wonderful, new feeling that made my chest feel light, and I basked in it, happy to be exploring this side of myself that I'd been keeping locked away.

"Do you think that would have happened if Taylor and I weren't here tonight?" Kendra furthered her questioning.

I thought for a second about how the night would have gone if Yasmin had come to my room and I was alone. I probably would have still been ashamed of my actions the night before, and been unable to get past it. We would have fought and if Yasmin confessed her feelings to me I probably wouldn't have known how to handle it and kicked her out. I would probably be crying at that very moment, instead of laying naked next to my friend in a post-orgasm haze. What Kendra was getting at was correct, having her there set the night on the best possible course.

"I don't think it would have, no," I admitted.

"No way," Yasmin concurred.

"I have a proposition for the two of you," Kendra said. "One that will unlock so many more pleasures than what you just experienced. A heightened state of sexual enlightenment. Would you be interested in that proposition?"

Yasmin and I didn't have to think this time. What I'd just experienced was the most incredible orgasm of my life, and if Kendra was saying that she could elevate that even more, I was all ears. Yasmin and I both spurted out "Yes" at the same time.

"Well, I think this evening's gotten a little off track, we were meant to be doing our assignment on animal behaviours seen in humans. However I think this proposition could even prove useful for that. You see, Taylor here is one of my good girls. She has given herself over to me and submits to me sexually. I tell her what to do and she does it. It's a symbiotic relationship.

"I get pleasure from gratifying beautiful women sexually, making them do things to each other that they once thought were depraved, and watching them experience the pleasures of that depravity. Taylor gets pleasure from the incredible orgasms she achieves, orgasms no man has ever given her, and getting to play with those same beautiful women. I suspect she's taken a particular liking to Yasmin here, her red hair and large ass really seems to be doing something for her."

Taylor's wide smile returned to her face as she nodded her head in agreement at Kendra's suggestion, looking straight at Yasmin with hungry eyes.

Kendra continued, "This dominant and submissive relationship is one seen in animal species too. Macaques have been known to be both dominant and submissive in sex, suggesting they're deriving pleasure from both roles. Now, to be one of my good girls is a little more elaborate than that, there's a few more facets to it. But I assure you, if the two of you submit yourselves to me, you'll experience sex like never before."

"So let me get this straight," I said. "Taylor is actually like… your sex pet?"

"If you want to call it that, sure. Taylor's one of my best girls," Kendra said as she used a finger to comb some of Taylor's hair behind her ear, looking at her adoringly.

"And you want Yasmin and I to submit to you so that we can have sex with a myriad of other women in whatever way pleases you?"

"In a sense, yes. But what I'm really asking is that for tonight you give yourselves over to me, and if afterwards you want to have sex with a myriad of other women in whatever way pleases me; then your friend will wax her little runway pubes off and the two of you will wear make-up whenever you see me and be ready for intense lesbian sex whenever I so choose."

"You won't regret it," Taylor said, her eyes not leaving Yas. "There's really no downside."

In my newly found sexual adventurousness and the strong desire to not have the night end just yet, I knew what my answer was. I wasn't sure whether I wanted to be one of Kendra's 'good girls', but at least for tonight, I was willing to follow her lead if it meant more passion and pleasure like what I'd just experienced. Part of me was worried about what Yasmin would say, whether she was interested in other girls or if it was just me she wanted to be with. And if I agreed it could hurt her feelings and diminish what she thought we had. However, my concerns were quickly quelled when Yas spoke before I could even open my mouth.

"I'm in," she said. Apparently she *was* interested in sex with other women besides myself, which was just fine and dandy from where I stood. I had plans to explore my obvious attraction to Kendra, and to continue the thrill I had gotten from following her demands earlier.

"Me too," I concurred. Taylor squealed once again, presumably ecstatic that she was going to get to have her way with Yasmin, who now looked back at her with similarly hungry eyes. I had a feeling the two would be making fast friends before the night was over.

"I'm glad to hear it," Kendra said. "Why don't you step off the bed and join me over here, Anita."

I looked down at Yasmin and we both giggled in disbelief that this night was actually happening. It was still crazy to me that a little over twenty four hours ago I didn't think I had any attraction to women and here I was about to fuck three of them. I climbed over Yas and got off the bed.

"Wait," Kendra stopped me before I started to walk. "You called Taylor my sex pet."

"I did," I replied.

"Well tonight you're my little sex pet too. So why don't you come over here, kneel in front of Taylor and eat her pussy so your red haired friend can watch."

This was what I had signed up for. I admit I did really enjoy the way Kendra spoke to me, the way she demanded it turned me on, and the thought of pleasing her filled me with joy. I walked over to the other bed where Taylor still sat in Kendra's lap, got down on my knees, removed Taylor's panties from around her ankles and spread the two pairs of smooth, feminine legs in front of me. Taylor's pussy blossomed for me as her legs spread, and I wasted no time in finding out what her nectar tasted like.

I licked up and down her bare cunt, spreading her labia with a flat tongue and targeting her clit with the pointed end. Taylor's hand immediately grabbed onto my hair and willed me closer, I shuffled forward a little so that I could oblige.

"Do you like watching your friend eat Taylor's

sweet pussy," Kendra posited to Yasmin.

"Yes," Yasmin sighed erotically, turned on by the sight.

"Then touch yourself while you watch them."

I paused for a moment in between licks and heard the familiar wet sounds of a pussy being masturbated. I pictured what Yasmin must look like, laying on the bed, one hand reaching down to flick her bean, the other playing with nipple that was still wet with her own juices, her head to the side watching Taylor's huge tits heave inside her crop top while I devoured her, my own rear staring back at her.

"That's a good girl," Kendra said in approval to me. "You can stop now."

I didn't really want to. In all the things I'd discovered tonight, the biggest thing that stood above the rest was that I loved eating pussy. The flavor, the skill to it, the pleasure it evoked in the woman I was going down on. The whole act was insanely erotic. Regardless, I honored my agreement to do what Kendra said, and stopped.

"Tell me Anita, when guys fuck you, what position is your favorite?"

"I like it when they fuck me from behind," I said without needing to think.

"You like it in doggy?"

"Yes."

"Interesting. Another point for the essay. Why don't you go and take that office chair from the desk and put it in the middle of the room, back facing towards your bed."

I got up from the floor and did as she instructed, and locked it in place so it wouldn't swivel.

"Climb onto it and lean over the back so you can see your friend."

Again, I complied and put my knees onto it, my arms resting on the top of the backrest, facing Yasmin who lay on the bed, looking at me with a lustful, excited look. She was still playing with herself gently, her lips parted as she watched me comply with Kendra's demands.

"Taylor, enjoy your red-haired meal."

Taylor didn't have to be told twice, she leapt up from Kendra's lap and stepped over to my bed where Yas lay, a look in her eye as if she was a lioness about to pounce on her prey. She pulled down the zipper on the side of her skirt and threw it away so that she was now bottomless. Then she reached down and took both of Yasmin's hands, pulling her up into a seated position on the edge of the bed.

Taylor lifted the crop top above her big tits, exposing them both but keeping the top on. Then she grabbed Yas by her red hair and pulled her face to her chest. Yasmin seemed very into it as she wrapped her arms around Taylor's lower back and brought them closer together as her mouth explored the hills and valleys of Taylor's generous breasts. Taylor giggled in elation at finally getting some sexual contact from Yas, playing with her bright red hair.

Kendra, still clothed in her black dress, stood from the bed and made her way over to me. While I was enjoying the sight of Yasmin and Taylor, I was feeling a little exposed in my crouched position on the chair, my bare ass and pussy poking out behind me in a submissive position. She lent down and whispered into my ear.

"I want you to watch everything my pet does to your best friend. You and her may have just had sex, but I want you to see the faces Yasmin's going to make as Taylor fucks her like she's never been fucked."

I was so fucking hot for Kendra. Her warm breath in my ear and the things she was saying made my cunt tingle in anticipation, my clit throbbing and begging to be stimulated. Yasmin's hands had wandered south and now played with Taylor's ass cheeks, coupled with the sight of her red curly hair in her chest I was made well and truly ready for orgasm number two.

Taylor tugged on Yasmin's hair, pulling her head back so she could lean down and kiss her on the mouth. "I'm going to go down on you, and do things you're going to enjoy but that you think you shouldn't enjoy. Give yourself over to them and tell me in great detail how much you like it, and how naughty you are for enjoying it." Taylor's smile had disappeared, replaced by a look of determination and seriousness. Yasmin nodded her compliance and Taylor dropped to her knees between Yas' legs.

Taylor used a hand to part Yasmin's lower lips and got to work with her tongue. At the same moment, I felt Kendra run a finger up my slick cunt and I moaned in approval, begging her to do more.

Taylor flicked her tongue in and out of her mouth with impressive speed against Yasmin's clitoris, attacking it with ferocity.

"That feels amazing on my clit," Yasmin said through a smile, enjoying a more practiced tongue between her legs.

Meanwhile, Kendra's expert hand got to work behind me while she kissed my shoulder-blades and nape of my neck. Her fingers explored the full length of my pussy, sliding between the labia and coating them in my wet. She slid her index finger into my vagina and I inhaled sharply at the sensation.

As if they were connected by some psychic link, I saw Taylor slip a finger into Yasmin's hole while she continued to lick her pink pearl, her nose nuzzling the pubic airstrip. Kendra added her middle finger inside me and brought her face back to my ear.

"Does it feel good to be fucked like a dog?" she asked me seductively.

"Yes," I said. Normally I would be offended by the comparison, but it was so fucking hot to give control to Kendra.

Yasmin leaned back on her hands, her tiny breasts and rib cage moving with the heavy breaths she was taking. She looked so pretty with her little button nose, cheeks flushed red, small figure and flowing ruby red hair dangling behind her. Regardless of what happened after the night was through, I foresaw a lot more steamy evenings between her and I.

Abruptly, Taylor stopped pumping Yasmin's snatch and stood up. She took Yas by the shoulders and pushed her onto the bed, so that Yasmin's head was at the foot end, pointed towards me. Taylor climbed on top, straddling the petite red-head, and lowered herself on top of her, running her hands through Yasmin's hair and kissing her deeply, her big tits pushing into Yasmin's small ones. Kendra kept sliding her two fingers in and out of my vagina while I watched their legs entwine and hands explore each other while they kissed passionately, their naked flesh pressing into one another. Yasmin's hands took each of Taylor's butt cheeks and squeezed.

After a long kiss, Taylor said to Yas, "Roll over onto your tummy so I can get a closer look at that spectacular ass."

Yasmin did so, flipping herself over beneath Taylor's legs, folding her arms in front of her and resting her head on them. Taylor lowered her wet crotch onto Yasmin's butt, and ground into it slightly as she kissed the back of Yasmin's neck and shoulders. Behind me, Kendra used her thumb to rub circles around my clit while simultaneously finger-fucking me. It felt really good and my abdominal muscles tightened in response. My channel tightened around her digits as she stimulated me closer to orgasm, and a soft moan escaped my lips as I listened to the wet sounds of her slick fingers pumping into me.

On my bed, I watched Taylor make her way south down Yasmin's back with kisses. She arrived at her plump derriere and sat up, looking down at it with admiration, cupping it with her hands.

"This part you're really going to want to watch," Kendra's hot breath said into my ear.

"Christ your ass really is something else, Yasmin."

Yas giggled at the compliment. "You can call me Yas. I make it a point that anyone who's about to lick my pussy can use my nickname."

"Oh, I'm not going to lick your pussy," Taylor said with a coy smile.

Yas made a puzzled look before Taylor grabbed her by her wide hips and pulled upwards, raising her bottom and forcing her to bring her knees up a little. I watched as Taylor leant down, used her hands to part the crack of Yasmin's gratuitous booty and extend her tongue into it, licking from the bottom to top, her pink tongue running through the deep valley of Yasmin's ass. Yasmin's expression turned from puzzled to shocked. And when Taylor brought her head back down to her asshole to lick it again, it turned from shock to unexpected pleasure. Taylor let go of Yasmin's ass cheeks and let them smother the sides of her face while she went to town on Yasmin's backside.

My face was firmly stuck in shock though. I'd almost forgotten about Kendra's magic hand playing with my pussy at the disbelief in what I was seeing. I had never, ever, done anything with my ass other than what it was intended for. I also couldn't believe that Yasmin was okay with being rimmed by a woman she'd just met, and yet, she seemed to like it, and did not protest. In fact just the opposite.

"Fuck that feels good," Yasmin said.

"Is it naughty?" Taylor's muffled voice said into Yasmin's bottom.

"It's so fucking naughty and dirty and *ohhh Christ*!" Yasmin let out a strained cry of pleasure. "But your tongue feels so good on my asshole. I fucking love it."

"Are you as naughty as your friend?" Kendra asked into my ear.

"Oh, I don't know," I said, very much hesitant.

"Why don't you ask your friend if she knows."

"Yas," I said, "Do you think I'd like it if Kendra did... that... to me?"

"Oh Ani, you've got to. It's the most amazing feeling. It's so taboo and hot," she replied through half-closed eyes and short breaths, she looked as though she was in heaven.

"I'll ask you again," Kendra said, "Are you as naughty as your friend?"

I decided to fight my hesitation. If I didn't like it then so what? I wouldn't do it again. The thought of the pleasure principle popped back into my head, reminding me to find immediate sexual gratification in whatever form it took. There didn't really seem to be a good reason to say no, so instead I replied, "Yes."

"Would you like it if I licked your asshole?"

"Yes," I sighed, as I was suddenly reminded of the sexual stimulation happening in my pussy.

Yasmin's face contorted in ecstasy on the bed. I could barely see Taylor's face, it was buried so deep in Yasmin's ample ass, digging with her tongue into my best friend's back door. Kendra's face moved away from mine and she positioned herself behind me, never stopping her finger-fucking and clit-rubbing. I felt her free hand grab a handful of one of my ass cheeks, and then the thumb of it ran up my crack, gliding over my tight, puckered asshole. A moment later there was a much warmer, softer appendage on it; Kendra's tongue.

She traced a circle around the rim of my hole with her slippery tongue, before flattening it and giving a slow, purposeful lick over it. I had to admit, it did feel pretty fucking amazing. Strange and unexpected, but so undeniably hot. Together with her hand working my pussy and the sheer naughtiness of the whole situation, I felt like I was on another plane of existence.

The sensual goddess licked over and over again while Taylor did the same to my best friend. Both of us moaning in pleasure at the feeling of having our asses serviced. If we were in Freud's oral stage before, we had definitely progressed to the anal stage now. My head briefly fell down onto the back of the chair before I forced myself to raise it, wanting to watch everything that Yasmin did. The familiar feeling of a rising orgasm could be felt in my loins.

Yasmin's sharp moans started to become louder and louder as she took her head off her arms and instead propped herself up on her elbows. I could see Taylor's arm pumping mechanically and figured she was fingering Yas the same as Kendra was doing to me.

"*Yes*, that feels so good, keep fucking me," she confirmed my suspicions. "Oh god your tongue is so good on my ass, please put it in me. Christ Ani, I can't wait to do this to you."

Taylor seemed to oblige as Yasmin's speech was cut off and her mouth made an O shape, her brow creased and eyebrows raised as Taylor's tongue penetrated her hole. Behind me, Kendra seemed to be trying to do the same thing, but not quite succeeding as my butt was clamped shut, I was still not quite sure how to react to the alien sensation and had not really relaxed. Undeterred, she probed my butthole over and over until I made a conscious effort to relax it, and her tongue slithered in with relative ease, filling the walls of the inside of my ass.

"Holy shit!" I exclaimed, and Yasmin laughed as if she was saying '*I know, right!?*'

I watched Taylor reach up with her free hand and pull Yasmin's hair, making sure she didn't look away from me. I imagined Yasmin was enjoying seeing Kendra behind me as much as I was seeing Taylor behind her. We were going to cum at the same time again, only this time it was with sexual deviants behind us. And this time it was me who arrived first.

The orgasm was like two bombs going off. First, one in my pussy, one I was familiar with, yet slightly different. It emanated from the spot that Kendra was rubbing inside my vagina, still clitoral in origin, but more intense. It went off like a hand grenade, causing a chain reaction in my asshole that was definitely *un*familiar to me. If part one of my orgasm was a grenade, this was a nuclear fucking bomb. I felt my ass contract around Kendra's tongue and she pulled it out, but continued to lick with great speed. I could feel my glutes vibrating and heard the sounds my wet pussy made to Kendra's hand as my cum spilled out. My eyes would have rolled back into my head if I wasn't so determined to watch Yasmin cum too. Instead, they just watered as I forced myself to keep them open.

Her experience looked similar to mine. She let out an almighty groan and tried to drive her head down, but Taylor's firm grasp of her hair prevented it. She pushed her fat rear as hard as she could into Taylor's face, begging for just an eighth of an inch more tongue to be inside her butt. Her ass cheeks jiggled against Taylor's face, before her back arched forward and brought her groin back down into the bed, causing it to pull away from Taylor's tongue, which seemed to act like a ripcord and make Taylor groan again as a second wave hit her. Taylor let go of her hair and withdrew from her cunt, mercifully letting her collapse to the bed, prone. She lay there facing downwards, her fabulous butt jiggling sporadically as aftershocks made their way through her. I similarly collapsed over the back of the chair, completely spent.

"Come here, Taylor," Kendra said. "I want to taste our new little redhead friend's ass on your tongue."

Taylor climbed off the bed and met Kendra in the middle of the room. They embraced, exchanging flavors with their mouths while Yasmin and I collected ourselves.

"Not too long now, girls," Kendra said, allowing us a short reprieve from the fucking so we could see straight again. "I haven't had my turn."

Yasmin wearily picked herself up from the bed, and I slid off the chair. We both went to the pair of lesbians making out in the middle of my room, the Goddess in the black dress surrounded by three of her naked good girls. Taylor reached around behind her and undid the zip down the back of her dress, exposing her lovely, olive-skinned back with a bra strap running across it. Without pausing from kissing Taylor, Kendra slid her arms out of her sleeves and pushed the dress down to the floor. She was pantiless, and stood there wearing only her bra. I could only see the back of her, but it was a lovely view. Her ass was large and round, although not quite as big as Yasmins. However, it was firmer, tighter, and held in place perfectly, the result of good genes and many hours at the gym.

I began kissing her neck and shoulders while Yasmin finished the job and undid Kendra's bra, which fell to the ground. Kendra did a half turn and gave Yas and I the full view of the front of her body. Her gorgeous, heavy breasts that were perfectly round with puffy pink nipples, the out-line of her abdominal muscles visible on her taut stomach, her wide hips and delta of trimmed, neat pubic hair adorning her pelvic mound. She really was one of the most stunning women I'd ever seen. Curvaceous, attractive and in charge.

The idea of being one of her good girls on a more permanent basis was seeming more appealing by the minute.

"My breasts require attention, girls," she said, demanding our mouths.

We didn't need to be told twice. Yasmin and I each took one of her boobs and covered them in saliva with kisses and licks. Taylor kissed her neck from behind and her hands explored Kendra's lower half, running over her hips and short bush.

Kendra placed her palm on the top of my head and pushed me down to my knees. I was apparently the chosen one to lick her pussy first, which I was quite pleased about. Kendra made her stance wider, opening her legs for me and granting access to the treasures within. I placed my hands on each of her thighs and leaned in with my tongue extended, making contact with her delicious snatch, my third for the night. Her nectar tasted as womanly as I would expect from someone like Kendra. As I enveloped her whole clit in my mouth, it activated my taste buds and stung my nostrils which were buried in her pubes. I heard her sigh above me and the feeling of pleasing Kendra filled me with elation and satisfaction.

I continued to play with her clit as much as I could, it was about the only area I could attend to in our current position. It was engorged with desire, I couldn't imagine how she'd gone through the whole night without having cum yet. Although from the sounds of it that was part of the fun for her, giving her girls pleasure before she got hers, teasing herself with the sexual acts she would make her subjects perform on one another. I loved every moment of eating her flower, satiated by her fragrant sex and filled with confidence as I made her moan.

"Yasmin, I desperately want to kiss your friend, but unfortunately that would leave my pussy unattended. Be a good girl and see to that." Kendra instructed.

Yas accepted Kendra's invitation and practically pushed me out of the way to get her turn at eating her out. I giggled to myself at her eagerness and stood up, complying to Kendra and kissing her without wiping my chin. Her own sticky cum spread around her mouth while I kissed her, dripping down between our chins and onto her voluptuous chest. She moaned softly into my mouth at the feeling of Yasmin licking her, and Taylor's hand which now played with her bosom. The three of us were determined to give as much pleasure to our mistress as possible.

"Taylor, honey, go and sit on Anita's bed head. My mouth will be with you shortly."

Taylor nearly jumped in excitement, and scurried off to my bed, where she positioned herself atop my bed head, legs spread wide.

"I hope you picked up some pointers on how to eat a girl's ass properly," Kendra said to me. "You got to experience it first hand from an expert while watching another, so I have high expectations. I'm going to go and lick Taylor's sexy little pussy on all fours. I'll trust you know what you have to do."

Kendra removed herself from Yasmin's begging mouth and climbed onto my bed. Yasmin's head followed her in disappointment that she couldn't continue the cunilingus. Kendra did exactly as she said and when on her hands and knees, delved into Taylor's smooth snatch. Taylor's lips pursed and eyes narrowed at the feeling as she let out a long exhale of satisfaction. I made my way over to them, climbing onto my bed and preparing myself to eat ass for the first time.

I positioned myself the same as Kendra, on my hands and knees, my feet dangling over the edge of the bed, Kendra's round ass, pink slit and pretty little brown pucker filling my field of vision. For an act I had considered lewd and uninviting not even an hour ago, I was keen to taste Kendra's asshole. I'd found myself loving the different flavors of pussy, and had sampled four in one night, counting my own. I couldn't think of anything I'd rather do in that moment than to lick this amazing woman's ass.

And so I did. I placed my face into the crack of her open rear, feeling the warmth of her cheeks against my own, and put the tip of my tongue onto her hole's opening. It was more of a salty taste, reminding me of olives. It was in stark contrast to the sweet flavors I'd been lapping up all night in my friends' groins. I liked it. It was different, in a good way. I slowly licked Kendra's asshole and ran the tip of my tongue around the outside of it to confirm. I definitely liked it. My licks grew more confident, as I remembered what Kendra's tongue had done to my ass, and tried to recreate it.

The memories brought back a familiar feeling in my own rear, and I longed to feel them again. Apparently I not only had some major lesbian tendencies in me, but also some anal desires as well. Freud would have a field day with this night! Fortunately for me, the longing for a tongue on my ass was soon relieved, as I felt a warmth behind me that could only be Yasmin's eager-to-please mouth.

Yasmin must have been feeling a little left out, and luckily for her, she'd been provided the perfect opportunity to fulfil her desire to rim me. With how short Yasmin was, she barely had to lean over to have access to my little brown star, and she grabbed me by the hips as she nuzzled her way between my cheeks.

The train of lesbians was a sight to behold. Taylor on the bed head, having her pussy eaten by her mistress, Kendra on all fours having her ass eaten by me, who was similarly in her favorite doggystyle position having my ass eaten by the small, red-haired woman standing at the end of the bed.

I believe the view was quite special for Taylor, who had the perfect vantage point to watch the rimming from her position atop the bed head, and I heard the sounds of her cumming, slightly rocking the bed with her uncontrollable movements. This set off a chain reaction in Kendra, whose asshole opened up as the rest of her body tensed, and I seized the opportunity to insert my tongue inside of her, like she had done to me.

The rim of her hole throbbed against my tongue, contracting and relaxing at a rapid rate, my tongue being forced out one moment and then sucked back in the next. Kendra made a terrific scream, muffled by Taylor's gash. Yas chose that moment to wrap her arms around my thighs, lift them slightly off the bed and bury her face as deep as she could into my ass, her whole mouth around my opening, and as her tongue pressed into it, she shook her head left and right, completely devouring my butt and setting off the next link in the chain reaction, me.

The three of us came spectacularly. Only Yasmin didn't, although I suspect she didn't mind. We all collapsed in a heap on the bed and Yas crawled up and snuggled my shoulder while we composed ourselves. The four of us in a naked heap. Our pussies tingling in the afterglow, our asses in a state of complete satisfaction, the nectar of four women's pussies and one ass running down the back of my throat. It was quite the night of self discovery.

But one night was nowhere near enough. My best friend and I both wanted more, and wanted to experiment further with other women. We wanted to see how far we were willing to submit to the great and powerful Kendra. We wanted to be good girls.

Yas waxed her pubes the following morning.

We got an A on our assignment.

THE END

SPOTTING A LESBIAN

Amanda

I had the little dyke this time. I had her dead to rights. I knew the little blonde slut had been up to something for months with that other woman she's always working out with, and I finally had proof. Brooke was finally going down.

I kept replaying the security camera footage over and over. It was taken the previous night when the gym was empty apart from the two of them. I'd been coming into work early for the last few days and checking the recordings before my shift started, trying to catch them in the act. There was always something about their passing glances, the way one would watch the other work out, how they'd spot each other just a little too close. Something about their energy just made me know they were fucking each other. If they thought they could have nasty lesbo sex in my place of work, they had another thing coming.

The recording didn't show much; just the tall, olive-skinned brunette spotting the short-haired blonde one from behind on the squat rack. Once the blonde finishes her set, the brunette whispers something in her ear and then the blonde turns her head to kiss her on the mouth. Then the brunette grabs her towel and walks out of frame towards the showers, and a moment later the blonde, Brooke, disappears towards the showers as well. What I wouldn't give to have a camera in there to prove it beyond any possible doubt.

I thought about what I should do with the footage. Lewd behaviour in the campus gym was strictly forbidden of course. I could show it to my boss and have both their memberships revoked. Although the footage didn't actually show them fucking, it just showed a kiss. The boss probably wouldn't go for kicking them out if he thought it could backfire on him with accusations of homophobia. Still, it confirmed my suspicions, and I needed to use it to get rid of them somehow.

I'd gotten to know Brooke's routine fairly well over the last few weeks of my investigation into her and the brunette. She was in most days during the daytime, but on Tuesdays and Thursdays she would come late at night, after the staff had gone and the gym was empty. Sometimes she brought the brunette with her, but mostly she was alone. I'd watched hours of her working out on security footage and in person. She was dedicated to her body, and would spend different days working different muscle groups. Her lonesome late night sessions though, were always dedicated to her abs and ass. Crunches and squats all night. With a body like hers she could have any guy she wants, I had no idea why the dyke would want her minge eaten by another woman.

With it being a Wednesday, Brooke walked through the doors in the afternoon with her gym bag strapped over her shoulder. I watched her enter and tried to hide my wicked smile as I had decided on a plan to get her out of my gym. I was going to go into the gym the following night and do some paperwork while I waited for her to arrive. Then, I would sit her down and confront her, show her the footage and threaten to show my boss if she and her brunette slut friend ever stepped foot in my gym again. Hopefully she'd be so embarrassed that she would take the opportunity to avoid further humiliation, and wouldn't call my bluff.

"Um... hi, Amanda," Brooke said and snapped me back to the present. I had been staring at her for far too long and she'd noticed.

"Hi," I replied, a little caught off guard.

"They've got you working pretty hard, huh?

Long day?"

"Oh, yeah something like that."

"Hey, can I ask you something? Do you have any tips for my glutes? I think my ass is looking a little flat."

She spun around and went up on her tiptoes, pointing her ass out to me through her tiny little workout shorts. The bitch was just messing with me, she knew damn well her ass was anything but flat. She did enough squats to see to that. It was perfectly round and firm.

"I think you should just continue whatever it is you're doing, it seems to be working fine," I said dismissively.

"Oh, thanks Amanda. I'm glad you like it," she said, misinterpreting my words as a compliment. Christ, it took every ounce of will to not expose her lesbian antics on the spot in front of everyone. But I had to wait until she was alone. I had to be patient. I watched her while she worked on her back and planned what I was going to say the next night.

✦✦✦

Work and classes on Thursday dragged on in anticipation of the lesbian slut-shaming scheduled to take place that night. Eventually though, the sun set and I took a shower to prepare myself for the night. I felt a strange, sexual urge while I was in the shower thinking about what was to come. Something about humiliating Brooke was kind of turning me on. It was an odd sensation for me to be feeling, but my pussy was getting wet and my hand made its way down my abs, through my sandy blonde pubes and into my slit.

I thought about the face she would make when I showed her the footage. I thought about her mouth opening wide and her brow creasing in shock while I jilled off. I thought about her begging not to show anyone because of how ashamed she was while I pressed my ass against the cold tile of the shower. I thought about her on her knees, looking up at me pleadingly and I pressed my hand against the glass to brace myself. Finally, I thought about her dropping her head and crying, her mascara running down her cheeks, and I came. The night promised to be a lot of fun.

I decided that rather than getting back into my smelly work clothes, I could go a bit more casual. In fact, I decided to go in showing a bit of skin, to see if I could make Brooke check me out, humiliating her all the more when the time came to expose her. I had a good set of tits and an ass that could almost rival Brooke's. So I put on a tight pair of light blue jeans and a tight, dark red halter top with a deep V. I decided to forgo a bra in order to show off my cleavage. I wrapped my long blonde hair up in a bun behind my head to show off my neckline and bralessness. It did seem to add a bit of nefariousness to my plan, making Brooke think about fucking me before I humiliated her for her lesbian affairs in the gym, but I didn't care. I wasn't the villain, she was.

I walked onto the college campus, my usual route to work, although I'd never done it with the sun down. It was late enough that there shouldn't be anyone in the gym anymore, but not so late that Brooke would be there already. As I approached I noticed the blinds were all down, protocol for the last staff member who left the gym. I used my swipe card to unlock the door, the same way any member would to let themselves in after hours.

As I closed the door behind me I heard the familiar metallic clank of a barbell being put back on the rack. Someone was still here. No matter, if Brooke turned up before they left I would just wait for them to go before confronting the dyke.

Except for one thing. It was her! Brooke had beat me there. It was dark but still earlier than I'd ever seen her there on a Thursday. What the hell was she doing here early? She looked at me from the other side of the gym, peering around various exercise equipment. I stood there frozen, not sure of what to do, this wasn't part of the plan.

"Amanda?" she called out. "Is that you?"

"Oh… yeah. Hi Brooke. I'm just here to do some paperwork I didn't get done earlier. Just uh… pretend I'm not here." I needed time to get ready, to cue up the footage, to make sure things went according to plan.

"Wow, they really do have you working hard," she replied, before turning around and lifting the barbell across the back of her shoulders, proceeding with her squats in front of the mirrors, her round bottom taunting me as she lowered each time.

I made my way over to the staff desk and signed in to the computer. I had a better vantage point of her from there. She always had on all this eyeshadow, blush and lip-liner, I don't know anyone else who gets so dolled up to go to the gym. She wore white leggings that proudly displayed her toned ass, the crevice between her cheeks visible at her lowest point in the squat, and then the outline of it observable when she stood back up. She had on a tight, sleeveless activewear top that bared her midriff and kept her smallish breasts in place.Her short blonde hair only just kissed the barbell bar across her shoulders. I found myself once again wondering why she would want some other woman going down on her when she could get any piece of cock she wanted.

Once again, she caught me looking at her in

the mirror. I felt her eyes look at my reflection and I quickly returned to my computer screen, refocusing myself to the task at hand. I found the footage of the brunette kissing her at the very squat rack she was on and played it again for my own benefit, just so that I was absolutely sure I wanted to do this.

Seeing her kiss that woman in the footage reignited my disgust in her though. I couldn't let her keep having repugnant lesbian sex in *my* gym.

"Hey Brooke," I called out. "Could you come here for a minute?"

"Sure, just a sec," she replied as she finished her set and mounted the barbell onto the rack behind her. She grabbed her phone and towel and wiped the sweat off her face as she made her way over to the staff desk.

"Have a seat," I motioned to the two chairs on the other side of the desk.

"What's up?," she asked as she sat down.

"Well Brooke, I'm afraid nothing good."

"Oh?"

"I happened upon some footage from Tuesday night that I've found a little disappointing."

"I see. Sorry I just forgot I have to send

someone a really important message, just give me two seconds and I'll be all yours," the dyke interrupted me, texting rapidly. I sat there patiently, unamused but unperturbed. "So sorry," she apologized. "You were saying?"

"Yes. I was," letting her know my disapproval. "Well I've found some footage from the other night of you and another member of ours that you might find interesting."

I turned the monitor towards Brooke and pressed play, watching her watch the video. That look of shame I imagined in the shower would be coming any moment now...

...but it never did. Brooke remained expressionless while she watched the video. Like she couldn't care less. Perhaps she was just in shock and didn't know how to react.

"Well?" I said, trying to prompt some shame out of her.

"Well what, Amanda? I'm not sure what I'm meant to be looking at."

I spun the monitor back around to me. I hadn't played the wrong part, it was showing Brooke walking off screen, following her brunette friend into the showers. What the hell was she talking about?

"You and the brunette. I've been watching the

two of you for quite some time. I know the two of you are fucking in the gym, and now I have proof. I thought I'd rather show you this in private, to give you the opportunity to quietly stop coming here, because I'm a nice person. I don't want to have to show this to my boss and make a whole thing of it. You know sexual relations of any sort aren't permitted in the gym, Brooke."

"I see," Brooke said. "But Amanda, seeing as you're such a nice person and all, how about you just don't bring it up with your boss, or better yet, delete the footage altogether. And I promise nothing untoward will happen in the gym again."

"I'm afraid I can't do that, Brooke," I said, becoming a little concerned with how according to plan this conversation was *not* going.

"Why's that?" she asked.

"Because it's against the gym rules. The gym that I work at. And I must uphold those rules at all times."

"It's not because you disapprove of two girls fucking?"

I was taken aback. This was getting out of hand. "Brooke, I'm not homophobic if that's what you're implying."

"Then what do you have to gain from showing

that footage to your boss?"

"Respect in my workplace. The feeling of doing the right thing. What do I have to gain from not showing my boss?"

"Something better," Brooke said ominously with a wry smile.

Just then the beep of the door card-reader sounded, and I felt the cool night air suddenly enter the room as the door opened. I spun around in my chair to see who was here at this hour and my heart skipped a beat.

It was the brunette.

Brooke's lover.

She donned dark gray activewear, the same style as Brooke did with the midriff showing. Her large breasts tested the limits of the top and her nipples were visible after coming in from the cool air outside. Her dark brown hair cascaded over her shoulders, her full lips not saying anything as she walked in. Christ, I must have inadvertently chosen one of their tandem workout/ hookup nights. She walked over and sat down next to Brooke in the other chair.

"Amanda," Brooke said, "this is my brunette friend, Kendra."

"A pleasure to meet you," I said, unsure of

what else to even say. The wheels had really come off. The chances of seeing Brooke beg seemed like they were rapidly diminishing.

"And you too, I'm sure," Kendra said politely. "Now, what's this about a video?"

How the hell did she know? The text message. Brooke knew exactly what I was talking about as soon as I mentioned having footage.

"Well, you see," I started, suddenly unsure of myself and caught slightly off guard by Kendra's confidence and poise. "Unfortunately, I have seen footage of yourself and Brooke engaging in... lesbian activities in this gym."

"Oh, the gym is anti-lesbian?" Kendra questioned.

"Well, no. I suppose it's more just sex that's banned in the gym," I said, suddenly finding myself on the defensive.

"I don't think you have us on tape having sex," Kendra pushed.

"Well you can clearly see in the video the two of you kissing and then going to the showers together."

"So what? What does that mean? We kissed, showered and went home. Doesn't sound like sex to me."

Oh God, she was calling my bluff. My plan was backfiring.

"Of course, we did have sex. Dirty, passionate, lesbian sex," Kendra said.

What the fuck? Why would she admit that? She just correctly pointed out I had nothing solid on them and she was giving me a confession. Why?

"But of course, you didn't want to use this footage to try and kick Brooke out of the gym. You wanted to use it for other reasons," Kendra stood up and made her way behind me, putting her hands on my bare shoulders. She leaned down so that her lips were at my ear, "You wanted to use the footage to try and have sex with Brooke."

"What!?" I said in disbelief at what I was hearing. "What the fuck are you talking about?"

"Brooke's told me about you," Kendra continued. "She's told me about how you watch her workout. She sees you in the mirrors."

"As recently as tonight," Brooke chimed in. I tried to maintain my composure but my cheeks betrayed me, flushing red.

"What exercise were you doing?" Kendra asked.

"Squats."

"Ooh, good choice, Amanda. There aren't many women that look as good as Brooke when she does squats," Kendra said, taunting me. "Brooke, honey, why don't you go and do another set."

Brooke got up from her chair and made her way back over to the squat rack, hoisting the barbell across her shoulders once again and squatting in those revealing white leggings that showed every square inch of her figure.

"I wasn't watching her because I wanted to fuck her. I was watching her because I was trying to figure out if she was a dirty dyke," I protested.

"Then why are you watching her now?" Kendra asked, "You already know."

"What... I'm not... I don't..." I couldn't form a coherent sentence as my eyes searched for anywhere else to look, but failed.

"It's always the homophobic ones that have the most burning desires. I bet you've masturbated to her, haven't you."

I watched Brooke go into a deep lunge forward, her ass compressing in the tight leggings, her boobs pressing forward against her top, her eyes watching mine in the mirror.

"It wasn't to her. It was to her shame, her begging-"

"Her begging?" Kendra said, spinning my chair around to face her. "Begging you to delete the video? Begging you to let her stay in the gym? Saying she'd do whatever you want?"

"Yes!" I said in frustration.

"Brooke, come over here and beg Amanda for what she really wants."

I heard the barbell placed back onto the rack again, and the next second Brooke was in front of me, on her knees. She placed her hands on my thighs and looked up at me with pleading eyes. Kendra standing behind her with her arms crossed.

"Please Amanda, I beg you to let me stay at the gym. I'll do whatever you want, I'll let you do whatever you want to me, I'll eat your pussy, I'll lick your asshole!" Brooke said.

I sat there in stunned silence. My mouth opened wide and my brow creased in shock. How had we gotten here?

Kendra spoke up. "Brooke and I will leave this gym right now and never return, if you can look me straight in the eye and say that your panties aren't wet."

I looked up at her, mouth still open. Confused. I was suddenly very aware of my panties and the damp spot that I could feel in them. I couldn't say it. It would be a lie and she would surely be able to tell. So instead I just sat there, looking up at her in silence.

Like an attack dog who'd just received it's command, Brooke thrust forward from the ground, a hand flying around to the back of my neck and her lips planting firmly onto mine. I sat there staring at her, my lips not moving, looking at her closed eyes and dark eyeshadow in front of me. I didn't push her off, I didn't want to. As if by their own will, my lips relaxed and parted slightly. Brooke locked hers in between and held my head there firmly from my neck.

My mind felt like a warzone. Scattered and loud and confusing. Why wasn't I pushing this dyke off me? Why were my panties wet? But as I felt my lips start to kiss Brooke back, I could only come to one logical conclusion: I was enjoying it.

Perhaps the brunette was right. Perhaps my hatred of Brooke all these months was actually hatred of myself for lusting after her. Perhaps my dismissal of Kendra was because I was jealous of what she had with Brooke.

Brooke's tongue fluttered across my lips, seeking entry. All the questions flying around in my mind evaporated and I thought only of her tongue. I opened my mouth in response and closed my eyes, letting our tongues encircle one another and dart into each other's mouths. Her mouth and tongue weren't like any other I'd kissed, they were soft, restrained and passionate. I felt butterflies in my groin and was increasingly aware of the wet patch in my underwear.

Brooke broke the kiss and stepped back, standing upright in her white fitness clothes while I sat there wide-eyed and breathless. Fuck she was hot. I felt suddenly okay admitting that to myself. Her figure was amazing and her pretty face with short blonde hair was so attractive.

"How wet are your panties?" Kendra asked.

"Soaked," I admitted.

"You should probably take them off then."

The suggestion was enticing. I wasn't the biggest fan of sitting in wet underwear, it seemed like the right thing to do for my comfort. So I kicked off my shoes, stood up, unzipped my jeans and pulled them down along with my panties, throwing them under the desk. I sat down again, still wide-eyed and not quite sure what the fuck was going on, or what was going to happen next.

"You weren't kidding, you're glistening," Kendra said, and I was suddenly aware of my open, naked legs. I crossed them in embarrassment at being bottomless in front of two women. "No, leave them open," Kendra instructed.

I don't know why I felt compelled to do what she told me, but I did. There was something about her sultry voice, her confidence, and femininity, that just made me want to comply. I uncrossed my legs and displayed my blonde, furry crotch for the two gorgeous women to see. They both stood there looking at me in approval. Brooke in her whites and blonde hair, Kendra the opposite with her darks and brown hair. I just kept thinking to myself, how did I get here?

"Brooke, why don't you show our unsure little friend just what a dyke can do," Kendra suggested.

Brooke immediately returned to her knees in front of me and kissed her way up one of my thighs. I gripped the armrests and raised my body against the back of the chair, as if I was afraid of what was coming, even though all I could think about was how much I wanted it. Kendra moved to my side, placed her hands on my shoulders and leaned into my ear again.

"Relax," she said calmly as she gently pushed me back down into the seat. "There's nothing to be afraid of. Brooke's going to take good care of you. She's going to help you come to terms with all of this. By the end of the night, you won't be confused anymore."

That sounded nice. If I just let Brooke do her thing I wouldn't have to feel like this anymore. I focused on my breathing and watched as the short blonde hair made its way towards my wet snatch.

A moment later and it had. Brooke stopped and looked up, but not at me, at Kendra to my side. Kendra gave some unspoken command and Brooke lowered her head. She took me into her mouth and I almost jumped out of the chair again, although this time not in fear but in elation. Kendra was at my shoulders ready to keep me in place though and I settled back in. It felt so fucking good having Brooke's soft mouth on my pussy. Brooke continued to lick and kiss all over my cunt, leaving no inch of vulva or labia unseen to.

She extended her tongue inside my vagina and curled it upwards, scooping out my cum as she withdrew and licked upwards to my clit. The only noise was my sharp breaths, the wet sounds of my vagina and the rustling of my pubes as Brooke's nose disturbed them. It was a beautiful sight seeing her pretty face between my legs, and I found myself wanting to see what the other parts of her looked like.

A hand made its way into the deep V of my halter top and began massaging my braless breast. It was Kendra's.

"Doesn't that feel nice?" she said. "Doesn't that feel easier than anger?"

She tweaked my nipple between her forefinger and thumb and I gasped a little. It did feel good though. I found myself reluctantly loving everything these two sexy women were doing to me. She continued to play with my boob while she spoke into my ear.

"You may have a few things wrong about Brooke and my relationship though," she said.

"You're lesbian lovers, what's to get wrong?" I said, looking up at her eyes, my brow creased at the orgasm that was swirling around in my loins, threatening to explode in the very near future.

"Brooke here is one of many of my lesbian lovers. She's one of my good girls."

"What? Your good girls? What does that mean?"

"It means she submits herself to me sexually. There's a handful of beautiful women around campus who do the same. I seduced them and unlocked desires they didn't know they had within themselves. In return they give themselves to me, and do whatever I tell them to do in order to have the most intense sexual experiences you could possibly imagine. Right now Brooke's teasing you, I bet by now you're getting desperate to cum, aren't you? But Brooke's not going to let you until I tell her to. Isn't that right, Brooke?"

"Yes, Kendra," Brooke replied into my snatch.

"So Amanda, this leaves you in a precarious position; wanting so badly to cum onto the face of the woman you've been lusting after for months, footage of you now on the security cameras being eaten out at work, confused feelings about your sexuality swirling around in your head. All these problems are solvable though, Amanda. All you have to do is give yourself over to me, submit to me, put me in charge of your sexual fantasies and I'll assure you they will be realized. Even the ones you didn't know you had. You'll be able to fuck Brooke here whenever you like. All you have to do is shave that hairy muff of yours and become one of my good girls. For now though, all you have to do is say the words."

"Okay!" I almost squealed, so desperate to cum.

"Okay...?" Kendra replied, coaxing me for more.

"I submit to you. I'll be one of your good girls or whatever the fuck. I'll do whatever you want, I'll shave what you want me to shave, I'll lick what you want me to lick. I'm yours as long as Brooke is too."

Kendra smiled, "Brooke, alleviate our new friend of her suffering."

At that moment Brooke sucked the whole top part of my cunt into her mouth and flicked my clitoris inside it. Simultaneously, Kendra twisted my diamond hard nipple just a little and placed her mouth on my neck, biting into it slightly. The combination of pleasure and pain immediately sent me over the edge and the swirling beginnings of an orgasm in my groin became a full blown whirlpool of tremendous energy, sucking in all it could before releasing it in a tidal wave of ecstasy, pushing down onto my clit and pubis.

I tried to cry out in pleasure, but Kendra covered my mouth with her hand, stifling my scream. We were in a campus gym after all. Brooke kept sucking on my clit and rolling it around in her mouth, every time a wave of bliss receded she would give it a flick and make a new wave crash down into me. My back arched upwards and my ass raised out of the chair, my tensed legs pushing it backwards, thankfully the desk was there to stop it rolling away or my head would have fallen out beneath me.

I rode out the climax with Brooke's mouth on my snatch and Kendra's hand over my mouth. I looked up at Kendra who only looked back at me with cool indifference. My tensed muscles suddenly felt weak and I collapsed backwards into the chair, my limbs splayed out to the sides. An aftershock shot up from my clit to my brain and I shuddered in delight and giggled at just how intensely I had cum.

Brooke looked up at me from the floor with her ocean blue eyes and wiped my love juices off of her chin, before licking her hand and swallowing, not letting any of the precious nectar go to waste.

My post-climax fog started to dissipate and was replaced with the inescapable reality that was dawning on me. I'd just allowed another woman to go down on me, I was a lesbian. What's more is that I too was now on tape having sex in the gym, and not just a kiss where I could maybe get away with it, but proper sex. My cunt was even pointed at one of the security cameras the entire time.

Excuses began to flood my mind. The dirty dykes tricked me. They turned my words around and seduced me, knowing that I couldn't expose them without exposing myself. It was all part of their plan to corrupt women and do whatever they wanted.

However, after taking one look at Kendra and Brooke, both staring at me, the cogs turning in my head trying to make sense of the evening, I dismissed every excuse that entered my head. As hard as it was to accept, the truth was in my wet pussy. I had loved every moment of Brooke tantalizing me, fucking me. I had been so obsessed with her lately not out of spite, but out of infatuation. This was all too much. I looked to Kendra for guidance.

"Am I a lesbian now?" I asked her.

"Do you feel like one?" she replied.

"I don't really feel different. Less angry, but otherwise the same."

"Having sex with a woman doesn't make you a lesbian, Amanda. You show me the straightest woman in the world and I'll show you another woman who could make her cum harder than she ever has in her narrow-minded life. The fact is you like having your pussy eaten, you like cumming. Doesn't every woman? It's just that tonight you were shown a different way of having your pussy eaten, and you came differently, and that makes you completely the same as every other 'straight' girl I've fucked."

She made sense, and it made me feel a little better. However, Kendra could see I was still struggling with it. She propped me up by the chin so I was looking in her eyes.

"Have you ever thought about what Brooke would look like working out naked?"

I felt a warmth return to my sensitive groin.

My clit twinged at the thought. I think I had thought about that before, without meaning to. While I watched Brooke work out, plotting against her, I would sometimes imagine what her ass looked like beneath her shorts when she did her squats, or her boobs when she did her dumbbell flys. But instead of lingering on these thoughts, I would catch myself and dismiss them immediately.

"I have," I admitted to Kendra. "Usually when I watch her do squats, I wonder what her ass and cunt look like."

"Why don't you take off Brooke's leggings, Amanda, and you can see for yourself."

My heart was suddenly beating a whole lot faster as Brooke stood up and looked down at me expectedly, her hands behind her back so that her boobs poked out at my head height. I raised my hands and stared at her groin with wide eyes. Unsure of myself, I let my hands collapse to my lap and searched for an excuse to not do what I so desperately wanted to.

"The door," I said. "Anyone could walk in."

"I flipped the lock when I came in," Kendra replied. "It's okay darling, it's what you want. Don't deny yourself the pleasures of a beautiful woman."

I searched for another excuse but came up

empty. Perhaps if I tried harder I could think of something but in my heart of hearts I knew I didn't want to. I reached out again and put my hands on Brookes bare, toned, midriff. A drip of sweat ran down the outline of her abdominals and was stopped by the waistband of her leggings, as if it was begging me to pull them down so it could continue its journey south. Brooke's flesh was warm, soft and slightly wet from her workout that I'd interrupted. Without further hesitation, I lowered my hands the few inches to her waist and curled my fingers into the inside of her leggings.

I grasped firmly, gulped, breathed out and pulled down on them. The activewear hugged her sexy legs so tightly that they peeled down, revealing Brooke's perfectly smooth pussy, the top of her slit visible from front on, a tiny hood shielding her clitoris. The leggings continued to peel down over Brooke's long legs and I had to lean forward to get them all the way to the bottom, finding myself inches away from her exposed crotch. I caught a whiff of her feminine scent mixed with the faint smell of salty sweat, and I felt the sudden desire to taste it on my tongue.

I had to refrain for now, however, as Brooke's undressing continued. Her leggings now lay bunched up on the floor as she stepped out of them, now as bottomless as me. I looked up and down her legs, my eyes lingering again on her pussy, as I became consumed with the thought of eating it.

"Does my ass look as good naked as you thought it would?" Brooke asked as she spun around, showing me her bare derriere.

"Yes," I said without question. It was as lovely as every thought I'd managed to repress in my psyche. It was so perfectly round and tight. There wasn't a lot of natural plumpness to it but her thousands of squats had it looking like it was carved out of marble. She stood up on her tiptoes and pointed it out a little, just as she had done when she was teasing me in her workout shorts the day before. She tensed her cheeks and I was pretty sure she could crack a walnut between them. She was so incredibly fit, while maintaining her femininity and sexiness. I unintentionally put a hand to my sensitive slit and ran a finger through it while I stared at her incredible ass.

Hearing the wet sounds of my finger on my slick pussy, she spun around and mounted me on the chair, her knees to either side of my waist, her shaved pussy hovering about my pubes. She took my hand and brought my finger into her mouth, sucking my juices off it.

"I'm sorry I just didn't get enough before, you're so delicious," she said in between licking my finger, causing my cunt to produce all the more honey for her.

Brooke threw her head back and used my finger to trace a line from her chin down into her cleavage, breaking a line through the fine layer of sweat on her chest. She let go of my hand and crossed her arms over her front, grabbing onto her white top and pulling it up over her head, exposing her firm but lovely breasts in front of my face. She grabbed both my hands with hers and immediately brought them to her hot tits. My mouth opened in hunger as I massaged her perky B-cups, and Brooke let out an "ooh" in appreciation.

"Go ahead, Amanda," Kendra said, coaching from the side as I fondled Brooke's fantastic tits. "Lick them, please her."

I did as Kendra told me to and shoved my face in between them, kissing her sternum as she shook her chest a little, her boobs smothering me. I reached around and took two handfuls of her tight rear, squeezing and pulling her forward into me. The front of her slit knocked into my bare stomach and I could feel it leave the tiniest wet spot just above my belly button. I flicked her nipples with my tongue as she lowered herself onto my legs and started gyrating on my mound, my pubes becoming moist with her sex. Once again my worries of sexuality and consequences were numbed completely by the feeling of the sexy little blonde nymph I had in my lap.

I licked the sweat off her tits, not minding the saltiness if it meant I could play with her chest. I loved the feeling of having her in my lap and my confidence was rising. I playfully put one of her erect nipples in between my teeth and gave it a slight tug. It had the desired effect and she ran her hands through my hair and moaned at the hint of pain.

"That's enough girls. Stop," Kendra commanded. But I had no intention of stopping. I kept flicking Brooke's nipple with my tongue, but Brooke was more compliant, perhaps trained better, and she immediately broke my hold on her ass and dismounted me, standing to await Kendra's next order. I admit, I didn't get the whole 'good girls' thing, but seeing Brooke obey Kendra like that, it did turn me on quite a bit. I imagined all the ways Kendra could fuck Brooke. All the depraved and degrading things she could do to her for her own enjoyment. I was intrigued.

"Brooke, our new friend here was promised the sight of you working out naked. Why don't you go over to the captain's chair and do some crunches for us to watch."

Without hesitation or expression Brooke walked away from us over to the exercise equipment against the wall. She was like a robot doing what its creator instructed it to without question. I watched her perfect, tight ass as it creased with each step she took away from me.

The captain's chair is a backrest that's suspended against the wall. There are two armrests out to either side with a grip for the member to hold on to and put all their weight on their forearms while they hang in the air. Then they lift their legs up and crunch their abdominals, targeting their obliques and lower abs.

Brooke hoisted herself into it and faced us again. Her thin, straight body suspended in the air while she rested on her arms. She crossed one foot over the ankle of the other and with her long, sexy legs she raised them straight out in front of her, tensing her abs as she did so.

It was the single sexiest thing I'd ever seen. Brooke wasn't shredded by any means, but she was toned to perfection in a way that retained her femininity while still looking fit as hell. The way her abs crunched as she brought her legs up, the slight grimace her face would make at the effort, the bead of sweat that ran down between her firm tits, the slight peak of pink pussy that I could see when her legs were at the top of her crunch, and the distinct upside down heart shape of her ass below her. Watching her work on her body without clothes on was everything I'd ever secretly hoped it would be.

I felt Kendra's hands tugging at the bottom

of my halter top and I raised my arms without resistance so she could slide it over my head, joining her blonde sex toy in nakedness, more and more willing to comply with every passing minute of this erotic evening. She leaned over the back of the chair and played with both of my breasts this time, softly drawing concentric circles around my areola as she slowly made her way inwards towards my nipples.

"Isn't she magnificent?" Kendra whispered into my ear.

I simply nodded my head in agreement.

"Do you like watching Brooke obey me?"

I nodded again. "I do. I'm a little jealous. The things I would do to that woman…"

"Submit to me and you'll do everything you ever dreamed of doing to her as well as everything you didn't."

She had both my nipples between the thumb and forefinger of each hand now. She lightly squeezed them as Brooke's leg reached the apex of her crunch. My back arched and I inhaled deeply at the sexual stimulation of two senses.

"Okay," I said. I was on a wild ride tonight, and I wasn't ready for it to end, I wanted to see where it took me. So I agreed.

"Do you want to see what she looks like when she squats?"

"Yes. So badly."

"Brooke, I think your abs have been seen to enough for tonight. Why don't you work on your ass for Amanda to see."

"Yes, Kendra," Brooke replied as she let herself fall from the captain's chair, her firm tits bouncing once as she landed on the floor with a thud.

"Come over here and do it in front of us," Kendra instructed.

Brooke obeyed, walking over and positioning herself about four feet from me. I remained sitting in the chair, enthralled by the display Kendra was making Brooke put on for us. The butterflies in my groin would flutter a little with every command that Brooke obeyed without question. The control Kendra had over her was so sexy, I wanted it for myself.

Brooke faced away from us, awaiting Kendra's order. Kendra stood behind me, reaching down with her hands and exploring the skin of her new fucktoy, planning how to use me.

"Begin," Kendra commanded.

Brooke lowered herself into a perfect squat, her strong thighs tensing, her ass poking out towards me causing her cheeks to part and giving me an eyeful of her asshole, her puffy pink pussy below. I was becoming more desperate to taste it with every passing minute. Kendra's wandering hand reached south and slid up the lips of my clit as Brooke reached her lowest point. I gripped the armrests as my body tensed at the feeling. I inhaled deeply and tried to take a mental photograph of Brooke in her naked squat, she was the sexiest I'd ever seen her in that moment.

Brooke stood tall again and squeezed her tight ass the whole way up. I was completely intoxicated with her. I wanted to eat her cunt. I wanted to grab her by the hips and shove my face between her legs. But I had to wait for Kendra to tell me to or it wouldn't happen.

The toned sex object repeated her squats for my visual delight while Kendra's clinical hand teased my pussy, her head next to mine, the curls of her long dark hair falling past my bare neck and brushing against my breasts. Just when I couldn't take it anymore, Kendra's head turned, and I felt her hot breath on my ear as she finally said the words I wanted her to say.

"Crawl over to her and lick up her pussy. Taste her. Savor her. Enjoy her."

Eager to please both Brooke and Kendra, I obeyed my new master. I slid down off the chair onto my knees and crawled over to the blonde bombshell. I covered the short distance and Brooke held her squat position for me. Her pretty, smooth snatch hovered just above my face, shiny with wetness and wanting. Wanting for me. I wanted her too, but as I was about to devour my first pussy, muddled thoughts began to make their way into my head again. I'd always found the thought of girls eating each other snatches disgusting, yet here I was, wanting to do it.

"Lick her, Amanda," Kendra commanded from behind me.

"Please Amanda, I need your hot mouth on my pussy. Please," Brooke begged.

That did it for me. Any confusion faded away with Brooke's sexy begging. I leant forward and delved into her downstairs delight. I instantly felt her wetness on my mouth, nose and cheeks as I satiated myself with her cunt. The flavor was not what I expected. I thought it was something I would have to overcome, to get over in order to pleasure the woman I was hot for. But it wasn't. She tasted incredible. I loved every drop of it that fell onto my tongue, I collected Brooke's sex and swallowed it gratefully. My mind was firing on all cylinders now as I was rewarded for my patience and lust. I loved eating Brooke's snatch.

"Good girl," Kendra said behind us, reminding me of what I was now.

"Fuck, Amanda, you eat pussy so well," Brooke said as she reached back and grabbed the bun in my hair, pulling me in closer.

I continued to hungrily lap up Brooke's nectar on all fours like a dehydrated dog. I moaned into her pussy in appreciation for the opportunity. Despite being in my place of work, on my hands and knees while an alpha woman told us how to fuck each other, it felt right to me, my sexuality felt expanded, like it had been in a cage for years and had finally been unleashed.

Kendra made her way over to us, standing next to us in her workout gear and enjoying the sight of me going down on a woman.

"Get down on your hands and knees Brooke so that I can help our new eager lesbian friend," Kendra instructed.

A day ago I would have taken offense to being referred to as a lesbian, but in that moment I couldn't have cared less, I just wanted more Brooke. Her cunt fell away from my face for a moment as she collapsed to her knees and then bent down as far as she could, her arms extending in front of her, propping her tight ass up into the air. Kendra swung a leg over Brooke and fell to her knees so that she was straddling the naked back of the blonde in reverse. She reached forward and grabbed my bun.

"I didn't tell you to stop," she said as she pulled my head forward and back into Brooke's pink. Happy to oblige, I returned to my meal, looking upwards through the crevice of Brooke's ass at Kendra to see if it was pleasing her. It was. "Tease her clit," she commanded.

I complied and focused my attention on the lower part of Brooke's pussy, which was engorged with arousal. I swirled my tongue around her tender button while I braced my hands on top of her marble calves. Above me, I watched as Kendra's hand joined me in Brooke's snatch and she pushed past my nose to insert her middle finger into her vagina. I expected Kendra to stiffen her finger and start pumping into Brooke, but instead, as she withdrew the digit, pulling it upwards and through the valley between Brooke's ass cheeks.

Kendra repeated the action a few more times until I realized what she was doing. She was coating her finger in Brooke's cum with each insert and was spreading it around Brooke's butt when she took it out. It didn't take long before the crack of Brooke's ass was shiny with moistness, her tiny pink asshole swimming in lubrication. Seemingly satisfied with this, Kendra's middle finger remained at Brooke's anal hole and she circled it around the outside of the opening, stimulating the blonde's rear.

"Let me in, honey," Kendra ordered, and just then I felt a slight shift in Brooke's weight while she exhaled slowly. This time Kendra did make her finger rigid as she slid it into Brooke's ass, quickly but gently until her entire finger was swallowed by the back door.

I had always found the idea of anal disgusting, but then again, I always found the idea of eating pussy disgusting and there I was with my mouth on one. It seemed to have an incredible effect on Brooke, who pushed back harder against my face as she groaned in pleasure, one of her pinned legs trying to twitch upwards at the feeling of Kendra entering her ass.

"Ooh, good girl. Your tight ass is so warm around my finger," Kendra said approvingly as she admired Brooke's hole stretching around her, accepting the full length of her middle finger.

Unexpectedly, or perhaps not unexpectedly, I found the sight incredibly arousing. The way Kendra degraded Brooke by laying her into the floor, having one woman eat her pussy and another finger fuck her asshole. The dirtiness of it. The forbiddenness of it. The pleasure of it. I was in heaven.

I kept attacking Brooke's pretty pink pearl with my tongue, flicking it with newfound confidence and determination at the sight of Kendra's finger moving up and down slowly into Brooke's rear hole. Brooke's quivering moans were now constant as she writhed in bliss at the feeling of having two women behind her.

All of a sudden her moaning stopped and I felt an increased amount of wet dripping into my mouth and down my cheeks, so much that it was dripping off my chin. I looked up and saw Brooke's tight ass cheeks quivering, Kendra beaming in satisfaction. Brooke was cumming silently. I sucked on her clit, taking it completely between my pursed lips as Brooke's whole body shuddered. Kendra withdrew her finger quickly and Brooke's hole closed up immediately, causing her to shake again.

She let out one, long, slow sigh as she rode out her orgasm. I let go of her sensitive spot and licked up the length of her slit, collecting her cum onto my tongue. As my head ascended, Kendra grabbed my bun once again and pulled me up to meet her. I put my hands onto Brooke's ass to support myself and kissed Kendra deeply, sharing with her the precious nectar while Brooke twitched with aftershocks beneath us.

"You know, Brooke and I have known for weeks that you've wanted to fuck her," Kendra said. "There was something about the way you looked at her while she worked out. Brooke recognised it because it was the same look she had when she used to watch me workout. I caught her masturbating to me in that shower just over there, and I used her for my own sexual gratification. I made her eat my cunt. I made her lick my ass. I made her do whatever I wanted. Do you want me to make Brooke do filthy things for your sexual gratification?"

I nodded desperately.

"Then you have to do something for me."

Kendra stood up from Brooke's back, allowing the blonde to stand up again. I stayed on my knees as I watched the two beauties embrace in front of me. Brooke's hands went to Kendra's wide hips and pulled down on her dark gray leggings. They peeled down over Kendra's lithe legs, exposing her large, juicy ass to me. A combination of good genes and hard work at the gym, Kendra's ass was something to behold. I'd always been so focused on Brooke that I'd somehow never stopped to appreciate Kendra's lovely, feminine body. Kendra turned and looked down at me, allowing me a view of her pussy for the first time. Unlike what she demanded of her good girls, Kendra's cunt had a trimmed tuft of pubes on her mound, a dark delta adorning a pretty pink slit. It occurred to me that it must have been a display of her dominance, being the only one who was allowed pubic hair. Her bodacious chest was still held in barely by her tight activewear top.

"Come with me," she beckoned as she and Brooke walked over towards the workout equipment. I got up from my knees and followed them.

She took us to a seat typically used for bench pressing. She sat down at the head of it, resting her back against the barbell that lay racked behind her. She spread her legs and I saw her lovely snatch flower open, the lips peeling to reveal the delights they housed.

"Amanda, if you want to use Brooke as your own filthy fucktoy, first you'll have to come and prove your devotion to me," Kendra posited.

Keen to see how else Brooke could be sexually used, I walked over to the bench. I lay on my stomach, my legs and groin splaying out behind me over the edge of the bench, as I lowered my mouth into the second snatch of the night.

Still glistening with Brooke's cum, my mouth went to work again in Kendra's. She tasted different to Brooke, but just as lovely. I probed her vagina with my tongue and explored her labia and clitoris, my nose being tickled by her neat bush. Kendra undid the bun in my hair and it fell down around my shoulders as she played with it and brushed it with her fingers while I pleased her pussy.

"Very good girl," she said approvingly. "You

have quite the natural talent for eating pussy, I'm glad to have you. Brooke, why don't you reward our new member."

I felt hands on the back of my thighs, Brooke's, she was kneeling down behind me. The next thing I felt was her tongue in my cunt once again. My brow creased and I moaned onto Kendra's clit at the feeling of having the tight blonde pleasing me for the second time. My cum mixed with Brooke's saliva dripped down into my pubes and onto the edge of the bench below.

"With your video, the one of Brooke and I kissing," Kendra began. "You wanted to shame her?"

"Yes," I admitted between licks.

"You like degrading her don't you? Having that power over someone."

"Yes, I love all the dirty and depraved things you make her do, make her take."

"Do you think it's dirty and depraved having her behind you now? Eating your pussy?"

"Yes," I admitted again.

"Can you think of any ways to make it more dirty? To humiliate her even more?"

I could. I thought I knew what Kendra was getting at. But I wasn't sure.

"Can I tell you something?" she asked rhetorically, "Brooke loves being degraded. So why don't you make her do something even more naughty and wrong."

Consumed with the thought of making the hot blonde please me, making her perform filthy fucking acts on me, I reached behind me and grabbed her short hair. I pulled upwards and her head followed, dragging her tongue into my crevice. Her long lick ran over my asshole and it pulsed in pleasure at the feeling of her warm, wet tongue over it. It felt good.

Brooke's hands moved from the back of my thighs and onto my ass cheeks, parting them so that she could have better access to my hole. The dirty lesbian had done this before. Her tongue knew just what to do and ran up and down across my pucker, the tip dipping in as it passed over.

"Oh Amanda," Kendra said. "You're such a naughty girl. Do you like the feeling of making Brooke eat your ass?"

"God yes," I exclaimed truthfully, gaining as much pleasure from exerting power over the hot blonde as I was from the act itself, even if that power was permitted to me by Kendra. If all I had to do was eat her tasty pussy, it was well worth it. I felt amazing having these two sexual beings at either end of me.

Brooke became a bit more aggressive on my back door, her movements faster and harder. I could feel the roughness of her flat tongue against my star as she pushed against it with her licks. The pleasure I was getting from debasing her was fading as the pleasure I was getting from being rimmed replaced it. I'd never felt such bliss in my butthole before but I was certainly enjoying the experience. I could feel tiny little sparks shooting down to the nerve endings in the rim of my ass, causing it to tingle in delight to the touch of the hot blonde's oral organ.

Kendra cradled my head in her pussy, running her hands through my loose hair and brushing it away from my face so she could see how she'd corrupted me, seduced me into becoming a lesbian. My mouth was hard at work on her clit, my nose crammed into her fragrant bush. I could see her abdominal muscles clench when I would use force on her bean, flicking it hard with my tongue. Between my rhythmic circling I occasionally attacked it, causing her to gasp and tense each time. I loved learning about Kendra's pussy, loved learning what worked for her.

"You're too good at that for someone who hasn't eaten pussy before," Kendra said approvingly.

"I love it," I responded between licks.

"Well good because you're going to be doing it a lot from now on."

I was happy to hear it, and I responded by giving her pink pearl another hard flick, causing her to jerk forward a little and pull my hair tightly. The sparks shooting down to my ass were beginning to feel more like thunderbolts as Brooke's wet tongue began to circle my hole and prod at it. Kendra must have been able to tell what was happening by the motion of Brooke's head.

"Relax your hole, let her in," Kendra ordered between heavy breaths; she was on the brink of orgasm.

I wasn't about to start questioning her commands now, so I did as she told me to and consciously unclenched my butthole, bearing down on the tight ring of muscle, causing it to open up. Brooke knew what to do and pressed her puckered lips against it. Her slippery tongue slid out from them and into my ass, overcoming the resistance of my ring and sliding in. My ass automatically clamped tight around her tongue, but I forced it to relax, allowing her to slither deep within my cavity. I was amazed at the sensation I got from it. Her tongue filled me up and began moving in and out, like Brooke was an anteater searching for nourishment.

I moaned onto Kendra's clit at the feeling. My

eyes rolled up and my ass was now fully charged for what was about to come. However, Kendra beat me to it by a second.

"Oh fuck that's hot!" she said as she pulled tighter on my hair while she watched Brooke ravage my ass. "You like having another girls tongue in your ass you slutty fucking lesbian."

Those were her last discernable words before she was rocked by her orgasm. Her abs clenched and she curled over. I could feel her heavy tits sitting on the top of my head as her pussy gushed into my open mouth. Kendra tried to restrain her cry as I made her cum, but she couldn't keep it in and she let out one, prolonged scream of joy.

I followed shortly after and all the perceived electricity that was being stored in my ass suddenly shot through every cell of my body. My legs shook and threatened to give out below me as I lost feeling to them. My stomach burned tightly as the electricity contracted my abs harder than any crunch. It coursed through my arms to my fingertips. My head felt like it was overloading as the surge of power rushed into it, and for a moment, I thought I would black out. The elation was almost too much. My mind could think of nothing else but as the shockwave subsided one thing was clear: my first anal orgasm would not be my last.

Brooke retracted her tongue from my hole and

I fell to my knees, resting my head on the bench, usually wet with the sweat of a hard workout, but now wet with the cum of one. Kendra rolled forward onto the bench as if she was a gymnast and licked the end of it where my cum had dripped onto, then she pulled my head up by my chin and gave me a deep kiss, ensuring I could taste myself on her. Brooke embraced me from behind and kissed my neck as she gave me a tight squeeze.

"You're mine now," Kendra said as she broke the kiss. "You're going to delete the footage on the security cameras from tonight and from Tuesday night. You're going to wax your hairy muff smooth for me. You're going to wear makeup at all times in case I should want to use you as my personal fucktoy. You're one of my good girls now, and you will obey me."

"Yes, Kendra," I replied.

THE END

SEDUCING THE RELUCTANT FRIEND

Aubrey II

It had been almost three weeks since my initiation into becoming one of Kendra's good girls. One of an ever growing secret club of women around the college campus that had been seduced by my sensual roommate, submitting ourselves for her pleasure, and of course, our own sexual gratification. It had been the most wonderful three weeks full of new experiences, flowering sexuality and satisfied holes. I was having the best sex of my entire life, and still basking in the newness of it all. It was like I looked at the world through a different pair of eyes now, like my lesbian awakening had made everything more significant. Every touch from another person, every flower I smelt, every flavor I tasted, it was like I was now experiencing it through the prism of being Kendra's good girl.

Kendra and I lived together just off of campus, in an apartment. I had become suspicious of her sexual proclivities, finding it strange that someone as drop dead gorgeous as her never had any visitors besides this one girlfriend of hers, Brooke. After broaching the subject with my best friend, Laura, I somehow got it in my head that the best thing to do was to hide in her closet the next time Brooke was around and try to catch the pair of them in the act. My suspicions were quickly proven correct as I watched Brooke gorge herself on Kendra's nethers. I thought I was safe in my hiding spot, but my mouth betrayed me, as a soft moan escaped my lips. Humiliated and exposed as a voyeuristic pervert, Kendra brought me out of the closet, both figuratively and literally. She opened my mind, my pussy and my ass to the exciting world of lesbian sex.

I was determined to share my new sexual revelations with Laura. I expected her to judge me though, as she was prudish, but I thought if I could get Kendra to seduce her as well, she would understand. Not to mention I had a newfound lust for my best friend with the way I now saw women. I'd always known Laura was attractive, but now I was attracted *to* her. I wanted to fuck her as much as I wanted to broaden her mind. Besides, the prudish girls are always the wildest in bed and I wanted to offer her to my mistress as a thank you for what she'd done for me.

I'd laid the trap, maintaining to her over the last three weeks that I'd not seen any more evidence of Kendra being gay, and that I wanted to introduce the two of them and get her opinion. Unfortunately, Laura had been incredibly busy with mid-semester exams, and I'd only seen her sporadically for quick coffee dates. Every time I saw her I yearned for her a little more, desperate to turn her. Finally, the night arrived where it seemed like it would happen.

Kendra and I sat in our living room, relaxing on the couches while we waited for our prey. I was already made up for the evening; lipstick, eyeliner and eyeshadow are a must for being a good girl. I was also freshly shaven anywhere lower than my eyebrows, another requirement of Kendra's. No one was allowed to have pubic hair apart from her, our mistress. I was also completely pantyless, which was not a rule to follow, but perhaps just me getting ahead of myself, too eager for the night's steamy promises and wanting to be able to quickly strip as soon as the time came. I wore a tight fitting white tank top that my puffy pink nipples could partially be seen through and some comfortable red short shorts.

Kendra sat opposite me, wearing similarly comfortable attire, although a bit more conservative. A breezy, blue-green skirt went almost to her knees, showing her lovely smooth, sun kissed calves. A tight black top that showed no cleavage clung to her womanly figure. It's tightness showed she was wearing a bra underneath, but with breasts like Kendra's, a bra was a must.

To me, Kendra was the essence of womanhood. Her dark hair that curled at the ends, huge brown eyes, button nose and full lips, made for a pretty face that was only half the story. Her body was incredible with her well endowed chest, olive toned skin and wide feminine hips that accompanied her plump but sculpted, perfectly round rear. A rear that I'd had the good fortune of putting my face into before, an experience I hoped my mistress would give my best friend soon enough.

"So your friend is coming over soon?" Kendra asked.

"Yeah, should be any minute now. I'm so excited to watch you seduce her. I have to warn you though, she gets shy around the topic of sex, she might be a bit harder to crack than most girls."

"Oh, please. Last week I made a self-hating homophobe eat me out while she got her first rimjob from Brooke. And besides, timid women are usually the ones with the most pent up sexuality. If she's as you've described to me, she'll have the same willingness to lick pussy as every other woman I've made one of mine."

"How are you going to do it?" I asked giddily. I couldn't hide my excitement at seeing Kendra work her magic and turn my friend into one of us.

"Well, she's in the same position as you were the other week, right? Trying to confirm whether I'm a lesbian or not?"

"Right."

"Well, she'll be analyzing my every move then while she tries to make up her mind. So I'm going to flirt with her, and make her seem like I'm interested. When I leave the two of you, you have to talk to her about it, don't let her think about anything but me. She'll say she thinks I'm into her and you have to make her doubt it, make it seem like she's the one who might have some lesbian leanings."

"Wow," I said, impressed but not surprised by her cunning, having fallen victim to it myself.

"From then, things will be running through her head, questioning herself. The rest should really take care of itself, just follow my lead."

My excitement had risen to fever pitch. I started to regret not wearing underwear because I could feel a familiar warmth in my groin as horniness and lust began to consume me. I prayed that any wetness I produced wouldn't be visible through my shorts. I had two new pleasures to look forward to tonight; getting to fuck Laura and getting to watch Kendra seduce another straight girl. Over the last few weeks, I'd been shared around with the other good girls, but I'd never gotten to see her seduce someone new. The only initiation I'd been a part of was my own.

"I'm so fucking keen for tonight! I'm struggling to wait."

"It shouldn't be much longer, dear," my mistress reassured me.

"I'm starting to get wet just thinking about what's to come. Kendra, may I have your permission to go and masturbate myself? I need to get some of this horniness out."

"No," Kendra denied my request. "You won't be having any orgasms tonight unless I get to see you fuck Laura. If we're not successful, you're going to bed hungry. Every drop of your cum will go to either her or myself, it would be such a waste otherwise."

The way Kendra spoke was not helping my horny predicament. I was dying to finger myself, or to have Kendra eat me out, or to grind my cunt into the fucking armrest. I needed a release, and every minute without Laura here was a minute longer I'd have to wait.

The intercom buzzed. Thank Christ. Laura had arrived. I practically leapt out of the chair and skipped over to the speaker by the door.

"Yeah?" I asked.

"It's me," Laura's voice crackled over the intercom from the front door downstairs. I hit the button and buzzed her in.

"Keep it together, Aubrey," Kendra reminded me, noticing my wide grin and skip in my step. "We have to play it cool or she'll get scared off."

"Yes, Kendra," I said, obeying my mistress and composing myself. I took a deep breath and settled down.

There was a knock at the door and I swung it open to reveal Laura. She stood there in a stripey playsuit, hand on hip, big grin on her face that was framed by her short, strawberry blonde hair.

"Hey there," she said through an adorable grin. It took every ounce of strength not to pull her in, push her up against the wall and kiss her.

"Come in!" I said as I hugged her with great restraint, my friend none the wiser about how wet I was between my legs. "I'm so glad you're done with exams, I feel like I haven't properly seen you in weeks."

"I know, I'm sorry, I feel like such a lousy

friend. I'm happy we're doing this."

"This is my roommate, Kendra," I introduced my mistress to my offering as we walked into the living room.

"Hi! It's nice to meet you, Aubrey's told me all about you," Laura said as she embraced Kendra politely.

"Oh well, hopefully there's still some things about me you don't know yet," Kendra said as she returned the hug, winking at me. "I love your playsuit! Your legs look incredible in it, I wish I had legs like that."

"You're kidding, right?" Laura said, in disbelief that someone that looked like Kendra would wish to change anything about herself.

"No, not at all! It's not often I see a woman with legs as sexy as yours," Kendra laid on the flirtation thick. Laura blushed, always uncomfortable with compliments about her figure, and she certainly wasn't used to receiving them from a woman.

The three of us made our way to the couches. Kendra and I sat to either side of the wide couch, giving Laura no choice but to sit between us, all part of Kendra's plan. We put on an episode of some TV show about vikings and enjoyed a platter of cheese and refreshments.

The night went on as we half-watched the TV and chatted about college, exams, parties, everything but boys really. Kendra continued her innocent seeming flirtations with Laura; making direct eye contact, paying her unnecessary compliments and one time, resting her hand on Laura's bare thigh as she was laughing. The last one definitely made Laura slightly uncomfortable, and I saw her force herself not to recoil out of politeness.

The TV show started to get a little steamier. A big hunk of a man was kissing one of the female characters passionately, and it was obvious where it was leading. Laura shifted her weight in the chair, being a little embarrassed about watching the impending sex scene with other people.

The viking hunk took off his shirt and stood there, muscles rippling in all his masculinity for his lover to enjoy. Just then I felt my phone buzz next to me. I picked it up to see a message from Kendra.

'Say something about him,' the text read.

"What a beast of a man! He's hot as fuck, don't you think, Laura?" I asked.

"Uh, yeah I guess," Laura said shyly.

"I dunno," Kendra spoke up. "He's not really

my type. I think she's quite stunning though. What do you think of her, Laura?"

"The woman?"

"Yeah, I mean, she's pretty gorgeous, she has that short blonde hair and a pretty face. I'm just admiring her is all I'm saying. You don't think she's pretty?"

"Oh, well yeah I suppose she is pretty."

"She kind of looks like you actually," Kendra said.

"Oh no, she's prettier than me," Laura retorted.

"No way, you're both quite beautiful but I think you actually have her beat. The similarities are quite striking though."

Kendra was exaggerating the similarities between Laura and the viking woman. They really didn't look that much alike apart from the same shade of hair color, but the comments did seem to be having their intended effect, as Laura blushed and struggled to make eye contact with anyone.

Just then the viking man ripped off his lover's clothes completely, leaving her stark naked and revealing the banging body she had underneath. Thank God for HBO.

"Oh wow," Laura said at the sudden full frontal.

"Oh her tits are amazing," Kendra began. "They're just the right size, big enough to have a handful but still perky. Do the similarities continue there, Laura?"

Laura didn't know how to respond to the overtly sexual question, so she just stayed silent.

"Oh I'm sorry," Kendra said. "I didn't mean to make you feel uncomfortable. That's kind of just how Aubrey and I talk to each other, don't we Aubrey?"

"Yeah that's true, we are pretty open around each other. She didn't mean anything by it, Laura."

"No it's fine, I'm not uncomfortable," Laura lied, trying to fit in. "They're not quite like mine, I guess. Hers are a bit bigger."

"They're more like mine," I said as I grabbed my own chest playfully, shaking my heavy boobs through my singlet. Laura and Kendra laughed, and I felt the air of uncomfortableness start to dissipate.

"My downstairs is a lot different to hers too!" Laura said with a bit more ease, motioning to the bush that the actress on screen had between her legs. Again, we all laughed, and I saw Kendra's hand go to her knee once more, lingering there for a little longer than before, her fingertips brushing Laura's thigh as she removed it.

"I'm not sure they had wax strips and razors back in those days," Kendra joked. "So you have to give them points for historical accuracy. Still, I would never let mine get to that level. Mine's always nice and trimmed. Aubrey doesn't keep any down there!"

Laura's head spun to me with an amused look. We'd never talk about those kind of things with each other, our sex talk had always been very restrained. Kendra was right of course, my pubes were waxed clean off, but what she was leaving out was that I had to maintain a hairless crotch in order to be one of her good girls.

I nodded my head to Laura, confirming Kendra's statement. Laura giggled and smiled at me before putting her hands out in front of her and sinking her head shyly.

"To be honest, neither do I," she confessed as she closed her eyes in embarrassment that she could be talking about something so private with other people.

"You don't?" I asked through a giggle.

"No, I guess I just think it looks neater. And most guys don't want to go down on you, so I keep it smooth to try and convince them."

"Ugh, imagine having to convince the person you're fucking to go down on you. Guys can be so selfish in bed," Kendra said.

"Yeah I guess, but what can you do, not get laid?" Laura said, the most comfortable I'd ever heard her talk about sex. Kendra sure had the effect on people that made them let their guard down.

"Well, I'm sure your pussy looks wonderful, Laura," Kendra said matter-of-factly. "And I think there are some other options to sleeping with selfish guys. Anyone who would be lucky enough to see *you* naked should be begging you to let them eat your pussy. If you'll excuse me, I just need the restroom."

Laura blushed again as Kendra got up from the couch, using my friend's knee to help her off it. As she disappeared through the door to her bedroom, Laura spun to me.

"Oh I think you might be right, Aubrey. I think she's a lesbian."

"You think? My suspicions have kind of died down the last few weeks," I played the fool.

"Oh, definitely. In fact, I think she might be into me," Laura said giddily.

"What, no way! What makes you say that?" I questioned.

"Are you serious?" Laura said with wide eyes. "Have you not been seeing the way she's been flirting with me all night? Complimenting my legs, comparing me to a woman on TV she finds attractive, talking about going down on me!"

"She wasn't offering, I don't think, Laura. She was just talking about how guys shouldn't be such selfish lovers. You know, guys? As in men."

"I've definitely been getting a vibe off her all night, Aubrey. You think it's all in my head?"

"I think you have confirmation bias and are seeing what you want to see."

"Why would I want to see Kendra flirting with me?" she rebutted.

"Well, maybe you're actually the one with the inclinations the other way. Have you ever thought of that?" I asked as I arched an eyebrow.

"Aubrey, please. You can't be serious."

"I don't know, the way you've been looking at her all night, blushing every time she says something nice about you."

"I've only been looking at her to figure out whether I thought she was gay or not! It's your lesbian theory I'm trying to prove here! And I always get uncomfortable when anyone compliments me, that doesn't mean anything."

"So how do you explain those?" I asked.

"What?"

"Your diamond hard nipples!" I said, stifling a giggle as I motioned to her tits, with two tiny bumps poking through. Laura covered them with an arm instinctively.

"Oh, so what? It's cold!" she offered an excuse.

"Whatever you say, Laura," I teased. "That coldness must have come on just as Kendra touched your leg, I guess."

"What are you two talking about?" Kendra asked as she walked back into the room, taking her place next to Laura on the couch and tucking her legs underneath her.

"Nothing!" Laura almost yelled, cutting me off as I opened my mouth to speak.

"Must have been a pretty intense nothing," Kendra quipped. I watched Laura's face, she looked like she wasn't even in the room anymore. She was clearly rattled by my accusation and trying to think to herself.

"Are you okay, Laura?" Kendra asked as she reached out with a hand and placed it for the fourth time on Laura's bare leg. Laura didn't flinch, just looked down at it with wide eyes.

"Yeah, I'm fine," she managed to splurt out unconvincingly.

"You don't look fine," Kendra said as she turned off the TV, feigned a worried look and wrapped her other arm around the dazed Laura.

"It's okay, Laura," I said reassuringly. "There's nothing you can't be open with us about."

"Aubrey, do you remember a few weeks ago when you said you thought hooking up with women was all part of the college experience?" Laura spoke up softly. Kendra looked up at me, grinning salaciously.

"Yeah?" I said, wetness growing in my shorts as I watched my best friend begin to give in to her dormant desires, preparing to take her first steps into lesbianism.

"I've been thinking about that a lot," she continued. "I think maybe I'm not making the most of my time at college, but I've never felt attracted to a woman before. That's to say, not until tonight."

"What are you saying, darling?" Kendra asked. Laura looked up at her to meet her eyes.

"I think I might be attracted to you, Kendra. I

don't mean to freak you out, and I'm not trying to say you're a lesbian, or that I'm a lesbian. It's just... Aubrey pointed out some things about my behaviour tonight and what she said kind of rang true."

"Oh it's okay. Here...," Kendra leant forward and planted a sweet little kiss on Laura's lips. Laura was totally caught by surprise by the gesture and sat there frozen. "Did that do anything for you?" Kendra asked.

"Oh my," Laura said, stunned. "It certainly did something for me," she covered her breasts with her arm again, her nipples must have gotten extra hard at the kiss.

"Would you like to kiss me again?" Kendra offered.

"Oh I, uh," Laura became uncomfortable, remembering that I was sitting on the other side of her.

"It's not a big deal, Laura," I said. "Watch."

I placed a hand on her thigh as I leant over her, Kendra mirrored my actions and our lips met in the middle, right in front of Laura's bewildered face. My mistress and I kissed briefly but passionately, our lips locking between each other softly.

Kendra broke the kiss from me and turned

to face Laura, who leant in and accepted her offer. They kissed again, this time more deeply, enjoying each other's mouths. Kendra's full lips pressed up against Laura's unsure ones, stripping away a layer of hesitation in my best friend. I ran my hand up and down her thigh with a light touch.

Laura pulled back from the kiss. "What's going on? I feel like I missed something."

"Well, that night a few weeks ago when Kendra was having her friend over and I ditched that date to see if they were fucking…" I said.

"Yeah?"

"Well, my findings might have proven more conclusive than I've been letting on," I admitted.

"You two are sleeping with each other?" Laura asked in disbelief.

"Something like that," Kendra interjected. "Just relax, Laura. Let Aubrey and I give you the best night of your life."

Laura's brow creased and she started to open her mouth but Kendra kissed her before she could object. The creased brow faded and Laura began to return Kendra's kisses, opening her mouth and allowing my mistress' tongue inside. Blindly, Kendra reached up and grabbed me by the back of the head, pulling me in. She pulled her face away from Laura and replaced it with mine.

Laura's shoulders tensed at the feeling of kissing her best friend, someone she'd never thought of kissing before. Still though, she returned my kisses and our mouths worked together. It wasn't long before her shoulders relaxed, and she brought a hand up to my cheek, cupping the side of my head. I flicked my tongue across her lips and she returned the gesture, enjoying herself.

Kendra's face was suddenly forcing its way between us as she joined us. Kendra and I lovingly kissed the apprehensive girl between us. Someone who was typically so prudish was now kissing two other women at once, an act I'm sure she never thought she would partake in.

It felt so good to be kissing Laura at last, to be making headway towards enlightening her to the pleasures that could be had with other women. It also felt good that my mistress was clearly enjoying my offering. Laura was another conquest for her, another woman with lesbian desires that she unlocked, another potential addition to her harem of good girls. For me though this was special, I could now be myself around my best friend again. There had been a lot over the last three weeks that I wanted to tell her, a lot of changes within myself. I was regularly eating pussy and having my ass tongued and finger-fucked and following the instructions of a sexual master that I completely submitted myself to. This was the final step in accepting myself for who I was and being comfortable with exploring my sexuality. It was a journey I looked forward to helping Laura along.

My hand that was caressing Laura's leg wandered further north, as I ran it underneath the cotton of her loose playsuit and almost touched her panties. Laura was skittish though, and she broke the kiss and pushed my hand out from her clothes.

"Woah! Aubrey! What are you doing?"

"Oh I'm sorry, I just thought…"

"Excuse Aubrey," Kendra said. "She's been a little eager for this moment all night. She might be rushing things."

"I'm sorry. I think I should go," Laura said as doubts entered her mind.

"Oh Laura, please don't go," I pleaded, seeing my opportunity to turn my friend begin to evaporate.

"This is getting weird, Aubrey," she said. "The two of you apparently planned this night to try and seduce me? I'm not sure what I feel right now."

"Stay and find out," Kendra said nonchalantly. "Your friend hid in the closet while she watched me have sex with another woman through the slats of the door. She discovered a lot about herself in that closet, when she came out, she was someone else, someone willing to give in to their sexual desires, regardless of whether she thought they were right or wrong. You should do the same."

"You want me to stand in your closet while you have sex with another woman?" Laura said, unsure if she was following what Kendra was proposing.

"I want you to stand in my closet while I have sex with Aubrey, as a matter of fact."

Laura sat there for a moment, not sure of what to say, weighing up the options she had of watching her best friend fuck another woman from the safety of a closet, or to run out the door now and deny her own impulses.

She stood up, turned to face the bedroom door, then the front door. She began walking and for a moment I could have sworn she was going to leave, but she changed her direction suddenly, and without speaking a word, disappeared through the door into Kendra's room.

"You almost ruined it with your hastiness," Kendra said as she reached forward and pinched my nipple through my singlet, twisting it a little.

"I'm sorry, Kendra," I apologized sincerely as I accepted my punishment, the sharp pain paling in comparison to my elation at seeing Laura choose to stay.

"It's okay. I seem to mostly be the target of your friends lesbian lust, she hasn't yet gotten past the thought of being with her best friend sexually. We'll change that. But for now, we need to go in and you will eat me out. If she likes what she sees, we'll know it."

"Yes, Kendra," I said, understanding the instructions of my master.

We got up from the couch and walked into her bedroom. It felt strange that the room seemed empty, yet I knew it wasn't. It occurred to me that I was in the exact position of Brooke three weeks ago, when it was I that hid in the closet, and Brooke out here, having to fuck Kendra and pretend that she didn't know I was watching.

Kendra walked over to the bed and lifted her black top over her head, her large breasts still housed by her bra, which hoisted them up and gave her the most unbelievable cleavage. In the last three weeks I'd seen Kendra naked many times but it always gave me a thrill to watch her undress. She wriggled her hips as she pushed the breezy skirt over her waist, letting it fall to the floor and stepping out of it. Now the woman who was previously the most conservatively dressed stood in only her black underwear.

Kendra really was a knockout in her panties and bra though. Her dark hair fell down and kissed the lumps on her chest, her toned stomach leading the eye past her feminine hips and down to her crotch, her thick thighs holding her up. She was insanely sexy, enough to make any woman reconsider their sexuality. I wondered what Laura thought of her figure from the comfort of the nearby closet.

Kendra beckoned me over with a finger and we embraced, kissing passionately, exchanging tongues and saliva. I reached around behind her and pressed my hands into her meaty rear. Kendra's ass was truly divine. It was plump and round but with all her work at the gym it held itself up extraordinarily well considering its size. I squeezed my two handfuls of booty and dug my nails into her juicy derriere. I also had been taught the pleasures to be had from what lay between those two glorious cheeks over the last few weeks, and longed to share that knowledge with my best friend. If it wasn't for the cotton panties obstructing my access, I would have run my finger up her crack then and there.

"Take off my bra," Kendra instructed. Not one to disobey my mistress, especially when the command was one I was happy to oblige, I brought my hands up and undid the clasp at the back of the bra. I pulled my body away from her a little so that she could roll her arms forward and allow the two firm cups to fall away from her body, revealing the exquisite globes that lay beneath them.

Kendra took a step to the side and faced the closet, showing off her breasts to the unseen voyeuristic eyes behind the slats of the door. I positioned myself behind her and began kissing her neck while my hands explored her front. I ran my fingers up the outline of her abdominal muscles, over her round hips and of course, cupping her copious breasts.

"Reach into my panties," she whispered into my ear so that Laura wouldn't hear her guiding me.

I ran a hand south and slid it underneath her black cotton panties. My hand continued over the trimmed pubes that adorned her mons and I ran a finger through her slit. It was warm with wanting but mostly dry. I used my index and ring fingers to grip her vulva and spread her lips open, running my middle finger up her slit again, this time finding the wetness within. Kendra's hips rocked back to my touch and ground her ass into my groin, her lovely rear pressing against me and almost causing more arousal than I could handle. My need for a release was reaching breaking point, I was so turned on.

Kendra gyrated against me while I moved my hand mechanically, stimulating her clit and coating my finger in her juices, her bush tickling my wrist. She breathed heavily into the air, squeezing her own nipples and making them erect. Laura was getting quite the show, from where I was standing I just caught a glimpse of her eyes between the slats of the closet door. They were wide with shock. It must have been something seeing her best friend do this to such an incredible woman.

Kendra grabbed me by the wrist and pulled my hand out of her underwear, trailing a line of cum up her midline, between her breasts and up to her mouth, where she licked the remaining trickle of nectar that clung to my finger.

Kendra spun around and pushed me down onto the bed so that I lay flat on my back with my legs dangling over the edge. She pushed down her panties and revealed the dark delta that was her muff, with the two pretty lips of her pussy beginning just below it. She stepped up onto the bed and walked over me, carefully placing her footsteps at my sides. When she reached my head, she spun around again and lowered herself to her knees so that her sweet pussy hovered above my face. She seemed to be staring directly at the closet door when she lowered her cunt down onto my desperate mouth.

I licked up the length of her snatch gratefully, collecting her cum on my tongue, activating my taste buds and giving me the fix I needed. I loved licking pussy, I loved giving another woman pleasure, I particularly loved giving my mistress pleasure.

"Open your mouth and stick your tongue out," Kendra commanded and I did so. "Now stay still."

Kendra started rocking her hips back and forth, grinding into my face with her pussy. Her abdominals tensed repeatedly as she used my face as a fucktoy, doing crunches to achieve the motion. It was messy, her slit spread juices all over my nose, mouth, tongue and chin. I collected every drop of the sweet cum and let it roll down the back of my throat. I moaned at the feeling of being used like an inanimate toy designed only for my master's sexual satisfaction.

She rewarded me with touching my pussy. Her hand reaching forward and rubbing my engorged clit through my shorts, soaking them in my sex. I moaned louder, thanking her for the stimulation.

I felt a drop of her cum run down off my chin and down my neck, collecting between my collarbones. I reached underneath her legs and behind her, spreading her ass cheeks and making her pretty little pucker visible. She took the opportunity to increase the swing of her hips, and at one end of the swing my tongue would lick her clit, while at the other it would graze her asshole. God, she was incredible, I never ceased to be amazed at the taste and sexuality of Kendra. I loved devouring every single part of her.

She held her hips forward, her abs holding the crunch, placing her ass onto my mouth and inviting me to eat it. I accepted my meal and rimmed her, pressing my tongue against her back door and wiggling it left and right. Kendra cried out in pleasure at the feeling of sitting on her subject's face, relishing my submissive tongue.

Without warning she released her crunch and rolled off of my face. Sitting herself down on the edge of the bed, facing the closet.

"Why don't you get up and see how our friend is enjoying tonight's presentation," Kendra instructed.

I obeyed my mistress and climbed off the bed, her wetness completely coating my face and dripping off my chin. I walked to the closet door and opened it, revealing Laura, who was pushed back against Kendra's hanging clothes, her playsuit around her ankles, one hand cupping a naked breast while the other was shoved firmly down her panties. She looked up at me with flushed cheeks and an open mouth.

"Holy fuck," she said to me through a heavy breath.

"It's funny," Kendra said from the bed. "This is practically the exact same way we found you, Aubrey, after you watched Brooke and I fuck on this very bed."

The irony was not lost on me. That night opened up a whole new world for me, and I was ecstatic to be on the other side of the closet this time, helping my friend explore her sexuality and guide her to becoming one of Kendra's good girls.

"Come over here, Laura," Kendra said. Laura obeyed her first command from her soon to be mistress and walked out of the closet, stepping out of her playsuit, wearing only her white panties, which were now see-through with cum at the front, showing the outline of her pussy. She walked over to Kendra and stood in front of her, her back to me.

"Take those off, you won't be needing them," Kendra motioned to her underwear, and again Laura did as she was told, pushing them down to the floor and kicking them away. I almost squealed in delight at seeing her obey Kendra. I admired her naked butt, gazing upon it for the first time. It was small and cute, a tight little package that I wanted to stick my face into.

"Kneel," Kendra said and Laura, seemingly enchanted by her, did so, getting down onto her knees between Kendra's spread legs. "You want to be a good girl and eat my pussy."

"I'd be happy to," Laura replied, the good girl part being lost on her, but the cunnilingus part most certainly not.

"So do it," Kendra invited.

Laura leaned forward and without apprehension began gorging herself on Kendra's wet slit. Now the only fully clothed person in the room, I watched the two naked women writhe in delight at the sexual act that was being performed. Laura enthusiastically licked up and down Kendra's cunt, enjoying her first taste of pussy, and Kendra sighed at the feeling of another virgin mouth successfully seduced into going between her legs. I wanted so badly to strip down and join in the fucking, but I knew I had to wait for Kendra's order.

Laura's own pretty little slit was facing me while she pleased my mistress, her labia jutting out from between her vulva, taunting me that I couldn't part them with my tongue. Her tiny pink asshole sat above it, an adorably small opening that matched the color of her skin so well that it was hard to spot. Seeing her naked and submissive drove me wild. I wanted to fuck her for eternity.

Kendra must have seen me staring at my best friend's nethers with yearning and beckoned me over to her with a finger.

"Kneel down next to your friend and give her a hand," she instructed.

I fell to my knees next to Laura, who didn't take her lips away from Kendra's sweet pussy. I kissed the inside of Kendra's thigh and made my way up to her clit, my face pressing against Laura's, who didn't even seem to acknowledge my presence, completely absorbed with eating the snatch in front of her.

I began teasing Kendra's clit with my tongue, extending it forward and battling against Laura's to flick the little button. Our tongues dueled for the privilege, flicking against each other and competing to give Kendra more pleasure. Eventually we found a compromise and I knelt more upright so that I could lick her love button from the top, while Laura bent down lower and licked upwards, tickling it from beneath.

Our tongues danced in tandem on Kendra's pink pearl, and it seemed to have the desired effect on her. She leaned forward to observe the two women tending to her bean, resting her heavy tits on the back of my head. I could feel the warmth of the underside of one of her boobs against my neck.

"Oh you girls are so good," she encouraged. "You're doing such a good job on my clit, I'm going to cum!"

Laura and I dared not stop, maintaining our wagging tongues like trained pets, serving our master in order to satisfy her needs. The hard tip of my tongue flicked Kendra's clit one way, while Laura's would flick it back the other, roughly attacking the little nub and causing Kendra's breathing to become heavier, her tits practically bouncing on the back of my head.

Kendra's orgasm arrived and I felt her boobs lift off my head as she leant back onto her elbows. She let out a deep, guttural growl of sexual pleasure as her butt lifted off the bed. Her muscular thighs squeezed together and forced my tits to cram into the side of Laura's face. My head was pushed off of her clit but Laura's remained, as the first time lesbian was suffocated in the combination of thighs, tits and pussy. I watched from above as her face disappeared amongst the flesh, and I saw Kendra's taut stomach tighten as she came, her contracting abdominals showing the faint outline of a six-pack.

"*Fuuuck!*" Kendra squealed in delight as she rode the waves of her climax. She cried out into the night air as she was made to cum by another 'straight' girl, her newest addition to her collection of subservient sluts.

Kendra released her tension and her body crashed back down to the bed, her legs falling to the side and releasing my chest and Laura's head, who almost fell backwards at the sudden freedom. She put her hands out behind her to stop her fall and her legs swung out so that she sat on her ass. She panted and looked wide-eyed as she caught her breath, the whole lower half of her face glistening with my mistress's cum. I wanted to lick every drop off of her.

"Come," Kendra said to Laura as she sat up, reaching down to her on the floor. The speechless Laura took her hands and allowed herself to be hoisted up and sat down next to Kendra.

"I can't believe I just did that," Laura said in disbelief as she stared into the middle distance, coming to terms with the fact that another woman's cum was drying on her face.

"You did amazingly well," Kendra said as she cupped my best friend's face and kissed her cheek. "Your friend and I are going to make you feel good now, but first, I'm afraid we haven't been entirely honest about our relationship."

"What do you mean?" Laura asked, confused.

"Well you see, I don't just have sex with Aubrey. I have sex with a whole group of women around the campus. They're my good girls, and they do as I say in order to have the most wonderful sex you could imagine."

"Aubrey, is this true?"

I nodded my head enthusiastically, "It really is something else, Laura. Giving myself to Kendra has been the best three weeks of my life. I've never had so many orgasms, or been so sexually explored, or felt so accepted. It's a great group of girls who sometimes... well, often... get together and fuck each other in whatever way Kendra tells us to."

"And you're like... their master?" she asked Kendra.

"Well, I prefer the term mistress. But yes, in a sense. Aubrey and the others live up to their full sexual potential under their subjugation to me. Your friend here wants that same pleasure for you, and brought you here tonight so that you could be seduced, and realize the thrill of sleeping with other women."

"Before, when you were sitting on Aubrey... was she licking your ass?"

"Yes, your asshole has nerve endings in it just like your clit. Properly stimulated, the sensations can be quite powerful. All my good girls have had intense anal orgasms."

"I want that," Laura said, surprising me at her willingness to be rimmed. I guess the theory holds up, the prudish ones have the most pent up dirtiness.

"You'll get it," Kendra said with a grin. "Lay back darling, by the time you come up, you'll be one of mine."

Kendra placed a hand on Laura's bare chest and gently pushed her down onto the bed. Kendra lay on her side next to my best friend and wrapped a naked leg around her waist as she began to fondle her perky tits.

"I think your friend is ready for you now, Aubrey," Kendra said. "Come and give her a kiss."

I climbed up onto the bed on the other side of the first time lesbian, still fully clothed and dying for an orgasm of my own, but ever the obedient slave to my mistress' desires. Laura looked up at me with contentment and wanting, enjoying Kendra nuzzling her breasts and craving my mouth. I lowered my head and jammed my tongue down her throat. She brought a hand up and grabbed my hair, pulling me in tightly as our tongues, which previously fought each other, now worked in harmony for each other's pleasure. I tasted Kendra's familiar flavors on her mouth, and ran my tongue in a wide circle, licking the outside of her lips to lap up the translucent coating before it dried.

"Would you like Aubrey's mouth on your pussy, Laura?" my domme asked my friend.

"Yes please," Laura begged as she pulled my head away to answer. I looked down and saw her legs squirming together in anticipation, turned on by the very thought.

"Aubrey, your friend needs your tongue to help her cum," Kendra said. "Oblige her."

I obeyed faithfully and got up from the bed. I walked to the end and spread Laura's legs apart so that I could kneel down between them, her bare pussy peeled apart in front of me, looking completely delicious. I looked up and saw Kendra watching me. She reached down and grabbed the top of my hair, and with a tug she pulled me into my best friends' crotch.

My mouth pressed against her lower lips, my head unable to move from Kendra's forceful hold. I slid out my tongue from between my lips and licked upwards between her labia. Above me, I heard Laura sigh into the night air while her butt clenched, pushing her pussy up an inch. It relaxed as she processed the shot of pleasure from having my tongue on her. Kendra released me and returned to Laura's chest, teasing one nipple while her mouth licked and nibbled on the other.

I licked up Laura's slit again and paid attention to her pussy this time. Her snatch had a flowery fragrance that was almost like lavender, but more harsh. The smell filled my nostrils and combined with the taste of her, the sweet, piquant taste of her that coated my tongue and filled my head with endorphins.

I proceeded to feed on her pussy and explore every inch of it with my tongue, keen to make up for all the years we could have been fucking but didn't. I ran it over the folds of her labia, dipping into her vagina, up her hairless vulva and brushing against her little clit. Every new action I performed was a new experience for Laura, and she would twitch whenever I did something she liked, her ass cheeks clenching together momentarily.

She breathed heavily as the sensations accumulated in her groin. Each lick, touch or nibble of her pussy and tits was another drop of water pushing against the dam, threatening to crack open and unleash the forceful flood of ecstasy that would be her orgasm. My mouth was coated in her fragrant nectar as I worked tirelessly at her pussy, my tongue flicking back and forth against her clit, my lips pursing to suck on it occasionally.

"You seemed very eager to have your ass eaten," Kendra pointed out.

"It looked so fucking hot, the way you made

Aubrey do it," Laura answered through sharp breaths.

"Have you ever had a rimjob before?"

"No, I always wanted to, but was too shy to ask any guy to do it?"

"Well then who better to ask than a girl. Go ahead, ask your best friend to please your asshole. She'll give you what you want."

"Aubrey," Laura said without hesitation. "Please lick my ass. I want you to do it so badly."

So I did. The underside of my tongue ran down from her clit, between her labia and over her taint, making its way to her tiny little pink butthole, covered in her own lubrication as it spilled out from her vagina. My tongue grazed the pretty little pucker and her butt clenched again, raising off the bed as she let out a sharp *'oh'* above me, forcing my face away.

Kendra brought a hand to her mons and gently pushed her groin back down to the edge of the bed.

"Just relax, Laura," Kendra instructed. "Keep still for Aubrey."

I extended my tongue back onto her asshole and I felt the hole squeeze tightly shut, but Laura successfully prevented her cheeks from tensing.

I rested my tongue on it for a second before licking up gently. I heard Laura make a longer sigh this time, as her body settled into place, accepting the wet organ slithering on her back door.

Kendra's hand moved down from Laura's mound to the top of her pussy, and her middle finger began circling her clit roughly, stimulating the little button while I attended to her ass. I placed my tongue flat against my best friend's hole and wagged it left and right, my saliva squelching against the tight crater.

I flicked my tongue back and forth against her opening, attacking it with my pointy tip, the softness of her knot contrasting the roughness of my tongue. I circled its outer rim eliciting moans of approval from Laura, whose hips started wiggling ever so slightly to the feeling of having me eating her ass and Kendra fingering her. I decided to try and probe into her ass with my tongue, pushing on her back door and trying to force my way in. Her clenched anus proved too strong though, and the strength of my tongue was no match for it. I thought about asking her to relax, but recognized her increasing writhing for what it was, her rapidly approaching orgasm, so I returned to licking her delicate little hole with a barrage of quick flicks.

Kendra's hot mouth on her tits, hand doing the dirty DJ on her clit and my wet tongue rimming her sensitive little asshole proved more than enough for Laura, who was sent over the edge in a powerful display. Her back arched upwards and hips bucked while she let out a series of borderline supersonic squeals. Her delicious honey leaked out of her cunt and dribbled downwards, where my thirsty tongue collected it and spread it around her pink knot. Her ass cheeks quivered as she tried not to clench them tight, imploring me to remain at her rectum. I heard the soft smack of her hands hitting the bed as her arms stiffened and she gripped the sheet to brace herself as the dam finally broke, releasing a powerful tidal wave of pleasure and satisfaction that surged through her entire body.

I remained at her ass even as the powerful orgasm died down, not daring to move until my mistress told me to. The order came in the form of her hand, wet with Laura's cum, gripping my hair and pulling me upwards.

"I want to taste her ass on you, stick out your tongue," Kendra said as she pulled me to her face. I poked out my tongue as she commanded and she took it completely in her mouth, sucking it between her luscious lips and sampling the saltiness of Laura's asshole mixed with the sweetness of her tasty love honey.

Laura lay below us while Kendra sucked the flavors off my tongue, her hands pinned to her sides while she twitched, her orgasm still winding down. She and I made eye contact while she watched Kendra enjoying herself. Perhaps she was processing the series of events that happened throughout the night to arrive at this moment. Perhaps she was in shock about the intensity of the orgasm that just emanated out of her pussy and asshole. Perhaps she wondered why she was enjoying watching her best friend be dominated, and was measuring her own willingness to submit. Perhaps it was a bit of all three.

"Wasn't that good, darling?" Kendra asked her after she was adequately satiated.

"That was... I've never... my ass felt incredible," Laura said, struggling to find the words.

"And don't you want more of that?"

"God yes," she replied emphatically.

"Then you're going to eat out your best friend for my enjoyment, and take your place as one of my good girls."

"Yes, Kendra," Laura said, a line she would be repeating a lot from now on. It was so sexy watching her submit herself to Kendra. I felt like there was steam coming off my pussy with how turned on I was at hearing the words, at seeing Laura become one of us, one of the girls.

"Aubrey, it's finally your turn. Strip down and go and sit on top of the bed head up there," Kendra instructed, motioning towards the top of the bed.

I just about jumped out of my skin at the command. Finally, I would be able to cum, my pent up horniness would have its release. I lept off the bed and pushed my shorts over my waist, wiggling my hips to get them the rest of the way while I lifted my singlet over my head and tossed it aside. It must have been some kind of record for stripping, and I finally joined my mistress and my best friend in their nakedness. I saw Laura's head rise from the bed so she could see me. She scanned me from bottom to top, taking in my hairless pussy, thin figure and largish tits, puffy pink nipples standing at attention. She looked at me with hungry eyes, ones I recognized. She was seeing her best friend in a whole new light; a sexual one.

I climbed back onto the bed and crawled over Laura who lay there inanimately, watching my naked body pass over her like an alien spaceship. Only it was her that would hopefully be doing the anal probing. I crawled to the bed head, spun around and perched myself on the thin wood frame, only wide enough to support the tops of my ass cheeks. It conjured up memories of when Kendra had instructed Brooke to do this very thing, and I, in Laura's position, fingered her ass while I ate her cunt to complete my initiation.

"Don't make her wait any longer, Laura, I don't think she can bear it," Kendra stated correctly. My pussy was flushed red from all the blood that had flowed into it over the last few hours, drops of cum already leaked out of my cunt, my clit was engorged and begging to be eaten.

Laura rolled over onto her stomach in front of me, then raised herself onto all fours and crawled up to me obediently. She didn't look at my eyes, instead, she looked squarely at my desperate gash and bit her lower lip. She didn't pause once she reached the top of the bed, she kept crawling until her mouth was at my pussy, and she opened it and poked out her tongue, pressing it against my clit and sucking the flesh around the little bean into her mouth.

I just about came on the spot. I let out a guttural groan of satisfaction as my stomach tensed and my eyes started to water at the feeling of finally having my clit stimulated, especially in such an extraordinary way. I braced my hands against the wooden bed head and looked at Kendra, who watched with glee at seeing her newest acquisition do her bidding. A lash of ecstasy shot up into my tummy and the only way I can accurately describe it is as a micro-orgasm.

Laura set her tongue to work and delved

into my snatch, exploring the nooks and crannies with her slippery muscle. She slid it into my vagina and I grabbed her by the back of her head, willing her to go deeper. She looked up at me with her full mouth on my pussy, tongue penetrating me, gratefully accepting the copious amount of honey that I was producing. I let go of her head and she withdrew her tongue, pressed her puckered lips against my hole and slurped out as much juice as she could. She really was fucking dirty.

I shifted my weight onto my hands and lifted my ass off the frame, allowing me to grind my pussy against Laura, face-fucking the strawberry blonde and covering her pretty face in my wetness. Her tongue and mouth felt amazing on my sex, better than I had even imagined. My prolonged horniness and teasing made every sensation feel ten times better than it normally would. I moaned and whimpered with pleasure as bolts of bliss radiated through my entire body thanks to my friend's enthusiastic mouth.

"You're going to lick Aubrey's ass, it's dying for some attention. Just do what I do," Kendra said from behind Laura as she herself got on all fours at the end of the bed.

I perched myself back on the frame as I wasn't sure I'd be able to hold myself up with what was to come. I watched Kendra grab Laura's tight ass behind her and spread her cheeks, admiring the pretty pucker.

"Oh my, what an adorable pink asshole you have, Laura," Kendra complimented.

Kendra lowered her head between Laura's rear and ran her tongue up the length of it. I could see her pink organ slide between the cheeks of Laura's ass, licking through her valley. It caused my friend to gasp in delight, and I felt her hot breath on my snatch.

"I told you to do as I do," Kendra reaffirmed as she began another lick.

Laura got the message and complied this time, reaching down with her tongue and licking from the back of my crack and forward, at my taint. The first ass she ever tasted was her best friend's, and she seemed to enjoy it. I was thankful I was sitting on the bed frame, as I surely would not have been able to keep myself up at the feeling of having Laura's virginal tongue run over my butt-hole. I pressed my head backwards against the wall and groaned as she licked my sensitive hole, one of my legs straightening out in front of me autonomously.

A few more licks over my ass and I was truly in heaven. I brought my head forward again and watched Kendra munching down on Laura's bottom, setting an example for how she should eat my ass. Kendra's head began rotating in circles and I felt Laura's tongue do the same as she rimmed me, her tongue swirling around my tight hole and buttering my back door with saliva.

I cautiously let go of the bed frame with one of my hands, moving it to my clit, finally able to masturbate myself. Of course, the fact that my best friend was eating my ass was a massive added bonus. I stimulated my little nub and pushed my back flush against the wall, careful not to fall off the frame in ecstasy.

The sight before me was incredible. My best friend on all fours in front of me while she delved into my back door, my mistress behind her, her face visible through the parted cheeks of Laura's rear end, her expert tongue devouring Laura's pretty pink knot.

Kendra used her hands to force Laura's ass cheeks further apart and dug her face deep down into the crevice. I had a feeling I knew what she was doing and I was soon proven correct as Laura mirrored the actions into my own anus. She pushed her face forward against my pussy to hold herself up while she used her hands to spread my ass cheeks as wide as she could on the edge of the bed head. Then she lowered her tongue and penetrated my tight ring with it. Where I had failed before, it seemed like Kendra had succeeded. Her tongue being stronger than mine, she overpowered Laura's tight clench and entered her ass.

I relaxed my anus to allow my best friend in, feeling her wet tongue probe into me. I rubbed my clit a little harder at the feeling and could feel the makings of my long awaited orgasm stirring in my loins. Laura's tongue filled up my cavity, I used every conscious effort not to squeeze too tightly and force her out. I allowed her to explore into my ass, moving her tongue side to side, filling me to the walls.

Suddenly her tongue withdrew from my butthole all the way to the tip, before pushing past my sphincter again and again, moving her head back and forth to assist with the tongue-fucking of my rear. I watch Kendra doing the same to her, her rigid tongue moving into and out of Laura's cute butt.

I kept circling my clit mechanically, feeling the orgasm swirling around inside me, threatening to go off. Laura slipped her tongue into me again, this time going deeper than before, which pulled the trigger on my orgasm.

I felt it in my pussy first, the explosion of ecstasy that radiated from my clit and fired in every direction. I put all my weight onto the hand gripping the frame as my hips jerked forward, I fought to keep feeling to that hand, making sure I didn't let go. My pussy gushed liquid sex as it finally had its release, the clear fluid leaked out of my pulsating channel and trickled downwards onto my friends face and hairline as Laura pushed herself as deep as she could into my groin. One of my legs tensed and straightened at the feeling as the shrapnel from the explosion in my pussy set off a bigger one in my ass.

It was like there were a million nerve endings in my butt and every single one of them was firing. My asshole squeezed shut around Laura's tongue, pushing it out, before opening up again and sucking her organ back inside. The effect was magical and I felt like I had reached nirvana. I collapsed down onto the pillows beneath me as I shook with pleasure, my limbs and stomach muscles tensing in tandem with my rectum. I was now face to face with Laura who's brow creased at the sight of me cumming in front of her, as her second orgasm began to assault her.

I watched her face contort and her heavy panting blew into mine as Kendra's insane tongue achieved its ultimate goal. Laura had a purely anal orgasm in front of me on all fours, her face not six inches from mine. It was so fucking hot watching her face as she rode out her wave of ecstasy, gasping for air and taking sharp, deep breaths in whenever she could find the presence of mind to do so. I reached up and touched her face as my own ridiculous orgasm subsided. She leaned forward and we kissed while Kendra finished up her work in Laura's behind. I could taste my own asshole on her tongue, and smell my own scent on her face.

"Are you excited to be a good girl?" I asked my best friend.

"I'm so excited. I'm so happy we did this," she replied enthusiastically.

Kendra crawled up to the top of the bed and kissed us both deeply on the mouths. I was elated to see Kendra accept my offering of Laura to her, almost as happy as I was to see Laura be so open and willing to submit herself to my mistress. I couldn't wait to share her around with the other girls. They loved it when new members joined.

THE END

RAVAGED BY THE OBEDIENT THREE
Andrea

Just to be clear from the beginning; I'm a lesbian. I've liked girls for as long as I can remember. Through my teenage years, my sexual encounters were very limited. Not due to any inhibitions of my own, but because of other girls around that time not being quite so confident in their own sexuality. College was the exact opposite. Even as a sophomore journalist, I'd already quadrupled my total sexual experiences in eighteen months compared to my whole life prior. Women were more open about their sexuality, and willing to experiment, and I was happy to take advantage of that.

It was the experimenters that I loved fucking the most; screwing the brains out of a girl who wasn't gay but not quite straight either, making her realize the pleasure of a woman's touch and tongue. It was a thrill to see a girl give in to her desires and open herself up to me. That's why when I caught wind of a rumored underground lesbian sex club that was going around campus recruiting women to submit to their domme leader, I was intrigued. It sounded like a story my readers would be interested in.

A good investigative journalist always pursues a story that is important to tell. I wasn't totally sure if this story was necessarily important to tell, but it sure sounded hot. Everyone knows sex sells, and uncovering some kind of lesbian sex cult on campus would certainly get me noticed, especially around the office of the college newspaper. I'd been writing at *The Verdant* since the start of the year, and struggled to find a story that would really shine. I thought there was a chance this could be my big break.

The story had come to my attention via a friend, Jack, who was at a party and heard the account courtesy of some blonde that was trying to fuck him. She told him that a couple of days before the party, she had been seduced by two members of the campus gym where she worked. She apparently tried to resist her urges but couldn't, and she had sex with both of them after hours in the gym, submitting to one and joining a league of women who did that kind of thing all the time. She said they made her shave her pussy bare and she always had to be wearing make-up in case their mistress ever desired to use her for sex. She then insisted she was straight and *had* to fuck him, before she ran out of the room crying.

I should have been offended when Jack recited the story to me, asking if it was true; because of course if there was an underground lesbian sex club on campus surely *I*, the only lesbian he knew, would be in it. But I wasn't offended, I smelt a story. It was likely just bullshit, a woman at a party telling guys something they would find hot in order to fuck them. But nevertheless, if it was true it would be big, and it at least warranted a little investigation.

That led me to the gym where the blonde from Jack's story worked. A batting of my eyelashes and parting with twenty bucks got the beefcake employee with poor gaydar to agree to show me the footage from the night of the blonde's alleged seduction into submissive lesbianism. Curiously, there was no such footage. The recording was blank, as if it had been erased. It was an anomaly that the crooked employee could not come up with any other explanation for.

Another twenty bucks and he let me see the log of members who'd used their swipe cards to access the gym after hours that night. At the time of the blank footage, there were three names who'd swiped in minutes after the recording went dark:

> *Brooke M.*
> *Amanda L. (employee)*

Kendra B.

Three names, one of whom was an employee, which tracked with Jack's story.

"This girl, Amanda. Why would an employee be here after hours?" I asked the beefcake.

"She could have just been working out. I sometimes come in early before work hours to get a pump on," he replied.

"I bet you do. What color is her hair?"

"Her hair? Uh, blonde I guess. Why?"

"It doesn't matter. Do you know these two other girls? Brooke or Kendra?" I questioned, feeling like a real journalist.

He smiled suggestively, "Oh yeah."

"How often do they come in?" I asked, hiding my repulsion at his tone.

"All the time, they're always working on their bodies," he said enthusiastically. Obviously these two were favorites of his to watch. "Hell, Brooke's here right now," he pointed over to the squat rack, where a blonde girl had a barbell across her shoulders while she stepped forward into a deep lunge, her firm ass tensing through her tight workout leggings.

She was really hot. I could see why the slovenly employee drooled over her. If she wasn't the subject of my investigation I would definitely have wanted to fuck her. Her firm ass wasn't the only thing tight about her as I ogled her in the mirror's reflection; she was toned with strong legs, a flat stomach that barely showed the outline of her abdominals beneath, thin arms that gripped the barbell behind her head and a nice set of tits that were held in place by her sports bra like fitness top. She was also pretty, with short blonde hair that cut off just above her shoulders, and perfectly made-up with lipstick and eyeliner, making her green eyes pop.

The make-up!

She looked like she was ready to go to a fancy ball straight from her workout, it was totally unnecessary for the gym. Again, this tracked with Jack's story. She could be the leader of the group, the mistress. Or she could be one of the submissives like Jack's girl from the other night supposedly was.

I exited the gym forty dollars lighter and sat on a bench with a good view of the entrance while I waited for Brooke to come out. Things in this story were beginning to line up, and it became more and more plausible by the minute. I hatched my plan while I waited for the pretty blonde to finish her workout.

I decided to keep my journalistic motives a secret. I'd go undercover to learn about this underground lesbian sex club. I figured a club that was meant to be secret wouldn't exactly be open to an interview, so infiltrating them and getting information from the inside would be the best way. I already had an in being a bonafide lesbian myself, and if I had to sleep with a couple of them then that was fine with me if they all looked as good as Brooke. Then, when it came time to write my story, I'd omit myself from it and say it was from an anonymous source. It certainly wasn't dangerous. It's not like they were drug dealers, these were my people, there was no risk to my safety.

Approaching them was a different story though. I couldn't exactly just go up to Brooke and say *'Hey, do you have a harem of women you use to do your sexual bidding? And if so, can I join?'* I'd have to figure out a way to organically insert myself into the group.

I decided I would have to first determine whether Brooke was the leader, as I figured I had no chance of being initiated unless it was by her. Soon though, my thoughts of infiltration turned into daydreams about the sexy blonde doing her lunges in the gym. I imagined her in the locker room stripping down and toweling off the sweat from her toned body.

I awoke from my daydream as the gym door

swung open and Brooke stepped out, a big smile on her face and gym bag slung over her shoulder. She walked off down the footpath away from me and I quickly jumped up from the bench to give pursuit from a distance.

I followed Brooke through the campus until soon we were walking down a street of apartment buildings about half a mile out. I was mesmerized by the sway of her short blonde hair as she walked briskly, almost as much as I was by the creases her toned butt made with every step, her back leg pushing the flesh of one cheek together into a perfectly round package I wanted to cup with my hand.

Being just the two of us on the empty street, my footsteps were in Brooke's earshot without the hustle and bustle of the college campus to drown them out. The fit blonde stopped and looked over her shoulder at me and I immediately took a turn up to the nearest apartment building entrance. I reached into my bag and pulled out my keys, pretending to fumble with them to find the right one. Brooke turned back around and continued walking, and I was quietly proud of my improvisation. I felt like a real investigative journalist.

I'd have to make an effort to be quieter though, she wasn't going to fall for that again. I gave her a little more distance and tried to make my footsteps as quiet as possible, sticking as close to the buildings as I could, should I need to duck into an alleyway at short notice.

Brooke reached a building and ran up the half a dozen steps to the front door, pressing a button on the intercom. I quickly sidestepped into an alley as I was prepared to do and watched her from my vantage point as she was buzzed in. Damn, no closer to finding out whether she was the leader or not. As desperate as I was to get the story out quickly and raise my journalistic profile, I reminded myself that good investigations take time, and that I had to be patient. Still, Brooke did look like she could be the leader of a lesbian sex cult, whatever that looked like. Her strong, commanding physique made me think she would be the one who did the dominating.

I exited the alley and turned to walk back the way I came in defeat. But the path was blocked. I almost walked straight into the woman who was standing there, hands on her hips. She was gorgeous, perhaps more so than Brooke. She had long, dark hair that curled at the ends, a beautiful face with a button nose and full lips, natural olive toned skin, wide, feminine hips and a pair of amazing tits that looked big even through her conservative top.

"Why are you following Brooke?" she asked me pointedly.

"Uh, what? I wasn't..." I stammered, caught off guard by the question.

"Yes you were. I saw you pretend to go up to that apartment building and then continue following her, and I did literally just see you come out of the alley you were watching her from."

"Okay," I said, now feeling discouraged about my investigative skills, having already gotten caught. "I was following her. I just had some questions I wanted her to answer."

"What questions?" the feminine beauty demanded.

"I'd just... heard she might be gay, and I..."

"Oh," she said, taking a softer tone all of a sudden. "I think I know what this might be about. You have some questions that you yourself want to answer too, I suspect?"

I really hadn't been going for that angle, but since the opportunity to get out of this conversation had presented itself, I decided to take it.

"Yeah! Exactly! I'm just... not so sure about some stuff, and I thought she could help me. How do you know her?"

"Oh I'm a close friend of Brooke's, she and I have a... special friendship."

Wait, had I just unwittingly bumped into one of Brooke's subjects? One of the girls that was a member of this secret club?

"I think maybe Brooke and I can help you," she said, her tone having gone from stern, to soft and now to sultry. I couldn't believe my luck, this was starting to work out after all. "Come back to this building tomorrow night at seven o'clock, apartment 14A. Now's not a good time, but Brooke should be available to answer any questions then. What's your name, by the way?"

"That would be amazing! My name's Andrea," I replied to the dark haired woman, immediately cursing myself for using my real name. I wasn't thinking straight as I tried to keep up with the turns the conversation took. "What's yours?"

"Kendra," she replied with a smile, and I had to stop my jaw from hitting the floor. She was the other woman from the gym list! She was there that night with Brooke and Jack's troubled blonde friend, Amanda.

Kendra sauntered by me and I watched as she walked towards the same building that Brooke had just been buzzed into. Her ass was fabulous too. Different from Brooke's in that it was much larger, perfectly round but still tight, and held up by her thick thighs, I could see that she definitely spent as much time on the squat rack as

Brooke despite having some genetic advantages. She pulled a key out of her purse and let herself into the building. It was curious that she lived there and Brooke had to be buzzed in. Perhaps part of the arrangement was that the mistress could stay at whoevers house she desires.

I seemed to have inadvertently set up some kind of guise as a straight woman who was unsure about her sexuality, and looking to Brooke for guidance. On the long walk home I considered the course of action I should take the following night in order to get the most information while retaining my cover. This plan would prove completely useless in the end, but I didn't know that at the time.

✦✦✦

They say a watched kettle never boils. I could certainly empathize throughout the entirety of the following day, which felt like the longest of my whole life. I couldn't stop thinking about the upcoming evening and the potential information it would bring, as well as the potential for getting laid. I'd given my plan a lot of thought throughout the day, and decided that I would come clean to Brooke when I went to her apartment, to an extent. I wouldn't reveal my journalistic motives, but I would say that I was a lesbian, and that I had caught wind of whatever club it was she was running and that I was interested in joining. This required less acting, less lying, and I thought that would make the evening more natural, and I was more likely to retain my cover if I wasn't going through the motions of pretending to be a confused straight woman.

This method also had the added bonus that there was a chance the night would lead to sex, which was on my mind more and more as the day progressed. As a journalist, it's dicey to get involved with your subjects like that, it allows bias to seep into your writing and brings up ethical issues about how you get your information. But as a horny lesbian in college, I needed to eat some pussy, and have my own eaten out by someone so into it that they ran their own secret club devoted to the concept. The thought of submitting to a woman was intriguing to me as well. Seducing curious women was usually *my* game, and as such, I was always the one with more experience, the one in charge and expected to lead. To put myself in the hands of another woman, and be her sexual putty to play with... well that seemed like a new experience I was keen to try out.

I wasn't sure how much of Jack's story was true, if any, but I thought I better give myself the best possible chance of being accepted, and just before leaving my dorm for the night of adventure ahead, I took a shower and shaved my pubes clean off. If Amanda had the details right,

I had to have a bare mound in order to be part of this group, and I didn't want to compromise my chances of getting valuable information, and valuable sex. I dolled myself up more than usual too, applying eyeliner, eyeshadow, some blush and a subtle lipstick. I slid on my white cotton panties and for the first time in years, felt the fabric against my hairless mons. I put on some denim short shorts to show off my athletic legs and wore a red halter top that bared my midriff.

I stared at my clock once I was ready, counting the minutes for what felt like an eternity before I could leave. Eventually the time came and I had to stop myself from walking too fast over to the apartment block off campus.

I arrived exactly at seven and pressed the button for 14A. I felt butterflies in my stomach, fluttering around with equal parts nervousness and excitement. A voice came over the intercom.

"Yes?"

"Um, this is Andrea... I think I met a Ke-"

"Come on up," the voice cut me off.

I heard the buzz of the door being unlocked and I entered the building. Sixty seconds later I was arriving at the door of apartment 14A, which was left slightly ajar for me.

I pushed it open and found a sight I did not

expect to find. The door opened onto the living room of the apartment, with the couches and television you would expect, but there was a table in the middle of the room, a table that did not belong there, a table that was put there specifically. It was set for two people and a single candle was lit in the centre. One chair was empty, and on the other sat Kendra, the dark haired beauty I'd met the day before. She looked at me with her full lips pursed into a wry smile.

"Come and join me, Andrea," Kendra said, gesturing to the empty chair opposite her.

I was expecting to be having dinner with Brooke, not Kendra. A little thrown, I slowly closed the door behind me and made my way over to the table, putting my bag down and taking my seat opposite the olive-skinned woman. I could hear the background noise of an oven whirring in an unseen kitchen around the corner, the smells of our presumed dinner filled my nostrils, causing me to salivate a little.

"You look confused," Kendra said.

"Oh, I guess I was just expecting to see Brooke," I admitted.

"Brooke will be joining us shortly. You look lovely by the way," she complimented me.

"Thank you, so do you," I said truthfully. She was in a simple but elegant black dress that showed a hint of wonderful cleavage that I had not yet seen on Kendra. Her heavy bosom was propped up nicely in the bra beneath, begging for a face to be jammed between them.

"Would you like a drink?" Kendra offered.

"Yes please," I said, feeling a little tense.

Kendra clapped her hand once and suddenly we were not alone in the room. From around the kitchen corner stepped a woman wearing high heels, black lace stockings, a tight french maid outfit complete with headpiece, and a black choker around her neck. It took me a second to recognize the woman as Brooke! Looking incredibly sexy in her getup, she walked over to us with her long, muscular legs, a bottle in hand, her face completely expressionless.

"See, I told you she would be joining us," Kendra said as Brooke poured our glasses before returning to the kitchen.

It suddenly dawned on me that I'd had it all wrong. Brooke wasn't the mistress at all, Kendra was. That made sense actually, Kendra exuded the grace and confidence of someone you'd expect to be in control. Brooke was one of her subjects, and had been ordered to dress up in the sexy french maid outfit as some part of Kendra's seduction of me.

"Wow," I said as I watched Brooke leave us and

return to the kitchen.

"She's quite something, isn't she?"

"Yeah, that she is."

"I know you have some questions for her, Andrea, but I think I can help you just as well as Brooke can," Kendra said suggestively as she took a sip of her drink.

"Well actually, I wasn't entirely forthcoming with you yesterday, and I think you may have gotten the wrong idea."

"Oh?" she asked with a raised eyebrow.

"Well you see, I'm actually gay myself, I always have been."

"I see, so you were following Brooke because you were interested in her sexually?"

"Well, yes and no. I can't say I'm not interested in her sexually because how could I not be, but that wasn't the main reason I was following her. I'd heard that Brooke was part of; and possibly the leader of; a secret club of lesbians who submitted themselves sexually to a single woman."

"That's quite the story, where might you have heard that from?"

"I can't reveal my sources."

"Your sources?"

Damn it, it was stupid to use journalism lingo. "My friend who told me about it, I can't betray their trust."

"I see. And what do you think now? Do you think Brooke is this woman that the others submit themselves to?"

"Well, I think by now my suspicions are pretty much confirmed, only by the looks of things I had a couple of details wrong."

"It looks like maybe you did," Kendra said, eyeing me cautiously as if she was deciding what to make of me. "I'm famished, would you stay for dinner to discuss this further?"

"Of course," I said, ecstatic with the way the night was progressing. The existence of this club was confirmed in my mind, and it looked pretty conclusive that Kendra was the leader of it all.

Kendra clapped her hands again and out stepped another woman from the kitchen. She wore the exact same outfit that Brooke had on earlier, and she was every bit as stunning as her blonde counterpart. She had long thin legs beneath her lace stockings, larger breasts than Brooke and long, light brown hair that was perfectly combed and fell down each side of her face.

"Who's this?" I asked curiously as I drank in the brunette. She had the same expressionless affect on her face as she obediently brought out a tray with pot roast and vegetables, laying it between myself and Kendra.

"This is Anita. She's a psychology student that I enlightened a little while ago," Kendra explained while Anita carved up the roast and placed servings on our plates, not making eye contact with either of us, as if she was a trained servant. "Anita had some unresolved feelings with her best friend, I helped resolve them."

Anita returned to the kitchen around the corner and left Kendra and I alone once more. I felt a pang of horniness in my groin and I crossed my legs beneath the table. I'd seduced many curious women before but the way Anita and Brooke acted, so obedient to Kendra, it turned me on. I often wouldn't see my sexual conquests more than once, after they'd successfully gotten their experimentation out of their system. What did Kendra do that made them not only stay around for more sex, but submit themselves to her completely.

"How many women do you have under your thumb?" I asked.

"A few," she replied coyly.

"And they'd really do anything for you, even serve you and your guest dinner in sexy outfits."

"Oh they do a lot more for me than that."

"Wow."

"So what was your business with Brooke then if you knew about our little arrangement. Did you intend to join?" Kendra probed as she put a piece of roast in her mouth, and I felt the night becoming something of a competition with her. The two of us were trying to get the truth from the other, Kendra probably trying to throw me with her sexy servants.

"Well I was certainly interested, I've slept with a lot of women around the campus over the last year or so, and the idea that there was a lesbian sex club that I hadn't even heard of intrigued me."

"Ah, but you did hear about it!" Kendra pointed out.

"Yes, I suppose."

"Who from again?"

"Nice try," I said with a smile as I ate a piece of broccoli.

"Well, however you found out, I suppose you've now figured out that it's absolutely true. I have seduced several women over recent months, and they have all pledged themselves to me in order to remain one of my good girls, and have sexual experiences they never thought possible."

"Your good girls, is that what you call them?"

"Yes. What else do you know about us?"

"Not much really, just that you have the rule that all women must be bare, downstairs."

"All except me," Kendra corrected as she took another sip of her drink. Pubic hair must have been some display of womanly dominance over the girls, that she was more feminine than them, that she could do what she wanted.

"And makeup, all the time?"

"Yes that's true too, I like my girls to look their best for me at all times in case I should feel the need to fuck one of them or make them fuck someone else or come over and dress up as a french maid to serve me dinner."

"That's all there is to it?" I asked, mentally taking notes that I would scrawl down as soon as I got home.

"Well, you're missing a few of the finer details, but that's all I'm willing to share," Kendra teased.

"What am I missing?" I asked.

"I'm afraid the only way you're going to find out more is if you became one of my good girls, and I have to say, half the fun for me is seducing a woman who didn't know she had those attractions in her, who didn't know the way other women could make her feel. I'm afraid we've never been sought out before, and especially by someone so confident in their homosexuality as well. The thrill just isn't there for me, darling, and I'm not sure you'd make a good fit."

My heart sunk as I felt the faucet of information starting to turn off. Perhaps I should have stuck with the confused girl act and let Kendra seduce me. It seemed she wasn't so interested in someone already out of the closet. I chewed on my pot roast as the feeling of defeat crept into my head.

"However," Kendra began, and I perked up again at the possibility of getting more from her. "I might be inclined to share a bit more information if you give me some."

"You want to know how I found out about you?" I asked rhetorically.

"It only seems fair, I'll share if you share."

I thought about my journalistic dignity, whether it was worth revealing my source, some girl I'd never met, in order to get the story. I decided it was. I needed this.

"Fine," I started. "A friend of mine heard it from a girl that was trying to sleep with him. Apparently she was seduced by you and Brooke in the gym she works at."

"Amanda, that confused little homophobe," Kendra said, perturbed.

"What will you do to her?" I asked, perhaps not really wanting to know the answer.

"I'll decide her punishment later. What is it you would like to know about our little club?"

"Well, I've had sex with plenty of curious women around campus. There's no shortage of girls looking to experiment in college. But in my experience, they almost always are happy with the sex, but run straight back to the nearest guy afterwards. How do you get these women to submit to you, what do you do differently?"

"Let me ask you this, Andrea. When you sleep with these women, what does the sex entail?"

"Going down on each other, some fingering, multiple orgasms."

"Enough for any curious young coed to get it out of their system," Kendra stated. "I make women give themselves to me, to allow themselves to be used for my sexual pleasure as well as their own. They give me every part of themselves for the experience; every thought, every erogenous zone, every hole."

"You mean..."

"Anal, yes," Kendra continued. "There are nerve endings in your ass that most women never have a tongue run over, or a finger put into. I make sure every one of my good girls has the most amazing orgasms of her entire life, largely due to the fact that I ensure no source of pleasure goes to waste."

"I've never done anything like that," I said as I put the last piece of roast in my mouth.

"Really?" Kendra said, her eyes getting a tiny bit wider as she leaned in. "Perhaps we could find some use for you after all."

I felt the faucet start to open again. I had an in. My lesbian proclivities weren't of interest to Kendra, but my anal virginity was. I considered the cost of going forward if Kendra willed it, whether I would want to have anyone around my ass, whether I would want to reciprocate. But I didn't have long to think, as Kendra clapped her hands once more due to our empty dinner plates.

Out from the kitchen stepped yet another new girl. Once again, she was in the same getup as Brooke and Anita, the lacey black stockings tight around her pale, thin legs while the choker around her throat lightly asphyxiated her. It occurred to me that it was less of a choker and more of a collar; she belonged to Kendra, she was her property. She had ruby red dyed hair that curled down past her shoulders and she looked as sexy as the two women who preceded her. She began to clear our plates and I was mesmerized by her actions, forgetting about my ass and thinking more about hers.

"This is Yasmin," Kendra introduced the redhead. "She's the friend who I helped Anita resolve issues with."

Fuck, Kendra had gotten both friends to submit to her as well. She must have been good. Perhaps there was more to ass play than I thought. Yasmin collected our plates and turned to take them back to the kitchen. As she turned I could see her plump rear eating the part of the maids outfit that covered her ass. She had a fabulously juicy butt, one that I would normally love sinking my fingernails into while grinding against a woman. I thought about what it would be like to put my mouth between it, and rim her the way Kendra said would bring the ultimate pleasure.

It was clear that if I wanted to get more information on this gang of obedient women, I was going to have to submit to Kendra, and be willing to eat ass. I really didn't want to let this story go, especially now that it was confirmed, so I decided I would do what it takes to find out what I needed. On a personal level, I was curious about how much I would like it, and decided to do what so many women had done for me in the past, and open myself up to the idea of experimentation. Maybe I had some anal proclivities I just didn't know about, maybe Kendra would be the one to unlock those proclivities, as she had done for an untold number of other women.

Yasmin's succulent derriere disappeared around the corner into the kitchen, and I was once again alone with the radiant Kendra sitting opposite me, now with no food in front of us, I was suddenly wondering where the night would go from here.

"What do you say to all those straight girls to get them to sleep with you?" Kendra asked me.

"They usually already want to fuck me, they just don't know how to go about it. I just tell them they could walk out of the room then and there, and remain curious for the rest of their lives, or they could stay and find out for themselves."

"And what about you? Are you going to walk out the door and wonder what this night could have led to, or are you going to stay and find out for yourself?" she said with a wicked grin, relishing seeing me debating with myself.

"I think I'm going to stay," I said with a dry mouth, a reaction my body usually reserved for the big decisions in my life. This didn't feel like a big decision, having sex with beautiful women wasn't something I would object to, but something was telling me this night was going to lead to big things.

"In that case it's time for dessert."

"What's for dessert?"

Kendra's grin widened into a cheeky, full smile.

"Neapolitan ice cream," she said gleefully.

On cue, the three vixen servants appeared from the kitchen, now without their french maid uniforms. They stood a few feet from the table and formed a line in front of us, putting their arms around each other's backs. They were now wearing only their lace stockings that ran almost to the tops of their thighs, as well as their choker collars, otherwise the trio were completely naked. Their tight, supple bodies pressed against each other, bare pussies on display, lovely breasts jutting out in front of them. The fit blonde, Brooke; the lithe brunette, Anita; and the juicy ruby redhead, Yasmin.

The trio all looked into the space between Kendra and I, awaiting command and remaining expressionless, perfectly trained. All different in their own physiques. Anita, the light brunette with largish C-cup tits hanging from her chest, her arm around her shorter friend Yasmin next to her, with dyed red hair and small breasts adorning her pale white chest, the ever sexy Brooke next to her with short blonde hair and a tight, thin body, her perky tits in between the other two in terms of size. Looking at their hair, I understood Kendra's quip.

My jaw had fallen completely open. The sight was incomprehensibly sexy. These three stunning women presented themselves to us, their exquisite bodies completely nude save for sexy stockings and chokers to signify their submission. My legs squirmed beneath the table as I drank them in.

"You ladies seem to have misplaced your maid clothes," I eventually said once I regained control of my mouth.

"Oh, there was only ever the one outfit," Kendra said, causing a fresh pang of horniness to shoot to my groin as I understood her implication. The three of them had been in the kitchen, cooking our dinner completely nude, swapping the one maid outfit between them when it was their turn to come into the living room. These girls really were willing to do whatever Kendra wanted. I imagined making three gorgeous women do that would have been quite the power trip for Kendra.

"So, which one do you like?" Kendra asked me, as if the three girls were pieces of meat, as if they weren't standing right in front of us.

"I like all of them," I replied, playing along with the tone of the conversation.

"Oh me too, darling. But if you had to choose?"

"The redhead, Yasmin. She's something else," I said, staring at the petite girl in the middle.

"A very fine choice," Kendra said as though I'd just picked out a cut of steak from a menu. "Be a good girl and step forward, Yasmin."

The redhead did as she was told, stepping forward as the brunette and blonde behind her closed the gap between them and linked up. Yasmin's thighs rippled with each step as she obeyed her mistress, walking right over to me so that she was maybe a foot from my chair. She looked down at me with the same cool, expressionless face as the other girls, as though she didn't have a thought in her head, only what her master told her to do.

"Pull your chair out and face her so you can get a proper look at her," Kendra said as I sat there wide-eyed, my head turned so I could take in the specimen next to me.

I pushed the chair back and spun it so that I was facing Yasmin. I sat back into my seat and bit my lip, completely forgetting about the story I was meant to be chasing.

"Go ahead, touch her, feel her body," Kendra encouraged. I reached out with one hand and raised it to one of Yasmin's small breasts, stopping an inch from the skin. I looked up at her to see if she was going to tell me to stop, but she looked me straight in the eye with her blank face. I cupped her breast, feeling the warmth of her soft flesh mould into the palm of my hand. I ran my hand down her midline, over her stomach, stopping just short of her bare mound and moving to her side over her hip, stopping at the hem of her lace stocking.

"Turn around, Yasmin," Kendra instructed. "Show our new friend your gift."

Without hesitation, Yasmin obeyed and turned, showing me her large, plump, pear shaped bum. It truly was magnificent, and I placed my hand onto it, cupping one of her cheeks and giving her a firm squeeze, digging my fingernails in just enough to leave a mark in the tender flesh. It was intoxicating having this power over someone, having another woman let me do whatever I wanted to them, even if she belonged to Kendra and was just on loan to me. I looked around Yasmin's side and saw the other two sensual women watching me. Brooke bit her lip just a bit, the first sign of the night that she could act autonomously at all.

I turned my attention back to the juicy ass

in front of me, the dark partition between her cheeks hiding a hole that I had a feeling was part of the dessert course. I felt a twinge of excitement at the thought of putting my face between her lovely ass, at trying a new sexual act with a woman.

"Do you still like her, or would you like to make another selection?" Kendra offered.

"No, she's perfect," I said.

"Then we're at the part of the night where I have to give you an ultimatum," Kendra began. "Are you willing to be a good girl like these three? Are you willing to be my servant in whichever way I choose, be it sexual or otherwise? Are you willing to open up yourself, your pussy and your rear to new experiences with beautiful women? Are you willing to eat ass for me?"

"Yes," I said, transfixed by the meaty booty staring back at me.

"Good, then you may eat your dessert."

In response to this, Yasmin moved herself against the table, facing Kendra. I turned my chair again so that I was facing the back of the redhead, as she bent over, placing her elbows on the table and standing on her tiptoes so that her ass raised a little, presenting herself to me as my final course, ready to be consumed. Her cheeks parted slightly and I saw the hint of a brown star between them, sitting atop the lips of her strawberry pink slit between her thighs. I looked over the top of the red hair to see Kendra, who was leaning forward on the table, looking onward with great anticipation. My dry mouth was completely gone now, as I salivated looking at the submissive beauty.

I leaned forward in my chair, reaching out with my hands and spreading her juicy ass as I did so. Without hesitation I extended my tongue and ran it up the length of her crevice, running over her asshole in the process. I briefly felt the taste of copper, as if I'd just licked a penny, the taste of my first butthole. I saw the red hair drop in front of me as Yasmin let out a little sigh of appreciation for having her back door licked.

I licked again, this time just up the inch or so either side of her entry, the copper like metallic taste activating my taste buds again. I recalled the first time I ate pussy, and the immediate response I had to it, the devout realization that it was definitely for me. I didn't have the same response as I tongued Yasmin's butt, but I did feel something. It was new and taboo and exciting. I was doing something I always thought I shouldn't do and the feeling of disobeying that instinct in order to obey Kendra was spectacularly naughty. I dared not stop.

The up and down motion of my tongue continued between Yasmin's butt, the inside of her plump cheeks pressing against either side of my face. I slathered a layer of saliva over her tight brown rosebud, enough that it oozed down to her taint. The sexy redhead let out soft *'mm's'* through closed lips as I beared down into her ass. I'd completely forgotten about my article, I was now a slave to my desires, and to Kendra.

"That's perfect, Andrea," Kendra said from across the table as she watched me gorge on her good girl's ass. "How's she doing for a first time ass eater, Yasmin?"

"So fucking good," Yasmin spoke for the first time, her words encouraging me to keep rimming her.

"Circle her hole with your tongue," Kendra told me, and I did as she said, ceasing my back and forth motion and running my tongue clockwise around the rim of her ass, the tiny crater of her entry in the centre.

"You, come here!" Kendra said, pointing at the brunette, Anita. Kendra pushed her chair back a little and pointed to the floor in front of her. Obediently, the naked brunette fell to her knees in front of her mistress, and put her head underneath Kendra's dress. I could see Kendra's dress bob up and down with the motion of Anita's head beneath it, as Kendra sat back and enjoyed the show while her slave ate her out.

I looked over to Brooke, who stood there alone now, arms at her side, watching the scene in front of her. She would surely be so turned on, desperate to finger herself, but she did not. She could not act without Kendra's say so. So she stood there and watched.

"Tend to her clit with your hand," Kendra told me.

I let go of one of Yasmin's generous ass cheeks and ran my thumb down her slit, which was delightfully wet with the cocktail of her own cum and any saliva that had dribbled down from her ass. I parted her supple lower lips with the pad of my thumb until I felt her sensitive little button of a clitoris. Using my thumb and the side of my forefinger I gave it a light pinch, causing Yasmin to jerk forward momentarily, pulling her delectable ass away from my tongue, before she returned to her previous position and my mouth once again made contact with her forbidden hole.

I circled her little button with my thumb in tandem with my tongue circling her back door. Her mouth must have opened because her *'mm'* sounds now became louder *'ah's'* as her stomach tensed with every revolution of her clit.

My favorite sounds filled the room. The sounds of women being pleasured. Yasmin's pleasure moans combined with the wet noises of her slick clit being rubbed, with the sound of my salivating tongue pressing against her asshole, with the muffled sounds of Kendra's pussy being eaten by Anita's mouth. I felt my own moistness between my legs and was suddenly dying to get my denim shorts and panties off, wanting to experience these anal delights for myself.

Yasmin's stomach tensed hard all of a sudden, her moans quickly turning into pants as I heard the thud of her hands hitting the top of the table, her hips undulating into me. I'd made enough women cum that I could recognize the signs. I pinched her sensitive nub hard and laid my tongue flat against her asshole, moving it left and right but never losing contact with the tiny entry, which slightly sucked in whatever part of my tongue that had the pleasure of being on it. I felt the ring of muscle in her anus contract and release rapidly, her asshole winking against my tongue in response to the attention I was giving it.

The redheaded nymph pushed back hard against me, causing my tongue to lick up the length of her crack as she collapsed backwards into my lap. Her head arched back onto my shoulder as she looked at the ceiling, the curls of her red hair tickling my face. Her legs were spread to either side of my closed ones and I reached around her with one hand to keep fingering her clit, my other hand also reaching around her to pinch the nipple of one of her perky little tits. I felt her large ass pushing back against my exposed midriff as she continued to squirm, riding out her orgasm on top of me, her cum spilling out of her cunt and into the crotch of my shorts.

Eventually, her writhing stopped, and her head lifted off my shoulder as she caught her breath. I held my hand against her pussy, not moving it, just holding it and feeling it's warmth and slickness in my fingers, her subservient, shaved mound resting in my palm.

"Feed her to herself," Kendra told me.

I did as she commanded and lifted the hand I'd used to finger her to Yasmin's mouth. Yasmin grabbed me by the wrist and hungrily licked her own juices off me, flicking her tongue between my fingers and taking them into her mouth, savoring her own flavor.

"Enough," Kendra said and the obedient sex pet ceased immediately. "Move back over there," Kendra said, motioning to Brooke standing by her lonesome as she reached under her dress and pulled out Anita by her hair. "You too."

Yasmin and Anita joined their naked blonde friend and they once again linked together. Brooke's face was still expressionless. Yasmin tried to do the same but she was still catching her breath, and her eyes had a post-orgasm glow to them. Anita looked a little put out at having to stop before Kendra could orgasm, her mistress' cum coating the lower half of her face, glistening in the candlelight. The three obedient beauties stood there naked once more, arms around each other's backs, long lithe legs covered in black lace beneath their hairless pussies.

"What did you think of your first asshole?" Kendra asked me.

"I loved it actually, a lot more than I expected," I said honestly, having enjoyed the dirtiness of the act, and the effect it had on my dessert.

"Good, there'll be a lot more for you to sample. These lovely ladies are now all going to pleasure you, they will act solely for your pleasure under my command, and you are mine now so you will do whatever I say, won't you?"

"Yes, Kendra," I said to my now mistress, dying to have a release of my own. I'd never had group sex before, and the thought of having these three absolutely stunning women all to myself was divine.

"Good girl," she said with a wicked grin. "I have something special in store for you. Ladies, undress and entertain our new member, I have to get some things out of my bedroom."

Kendra got up from the table and disappeared

behind a door as her three servants let go of each other and stalked towards me. Anita took my hand and led me out of the chair, standing me up as the group of naked girls surrounded me. The brunette took my head in her hands and began kissing me, our tongues dancing between our mouths as I tasted Kendra's fragrant sex on her while she tasted her best friend's asshole on me. Brooke pawed at my chest while Yasmin's hands cupped and caressed my ass through my shorts.

The next thing I knew Brooke was tugging at the bottom of my halter top, pulling it up, and I lifted my arms to let it over my head. Meanwhile, the redhead unbuttoned and unzipped my short shorts, forcing her hand down the front and cupping my warm pussy through my panties, which by now were completely soaked. Her hand felt good on my sex and I bit Anita's bottom lip at the feeling of being touched where I wanted to be touched. Brooke undid the front clasp of my strapless bra and it fell to the ground as Yasmin pushed down my shorts.

Anita stepped back and looked me up and down, taking in my supple breasts and slender frame, my white cotton panties essentially see through with how wet they were, my moist camel toe betraying any mystery of what lay beneath.

"I think they may as well come off too, Yas. It's

what Kendra would want," the brunette said to her friend, the first time I'd heard her say a word all night.

Yasmin obliged and pulled down my panties, and I stepped out of them, joining the three of them in their nakedness, save for their stockings and choker collars.

"Already shaven," Anita pointed out, looking down at my hairless groin. "Kendra will be pleased."

The brunette stepped in to kiss me again while Brooke and Yasmin planted soft kisses around my neck and shoulders as their hands explored my naked body. I could feel the lace of their stockings brushing against my bare legs, the heat emanating from their pussies onto my upper thighs.

Suddenly, Brooke grabbed a handful of my hair and pulled my head back firmly, taking my lips away from Anita's face. I looked out of the corner of my eye at the blonde who was holding me as I felt the sensation of leather be wrapped around my neck.

"You're like them now," I heard Kendra's voice behind me as she tightened the leather choker around my neck. "You're my good girl and you'll do as I say," she clasped it behind my neck so that I could feel the pressure of the collar without feeling discomfort, a constant reminder that I belonged to her and signifying her dominion over me.

It felt fucking hot to put my body into the hands of someone else. Having always been in the driver's seat during my sexual encounters, submitting myself to Kendra was a welcome new experience. The thought of my article entered my mind, but I quickly dismissed it, not caring about my journalistic ambitions for the time being, caring only about sex.

"Turn around," Kendra said. I did so and saw her standing there, still in her black dress, holding a pink strap-on dildo in her hand, the leather straps dangling below it.

"Brooke, put this on," she said, handing it to the toned blonde. Brooke placed the strap-on at her mound, and fastened the leather straps around her waist and legs, an act she'd clearly done before. "Go and sit on the couch, our new friend will be with you shortly," Kendra instructed.

Brooke took her seat as instructed, her pink jelly cock swaying around as she walked and pointing up as she sat down. While I surprisingly enjoyed my ass-eating exploits on Yasmin, I quietly hoped that Kendra didn't intend to make Brooke put the thick dildo up my ass. Still, I had submitted myself to Kendra already so I had to trust in my mistress that she would provide me the pleasure that made so many other women give themselves to her.

Kendra walked up to me and placed her hand on my snatch, her middle finger wiggling between my labia while she looked at me possessively, as if she was testing her new piece of property.

"Good," she said approvingly. "Nice and wet already I see, and nice and smooth. You're going to fit right in with the other girls. Go over and sit on top of Brooke so that she can fuck you," she commanded.

I smiled as I felt a thrill shoot through my body at being told what to do. It was so hot and kinky and I couldn't wait to be fucked. I obeyed my mistress and made my way over to the sexy, tight blonde sitting on the couch, her pink plastic dick waiting for me. I climbed on, putting my knees to either side of Brooke so that I was straddling her. The dildo pressed into both our stomachs as I came in close to kiss her. This was Brooke's first bit of physical attention for the night and she seemed happy to receive it, returning my hard kiss with equal force, our lips pressing against each other.

Her lips parted and I followed suit, allowing me to stick my tongue into her mouth as she reached down and ran a finger through my slit, applying a little bit of upwards pressure, signalling me to raise my body up. She then grabbed onto the plastic cock and maneuvered it into the space between us, running it's head back and forth through my cunt, collecting my natural lubrication.

Brooke placed the head of the dildo at the entrance to my vagina, and I could feel the round bulb between my lips, asking for permission to enter. I lowered myself onto it slowly, feeling the girth of the strap-on as my hole stretched around it, penetrating me. It entered me with ease and my wet pussy slid down the plastic pole, my cum lubricating it as it did so. I accepted all eight inches of the fake cock while I pressed my forehead against Brooke's, looking into the blonde's eyes as my hot breath blew into her face.

I sat on top of her for a moment, feeling the entire dildo within my body, the plastic pushing against the walls of my channel. I looked at Brooke, who for the first time showed a hint of a facial expression, with some distinct glee behind her eyes. I wasn't sure if it was for seeing me take the dildo like a pro, or because I was obeying my new mistress the same as she was. I looked down at her leather choker and felt my own around my neck. I was the same as Brooke now, an obedient lesbian, a slave to the wills of Kendra.

I tensed my thigh muscles and raised myself

up, feeling the dildo sliding out of me as I did so before letting my weight pull my body back down and take it once more. My vagina was stretched enough to accept the girth of the strap-on comfortably now and I began to bounce up and down on it, enjoying the feeling of some sexual stimulation of my own. It wasn't often that I'd used toys as part of my sex play, but I always did relish the feeling of having my pussy stuffed while a woman went down on me. The strap-on was a little different, but I enjoyed having Brooke below me, her perky tits pointing up at me, her pretty face looking up at me in astonishment.

The ribs of the dildo rubbed against my g-spot and felt amazing as they entered and withdrew from my pussy. I braced my hands against Brooke's shoulders while I rode up and down on her, increasing my speed, my thighs starting to burn.

"That looks wonderful, Andrea," Kendra said from behind me. "But stop bouncing for a moment and let Brooke fuck you herself."

I took the full length of the fake cock and stopped again, my thighs thankful for the reprieve. Brooke slid down the back of the couch a little and I shifted my knees back a couple of inches so that I moved with her.

She tensed her considerable abdominal muscles and pushed me up into the air a few inches. For someone as fit and toned as Brooke, I shouldn't have been surprised at her strength, but I was, as she used her thighs and abs to slide the dildo in and out of me. I held onto her shoulders still and moaned into the air as the pink cock fucked me from beneath.

Brooke continued to pump into me while she reached behind me and grabbed my ass, giving it a firm squeeze and digging her fingernails into it as I had done to Yasmin earlier. Although my cheeks were already spread due to my cowgirl position, Brooke spread them further, her pumping never stopping.

It was then that I felt a wet tongue on my ass. Someone's slippery organ slid over my back door and caused my eyes to go wide at the unexpected sensation.

"I thought it only fitting that Yasmin should return the favor you gave her," Kendra said.

So it was the redhead who was munching down on my rear. I quickly got over the unexpectedness of it and began to enjoy the feeling of her sweet little tongue flicking over my pucker. It felt amazing while Brooke continued to fuck my pussy at the same time the filthy redhead devoured my behind.

"Oh fuck," I sighed as I enjoyed the feeling of two women attending to me.

Brooke took the opportunity of my heaving tits in front of her face, and she buried herself between them while she fucked me and held my ass open for Yasmin. Her hot mouth lavished saliva all over my mounds, flicking and nibbling my nipples. I thought it couldn't get any better. I was wrong.

"Sit on the top of the couch so that Andrea can be a good girl and eat your pussy," Kendra said out of sight. I felt the presence of a third body looming near, and the next second I saw Anita's long, lithe legs climbing up onto the couch. She sat herself on the top of the couch's backrest, perched just above Brooke's head, and she spread her sexy legs to either side of the muscular blonde, affording me easy access to her pussy.

I dove in immediately. I would eat pussy for a living if I could, and unlike eating ass, I was already intimately familiar with the art. I pressed my face into her cunt and licked the length of her labia repeatedly, exploring the sumptuous snatch for sensitive spots. I devoured the brunette's pussy while the ass play, tit sucking and dildo fucking continued, completely elated with the most incredible sex of my life. I felt the butterflies that had been present in my stomach all night begin to flap harder, causing a stir in my lower tummy.

Anita was wet, like, really wet. Her cum oozed

out of her slick pussy faster than I could lick it up, and it dribbled down onto Brooke's forehead and hairline. As if alerting the blonde to a new meal, Brooke relinquished my tits from her mouth and tilted her head back, pressing her chin and tongue upwards into Anita's hovering asshole, which was already coated in her nectar and began to dribble down the side of Brooke's face and neck. Brooke's abs tirelessly crunched below me, driving the plastic dick in and out of me while all I had to do was remain still and enjoy the ride.

I took a brief moment to turn my head, curious as to what my new mistress was doing. I expected to see her stripped nude, masturbating herself to the lesbian orgy she'd directed. Instead she had turned her chair at the dinner table towards us, and just sat there, her hand at her mouth, watching us hungrily without touching herself. Enjoying the show of her newest acquisition having her holes filled with dildo, tongue and pussy.

I returned to my post at Anita's snatch, with a seemingly endless supply of cum seeping out of it, trickling down onto the eager blonde's face, neck and tits below. I could see the glistening lines running down Brooke's chest where the precious juice had spilled down onto her. I could also see the light pink underside of Brooke's tongue as it darted around Anita's pucker. Sick of me watching the scene, the brunette used both hands to grab my hair and pulled me back into her cunt, groaning with pleasure as my tongue went back to work.

Behind me, Yasmin's tongue pressed against the ring of my anus with greater force. She was no longer licking, she was probing, trying to overpower my clench. The tip of her tongue entered my crater and she seized the opportunity, and using all the strength her tongue could muster, she slithered inside me. The sensation of her slippery organ entering me caused a wave of bliss to surge from my asshole to my head, making me moan into Anita's soaking pussy and to bear down on my butthole, causing it to open up for the sexy redhead.

Yasmin started making muffled groans into the crevice of my ass, and I could feel the vibrations tickling my ring as her tongue repeatedly penetrated my bottom. She was loving eating my ass as much as I was loving having it eaten, which seemed impossible. Her soft, strong tongue filled up the space of my ass while the pink dildo below filled up my tight cunt, and the feeling of having both holes pleasured by such gorgeous, sexy women was a feeling like nothing else. The butterflies flapped harder as I neared orgasm.

Anita was the first to cum however. Satisfied

by my expert mouth on her pussy and Brooke's eager tongue rimming her asshole from below, I felt her pull my hair tighter and she let out a sustained, long moan that, while it gave the impression of agony, sounded to me like she was in heaven. Her stomach squeezed as she leaned forward, her bountiful breasts resting on the back of my head between her hands. Then she quickly jerked back as the orgasm released, her legs straightening to either side of Brooke's short blonde hair. She let out a guttural groan above me and her pussy gushed into my mouth and onto my chin, the translucent liquid dripping down and coating Brooke's perky tits and neck.

Brooke let go of my ass and rubbed her hands around her own chest before grabbing both my tits. Her lubricated hands squished my lumps and she pinched both my nipples, while her pink dildo slid deep inside me. I lapped up as much sex as I could off the cumming brunette in front of me, while the petite Yasmin pushed her pretty tongue as far into my asshole as she could.

It was too much for me and my orgasm arrived with thunderous ferocity. The butterflies in my stomach turned into something else entirely, like there was a ball of kinetic energy inside me that burst, sending a flood of endorphins in every direction and escaping out of my ass and pussy. My core tightened around the plastic dick that Brooke rammed into me, holding it in place while my asshole began to quiver around Yasmin's soft tongue, pulsating rapidly as she attempted to bury it even a millimetre deeper, her organ writhing inside my anus.

I sucked up a mouthful of Anita's clitoral flesh and pursed my lips around it as my eyes squeezed shut and I moaned tensely onto her pink button while she kept cumming. My back arched upwards, my spine feeling like it had become electrified with the sharp but pleasurable pain of Brooke pinching my nipples.

I'd never felt any orgasm so intense. I'd never felt such pleasure in my butthole, and as if in a fleeting instant of crystal clear clarity, I understood why all these women gave themselves to Kendra. I had already given myself to the sensual mistress in words, but in that moment I gave myself to her in mind as well. While the nerves in my ass fired a million times a second at having been pleased for the first time, and my pussy seeped cum down the sides of the strap-on, and my mouth filled with the slippery clit of some sexy brunette I'd only just met, I truly became Kendra's good girl.

Wave after wave of the orgasm crashed downwards into my lower region, while my head felt like it was floating. Anita's climax wound down and she forced my head off her sensitive clit, pushing me down to meet Brooke, and we kissed deeply as I continued to cum. I moaned into her mouth now, tasting Anita's salty asshole on her tongue while my head pressed into the brunette's open cunt, her glistening cum getting in my hair, not bothering me in the slightest.

Yasmin withdrew her tongue from my rectum and I felt my body relax as my orgasm began to die down. Every muscle now burned without the intense ecstasy to hold me up, and I slid down the remainder of the length of the strap-on, sitting on top of Brooke, her strong abs finally able to rest.

Even as the orgasm subsided, and exhaustion crept through my body, I still felt like I was floating. My head remained foggy with dopamine and endorphins and for a moment I forgot where I was, just that I was kissing a blonde girl and that I felt a delightful new satisfaction in my ass.

"That was incredible, my girls," a sultry voice said behind me, and it brought me back to reality as I came to my senses. The voice was Kendra's, I was kissing Brooke, we were in her apartment.

Anita, Brooke and I were in a heaving pile of nakedness on the couch as we caught our breath. I pressed my hands against Brooke's shoulders and slid off of the strap-on, collapsing onto the couch next to the toned blonde. Anita climbed down off the back of the couch and fell down on the other side of Brooke, all three of our chests heaving as we sucked in big gulps of air. I saw Yasmin on her knees between Brooke's parted legs, her chosen vantage point for rimming me. She watched the three of us panting with glee, happy to see me and her best friend cum.

"Don't let any of that cum go to waste now, Yasmin," Kendra said from her chair.

Yasmin crawled forward and closed the distance between her and Brooke, before taking the pink dildo into her mouth, giving it a blowjob for the sole purpose of licking my flavor off it. Brooke watched as the redhead worked her fake cock, licking up its shaft and sucking on it.

"You two, come here," she said to Anita and I. Exhausted, but determined to do as I was told, I picked myself up off the couch along with Anita, and we made our way over to Kendra as she stood from her chair.

"Help me out of this dress, Andrea," she instructed as she pulled the nude brunette in to kiss her.

I'd seen three stunningly attractive women naked tonight, and watched them debase themselves in unbelievably sexy ways for my sexual gratification. I was exhausted from the intense sucking, fucking and rimming that had taken place already, yet the thought of seeing Kendra naked completely reinvigorated me. I was eager to see what the curvy mistress was concealing beneath her black dress, and I made my way around to the back of it to pull down the zipper.

The zipper fell and exposed her lovely, olive-skinned back, smooth and sensual in the way it moved. Her shoulder blades undulated as her arms reached around Anita to feel the body of her slave, tiny bumps of her spine just visible beneath her sun kissed skin. Kendra removed her hands momentarily from Anita's ass and she slipped them out of the short sleeves of the dress, allowing the top half to fall to her waist. I pushed the dress down and she wiggled her hips side to side to assist me. I saw the dress all the way to the floor, falling to my knees, and when I looked up I saw a thing of absolute beauty.

Kendra's sumptuous, pear shaped ass was almost as big as Yasmin's and almost as sculpted as Brooke's. It was more than two handfuls of booty, and seemed to defy gravity with it's pertness, remaining off the backs of her thighs. She wore black lace panties that matched her bra, and her generous ass swallowed much of them, disappearing between her lovely cheeks. I reached out and cupped the magnificent rear, taking a cheek in each hand and pushing them together, marvelling at its paradoxical firmness and softness. I looked past my mistress' hips and saw the blowjob still taking place on the couch, Brooke having caught her breath and playing with Yasmin's dyed red hair to get a better view of the lips sliding up and down around her strap-on.

I tugged at the sides of Kendra's lace panties as I saw Anita's hands reach around to the clasp of her bra. I pulled the panties down, peeling them out of her crevice and letting them fall down the rest of the way across her thick thighs.

I wanted to reach between her cheeks and taste her asshole, to please my mistress, to be a good girl. But I knew I would have to wait for the command, so I remained on my knees looking up as she made out with Anita, rolling her shoulders forward so that her bra fell to the ground, joining the dress and panties around her ankles.

Kendra broke from her kiss with Anita and turned around, stepping out of her clothes as she did so, and faced me head on. I looked up at my mistress with astonishment at her femininity and beauty. The first thing I saw was a neat delta of trimmed pubes sitting atop her pussy lips, with no sign of hair on her vulva. My eyes continued north over her taut stomach; the edges of her abdominal muscles visible; to her large breasts that hung from her chest. They were lovely round mountains with pink, puffy nipples that completed her perfect picture of womanness.

Kendra reached down with a hand and pulled me up off the floor, bringing me in for a deep kiss as her hands ran over my back and buttocks, pulling my groin against hers so that I could feel her pubes tickling my bare mound, another display of her dominance over me. Kissing her filled my head with elation, finally being able to be close to my new mistress, fortunate to be chosen by her as one of her good girls. Her body felt warm and right as it pressed into mine, and I was grateful to be subservient to her.

After a moment, Kendra pulled her face away from mine and began walking to her bedroom door.

"The four of you, in here," she said commandingly.

Yasmin popped the pink dildo out of her mouth and stood, as Brooke lifted herself off the couch. The four of us collared good girls all did as we were told and walked together towards the door, eager to please Kendra in whatever way she would let us.

I walked through the door first to find Kendra sitting on the end of her bed, leaning back on her hands and looking expectantly at me as her three other pets made their way in behind me.

"Anita and Yasmin, come here," she said, and I felt a pang of disappointment at not being chosen. The two girls walked over to Kendra and sat down to either side of her, and she took turns embracing them with kisses. Behind me I felt Brooke poke her dildo against my ass playfully, and I smiled to myself.

Kendra made direct eye contact with me and made a *'come here'* motion with her finger. I walked over to her and she parted her legs, indicating where she wanted me to go. I dropped to my knees, finding myself inches from her inviting and fragrant pussy.

"Don't just look at it, eat it," Kendra said sternly above me while she guided the heads of Yasmin and Anita to her tits, the obedient pets taking one breast each in an effort to please their domme.

Excited to be the one to eat her pussy, I leaned in and placed my mouth against her hot slit. Her lovely fragrance was trapped in the short hairs of her pubes, and I pushed my nose against them while I licked her clit, inhaling her womanhood. My tongue went to work right away around her pink pearl and her wetness was added to the layer of Anita's that had dried around my mouth.

Kendra tasted absolutely wonderful. She had the most delicious pussy I'd ever eaten, and I had eaten a lot. Her sex vaguely reminded me of lavender but with a sharpness to it that stung my tongue and opened up my nostrils, which only served to breathe in more of her and elevate the experience. I could eat her snatch for hours.

Kendra lay down onto her back, the two bobs of brunette and ruby red hair on each of her tits lowering with her. She breathed heavily into the air as my experienced tongue darted over her love button.

"God, Andrea, that's quite a tongue," she said appreciatively, her compliment filling me with joy. "As wonderful as it feels on my clit, I'd love to see what it can do to my ass."

Kendra shuffled her butt forward a little bit, so that it was perched on the very end of the bed, moving side to side so that her cushion-like cheeks spread open slightly, revealing her tight brown bud between them.

I lowered my tongue through her labia, immediately obeying my commander and eager to taste her ass. My tongue ran over her taint and I rested it against her pucker, savoring the flavor of it. Her asshole tasted similar to Yasmin's, and the familiar taste of copper activated my taste buds again. However, Kendra's had a salty quality to it, a bit more of an aggressive taste than Yasmin's. I loved it.

I began moving my tongue back and forth over my mistress' rim, feeling it pulsate to my touch. Suddenly, the familiar short blonde hair of Brooke hovered above me. She had positioned herself to the side of Kendra, laying over top of

Anita's groin in order to get to Kendra's clit, her plastic dick dangling below her still.

The two of us tag-teamed our master, Brooke tending to the soft flesh of Kendra's pussy while I licked the rough, ridged surface of her ass-hole, craning my head upwards to reach it which caused my choker to pull tight around my throat, but I didn't care. I welcomed the discomfort for the opportunity to rim Kendra.

Kendra lay there while her four subjects tended to her most erogenous zones. The enlightened best friends nibbled and licked at her nipples while Brooke and I took care of her lower half. Kendra had the same response anyone else would have to four people pleasing them, her moans gradually becoming louder and her pussy leaking more and more deliciously sweet cum down over her taint and onto her asshole, where I licked it up gratefully.

I did as Yasmin did to me earlier and pushed the tip of my tongue directly into her tight hole. I prepared myself to have to force my way in as the redhead did to me however Kendra seemed to consciously relax her anus and I felt the ring of muscle preventing my entry loosen a little, allowing me to slip my tongue in with relative ease. Her flavor was extra strong on the inside of her ass, and her saltiness assaulted my taste buds. I was grateful for her excess cum leaking down to make the taste more palatable. Mostly I was just happy to be inside of her, and I pushed as much of my tongue in as I could, the length of my organ pressing against her anal walls and filling her cavity while her sphincter choked the base of my tongue the same way my collar did to my neck.

I withdrew my tongue almost all the way, leaving just the tip of my tongue inside her crater, before pushing it back in and filling her up once again. I loved hearing the sound it made as it slid inside her tight hole, while Brooke's flicked around her pink pearl, mixing with the sounds of the best friends' mouths on Kendra's tits and of course, Kendra moaning into the night air.

My stiff tongue continued to fuck Kendra's butthole and it was like I could feel her orgasm stirring inside of her, like my tongue had penetrated her deep enough to sense the impending explosion of ecstasy. Kendra repeatedly contracted and relaxed her ass for me, pushing my tongue out momentarily before sucking it back inside her.

"The four of you feel so good on my body. My holes love your tongues, ladies, as do my tits. Keep going, make me cum," Kendra said, confirming my suspicions.

Suddenly, her butthole opened a little wider than what she could control herself, sucking my tongue in as deep as it could go, practically swallowing my wet organ and pulling my bottom lip up to her entrance. It was as if her asshole had a gravitational pull, a black hole sucking in anything around it, and it held open for a moment, signifying the beginning of my mistress' climax.

Kendra's thighs spasmed to either side of me, the stunning woman fighting against the pleasure to keep them open, not wanting anything to prevent Brooke and my mouths from being on her. Her ass closed tightly shut, my tongue being forced back into my mouth while I kept pressure on her tiny hole. Cum leaked out of her pussy and with Brooke remaining loyal to her clit, it dribbled down onto my nose and into my open mouth while her butthole sucked me back in and held me there.

She cried out loudly into the air while the best friends' muffled moans could be heard on her tits, the pair licking and biting her nipples. Kendra's whole body shook as the almighty orgasm ripped through her, every bit of flesh rippling as she convulsed in ecstasy.

It was the hottest thing I'd ever been a part of. It gave me immense satisfaction to watch my master cum like that, to debase myself by eating her ass in order to please her. Having amazing, passionate, dirty lesbian group sex was the most incredible experience of my life, and I planned to do more of it.

Kendra's orgasm continued for some time, wave after wave crashing into her and causing her body to contort in all manner of wonderful ways, her cries of pleasure our reward for being such good girls.

As the violent climax subsided, Brooke grabbed me by the hair and pulled my head back, kissing me deeply between Kendra's legs in an effort to taste her asshole vicariously via my tongue. Anita and Yasmin mirrored our actions over Kendra's chest, their mouths pressing into each other passionately as the two lovely globes of flesh glistened with their saliva below them.

Kendra sat up, kissing each of her subjects in appreciation of our efforts. The five of us sat huddled around the edge of her bed, all of us satisfied, our holes having been used and fucked, our faces and bodies wet with each other's cum and saliva. The aroma of lesbian sex hung strong in the air, my favorite smell.

"It seems one of us still hasn't been seen to," Kendra stated.

Confused, I ran through the events of the evening. I devoured Yasmin's plump ass and made her cum, I also ate out Anita's pussy with great precision, I'd been fucked and sucked and of course Kendra had all four of us tend to her.

Brooke was still left! I looked over at the excited face of the toned blonde, her short hair falling behind her as she looked up to her mistress from the floor. Kendra leaned down and reached to the side of Brooke, unclasping the leather straps of the wearable dildo. She offered it to me.

"Would you do the honors, my newest good girl?" she asked me.

"Yes, Kendra," I replied gladly, taking the pink dick from her and fastening the straps around myself while I looked at Brooke with insatiable hunger. Brooke met my gaze with horny anticipation for her impending fucking.

I never did write the article.

THE END

CUFFED AND TONGUED

Allison II

The first day of spring was an uncharacteristically warm one, so Taylor and my sentiment of spending it at the park was apparently shared by everyone in a ten mile radius of the college campus. The place was packed, not that we minded; half the reason we went there was to see all the sexy women shed some of their winter layers and work on their bodies in tight clothes that showed plenty of skin. Taylor and I found some shade under a tree and let our eyes feast on the veritable cornucopia of women we'd like to fuck.

Of course, this was the first time I'd had the inclination to do this. A mere two months prior I would have been more interested in the male joggers, rather than their female counterparts, but a lot had changed since an evening in my friend's hot tub. I poetically thought of the last winter as the end of a sexual chapter of my life, one dominated by disappointing boys and faked orgasms. Now my sex life was dominated by being dominated, specifically by one woman; Kendra. She opened up my world to a plethora of new experiences and pleasures, and all she asked for in return was my submission, which I was happy to give. Under Kendra's thumb, we'd seduced a harem of women into our little club, enlightening them to the pleasures of lesbian sex, submission and anal play. My best friends Brooke and Taylor were now more than best friends; we were lovers together, students under Kendra's tutelage, followers of her church. It was really a shame that we hadn't been open to those experiences sooner, and that we spent so long having less fun together than we could have, but at least now we had each other.

"Christ, I'd like to eat her ass!" Taylor exclaimed a little louder than she should have. I noticed the jogger she was referring to, and the statement was justified. The woman had a long, sandy blonde plait bouncing around behind her head that went almost all the way down to her supple, round ass. With every stride she made, the fullness of one cheek's flesh could be seen pressing against her tight fitness shorts for a split second before the leg moved forward and the same effect would happen for it's twin.

The woman turned her head and gave us a sideways glance as if to see if she'd really heard what she thought she did. Her furrowed brow and pursed pink lips showed an expression of confusion more than disgust. It wasn't exactly a comment she'd be used to hearing from two femme coeds at the park. Taylor and I played coy and avoided eye contact, pretending the remark hadn't just come from one of us. As soon as the jogger was out of earshot the pair of us burst out laughing.

"Taylor!" I scolded her. "Try to be a little more subtle at least!"

"I'm sorry, I can't help myself," Taylor protested between laughs. She always had been the excitable, outgoing one of the group. She was the wild party girl who said what she liked and never worried much about the consequences.

The laughter subsided and Taylor lay herself down, resting her head in my lap. I stroked her hair lovingly, admiring her pretty face which as always, wore make-up to accentuate her features. One of the conditions of entry into Kendra's little fan club was to always look our best. It was a condition that all the good girls took seriously, as we would never want to displease our mistress.

"Can you believe the last couple of months?" I asked her.

"Not at all. They've gone by so quickly," she replied gleefully.

"Do you miss cock at all?"

"You know I haven't gone anywhere near two months without a dick since I was sixteen... but I don't miss it one little bit. Being with you and Kendra and Brooke and all the other girls we get to seduce is just the most fun I've ever had in bed... or in a hot tub... or in a library for that matter," Taylor chuckled.

"I don't think that last one is a very high bar," I remarked. "I'm the same though, not that my sexual escapades were anything like yours prior to our initiation but everything seems so radiant and full of light now, even the mundane everyday activities. I comb my hair as Kendra's good girl, I brush my teeth as Kendra's good girl. It makes everything brighter."

"I guess that's why Kendra calls it being enlightened, but I know what you mean. How could anyone want anything else?"

"Well, you heard what Amanda did, right?"

"Yeah, blabbing her mouth at a party about the little queer club she was in to try and get a guy in bed. Fuck her, how could she risk breaking up what we have going?"

It was rare to see Taylor angry, it only ever happened when she was defending someone she cared about.

"I think there was a little more to it than just trying to sleep with some guy," I said. "She's so hot she hardly needs a lesbian story to get a guy in bed. I think she's still coming to terms with her sexuality and was ashamed of letting herself be seduced by Brooke and Kendra."

"Oh please, that girl is so in love with Brooke. And she didn't seem that ashamed when my tongue was up her butt. She better come to terms with it pretty damn fast if she's going to continue having fun with the rest of us. Do you think Kendra will kick her out?"

"I doubt it somehow. But I think there will definitely be some form of punishment."

"I hope so. I hope I get to be part of it."

"Taylor!" I said playfully, leaning over her so that my hair tickled her face. "I've never seen you so vengeful, it's kinda hot!"

She pinched my thigh in retaliation with a cheeky grin on her face, her eyes beaming up at me.

"Then why don't we get the hell out of here," she suggested. "A day like this should be spent with our faces in each others pussies, not sitting under a fucking tree. Besides, all this fine ass running around is making me wetter than a fish."

"Lovely," I replied sarcastically at her crude remark when something out of the corner of my eye caught my attention. "Wait, shush, that girl is coming back!"

"What girl?" Taylor asked as she turned her head in my lap to see what I was looking at. The jogger with plaited hair and a munchable ass was making her way back along the footpath, panting heavily and walking now, cooling off.

Taylor and I stayed silent as she walked past us, seemingly slowing down as she got closer. She pretended to be checking her running stats on her fitness watch but I could see she was looking at us out of the corner of her eye. She passed us and her gait picked up again.

"I mean, I still want to eat her ass, but I'm willing to settle for yours, Allison," Taylor said, mistakenly thinking the jogger was out of earshot.

"Taylor, for fuck's sake!" I whisper yelled at her, as I saw the jogger spin around and start walking back to us.

"Are you talking about me?" the jogger asked as she approached.

"I'm really sorry about my friend," I tried apologizing on Taylor's behalf.

"Yeah, sorry about that, I have volume control

issues sometimes. At least that's what my neighbors say," Taylor joked as she sat up from my lap, trying to make light of the situation.

"That's kind of a weird thing to say about someone you don't even know," the jogger said through panted breaths. Although she could have been justifiably pissed off, there didn't seem to be aggression in her words.

"Oh it's not that weird if you knew some of the shit we get up to, especially to girls as drop dead gorgeous as you," Taylor doubled down on the flirty talk. I envied her ability to be upfront with people. I'd witnessed her play this game with plenty of boys over the years, but lately I'd been seeing her play it with girls and I found it a lot more interesting.

"Jesus, you're confident," the jogger said as she placed a hand on her cocked hip and caught her breath. Taylor's flirting apparently had her interested. "What makes you think I'm even interested in girls?"

"In our experience, every girl is interested in girls. Especially the ones who say they aren't. So which one are you?"

"Well now there's no answer I can give that would make you think I'm not. Even if I was to say I'm not interested then by your own twisted logic you'll interpret it as I am."

"Huh," Taylor feigned puzzlement. "I guess that's true. So do you want to come back to my place?"

"Sorry, I'm not interested in girls, and I'm certainly not interested in having my ass eaten by one. Interpret that how you will," the jogger said as she turned and began briskly walking away. A pang of disappointment hit me, as although I hadn't been as vocal as Taylor, the jogger did have an ass I'd love to bury my face into, and for a moment I thought my friend had her on the hook.

"Jog your fine ass over to 516 Stonewall Rise when you change your mind!" Taylor called out after her, but the jogger's head never turned.

"I'm sorry sweetie," I said sympathetically as I pressed a kiss onto her cheek. "I thought you had that one too."

"Text Kendra will you? Tell her to meet us at mine in an hour and that we have a present for her," Taylor said confidently. "Come on, we better get home."

✦✦✦

"I really think you might have misread that exchange," I said as Taylor closed the front door behind her. We entered the living room just off the entryway and she spun me around, wrapping her arms around my waist and planting a kiss on my lips. Even after all the girls I'd fucked over the last two months, I still felt butterflies and nervousness whenever I'd kiss Taylor or Brooke. As much as I loved it, it was still a taboo feeling kissing my best friend of so many years. We'd spent so long talking about our boy crushes, now the time we'd use for talking was spent eating each other out.

"Well I guess we'll see, won't we," Taylor said, still confident in the fact that the jogger would be knocking at the door any minute.

"Kendra's gonna be mad when she turns up with no present waiting for her."

"Oh, I dunno I can always put something together," Taylor said as she let go of my waist and practically skipped to her room, returning with a pair of handcuffs dangling from a finger. "Namely, your wrists behind your back," she said with a brash grin spread across her lips.

"Woah, Taylor I've never done anything like that before," I exclaimed, but after so many years of friendship, she could see in my face the excitement I felt at the idea.

"Two months ago you'd never eaten a woman's ass and now you can't stop licking the booty," she said as she sauntered over to me, exaggerating her speech playfully. She reached around me and spanked me lightly with one of the metal cuffs. "It'd be fun. Kendra got me these as a present. She's a very practical gift-giver. I'm sure she'd be thrilled to see I'm using them."

"I'm sure she would," I giggled. "Let's see, you might not even get the chance if your jogger friend shows up."

"Or maybe it would be the perfect opportunity," she replied coyly as she turned and poked her cute little bum out at me before making her way back to her room to return the handcuffs to their hiding place.

The doorbell chimed.

"No fucking way!" I exclaimed. An excited Taylor came bursting from her room, her big tits bouncing on her small frame.

"Is it her?" she asked eagerly as she ran to the front door.

I peered around the curtains of the living room window to see who was standing outside.

"It fucking is!" I half-shouted as I ogled the jogger standing nervously by the front door, playing with the end of her plait and still wearing her fitness gear. "It looks like she ran here. Taylor you little minx, how the hell did you pull that off?"

"I guess this body is just too irresistible, even

for the straightest of women," she proclaimed as she struck a proud pose. "Come here!"

I quickly made my way to the entrance and Taylor opened the door, trying with futility to hide her excitement for devouring the meal on the other side. The jogger was definitely unsure of what she was doing, I thought she might make a break for it at any second. Taylor refused to speak first, forcing the jogger to eventually make eye contact with her.

"My name is Dana," she announced. "I'd like to come in, but you're not eating my ass."

"Hi Dana, I'm Taylor," my petite friend replied. "You're welcome to come in, we won't do anything you don't want."

Dana stopped fiddling with her sandy blonde plait and came inside, fists clenched, shoulders up in defense mode. She kicked off her runners and socks at our request, nearly falling over as she did so due to the refusal of Taylor's shoulder to brace herself on.

"There's no need to be nervous, Dana," I assured her. "You'll be well taken care of. I'm Allison by the way."

"Yeah I remember from the park," she said as Taylor closed the door behind her. "So what, you two are a couple that just goes around picking up girls at the park or the supermarket or whatever?"

"Hmm, there's a little more to it than that, but don't worry about it for now," Taylor answered with her permanent grin still plastered on her face. Taylor revelled in these moments, the anticipation before the unsure girl gives herself over completely. I'd first seen the look in Brooke's hot tub when it was me who was about to give in to my dormant desires. Back then I was confused by Taylor's behaviour, now I shared it, although I didn't wear my heart on my sleeve like she did.

"So what do we do now?" Dana asked.

"Come with me," Taylor grabbed her by the hand and led her towards the bedroom. I grinned at the prophetic double entendre she'd inadvertently made as I followed the pair.

As soon as they were in the room and without letting go of the nervous blonde's hand, Taylor spun around and looked up at Dana, who towered over her by almost a whole foot. Taylor raised a cautious hand and placed it on the exposed part of Dana's chest, just above her cleavage.

"Is your heart beating faster now or when you were on your run?"

"Definitely now," the attractive jogger replied.

"Well you'll have a better workout here than at

the park in that case. Have you ever kissed a girl before?"

"Only at a party. I liked it, but I was pretty drunk, so I liked everything."

"I think you'll find you like it sober too," Taylor said as she stood on her tiptoes and pressed her lips against Dana's, never letting go of her hand. Without breaking the kiss, Taylor moved her hand from Dana's heart to her breast, cupping her bosom and running her thumb over her nipple through the fabric of the running gear. The move seemed to have it's intended effect and Dana let out a soft moan of approval before breaking away from the kiss.

"I've uh... run a few miles today, can I use your shower?" Dana asked.

"Oh, we don't mind," I said as I stepped forward. "We'll get you clean in a little while, let us enjoy you like this for a bit. Your scent is intoxicating," I leaned in and kissed her myself, tasting her full lips and inhaling the pheromones steaming off her body as the sweat evaporated off her skin.

Taylor let go of Dana's breast and started twirling her plait around her finger while I kept kissing the reluctant jogger. She seemed enchanted with Dana's hair, running her hand up and down its length before tugging on it gently to guide the blonde away from my lips and back to hers.

"I love playing with this," Taylor said as she wrapped the plait around her hand. "It's like a length of rope," she stated, looking at me with a look in her eye that suggested a plan. I had some idea of what she was insinuating as my mind was cast back to the pair of handcuffs she had hidden somewhere in the room. Taylor clearly had some bondage proclivities she wanted to explore, and admittedly, the thought enticed me as well.

Taylor pulled Dana to her lips again, her hand lost in the tangle of the blonde's plait. The move exposed the nape of the jogger's neck and I seized the opportunity, planting kisses along it and sampling the salty but alluring taste of her sweat. I could hear Dana sighing her approval into Taylor's mouth, as my petite friend's magic tongue was granted entry between the previously hesitant woman's lips. Their kiss grew more intense as Dana's inhibitions began to fade, melting away into a pool of sexual desire.

My confident best friend pulled back on the knot of hair, forcing Dana to look up at the ceiling while Taylor went to work on the other side of her neck, mirroring my actions. Dana moaned above us, relishing the feeling of having our mouths kiss and suck on her pretty neck.

"That feels incredible," Dana admitted.

"Oh, we're just getting started," Taylor chuckled onto her neck.

"We need to lose some of these clothes, I want to taste her all over," I suggested, looking across to my friend who bit her lip and nodded slightly in agreement.

Taylor and I each grabbed a side of Dana's top and pulled upwards. The blonde raised both her arms and allowed us to pull the garment over her head, exposing her lovely, pert tits beneath, adorned with erect nipples. A bead of sweat was dislodged from her collarbone and traced down the length of her chest, nestling itself between her luscious breasts. Taylor and I revelled in the display of femininity before us, a sight neither of us ever tired of.

As I disposed of the now useless fitness top, Dana suddenly became aware of Taylor and my ogling of her, and wrapped her arms around her chest, shielding her beautiful breasts from our view.

"Oh baby, don't be shy," Taylor protested with pursed lips as if she was a child who'd had her favorite toy taken away. She put a hand on Dana's arms to try and coax them away but Dana held firm.

"Sorry, I don't really know what I'm doing," Dana said with a creased brow, the threat of regret and reluctance reappearing.

"No, it's our fault. We're just big perves," Taylor remarked. "We shouldn't have made you get undressed first. Allison and I will do it with you, okay?"

The unsure Dana thought for a moment before nodding her head in agreement. Taylor and I would have to be more careful. We certainly didn't want to scare away the sexy jogger before our mistress arrived. Taylor and I both shed our tops and bras, equalling Dana in her nakedness in an effort to make her more comfortable. I noticed Dana bite her lip lightly as she stole a glance at Taylor's big tits. For such a short, thin framed girl, Taylor's boobs were the only big thing about her, besides her personality. Taylor's naked chest was definitely a sight that would make any straight girl think twice about their sexuality.

"Come over here, beautiful," I said to Dana, touching her on the shoulder reassuringly as she let her hands fall away, becoming more comfortable in her toplessness. I guided her to the edge of the bed and sat down next to her, wrapping one arm around her waist. "You're going to want a good view of this."

Taylor giggled, not only comfortable at being ogled, but thriving on it. She faced the pair of us on the edge of the bed and dropped a leg, swinging her hips to the side and raising both arms above her head, giving Dana a seductive look that went largely unnoticed, as the blonde's eyes didn't leave the globes hanging from Taylor's chest.

"Quit teasing us, bitch," I playfully scolded my friend. "Take those pants off already."

"If you insist," Taylor replied as she unbuttoned her jeans. Her tight stomach tensed as she looked down to wrestle with the tricky button. She had success and wriggled her hips side to side as she pushed the constricting denim down past her knees. "They're too tight, will you give me a hand, Dana?"

Without waiting for a response, Taylor turned around, flashing her tight little butt at us with only a black thong to leave anything to the imagination. The seductive brunette dropped onto all fours and kicked her lower legs up and down, the restrictive jeans clinging to her calves. She looked back at Dana over her shoulder in anticipation.

Dana's hesitance was well and truly melting away again, as she needed no words of encouragement from me. She slid down from the bed and crawled over to the waiting Taylor, grabbing the bunched denim and peeling the remaining length off of her pale legs.

"That feels better," Taylor said thankfully,

smiling over her shoulder at the blonde in her submissive position, wearing only her thong. "If it's not too much to ask, would you mind finishing the job?"

I could just about hear Dana gulp, but the wide eyed blonde reached forward nonetheless and gripped the waistband of Taylor's thong. I sat patiently on the bed, growing aggravated with my pants. The familiar warmth that had been stirring in my groin was now soaking my panties, and I was desperate to be naked, but I would have to wait my turn. Dana obligingly pulled the thong down Taylor's thighs, peeling the fabric out of the crack of her butt to reveal the cute little asshole beneath, one I'd feasted on many times over the last few weeks. Taylor's pretty pussy lay neatly beneath it, hairless and looking gorgeous as ever with its rich pinkness contrasting her pale white skin around it. Taylor lifted her knees enough to allow Dana to slide the thong down her calves, and then over her feet so that she was completely nude in front of her prey.

"Well, do you like what you see?" Taylor asked. Dana only nodded in approval, unable to find the words. Taylor remained on all fours for a moment to let the jogger take in the sight before her. I saw her clench her ass muscles so that her butthole winked a bit, and I knew that now she'd broken down the defences of Dana's lesbian reluctance, the next task would be to break down her anal aversions. She had to make her butthole seem as appealing as possible, and she was doing a great job, although I might have been a little biased.

Having given Dana an eyeful for long enough, Taylor spun around onto her butt, putting her hands out behind her to prop herself up, giving her conquest the full frontal view. The wide-eyed blonde seemed to enjoy it just as much. But before Taylor's tits even had enough time to stop jiggling, she thrust herself forward and began crawling towards the stunned blonde. Seemingly unsure of what to do, Dana fell backwards onto her ass, and crawled back away from the encroaching Taylor. Eventually she reached the bed and couldn't crawl any further, and the naked Taylor reached her, putting her hands on the jogger's muscular thighs and kissing her on the mouth.

Dana was still definitely nervous, but appeared to be loving every second of the seduction, as she kissed Taylor back with equal passion. I remained perched on the edge of the bed, enjoying watching Taylor work her magic but finding it increasingly difficult not to join in. Taylor's hands moved to the sides of Dana's workout shorts and pulled. Dana raised her ass off the floor a little to allow the petite brunette to remove both her shorts and panties in one motion, joining her in her nakedness.

"Spread your legs for me, baby," Taylor implored. "Let me do what I do best."

Dana complied, spreading her legs on the carpeted floor, her vagina glistening in a combination of sweat and love juices. Taylor looked up at me and as if linked by a psychic connection, I could tell what she was thinking. Dana had a light triangle of pubes that matched her sandy blonde hair color. They were trimmed and neat, but they would have to go before our mistress arrived. Kendra liked her good girls to be clean shaven. Nevertheless, it was no problem for us and Taylor dove in to enjoy her hard-earned meal.

The response from Dana was instant, as she threw her head back in ecstasy and let out a yelp that could almost be mistaken for pain if it wasn't so obviously pleasure. Taylor buried her face into the blonde's snatch, her ass jutting out behind her making a love heart shape from my vantage point. It was a fucking sexy sight seeing Dana having what was undoubtedly the best oral of her life... so far.

Dana writhed in pleasure, her tits heaving as she took in deep breaths. She was going to cum quickly, I could tell already. The sight was too much for me as my legs squirmed, crossing and uncrossing with the need to have a face between them. I stood up and tore down my shorts with lightning speed so that I was finally as naked as the other two. Suddenly not caring about easing Dana into her first lesbian experience, I stepped over her with one leg so that her eyes were level with my bare cunt. Before she had time to register what I was doing, I pushed her head back so that it lay on the edge of the bed, facing up towards the ceiling. I placed one knee to either side of her shocked face and lowered myself onto her open mouth.

I was so wet that I felt a bit of cum drip off my glistening snatch and fall into Dana's mouth below a moment before I reached it. The taste must have agreed with Dana because she wasted no time ravaging my pussy the second it touched her lips. She was definitely on board with the lesbian experience as she got eaten out by Taylor while licking up the length of my pussy. The lamb on this lesbian spitroast. The inexperienced blonde was hungry it seemed because her enthusiasm for cunnilingus was almost unparalleled. I remembered how eager I was the first time I tasted pussy, the deliciousness of it catching me by surprise and whipping me into a frenzy of desire for more.

I let out a sigh of relief as I was gratified at last for my patience. Dana's pretty face creased as she moaned into my vagina, her new task doing little to delay the inevitable orgasm that was coming for her like a freight train. She reached around my legs and clung onto my thighs, a grip which I felt tighten suddenly as she let out a sharp squeal between my legs as the train hit her.

Her lips pursed tightly around my clit as the orgasm crashed through her, so tight that it hurt me a little.

"Ooh, gently, gently," I coached her, and she forced herself to release the grip she had on my clit.

Instead, her head rocked left and right as she shook violently beneath me, smearing my cum all around her mouth like messily applied lip-stick. She kept inhaling and exhaling sharply as she struggled to catch her breath, a fresh layer of sweat appearing on her brow. The jogger rode wave after wave of ecstasy until eventually, the grip on my thighs relaxed, leaving white im-prints on my skin, and her orgasm subsided.

Dana's hot, exhausted breath blew up on my unsatisfied vagina while she recovered from her first orgasm given to her by another woman. Her arms fell to the floor as she tried to catch her breath and it became clear my chances of her sexy mouth finishing me off were rapidly dimin-ishing.

"New personal best," Taylor gloated from the floor behind me, obviously happier than I was with Dana's ability to climax quickly. "You look sexy as fuck when you cum, and I want to see it again, but you can't tease Allison like that. You've gotta finish the job."

"You read my mind," I looked over my shoulder at my best friend on the floor, who gave me a wink as she wiped the quivering jogger's cum and sweat off her mouth with the back of her hand.

"I want to," she spoke up from beneath my cunt. "Just tell me what to do."

"Come on, get up," Taylor instructed. "Why don't you face us, Allison."

I turned on the bed, still kneeling, and saw Taylor stroking Dana's plait while placing soft kisses on her cheek. Dana looked at me with a bewildered look in her eye, like she was hypnotized. Still panting heavily, she looked at me like a meal she wanted to consume. The hesitant jogger had had a taste and was now drunk on lesbian lust.

"You're doing so good, baby," Taylor said encouragingly, "You're going to do so much better though."

Taylor stepped over to the bed and gave me another wink before pushing me down onto my back. I giggled as she led the mesmerized Dana over, and positioned her on her knees a few inches further up than my head. I wasn't sure how Dana was meant to eat me out from there but trusted my best friend had a plan. The miniature sized nymphomaniac then grabbed underneath my legs and flipped them over, curling my body so that my weight balanced on my head and shoulders, my rear pointing straight upwards with my pussy facing the head of the bed, facing Dana. My legs dangled downwards to either side of my head, luckily Taylor knew I was flexible.

Taylor reached over the top of me and took Dana by her long plait, pulling on it gently and leading the jogger towards my snatch like she was on a leash. Dana didn't need any further instruction and returned her mouth to my pussy above me, maintaining her former enthusiasm for eating cunt. She moaned onto my slit, apparently appreciating my taste.

"Oh, you'll make such a good girl," Taylor marvelled at the hopefully soon to be inducted lesbian.

"Christ, Kendra's going to fucking love you," I said as I lavished Dana's tongue swirling around my clit.

"Who's Kendra?" Dana managed to say with a face full of muff.

"Don't worry about it," Taylor said, and the preoccupied Dana seemed happy to dismiss it. "Don't you think this asshole looks so pretty?"

Taylor traced a finger around my skyward

pointing pucker, displaying it to Dana, who didn't reply. The eager jogger was still butt-shy it seemed.

"Well, I think it's pretty," Taylor continued, unperturbed by Dana's lack of response. "I think it looks good enough to eat," she said before I felt her warm tongue press against my rim and swirl once.

My abs tensed and I let out a whimper of appreciation at the attention given to my ass.

"See how good it makes her feel?" Taylor teased Dana, who's lips still didn't leave my pussy, but eyes seemed curious about what Taylor was doing at my back door.

My old friend returned her tongue to my asshole while my new friend kept licking and nibbling on my clitoris. I was powerless below, my legs dangling to either side of my head while the two beautiful women satisfied my nether regions. It wasn't long before the orgasm that Dana had started working on before was about to be realized at last.

I came hard. In the position Taylor had rolled me into; my pussy and ass was my apex, and the orgasm radiated from the top down. I let out a guttural groan as the orgasmic energy reached my head at the same time it reached my toes. My abs tensed, rolling me up even tighter and pushing my hips further towards Dana. The two sexy tongues followed, and a cocktail of my own cum mixed with Dana's saliva dripped down from my pussy all over my tits, neck and open mouth, the taste only enhancing the pleasure.

I rode out the incredible climax before Taylor relinquished her tongue from my asshole and stepped off the bed, allowing me to unroll myself and splay my body across the bed as I sucked in deep gulps of air, swallowing the delicious cum cocktail in the process and savoring the taste of the orgasm. Taylor climbed on top of my heaving body and licked at my neck and chest, not wanting the precious nectar that had spilled all over me to go to waste.

"That was… wow," Dana said in shock. "I just had the best orgasm of my life but that somehow looked even better."

"I can assure it was babe," Taylor said as she stood at the edge of the bed having licked my chest clean, the pair having their conversation across my temporarily paralyzed body. "And you know why."

"Is it really that good having your ass licked?"

"Yes," Taylor said confidently.

"Yeah," I managed to pant out.

"I think I want to try it," Dana admitted

nervously, like she was telling a secret. Taylor's trademark grin spread from ear to ear.

"Oh that can be arranged," Taylor said. "Kendra will be here soon, then you'll see."

"You said that name earlier. Who's Kendra? Is she coming here? Now?"

"It's kind of complicated to explain. But Kendra did for us what we just did for you, and then some. In return for the best sex imaginable with all manner of beautiful women, Allison and I give ourselves to her."

"What do you mean give yourselves to her?"

"We submit ourselves to her. We do whatever she tells us to, and we have the most fun doing it."

"Wow, that's... kinky," Dana said, unsure of what she was hearing.

"It sure is," Taylor said, raising an eyebrow. "We're her good girls. And I think you'd make a perfect good girl, Dana."

"Oh, I don't know about all that-"

"Don't worry," Taylor raised a hand of interruption. "You won't be made to do anything you don't want to. What's going through your head right now is what went through every good girl's head the first time they met Kendra. I assure you, if you just go with it for this afternoon, your mind will be made up by the time night rolls around. So what do you say? Do you want to meet Kendra and have your asshole licked and enjoy the most sensational orgasms of your entire fucking life?"

Dana's brow was creased, she was trying to process all the information she just heard, weighing up all the options. Taylor and I already knew the decision had been made though. She'd had a taste and there was no way she was backing out now.

"So to be a good girl... do you have to do anything else?"

Taylor almost squealed in excitement. "Well, now that you mention it, why don't we get you cleaned up before Kendra gets here."

My friend extended both her hands and helped me off the bed, before leading the two of us to the ensuite bathroom and running the shower. The three of us got in and washed away the evidence of our sexual activities. The cum, sweat and drool all washed off our bodies and down the drain. Taylor passed around the body wash and we washed each other's smooth skin, laughing as we inadvertently tickled one another and explored our bodies, lathering soap over one another, pausing intermittently for quick kisses. Taylor picked up her razor off the ledge.

"There *is* one thing we have to do before Kendra gets here," Taylor said, razor in hand, pointing cheekily down at Dana's neat pubes.

"What, I've gotta be shaved, like you two?"

"It's part of being a good girl," I replied.

"But I'm not a good girl. I like my pubes! There's not many of them anyway!"

"I know but it will make a good first impression if you're shaved. Pleeeeeease, for me?" Taylor pleaded.

"Fine," Dana relented, powerless against Taylor's cuteness. "Give me the razor."

"No, I'll do it!" Taylor exclaimed. "It'll be so sexy. Turn around and come here."

Taylor positioned herself up against the shower wall and Dana spun around, backing into the much shorter brunette, who could just peer over her shoulders when she stood on her toes. Taylor then used one hand to maneuver some of the soap suds onto Dana's mons, lathering up her pubes before reaching around with her other to shave off the trimmed bush.

With careful but confident motions, Taylor expertly shaved the unsure jogger bare. Wiping away Dana's pubes and with it, some of her sexual autonomy, an important step in submitting to Kendra. She washed off the remaining soap suds to reveal Dana's now hairless snatch.

"Now we all match," Taylor said, proud of her work as she returned the razor to the ledge. "What do you think?"

"I think I haven't seen my pussy hairless since before puberty," Dana replied, running her hand over her mound. "I kind of like it though, it's so smooth. I can't wait to meet Kendra. I wonder if I'll like having my ass licked as much as you two seem to."

Taylor grabbed Dana's hips and spun her around so that they were facing each other, even though Taylor's face was only boob height on Dana. "Oh I'm confident you will," she said with a grin as she rubbed her hands all over Dana's tight, soaped up body. She reached around and lathered soap all over Dana's backside, before pushing her middle finger in between her ass cheeks. "How does that feel?" she enquired.

"Naughty," Dana responded with a giggle. "I've never had someone else's finger there before."

"Well if you expect us to eat it, it's gonna have to be nice and clean," Taylor said as she moved her middle finger up and down the crack of Dana's butt. "Inside and out," she said as she pushed the very tip of her slippery finger into Dana's virgin hole.

"Oh," Dana gasped, grabbing the petite brunette's shoulders as she rocked forward in surprise. "That feels nice."

Taylor smiled and nodded her head, before taking the opportunity of the slightly bent over jogger to kiss her deeply on the mouth. She removed her finger from Dana's derriere and I took the shower head to rinse the sexy, round booty.

"I think she wants you, Allison," Taylor suggested to me between kisses, as she grabbed an ass cheek in each hand and spread them ever so slightly. The ravine of Dana's succulent ass looked so inviting to me.

I returned the showerhead to its hook and dropped to my knees on the shower floor, licking my lips as I gazed upon the perfect posterior. Taylor pulled the cheeks apart a little more and I dove in, I briefly teased the forbidden opening with the tip of my nose before giving one long lick up the full length of Dana's toned but juicy ass.

"Mmm," I heard from above me over the sound of the running water.

"Oh, she bit my lip!" Taylor exclaimed. "I think she likes it."

"Mhmm," Dana agreed as she kept searching for Taylor's mouth to kiss.

I worked my magic on Dana's tight, puckered asshole. My tongue bathed it in saliva as I tasted her perfectly clean butthole, with only a hint of soap present on my initial licks. I moved the flat of my tongue repeatedly up her ass before using the harder tip of the appendage to circle around the rim and probe her pucker as much as she would allow, which wasn't much.

Taylor spread her cheeks as much as she could to allow me the greatest access, as I kissed her on the hole and rimmed her expertly. The jogger kept moaning into Taylor's mouth as her thighs and calves tensed while my tongue tickled her asshole.

"Holy shit that feels amazing," she exclaimed in disbelief.

"Don't cum yet, I was the one that wanted to stick my face in your ass in the first place, remember! Allison, give me a turn!" Taylor said as she slipped out from between Dana and the wall.

I stood and let her in as she pushed Dana up against the cold tiled wall before grabbing her by the hips and pulling her succulent ass towards her so that she could plunge her face into it. Taylor looked like a famished dog had just been given a T-bone steak. She pushed her face into Dana's crack as hard as she pulled back on Dana's hips, desperate to lick every inch of ass on offer.

The side of Dana's face was pressed up against the shower wall, her hands pressed against it to either side of her head, her brow was furrowed and her eyes were closed and she let out soft whimpers of pleasure as she tried to come to grips with the new sensations she was experiencing. No one ate ass like Taylor and it looked like she was giving Dana the platinum service. Taylor didn't just move her tongue when she rimmed a girl, her whole head would move with enthusiasm for her favorite act. Her deviant mouth never left the reluctant jogger's bottom as her head moved left and right, up and down and then in a circle, mirroring the movements of her tongue.

I saw Dana shift her weight onto her heels as her toes curled and the orgasm ripped through her body. Her first anal orgasm would be a high should would chase forever, there's nothing quite like it. Her eyes opened, staring at nothing as her hips rocked backwards and forwards, Taylor's head following, still gripping her sides. Taylor's muffled screams of delight in Dana's ass mixed with the sharper, broken yells of the jogger reverberating around the shower.

Wave after wave of ecstasy shot through Dana's body from her asshole and she had no choice but to ride them. Eventually, she had to reach back and push Taylor's head away from her ass.

"Please, no more," she mustered before turning against the wall and sliding down it. The satisfied face of Taylor watched her collapse into a heap on the shower floor, immensely proud of her efforts and incredibly happy she got to live her day-long dream of eating the joggers ass.

After a couple of minutes to let Dana pick herself up off the floor, the three of us finished our shower in earnest and toweled ourselves off. Even though I was completely dry, there was still one part of me that remained wet, as watching Taylor rim Dana in the shower only made me hornier for another climax. Although by my count, Dana was up to two now, I'd had my one and poor Taylor was so far neglected. I didn't feel too bad though, as I was sure that would be remedied by the time the afternoon was over.

Giggling and each wrapped up in a towel, we opened the door back to Taylor's bedroom and found a familiar, exquisitely feminine figure sitting on the edge of Taylor's bed.

"Kendra!" Taylor squealed as she did a little jump of happiness at the sight of her mistress.

"Hello, girls. Sounds like you've been having fun without me," Kendra's sultry voice replied.

"This is Dana," I spoke up. "She's been spending the afternoon discovering the joys of a woman's tongue."

"We found her at the park, we thought she'd make a nice present for you," Taylor said, eager to see Kendra's reaction to her gift.

"Hi," Dana said as she sheepishly raised a hand, her former nervousness somewhat returning at the sight of the sexual master we'd been telling her about.

"Hello, Dana," Kendra replied as she got off the bed and strutted over to us, stopping in front of the jogger and making intense eye contact, as if she was scanning her eyes for something. "A present for me? It's not even my birthday."

"Well, we just wanted to thank you," Taylor said, a hint of hesitance in her voice at Kendra's underwhelming reaction. "You've done so much for the two of us in the last couple of months, and all the other good girls. We just wanted to show our appreciation."

"Take off your towel," Kendra commanded. Dana looked to Taylor who nodded hurriedly before she obliged. The freed towel fell away from her fit body into a heap on the floor, and Dana stood naked before us, her magnificent round breasts, flat stomach and newly shaven pussy on display. Kendra looked her up and down, assessing the gift.

"I love it," she finally said with a smile, causing

Taylor to sigh in relief. "She's perfect my darlings. May I ask, was her pussy already clean shaven?"

"Not quite, we just did that in the shower. Dana was eager to meet you and happy to meet the requirements before we presented her," I said, bending the truth somewhat.

"Is that so?" Kendra asked rhetorically as she reached around the back of Dana's head and pulled her in for a sensual kiss. Kendra's full lips enveloped Dana's mouth as the two exchanged tongues, my mistress enjoying her offering. "Hm, I can taste Allison's pussy on your mouth, but not Taylors. Have you been neglected my pet?"

"We've just been preoccupied with showing our new friend what a good girl can do," Taylor responded.

"And are you enlightened?" Kendra asked Dana, who nodded shyly.

"She's been a little hesitant to eat ass," I chimed in. "But after what we just showed her in the shower I think she's ready to try it for herself."

"So Taylor hasn't cum yet and our new friend hasn't rimmed anyone. I think we can rectify both issues at the same time."

"Can we use your present?" Taylor's eyes

widened with anticipation.

"Use Dana? I certainly intend to."

"No I meant... the present you got me."

"Oh," Kendra said, remembering what Taylor was talking about. "I don't see why not. Tell me where they are while you and Allison get rid of those pesky towels. And give Taylor some attention, girls. It sounds like she's been starved of it."

Taylor giggled as she and I let our towels join the other on the floor. She told Kendra where to go as I turned her to face Dana, her conquest. Dana had to lean over to kiss my short friend while I pushed her hair to one side so that I could lick and nibble the nape of her neck. The little sex kitten in the middle of the lesbian sandwich was loving having the attention on her at last, and she let out squeals of excitement as my hands reached around and fondled her large breasts. I heard a drawer open and close as Kendra retrieved the kinky present.

I stepped out of my mistress' way and she took my position behind Taylor. Holding the handcuffs between her teeth, she placed both hands on Taylor's shoulders and ran them down the length of her thin arms, grabbing her by the wrists and pulling them into an X shape across her lower back. She took the cuffs from her mouth and locked them both into place around

Taylor's wrists. Taylor let out an excited giggle as the cool steel locked into place around her skin. The bracelets signified her submission to Kendra, the loss free will of her arms mirroring her status in the sexual hierarchy that came with being a good girl. We could do whatever Kendra told us to do to her, and she'd just have to take it.

Kendra grabbed Taylor by the hair and pushed her by the wrists over to the bed. Taylor let out a little yelp of pain but her smile showed how much she was enjoying the rougher than usual play. Kendra made a come hither motion with her finger towards Dana and I and we obliged. The three, freshly cleaned, hairless from the head down, bare naked women were putty in Kendra's hands, just the way she liked it. It wasn't uncommon for Kendra to keep her clothes on while she ordered her good girls into all manner of sexual scenarios. She enjoyed the power of being the boss, as well as denying us all the view of her magnificent curves, teasing us until it came time for her to cum.

My mistress pushed on Taylor's head and bent her over the bed, the cheeks of Taylor's cute little ass parting with the movement, the engorged pink lips of her vulva below, begging for attention. The tiniest sliver of cum could be seen in the unparted slit of Taylor's innie cunt, her patience coming at the price of being unbearably horny.

"If you want to be one of my good girls, you're going to have to learn to eat ass," Kendra informed Dana. "And if you want your own ass eaten regularly by the most beautiful women imaginable, you'll be my good girl."

"I'm ready. I want to," Dana said as she took a deep breath in and clenched her fists, accepting her fate and powerless to Kendra's wiles.

Kendra took her by the long plait of hair, apparently sharing a penchant for it with Taylor. "I like this, it's like a lesbian leash that lets me direct your face into any pussy or ass I choose."

And with that, she pulled on it firmly but gently, bringing Dana down to all fours behind the cuffed Taylor.

"I want you to lick her from end to end. Show her how grateful you are for bringing you here."

With a short pull of hair that was quite frankly unnecessary, the plenty grateful jogger extended her tongue and licked Taylor upwards from her clit, right through the crevice of her ass. Taylor moaned into the duvet as she finally had a tongue on her.

"What do you think of her?" Kendra enquired.

"She tastes heavenly, all of her," Dana replied, hunger in her voice.

"Keep eating her while I talk to Allison for a moment."

Kendra let go of the plaited hair and walked towards me. The slippery sounds of Dana's face running up and down Taylor's most erogenous zones continued in the background, mixing with Taylor's cries of joy into the bed, her shoulder blades writhing as her arms involuntarily pulled on their shackles.

"You found her at the park?" Kendra asked me.

"We were watching all the sexy joggers go past and fantasizing about what we'd do with them. Taylor accidentally fantasized out loud as this one went past."

"It's rare Taylor does anything by accident when it comes to fucking other women. Our new friend seems to be loving exploring her derriere. Do you think she's been enlightened enough to join our little gang?"

"She definitely has a lot of potential. She was a little hesitant at the thought of submitting to you, but I'm confident that you can convince her. She just needs your magic touch. It's not like you to be questioning a new member. Is this because of Amanda?"

"We're not talking about that now," Kendra dismissed my question. "I have an idea for our new friend, one that should wipe out any semblance of doubt. Stop now, Dana," she called over to the eager inductee.

But Dana didn't stop, she couldn't bring herself to take her face away from Taylor's pretty pink pussy and asshole. Taylor closed her mouth in an effort to stifle her cries of pleasure, hearing the command and knowing that Dana should have stopped eating her out, but powerless to move away thanks to her cuffed hands.

Kendra walked over swiftly to the pair and pulled back on Dana's plait, forcing the jogger's head back to look at her.

"When I tell you to do something, you do it, no questions," Kendra instructed firmly but without anger.

"Okay, I will, I'm sorry Kendra, I couldn't help myself," Dana pleaded from the floor.

"In the future you *will* help yourself, understand?"

"Yes, Kendra."

"Good," Kendra relinquished Dana's hair from her grip. "Now, it doesn't seem fair that Allison and I should have to miss out on the fun. Taylor, climb up on the bed and put your ass up."

My best friend obeyed her mistress, pushing

herself up onto the bed quite gracelessly without the use of her arms. Her head pressed into the mattress as she rested on her knees and pointed her cute ass into the air, Dana's saliva still wet in her crevice. She stayed in the position silently and awaited the tongue of Kendra's new fucktoy.

Kendra pulled Dana off the floor by her hair and instructed her to climb on the bed near Taylor's head. She guided the unsure jogger's leg over Taylor's body so that she straddled the back of the petite sex kitten's head.

"Sit on her," Kendra commanded. "Don't worry, she likes it, don't you Taylor."

"Yes, Kenda," Taylor agreed into the bed.

Dana's bare pussy lowered onto Taylor's head, and she allowed some of her weight to force my friend further into the duvet. Taylor didn't protest, in fact, she let out a pleasure moan at the feeling of having Dana's warm crotch in her hair, and the pressure of a new lesbian holding her down. Kendra pushed Dana so that she bent to the same angle of Taylor's back, the jogger's breasts pushing into Taylor's flesh around her sacrum, just out of reach of Taylor's cuffed hands.

"Well, keep eating her asshole," Kendra instructed.

Dana was more than happy to oblige, returning to her previous post albeit from a new vantage point. She spread Taylor's ass and nestled her open mouth between the tight butt cheeks of my best friend, probing and swirling her tongue around Taylor's pretty little star. The result was instantaneous as I heard Taylor's muffled cries into the bed from beneath the crotch of the woman straddling her head and tonguing her ass.

Kendra made her way back over to me, shedding her clothes with every step until she was completely naked. Kendra in the nude was really a sight to behold. Her olive skin, feminine curves and dark, curly hair falling down around her shoulders accentuated her best features; her full, luscious lips; large, round tits that begged to be played with; and her delicious pussy, adorned with a delta of neatly trimmed black pubes, a display of dominance over her cleanly shaved harem. I knew that behind her was everyone's favorite feature of all: a plump, juicy rear end that was almost impossible in it's perfection. It caught the eye of Dana, who's tongue momentarily stopped servicing Taylor's ass to watch the sexual goddess walk toward me. If her mouth wasn't already open it sure would have ended up that way as she saw the sway of Kendra's hips, and the curvature of her fabulous butt.

"What do you say we join the party, my pet?" Kendra said as she took my head in her hands and kissed me lovingly.

"Yes, Kendra," I responded. My favorite two words to say, as it always preceded sexual bliss.

"Why don't you tend to Taylor's clit? I'm going to see if I can make a convincing argument to our new friend's ass."

My mistress and I walked over to the pair on the bed. I took my position behind Taylor, holding onto her calf muscles and going to town on her pussy. I cleaned up the cum and saliva from Dana's previous haphazard oral, licking around her vulva to tease, before running my tongue through her pretty pink slit, paying close attention to the little button at the bottom. I felt her calves tense as I flicked the sensitive nub. The wet noises of Dana's eager tongue pleasuring her asshole could be heard above me. I felt jealous of the reluctant jogger getting to give her first rimjob, but I was more jealous of Taylor, the patient little nymph was getting the star treatment today, and seemed to be loving being bound by the cuffs.

At the other end of the bed, Kendra positioned herself above Taylor's head, spreading her legs to either side of Dana's, which straddled the back of her sex pets head. Kendra placed her hands on Dana's hips and lifted the jogger off of Taylor's head, revealing a wet patch in Taylor's hair where Dana's pussy was. Taking the weight off of Taylor's head allowed Kendra to pull her up by the hair and slide her pussy beneath the face of the delirious slut. Hungry for her mistress, Taylor immediately started her oral acrobatics in Kendra's cunt. The trimmed hairs of the only pubes in the room tickled her nose as she thirstily lapped up any cum she could get her tongue on, her own body weight forcing her face deep into the pussy below.

With her pussy being tended to, Kendra returned her attention to the prospective new good girl. She pulled on Dana's hips and brought her ass up to her face. Cleaned in the shower with soap and two tongues, this was the moment we'd been preparing Dana for. Kendra wrapped her arms completely around the top of Dana's thighs, pulling her ass the rest of the way and diving in with her exquisite tongue.

The move had its desired effect on Dana, who's face I watched above me. Her eyes widened and she momentarily ceased rimming Taylor to bask in the undeniable ecstasy of having Kendra in her butt. I remembered the first time I had Kendra eat my ass one night in a hot tub, I never thought it was possible to feel that good, especially not from a place that had previously been completely off-limits. It was a whole new world that Dana was being opened up to and she seemed to be loving it.

I ate Taylor's snatch, who in turn devoured

Kendra's, who was rimming Dana, who licked Taylor's asshole with vigor. It was a wonderfully sexy lesbian pretzel that Kendra had orchestrated, with the handcuffed Taylor very much the center of it. I increased the speed of my licks up and down Taylor's pussy, which was becoming increasingly messier as cum spilled out of her and her orgasm neared. Dana's rimming efforts above me were becoming less directed as she struggled to maintain concentration on the pretty butthole before her. Kendra's expert tongue was almost doing too good a job, and my mistress added a hand to the mix, rubbing her thumb in circles around Dana's engorged clit while she swirled around her ass with her tongue.

"You have to relax your ring," Kendra instructed from behind the rapt inductee. "Let me in."

I saw in Dana's face that she made a conscious effort to relax her asshole for Kendra's probing tongue. She surged forward and let out a surprised *ohhh* as Kendra's tongue slipped inside her bottom.

"Oh my god," Dana said between licks of Taylor's butt.

I smiled up at her with Taylor's clit in my mouth, giving her a knowing giggle as if to say '*I know right?*'

Taylor's low, regular moans into Kendra's snatch suddenly became faster and higher pitched as she became overwhelmed by the sexual attention she was receiving. Cum poured out of her vagina and onto my waiting tongue, as I collected every drop of her nectar that I could. Above me, I could see her butthole squeeze and relax rapidly and uncontrollably as the orgasm rocked through her, causing every muscle in her body to contract and flex involuntarily. Her sex seizure continued as I gave her one final lick up the length of her pussy and met Dana's tongue at her asshole, kissing the beautiful jogger hard, trading her Taylor's cum for the taste of her ass on Dana's mouth.

Dana's third climax of the day followed as I was kissing her. She bit down on my lip as Kendra's moist tongue fucked her ass, and her clit was pinched and assaulted by Kendra's expert hands. The poor girl really didn't stand a chance, this would definitely convince her to submit to Kendra and join us as a good girl. If not, she'd have to have major self-loathing issues to deny herself more orgasms like this.

Dana's orgasm subsided eventually, and Kendra withdrew her tongue from her rear so that she could slide off of Taylor's back and collapse on the bed next to us. Below her she revealed Taylor in the most sexy submissive position. Cuffed, ass up in the air, head buried in the crotch of her mistress, shaking occasionally as aftershocks of her orgasm electrocuted her. Her hair was wet with cum, as was her shoulder blades and neck after Dana's messy finish. Her ass and pussy glistened with Danas and my saliva, along with her own cum, a light sheen of sweat covering her body. The smell of the satisfied sex pet filled my nostrils. Taylor was definitely in her happy place.

Kendra reached over to the bedside table for a key and uncuffed her, permitting Taylor to lie on her back, her big tits jiggling whenever an aftershock would make its way through her. Dana and Taylor lay next to each other but opposite ways, trying their best to catch their breaths.

"What did you think of the handcuffs, my dear?" Kendra asked the exhausted Taylor.

"They were so good," Taylor responded. "It adds a whole new dimension to submitting to you. I loved having my own weight force my face into your pussy, it was so hot. I can't wait to use it on one of the other girls."

"Oh, I have someone in mind. I'm glad you liked your present."

"Did you like *your* present," Taylor asked, desperate for validation from her mistress.

"I loved it, my pet, thank you. Dana's virgin ass was so wonderful to enjoy. Did you enjoy it,

Dana?"

"Holy shit," Dana managed to say between panted breaths. "I never knew I could feel like that. I never knew I could feel so much ecstasy from having my ass played with."

"Would you like to have more of that ecstasy?"

"God yes. I'll do whatever you want. I'll submit if that what it takes, you can bind me, tie me, fuck me, do what you want with me. Just promise me more orgasms like what I've had today and I'm yours. I'll shave my pussy every morning with a fucking smile on my face if it means having sex with gorgeous women and having my ass licked on a regular basis."

Kendra gave me a look as Taylor burst out laughing on the bed.

"What's so funny?" I asked.

"*I'd like to come in, but you're not eating my ass,*" Taylor said in a mocking tone, repeating Dana's words from earlier in the afternoon. "Two hours later and you're a little butt slut!"

Dana joined Taylor in her uncontrollable laughter. "What can I say? I'm a convert."

"You're a good girl now," Kendra pointed out. "And your work's not done for the day."

The laughter of the pair on the bed died down,

and the three of us looked at our exquisite mistress at the head of the bed. She had yet to cum this afternoon, and it was time for her subjects to show their appreciation. We were all more than happy to oblige her, to please her, to submit to her. Every time I got to be a part of enlightening a new good girl to the pleasure of lesbian sex and ass play, I felt so grateful for everything Kendra had shown me.

What an incredible two months it had been.

THE END

THE
PUNISHMENT
OF AMANDA
Amanda II

I glanced down at my freshly shaved pussy as I stepped out of the shower and sighed. I had done everything Kendra had asked of me; I kept my downstairs hairless, wore make-up at all times, I submitted myself to her and followed her every command, and answered her every message when she wanted to use me for sex. It had been over two weeks since her last message, and I was frustrated and horny. Had I done something wrong? I yearned for my mistress, and for Brooke, another loyal subject of hers that was instrumental in my subservient lesbian turning.

As I toweled myself off I reflected on the night it all changed for me, and the shame I felt about my behaviour. I worked at the gym located on the college campus, and for a while I had suspected two of our members; Brooke and Kendra;

of having lesbian exploits in the gym after hours. I captured some inconclusive evidence on camera and used it to try and blackmail Brooke into cancelling her membership.

I didn't even know why I hated what they were doing so much. At the time I rationalized it as not allowing gym members to break the rules, but that night it was pointed out to me that I was jealous of Kendra, and that I really wanted Brooke for myself. I'd never had feelings of attraction towards another woman and it was still something I was coming to terms with. But nevertheless, I allowed myself to be seduced by her and Kendra, the leader of a cult of women around campus that regularly fucked each other and seduced new members, with a particular focus on ass play.

I submitted myself to Kendra out of a deep desire to keep having sex with Brooke, and for a time everything was great. I would receive a message from Kendra every few nights and I would go where she told me, eat whichever pussy or ass she instructed, and in return I got to have incredible sex with Brooke and the other gorgeous women who let themselves be fucktoys for their mistress to play with.

But my phone had gone silent, and I had to make do with thoughts of Brooke's fit body to masturbate to every night. I started applying my make-up in the mirror, getting ready to go to dinner with my parents in a few hours. Really though, I was getting ready early in the probably futile hope that my phone would buzz and I would have to cancel my dinner plans.

Almost the moment I had finished the thought, my phone vibrated on the counter. My heart skipped a beat and I almost knocked it off in my rush to see who the message was from.

It was Kendra! Finally! I opened up the message, my heart racing and adrenaline running through me at the thought of getting to eat some gorgeous girl's pussy.

'*Meet at Taylor's house in twenty minutes*' was all the message said. It wasn't unusual for Kendra's texts to be brief.

'*I have dinner with my parents tonight, should I cancel?*' I messaged back.

'*No need*' was all I got in return. My heart sank a little, whatever this was for it was obviously going to be brief. It wouldn't be an all night long sex romp that we sometimes had, but it also didn't sound like there was a new girl to seduce, that usually took some time. Whatever it was, I better be getting fucked, or else I'd have to voice my frustrations.

I finished getting ready, putting my long blonde hair up into a bun, throwing on a black lace bra with a matching thong, and covering up with a tight red sweater, a denim skirt and a pair of high heels appropriate for dinner with the folks, I could probably go straight to the restaurant after the sexual exploits that awaited, as long as I had a mint first.

I almost forgot to lock the door behind me in my rush to get over to Taylor's. It was a quick drive and I arrived exactly eighteen minutes after Kendra's message. The good girl in me knew I should wait for the extra two so as to not displease my mistress, but I was too excited. I leapt out of the car and knocked on Taylor's front door.

Taylor answered the door. The little firecracker brunette usually had an ever present grin on her face and a spring in her step but tonight her face was blank. She offered me no smile or greeting.

"Hi Taylor, long time no see," I said to the petite nymph. No one relished obeying Kendra more than her, she was normally so full of energy and had an unquenchable thirst for pussy and ass.

"Come in, Kendra's waiting for you in the living room," she said with an uncharacteristically dry voice.

I entered the house, suddenly very unsure of what was going on. Whenever I was called to a lesbian fuck session there was usually so much warmth and love, but Taylor was giving me very cold vibes.

Taylor followed me into the living room, where Kendra was sitting in the middle of the couch. She extended her hand, gesturing towards the armchair across the room. I noticed the coffee table had been pushed off to the side of the room, leaving a noticeably large space of carpet between myself and Kendra. Taylor leant against the entryway to the room, not joining the two of us.

"Kendra, what's going on?" I asked as I sat, confused by the weird tone of the evening.

"Amanda," she finally said, "do you like being my good girl?"

"Well, yes, of course," I said truthfully.

"That night in the gym you pledged yourself to me, and in return I've opened your world to a whole range of new experiences. You've been sucked, fucked and licked by every good girl I have, and you seem to have loved every second of it."

"I definitely have. Since I submitted to you I've been having the best sex of my entire life. Far better than I thought was even possible."

"So then you wouldn't do anything to compromise that arrangement, would you?"

My brow creased, I was confused by her question. "Of course not," I replied.

"So then why do I have a journalism student snooping around? Investigating a 'secret lesbian sex club' on campus?"

"I... don't know. I don't even know any journalism students. Are you accusing me of something?"

"You haven't been running your mouth at parties about what you do with us? Trying to seduce guys with your story?"

My heart sank.

Fuck.

I suddenly knew exactly what bush Kendra was beating around. About three weeks prior I was drunk at a party, feeling particularly insecure and confused about my sexuality, ashamed of the things I'd been doing, the things I'd been undeniably loving. In my inebriated state I'd tried explaining it to some guy I wasn't even into, just wanting him to fuck me so that I could feel normal. It was a low point for me, and now it was coming back to bite me in the ass. I closed my eyes in shame.

"So you *do* know what I'm talking about?"

Kendra enquired as I sighed.

"Yes," I admitted. "Kendra, I'm so sorry. I was drunk and didn't know what I was doi-"

"Save it," my mistress interrupted. "I know you've had a harder time than most accepting your newfound love for other women, and I understand that that's compounded by some strong feelings for Brooke in particular."

I tried to interject but Kendra simply raised a silencing hand and continued.

"But your actions have put the entire group in jeopardy. We keep our private stuff private, free to explore our sexual proclivities without having the eyes of every horny boy on us in class, and without girls bitching behind our back because they're jealous they haven't been satisfied in the way we offer. All of you girls submit yourselves to me, and that's a role I take seriously. I have to protect my good girls, and there's no room for anyone who doesn't share that sentiment."

"I do share that sentiment. I'm really so sorry," I felt tears welling in my eyes. "Please don't kick me out. I'll do anything you want!"

"You already do anything I want," she replied dismissively.

"Just tell me what to do to make it right," I pleaded. Kendra squinted at me, assessing my genuineness and decided what she wanted to do. My heart raced and I tasted metal in my mouth as I felt all the goodness of my time as a good girl slipping away… Brooke slipping away.

"You'll have to pay your penance. You'll have to prove to me and all your fellow good girls that you deserve to stay."

"I'll do anything," I pleaded. Desperate to remain in the group.

"Let's begin then. Come and stand here in front of me and take off your sweater," Kendra instructed.

I practically leapt off the chair, eager to pay the price but nervous about what that might entail. I stood in the middle of the room and pulled my sweater over my head, tossing it to the side and waiting for my next instruction in my denim skirt and bra. The coffee table to the side was beginning to make sense, the living room would be the stage for my recompense.

Taylor entered the room and it occurred to me that she'd just ducked out of sight for a few seconds. She had something shiny in her hand, but I couldn't really see what.

Kendra stood and Taylor passed the object to her, which she held behind her back, out of my view. My mistress strode over to me and grabbed me by my cheeks, squeezing my mouth, the tears of shame in my eyes threatening to break free.

"How dare you," Kendra said spitefully to me, the first time I'd ever heard actual anger in her voice.

"I'm so sorry," I whimpered as she let go of my face.

"Put your hands out in front of you," she commanded.

I obliged and her other hand revealed the object she was hiding behind her back. A pair of handcuffs with a longish chain between them. My mistress fastened the cuffs around my wrists, locking the cold steel into place tightly. She looked upwards and my eyes followed hers towards the ceiling. I hadn't noticed it before, but there was a metal hook secured to the roof of Taylor's living room!

"Taylor's parents are letting her have some friends live here now. As you can see, we've started remodelling already. Throw the chain up there," Kendra told me.

There was a moment of hesitation, as I thought about the implication of being chained to the ceiling. I would be trapped in the middle of the room, vulnerable to whatever punishment Kendra decided to dole out. The moment passed though, and I threw the chain over my head, extending my arms upwards as the chain looped around the hook on the first try. There was only the slightest amount of slack in the chain with my arms above my head, even with my tall frame my arms were almost at full extension.

"It's not just me you have to make amends to, Amanda," Kendra said as she reached around behind me, under my denim skirt and pushing a finger between my ass cheeks, forcing a bit of the lace thong into my asshole, causing me to wince. "It's all of them as well."

One by one, each of the good girls filed into the room. Allison, Laura, Aubrey, Anita, Yasmin and two new girls joined Taylor standing in front of me. Last to enter was of course Brooke, the one Kendra knew I cared most about. Seeing the look on her face as she stood with the other good girls was too much, my eyes were overwhelmed and my shame tears spilled down my cheeks silently.

"There's a couple of fresh faces you wouldn't recognize," Kendra said, her unmoving finger still pressing into my anus. "That's Dana, a gift to me given by an appreciative Taylor. Someone who knows how to serve her mistress," she said, motioning to a tall, fit looking woman with a long, sandy blonde single plait behind her head. "And that's Andrea, she's a journalism student," Kendra half-whispered into my ear as her finger pressed a little harder against my hole. The unfamiliar face with the pixie cut was obviously the one that exposed me, Kendra must have turned her into a good girl to stop the story getting out.

"I'm so sorry everyone, I really can't express…" I tried to find the words. But they weren't enough, so I just stopped. I would have to endure the evening to prove myself.

"Who has the marker?" Kendra said as her finger withdrew from my ass and she positioned herself behind me.

"I do, Kendra," said the ever obedient Yasmin. The dyed ruby redhead with the naturally plump bum stepped forward from the group, I red magic marker gripped in her hand.

"Do the honors, my pet," the mistress instructed as she reached around my chest and undid the front clasp of my bra, the lace cups splitting apart and allowing my breasts to fall out. Unable to remove my bra with my cuffed hands chained to the ceiling, Kendra let the bra hang around my shoulders.

Yasmin uncapped the pen and pressed it against the skin of my chest. She wrote the word 'TRAITOR' in bold red letters across the top of my tits. She gave me one a scolding look before returning to the group of girls.

"Who else wants a turn? How about you, Taylor, seeing as you were good enough to host this little event," Kendra called forward one of her star pupils.

Yasmin passed the marker to Taylor who stepped up to me, a scornful look on her face as well.

"Where shall I mark her, Mistress?"

"Hmm," Kendra pretended to think for a second, before dropping to her knees behind me, ripping down my denim skirt and then my thong to my ankles with two swift motions. Her hands stroked my bare legs as I stood naked and helpless before the group of girls I cared for so deeply. "Make sure she knows who her cunt belongs to."

Taylor got on her knees in front of me and reached up to my bare mound with the marker. Across my mons she wrote 'KENDRA'S' and drew an arrow pointing down to the tip of my slit. She capped the pen and returned to the group, as Kendra stood up behind me.

"Do you think that's too far, Amanda?"

"No, Kendra. I'm grateful for the opportunity to prove myself," I said, happy to be branded a traitor if it meant remaining a good girl.

"How else do you think you can prove yourself?"

"I'll do whatever you want," I said with a quivering voice.

"If I was to instruct each of the eight girls in front of you to come and spit on your tits, would you take it? Would it be worth the humiliation?"

"Yes," I said resoundingly.

"Well, you heard her, girls."

One by one, each woman took their turn to step up to me and spit on my chest in disgust. Their spittle covered the red traitor label, drizzled down my tits and cooled in the brisk air. My tears stopped flowing as I stood there hanging from the ceiling, enduring the humiliation and shame to keep my spot in the harem. It made me feel awful having the women I cared so much about doing this to me, but I deserved it. So I took it without protest.

Once again, Brooke was last in the line. She looked at me in the eyes, pain and sadness could be seen in hers. For a moment I thought she wouldn't do it, but she had to comply. Her spit landed on my left tit, and even though it was only saliva, I could swear it stung a little. Brooke didn't look at me again, she just turned and walked back to the group to watch whatever else our mistress had in store for me.

"Good girl," Kendra whispered into my ear. The words every member loved to hear from her. We lived to please her, and would do whatever she wished to be praised.

"Thank you, Kendra," I said, embarrassed but grateful.

"There's only one thing. The spit of the girls will wash away, as will the marker... eventually. I think you need a more constant reminder of your place."

And with that, I felt the coldness of steel on my throat, and leather around my neck. Kendra clasped the choker into place, a steel heart being the centrepiece at the front. It was tight enough to not restrict my airway, but applied enough pressure that it was impossible to not be aware of it.

"You're going to wear this from now on, do you understand?"

"Yes, Kendra."

"Good. You're doing a wonderful job paying your penance, Amanda. There's going to be a bit more to endure though before your night is through."

"I'm willing, Kendra."

"I'm glad to hear it. Andrea, would you bring forward the toy."

From the harem of Kendra's sex pets stepped forward one of the new girls I didn't recognize, Andrea. The journalism student who must have caught wind of my blabbing at the party and decided to investigate. She was pretty, thin, as tall as me with a pixie cut that curled around the bottom of her ears. She wore dark eyeshadow and dark red lipstick that made her mouth look so sexy, so inviting, so fuckable. In her hand she was holding a strap-on pink dildo by the shaft, the leather straps dangling below.

"Open your mouth," Kendra whispered in my ear, her hot breath tickling the nape of my neck.

I complied and opened my mouth slightly, before Andrea jammed the dildo into it, forcing me to take at least half its length so that she could let go, and my lips held onto the plastic dick.

"Good girl," encouraged Kendra as she stepped around to my side and grabbed the base of the strap-on. "I'll hold it so that you can suck, and trust me, you're going to want to get it nice and lubed up for where it's going. Andrea, why don't you give her a hint."

I didn't need a hint, I already knew where it was headed, but I was grateful for any extra lubrication I could get. I started blowing the plastic cock as messily as I could, spreading my saliva along as much of its length as I could without gagging. Meanwhile, pixie cut made her way around to my rear, dropping to the floor and holding on to my thighs.

Her tongue confirmed my suspicion when I felt the wet organ on my asshole. I rocked my hips back to allow her greater access while she pushed her face into my butt, working up a nice lather of saliva on my tight pucker. Kendra held the dildo steady for me while I continued my jaw workout, saliva dripping out of my mouth in my attempt to coat the toy, although half of it dripped down to the floor.

An excitement started to brew amongst the onlookers, whose faces began to turn from scornful to interested. I saw a couple of sets of legs begin to squirm as they watched me hanging by handcuffs from the ceiling, desperately lubing up a floating dildo while I got rimmed, my bra still hanging off my shoulders, skirt and panties around my ankles, branded, spat on and choked. Kendra looked pleased at my commitment to remain one of her good girls.

Pixie cut was doing a fantastic job on my back door. Her strong tongue slid over my tiny ring repeatedly, occasionally pressing into it with the tip. She was clearly a fast learner under Kendra's tutelage. The sexiness of the whole situation suddenly dawned on me, and my feelings of shame lifted briefly for me to appreciate just how fucking hot this was. I felt my pussy moisten and let myself enjoy the sexy journalist's warm tongue in my ass. Even blowing the pink dildo while Kendra watched so closely turned me on. Just because it was meant to be a punishment, didn't mean I couldn't enjoy it.

"You probably guessed Andrea was the student who sniffed us out thanks to your loose lips," Kendra said to me. "Luckily for us, she was more interested in being fucked by beautiful women than she was in publishing a story. She was gay already, but ignorant to the pleasures of anal play. That was until I had my way with her."

The energy in my audience was definitely rising, I was betting a lot of their clothes were starting to feel very restricting. Yasmin's hand was up Anita's skirt from the rear in an attempt to be subtle. Anita was trying her hardest to keep a straight face.

"Who should do the honors?" Kendra pondered as she removed the dildo from my mouth, dripping in saliva. "Maybe Brooke? No, not yet. I think Laura can have the first helping."

Kendra snapped her fingers and I felt Andrea's tongue retreat from my rectum. She danced back to the group, passing Laura as she stepped up to the plate. Kendra handed the strawberry blonde the strap-on and with a passing glance, Laura took her place behind me. I heard the straps fasten around her waist and legs, and I mentally prepared myself for what was to come.

Laura placed the tip of the plastic dick against my tightest of openings. I'd had a finger or two in my ass before and enjoyed it, but having a whole dildo stuffed up there was uncharted territory for me. I paradoxically tried to relax my sphincter at the same time I braced myself for the punishment my butthole was rightfully about to receive.

"Remember, Amanda," Kendra said, "you can stop this at any time, just say the words. Of course, that will mean you're *not* really willing to do whatever it takes to stay one of my good girls, but the choice is ultimately yours. Laura, do it."

Laura placed one hand on my hip, while her other guided the dildo into me. She slid it inside my ass slowly but steadily, my asshole stretching unwillingly to accept it's girth, the saliva on both the dildo and around my ass helping the smooth motion. I felt a searing pain in my rear and cried out. My ass accepted about half the length of the cock before Laura stopped pushing. My ass crammed full of silicone tried its best to acclimatize to the rectal stretching, as the white hot pain in my ring reduced to a more tolerable, throbbing ache.

Laura pulled back and I felt the dildo begin to slide out of me, which was a lot less painful than when it was pushed in, almost enjoyable. All but the tip of cock was pulled out before it began its return journey into me. The searing pain re-turned as it slid further into me this time, and I breathed deeply through it all.

I knew I could stop this at any time, make the pain end, but I didn't want to. I deserved this, it was my price to pay for what I had done, and it wasn't as bad as the pain I'd caused. More than anything, I just wanted to stay a good girl, so I let my ass be rammed over and over by the pink dildo. My silence was my consent, I was happy to oblige.

My stretched ass began to become used to it's pink invader, and the pain subsided. It was still present, but bearable, and unexpectedly, I began to take enjoyment in it. I'd had orgasms with fin-gers in my ass before, stimulating the nerves in-side my rectum, and the ass-fucking was starting to have the same effect, the pain adding another dimension to the pleasure. Not to mention it was naughty as fuck having Laura cram the plastic up me. It appeared to please my mistress too, who was getting off on the ultimate act of submis-sion. I never protested once.

"Good girl, take the full length of it for me," she said with an entranced look on her face.

"Yes, Kendra. I'll gladly take it all for you," I said through panted breaths, enduring but en-joying the smooth motions of my butt-fucking as Laura sank the entirety of the shaft between my cheeks.

"What do you think girls? Has Amanda proved she's willing to be a good girl from now on?"

There were mutterings of mixed levels of approval from the crowd, who I suspected were mostly just wanting to fuck each other by this point. They were worked up into a complete sexual frenzy watching my rough submission.

Kendra waltzed over to the group, parting them and returning to her seat on the middle of the couch behind them. The harem followed, some joining her on the couch, some on the floor in front. Aubrey and Allison sat to either side of their mistress, stroking her hair and placing soft kisses on her neck, Taylor and Dana each sat next to a leg, running their hands up and down her calves. Kendra seemed completely uninterested in the touching, her eyes remaining firmly on my face as I lurched forward with every push into my anus, inhaling sharply every time.

"I think you should be fucked by the person you hurt the most," Kendra spoke. "Laura, unstrap yourself and come and join me. Brooke, you're free to punish her."

Laura pushed almost the whole length of the dildo up me before unstrapping herself, leaving the pink cock jammed in my ass, the leather straps touching the backs of my thighs as they dangled freely. The strawberry blonde went and joined the others on the floor as Brooke stood from the couch, staring me dead in the eyes as she made her way over to me. My eyes searched hers for forgiveness but found none. Not yet.

The fit blonde that I cared for so deeply stood close behind me and fastened the straps of the dildo around her shorts. Both of her hands grabbed me by the hips and the fucking began.

She was rougher than Laura. Instead of smooth motions, she took her time pulling the cock out before ramming it back in with full force. My ass remained stretched around the plastic but it was starting to dry out, making the sharp pain began to return as Brooke punished me.

"Please," I begged Kendra, "I need more lube. It hurts."

"Up to you, Brooke," Kendra said.

The blonde paused for a second, my ass stuffed with the thick dildo, before she pulled it out completely. My stretched asshole closed immediately in its absence, my sphincter relishing the reprieve. Brooke bent down behind me and spread my ass cheeks, before spitting once onto my ring. That was the best I was getting and I took it gladly.

Before I knew it, the dildo was back at my punished butthole and forcing its way in.

"Ooohhhh," I screamed out in equal parts pleasure and pain. My feet left the floor slightly as my ass accepted the unrelenting cock, hanging my weight completely from the hook above.

"I think she's starting to like it," Kendra mused.

I bit my lip and nodded my head admittedly.

"Anita, crawl over and help her enjoy it a little more."

The loyal sex slave crawled towards me on all fours, running her hands up my legs when she reached me. She looked at my shaved cunt as it jolted forward rhythmically with Brooke's fucking. She placed her hands over Brooke's on my hips and threw her face into my pussy.

The feeling of her tongue on my sopping wet snatch was heavenly. She moved her head backwards and forwards to keep her mouth on me while I helplessly rocked to the movements of the anal pounding Brooke was giving me. Her lips pursed around my engorged clit and it looked hot as hell from my position. My shaved mound with 'Kendra's' written across it, the red arrow pointing down the gorgeous woman hanging off the clit that belonged to my mistress.

Anita slipped two fingers into my vagina

effortlessly, that orifice much more used to things being put up it. She pumped away while she suckled on my pink button. Every time Brooke pushed in, I felt the incredible mix of pleasure and pain in my asshole, which alternated with Anita's fingers in my snatch. As Brooke pulled out I felt a wonderful light sensation in my butt that paired with Anita's lips sucking on my clit.

The double penetration and clitoral stimulation proved too much for me, and my orgasm appeared suddenly and viciously. It tore through my body as my feet lifted off the floor once again, I screamed out into the air as I achieved nirvana. I felt all my guilt and shame pour out of me, my cumming cleansing me of my sins as I was relieved through my pussy and ass. Anita sounded like a thirsty dog as she messily collected the cum gushing out of my cunt. My asshole spasmed around the thick dildo penetrating it as Brooke pushed it in as far as she could go and paused, squeezing my hips and holding me as I shuddered, suspended in the air, the chains of the handcuffs rattling as I convulsed.

My eyes squeezed shut as the climax exploded over and over again within me, enhanced by the dull pain in my stretched asshole, my pussy singing from Anita's stimulation of it, my shoulders burning from holding me up. The intense orgasm only served to strengthen my resolve that the humiliation and pain was worth it. Nothing and no one could make me cum like these girls, in all the ways I never expected. I felt the spine tingling orgasm subside after who knows how many waves of ecstasy crashed through me.

"Fuuuuuck," I said, exasperated as my legs found the floor again, but were too wobbly to keep me up. Instead I let myself hang by the handcuffs, my head falling as my body rebooted itself. Even after the copious ass play and minge munching I'd had done to me lately, no orgasm came close to that one. That was something else.

At Kendra's command, Anita withdrew her fingers from my snatch and put them in my mouth. In my daze I tried to lick my own cum off of them, but I did so lazily, unable to process information just yet.

Kendra told Brooke to unstrap herself and she did so, leaving the dildo inside me as she and Anita rejoined the others by the couch. I hung there helplessly as I regained my senses, becoming aware of where I was, what I was doing, of the cold dried saliva on my chest and my ring stretching around the plastic dildo inside me.

I hung there helplessly as Kendra made me watch her harem undress each other and lick, suck and fuck together in an orgy of lesbian lust. This was the worst torture of the whole night, as

I was unable to join in. I just had to hang there and watch Allison's tongue rim Brooke's fit ass instead of mine; Yasmin burying her face into Taylor's big tits instead of me.

The eight subjects were contorted and controlled by their sexual puppet master into all manner of impossibly sexy positions. What I wouldn't give for someone to come over to me and offer me their cunt, or to come over and work the dildo in my ass again. But this was all by design, of course. My favorite women in the world had degraded me and made me cum, and I was unable to return the favor. I just had to hang there and stew in my guilt, knowing that if I didn't behave from then on I'd *never* be able to join them again.

It reminded me of why I endured what I did though, reminded me that it was worth it. I would do it all again a dozen times to remain part of this group. I would be humiliated and butt-fucked every day to stay a good girl.

Buttholes were explored, cum was exchanged, Kendra even ordered Brooke and Andrea to trib each other at one point, that was one I was particularly jealous of. Once every girl had been adequately satisfied, Kendra finally instructed Dana to release me.

The new girl stood naked on a chair to reach the hook on the ceiling, and I had to find the strength in my legs to hold myself up to give her enough slack to pull it off, before I collapsed to the floor in a mess of horniness and exhaustion. I was naked save for the undone bra around my shoulders, and the dildo remained sticking out of my ass. I dared not try to remove it until Kendra gave me permission.

"Oh, my pet," the now naked Kendra said from the couch, surrounded by a sea of nude women, her pussy the only one with pubes, as it was forbidden for anyone else. "You've done such a good job, been such a good girl. I think we're almost all ready to forgive you."

'Almost?' I thought. *'What more could she do to me?'*

"Brooke, come and straddle me for a minute and give me a kiss."

The fit blonde bombshell did as she was told and picked herself up off the floor, went to Kendra in the middle of the couch and placed a leg to each side of Kendra's wide hips, kissing her mistress deeply and lovingly. Her perfect round ass pointed out at me, the folds of her slit visible beneath a tiny brown hole that glistened with the saliva of the women lucky enough to eat it.

Kendra's arms wrapped around Brooke's tight body as they kissed, pulling her pupil in closer, causing Brooke's pussy to push against the triangle of pubes on her mound. Kendra made a come hither motion to me. I mustered the strength to crawl over to the couch, the handcuffs clinking beneath me, the dildo causing pain in my ass every time a knee moved forward, every other set of eyes in the room watching my every move.

I reached the base of the couch between Kendra's spread legs, and inhaled the sex of both my mistress and Brooke as they made out. The tang of their scents stung my nostrils pleasantly, and I sighed at the olfactory stimulation. Kendra reached her hand down and ran her middle finger up Brooke's pretty slit, accumulating the blonde's cum and continuing the motion until she reached her asshole, which she circled her finger around, spreading the delicious slickness like a condiment.

Her hand reached out and I raised my head so that she could grab a handful of my hair. She pulled me in and I ran my tongue thankfully up Brooke's ass. It was always a fantastic treat getting to rim Brooke. I got off so much on performing such a lewd act on another woman and Brooke's firm, toned butt squeezed against my face in the sexiest way.

I circled the tight balloon knot, tasting a mixture of her sweet cum mixed with the slight saltiness of her asshole. Her crack was like crack to me and I devoured every inch of it.

"She looks so hot with that strap-on hanging out of her ass," I heard Aubrey's voice say to my right.

"It looked like she enjoyed it, I think I want to see if I can fit it up my butt next time," Yasmin said to my left.

"I'll fuck you with it if you want," the recognizably excited voice of Taylor responded.

They all watched me tongue Brooke's ass while she ground her clit into Kendra's mound. I could hear the familiar wet sounds of girls kissing and pussies being rubbed surround me as my audience watched on in insatiable horniness.

I moaned into the tight rear end in appreciation of its taste and the effect it had on Brooke. She kept making out with Kendra heavily above me, their tits mashing into each other, her clit rubbing against and moistening her mistress' neat pubes.

Brooke came for me. Her pucker seizing uncontrollably, opening and closing. I took the opportunity to push my tongue inside her and let her sphincter do all the work, squeezing my organ out before sucking it back in over and over. Cum spilled out of her pussy and trickled down onto Kendra's open snatch below it. Kendra broke the kiss and sucked on her neck as she exhaled deeply with only a hint of voice.

Even without seeing it, I could feel the sexual energy around me lift as the wet noises intensified, indiscriminate moaning surrounding me as a select few came themselves while watching the performance in front of them.

Once Brooke's orgasm subsided, she whispered something inaudible to Kendra and I saw my mistress nod. The fit blonde dismounted our sexual master and walked to my rear, withdrawing the dildo from my anus and letting my hole relax, a little worse for wear but definitely satisfied.

With that, she helped me stand up and undid my handcuffs, letting them fall away. She held me in her arms, embracing me tightly.

"I forgive you," she whispered in my ear before pecking me on the cheek.

The words meant the world to me, the final piece to my forgiveness, I'd made things right with Brooke and endured the night of punishment.

Kendra did give me one last instruction though; she forbade me from showering until the next day. And so I clasped my bra, slid my panties and denim skirt back up, retrieved my red sweater and left Taylor's house a forgiven woman, free from guilt or shame and still a good girl.

Later on, while I sat there in the restaurant with my parents; my sweater hiding the dry saliva and traitor label, my throat lightly choked as a constant reminder of my submission, my ass sore from being roughly fucked, and my wrists red from tight handcuffs; I was the happiest I'd ever been.

THE END

THE LESBIAN HAREM HOUSE

Erin

It was a boring summer's day at work. The department store was practically empty as people enjoyed the warm weather, soaking up the sun by the lake or at the park while I wandered the aisles of the shoe section, neatening the boxes and praying for a customer to need some assistance.

Out of the corner of my eye, my prayer was answered as I saw one of our regular customers, Kendra, browsing through the lingerie section nearby. I turned my head and watched the gorgeous woman assessing the sexy underwear on the racks.

While I was straight, I'd always held an innocent infatuation with this particular woman. I'd helped her many times with her shopping in the past, and each time I was taken aback by her femininity and grace. Her skin was flawless and had the most lovely olive color, as if she'd somehow just stepped off of some Mediterranean beach before coming into the store. Her wide hips always swayed a flowing skirt or dress and today was no exception, the knee length white linen of her skirt dancing around her lithe legs as she moved.

Besides her undeniable beauty, I always enjoyed helping Kendra. The way she spoke and carried herself made her very pleasant to talk to, and I always got a kick out of pleasing her, certainly more than I did with any other customer. I cursed my manager for placing me in footwear instead of underwear today.

Instead I just silently watched on from my vantage point between the shoe aisles. She rummaged through bras, occasionally picking one out and holding it against her ample bosom to roughly see if it would fit. She smiled and waved to some unseen person over the top of the racks, before being joined moments later by her friend.

Kendra often had one or more friends accompanying her on her shopping trips. They came in all shapes and sizes but always had one thing in common; they were pretty as hell. The girl with her at the time was no exception. I'd seen her before but didn't know her name. Whenever I helped Kendra pick something out, her friends were seemingly very shy and would never speak unless asked something. This girl had straight, light brown hair that came just past her shoulders, and wore a summer dress with white flowers printed onto a yellow background. She was short, petite, some would say, although her breasts seemed bigger than her frame would suggest underneath her dress.

I remembered the friend now. I'd helped Kendra one day pick out some new fitness gear and she was with her then. I remember it struck me as particularly odd how quiet she was around me when she seemed so animated and bubbly with Kendra. The same was true today, as she broke out into a big smile and wrapped her arms around the gorgeous woman, standing on her tiptoes to reach around Kendra's neck. Yet I bet if I sauntered over to the pair she would barely register my presence.

What are you doing, Erin? I cursed myself for spying on the attractive customers. What did I care if Kendra's friends ignored me, I wasn't one of her pals, I was a shop assistant that occasionally helped her. I was no more than an employee of the service industry to her. My thoughts about her friend were starting to resemble something like jealousy, which was an odd emotion to be feeling about the friend of a customer who's name I didn't even know.

I turned my attention back to the shoes, bringing them forward and straightening the boxes.

Still, I couldn't help but steal the occasional glance at Kendra and her friend nearby. The way they interacted was so unusual. They were comfortable around each other, but it was almost as if there was a friendly boss and employee dynamic between them. Kendra would hold up the various pieces of lingerie she chose against her friend's body, yet her friend never picked out anything for herself, and just let Kendra hold the underwear against her without even making her own assessment. It was as if they were buying lingerie for the friend, only the friend had no say in what she got.

You're doing it again, idiot. Damn it. My inner monologue was right, I had no reason to be looking over at the pair and needed to remain focused on my monotonous task at hand. I pushed Kendra and her unnamed friend out of my mind and placed a mental ban on myself from looking at them again.

The shoes needed me. They were unkempt. It was a disaster zone. *Just keep working the shoes, Erin.*

"Hi, Erin," the voice startled me. I spun to find the tall, almost too beautiful Kendra standing face to face with me. "Sorry, I didn't mean to frighten you!"

"It's okay, I was just off in my own little world," I replied, frazzled by my girl crush seemingly apparating next to me. "Hi Kendra, how are you?"

"I'm great, we've just been looking for some new lingerie."

"Find anything you like?"

"Yeah, we got a couple of sexy pieces," Kendra said. Her friend stood behind her and to the side a little, the previously bubbly girl now silent as a church mouse with a completely uninterested look on her face. She held up the lace panties and bras they'd selected for me to see.

"Very nice. Is there anything I can help you with today?" I asked hopefully, wanting to spend as long as possible with this particular customer. My heart was beating faster and louder than usual, I could hear it in my eardrums. Although that was likely because of the fright she'd just given me.

"Well actually, I was here the other day and picked out a pair of really hot leather boots. Only there were none in my size. The shop assistant was very helpful and was kind enough to order some in for me. I was wondering if they might have arrived?"

I loved the way she talked. So elegant and well spoken with just a hint of a European accent, too faint for me to place. "I'll go and have a look out the back for you," I replied with a smile.

"You never know what fun you might find in the back," Kendra said with a wink. The joke flew over my head, but her friend seemed to get it. Her girlish giggle was the first voice I'd heard from any of Kendra's friends without eavesdropping.

A short time later I was moving through the ghost town store on my way back to the pair in the footwear aisle, box in hand with Kendra's order inside, surprised I didn't have to watch out for tumbleweeds on the way. I'd snuck a peak and they were indeed hot, or at least they would be on the dark haired beauty. As I approached the aisle, it occurred to me that my heart was still beating like a drum despite there being plenty of time since the fright. *What is the matter with you, Erin?*

I rounded the corner to the aisle and the two of them jolted suddenly and adjusted themselves. I could have sworn I'd just seen Kendra's hand up her friend's dress for a split second. Surely not. I must have been imagining things, although the pair did look as though they'd just been caught doing some unknown crime.

"Is that them?" Kendra asked, not allowing me time to dwell on what I'd just seen or for any awkwardness to set in.

"Uh, yeah, size eight?" I replied, snapping out of it.

"That's me!" she said with a smile. I offered the box out to her. "Oh, Taylor will take that."

The light brunette scurried past her and took the box from me, adding it to the collection of all their other purchases in her hands.

"So, Taylor is it?" I asked, bemused by the fact that I'd finally learnt the name of one of Kendra's friends. "You know, I don't think we've ever had the pleasure. I must have assisted you a dozen times, Kendra, but I don't think I've ever met any of your friends."

"Well, 'friend' isn't quite the term I'd use to describe Taylor, or any of the girls that are in here with me," Kendra replied nonchalantly.

"What do you mean?" I asked, my brow creasing slightly in confusion.

Kendra leaned in so that her face was right next to mine. I got a whiff of her intoxicating perfume as she whispered in my ear, causing the hairs on the back of my neck to stand up. "Taylor is my submissive, she does what I say in exchange for my sexual domination. Same as all those other pretty girls you see with me."

I burst out laughing. That was the most ridiculous thing I'd ever heard. She was trying to tell me that a woman as beautiful as her was a lesbian who dominated what amounted to a harem of other almost as beautiful girls... who she then used to hold her shopping.

"Yuh-huh, can you imagine?" I said as my laughter died down, suddenly noting that I was the only one that found it funny. Kendra remained at my side and Taylor just stood there, staring blankly at me.

"You don't believe me?"

"Kendra, that's the most ludicrous thing I've ever heard. I have to give it to you for playing the long game though. Do you ask every one of your friends to be silent when you come and talk to me?"

"Taylor, why don't you show Erin here how serious I am," Kendra said, looking around us to see if anyone else was nearby. "Get on the floor and show Erin your pretty plug."

"Kendra please, the joke's over, there's no ne-" I stopped mid sentence as Taylor spun around and dropped to the floor on all fours. What the hell was she doing?

With barely a moment to process what was going on, Taylor reached back and pulled her yellow dress up over her ass, exposing her naked crotch below! Devoid of panties, her hairless snatch stared up at me, a pink slit down the center of her bare vulva. Above it, a light pink heart shaped jewel covered her asshole. It took me a moment to register that it was the end of a buttplug!

"Taylor here is in anal training," Kendra said as she walked over to the light haired brunette on the floor. She reached down and with two fingers massaged the heart shaped end in a circle, no doubt causing the plug to move around inside Taylor, who's hips wriggled at the feeling. "I have a big thick strap-on she's dying to have in her."

I stood there, mouth hanging open, completely speechless at the display before me. I'd gone from barely speaking a word to any of Kendra's friends to seeing one completely bottomless with a plug up her ass in the middle of the shoe aisle! What was more, it confirmed what Kendra said was completely true! Taylor was submitted to her, and had to do anything she said in exchange for Kendra's sexual domination, apparently along with the half dozen other girls Kendra had accompany her through the doors of the department store.

Perhaps even more curious than the submissive lesbian harem revelation, was the fact that I felt a pang of arousal shoot up from my pussy as Taylor showed off her own as well as her plugged asshole to me. My stomach muscles contracted as the unexpected feeling electrified my groin for a second. *What the hell is wrong with you today, Erin?*

"I think we've convinced her," Kendra said with a giggle at my shocked expression. Taylor stood up off the floor and her dress fell back into place down her legs, giving her the illusion of modesty. "What do you think of that, Erin?"

"I uh... um, it's..." I stammered, unable to form a sentence.

"So now you know why the 'friends' you see me with never talk to you. I've instructed them not to because I want you all to myself," she said with a grin. "Say, Erin, I spotted a dress on the rack over there I think I'd like to try on, could you show me to the change rooms?"

I knew she knew where the change rooms were, but I was just thankful to have some familiar footing on which I could form a coherent response. "Yes, of course. Right this way."

I turned and walked out of the footwear section, grateful that my face was now hidden from the two apparent lesbians in tow. My eyes were still wide and my fists clenched in shock at what I'd witnessed, as well as the light, tingly feeling in my groin. As I walked, I felt a familiar slickness between my legs. *Are you actually wet right now? Why the hell are you wet?*

I was too preoccupied with myself to notice Kendra pull the first dress she saw off the rack as we meandered through the apparel towards the change rooms.

There was no attendant at the entry, the store was too quiet to warrant one. I faced Kendra but avoided eye contact as I outstretched an arm, gesturing her to the hall of change rooms. "Any one you like," I mumbled.

"Thank you, Erin. We won't be long. Will you wait for us? I don't want any other shop assistant," Kendra said.

"Of course," I mumbled again as she passed me, her hand squeezing my upper arm on the way through. Her touch set my skin on fire, lighting up my whole nervous system. How the hell was she doing this to me?

Taylor followed her domme inside and they closed the door behind them. I heard whisperings and jostling around while I waited patiently for them. I hoped they weren't having sex, that would be incredibly uncomfortable for me to have to break up, especially in my current confused state.

Another pang hit my nethers at the thought. *What if they were having sex? Wouldn't that be hot? You could even join i-*

Fuck! I couldn't think like that. They're customers and more importantly they're... girls. I shouldn't be having these thoughts about them.

"Hey Erin, would you come in here?" Kendra's voice called over the top of the change room door. "I want you to have a look at this for me."

"Um, if you come out here I'd be happy to give my opinion," I replied, staving off my thoughts of the two of them doing something untoward.

"No, I want the mirror. Just come in!" she said with a reassuring, playful tone.

Perhaps against my better judgement, I found myself walking to the door, my hand reaching out to push the wooden panel and hopefully just find Kendra dressed in her prospective purchase.

The door swung open and that was most certainly not what I found. My jaw muscles apparently were not working, because my mouth fell open again at the sight of the butt naked Taylor standing in the middle of the room, staring at me blankly. Kendra was off to the side, still dressed in what she was wearing before, watching my reaction with a pleased smile on her face.

"Come inside, Erin. Close the door behind you," Kendra instructed.

"Oh I don't know, I better-" I trailed off as I began to back out the door.

"Now, now, Erin. The customer is always right. You've been so helpful to me every time

I've come into the store. Aren't you going to keep being helpful to me?"

I gulped. It was as if there was some unseen force making me want to do what Kendra told me, some invisible hand behind me, pushing me in. I stepped inside the cubicle and closed the door, pressing myself up against the back of it, petrified at what might happen next.

"Good girl," Kendra said with her wry smile. "Don't you think Taylor's pretty?"

I looked at the petite naked brunette in front of me. Her large tits confirmed what I already suspected about her cup size. I looked at her tight stomach and neat little line of her slit part way up her completely shaved groin. In the mirror behind her I could see her pert little bum, her cheeks small in size but enough to conceal the buttplug that I knew was inserted between them. She looked back at me with indifferent eyes that wore a rather heavy amount of eyeshadow. In fact, the amount of makeup she wore made her look as if she would be more suited to a nightclub environment rather than a department store.

I nodded my head slightly, unable to form words with my mouth. Kendra moved from the side of the cubicle over to me. I pressed myself harder against the door as she looked down my button-up shirt before looking at me directly in the eyes.

"There's no need to be afraid," she said softly as her head moved in and she pressed her lips against mine. Unable to react in any way, I felt her soft, full lips kiss me sweetly. It sent a wave of pleasure shooting out from my brain and down my spine, my back arching against the door.

This is a customer that's kissing you right now. You're at work. She's a woman! Were all thoughts that melted away as my mind focused only on the enjoyment of having Kendra kiss me. Regaining some small part of motor function, I let myself kiss her back, our lips moving over one another as her hand came up and cupped my cheek.

My body felt alive for the first time in a long time at the lesbian kiss. As if I was Frankenstein's monster reanimated by a lightning storm, I felt pleasure everywhere. My back was permanently arched, my fingertips tingled with delight, the butterflies in my stomach were whipped up into a frenzy. I pushed aside any creeping thoughts that this was wrong and let myself enjoy it.

Painfully, Kendra broke the kiss. "Would you like Taylor to eat your pussy?" she asked, her breath mixing with her perfume and assaulting my nostrils with the prettiest smell.

"I... uh," I stammered again. My mind was saying no but my pussy screamed yes, my mouth was caught somewhere in the middle of that.

"You don't have to say, just nod."

I did as she said, my pussy winning the tug of war and my head nodding vigorously to confirm what she already knew.

"Taylor, my dear. Show Erin the services I provide."

The naked Taylor said nothing in response. She simply walked up to us and dropped to her knees in front of me. Her hands reached up my black pencil skirt, causing my hips to wriggle at the new sensation of having a woman's hands up there. Her fingers curled around the sides of my cotton panties and pulled them down, wrestling them over my shoes as I lifted one leg at a time to assist her.

"Let me see those," Kendra said down to Taylor, who reached up to hand her the panties. Kendra inspected them, inhaling my scent off of them and giving the inside a lick. "Oh she's plenty wet already, Taylor. Enjoy."

With that, Taylor pushed up the sides of my uniform skirt, bunching the fabric up above my hips so that it wouldn't fall down again. My pussy was on display, this naked girl about to lick it, her domme Kendra to my side, watching the show. This was by far the naughtiest thing I'd ever done, and I was loving every second of it, even if it did confuse the hell out of me.

Taylor's hand brushed through my thick but neatly trimmed pubes. She seemed somewhat perturbed by the dark bush, and she looked up at Kendra, as if asking for permission.

"They're fine for now, darling. Eat her pussy," Kendra gave the command.

Taylor grinned as she heard the words before diving in between my legs. She placed a hand on each of my thighs as her tongue explored my pussy. I nearly collapsed as my legs shook with uncontrollable ecstasy. The feeling of having the submissive little sex kitten eating me out was incredible. I shifted my stance so that my legs were further apart and allowed her greater access to my snatch.

The sounds of her tongue licking at my wetness filled the changing room, as Kendra undid a couple of my shirt buttons and slid a hand into it, fondling a breast over my bra. Taylor felt so good on my pussy, her lashing tongue flicking out and applying pressure in all the right places.

"I told you I wanted the mirror," Kendra whispered into my ear, turning my attention to the wall ahead of us. I saw the reflection of the submissive Taylor devouring my furry crotch, her own slit behind her looking moist with horniness, her vulva puffy and flushed with arousal, her pink heart-shaped buttplug staring at me.

Watching the erotic scene unfold in the mirror was too much for me as Taylor's expert tongue circled my clit. Having these two women seduce and fuck me at work was the hottest thing that ever happened to me. I came hard against the change room door as Kendra tweaked my nipple through the fabric of my bra at the same time her submissive sex pet pressed down hard on my pleasure button. Cum spilled down the insides of my thighs as I tried my hardest to suppress my scream. I was normally quiet in bed, but the climax that these two women teased out of me demanded I cry out in pleasure, necessitating Kendra to place her other hand over my mouth to stifle the scream.

My body quivered against the door and my legs gave out, I slid down the length of wood, falling onto my bare ass, unfortunately pulling myself away from Kendra's fondling hand and Taylor's sexy mouth. In my crumpled state on the floor, I met Taylor's gaze, her previously blank face now smiling ear to ear as my cum glistened around her mouth like translucent lipstick.

"You're always so willing to go above and beyond to help me, Erin," Kendra said from above. "You're most of the reason I keep coming back to this store, you know."

I didn't respond. I couldn't. I was dazed and

trying to come back to my senses as guilty thoughts crept back into my mind in my post-orgasm clarity.

"Get dressed Taylor. Let's finish our shopping, I saw some panties that I think would look lovely around Yasmin's juicy butt."

Taylor stood up and collected her dress off the bench, leaving me with an unobstructed view of myself in the mirror, my uniform bunched up over my hips, my shirt unbuttoned and my pussy glowing in satisfaction. Once Taylor's dress had been slipped back on, her big tits, shaved pussy and buttplug concealed, I stood up to let the pair out.

"That was just a taste of what I offer to the girls who submit to me," Kendra said as she opened the door with one hand, offering a piece of paper to me in the other. "Take this, if you're interested in more, shave your hairy snatch bare, dress yourself up nicely and come to this address at eight o'clock tonight. You can watch Taylor's anal training be put to the test."

I took the piece of paper from her without saying a word, and with that, the pair stepped out. Taylor flashed me a cheeky grin as she closed the door behind her. "See you tonight," she said, the first words I'd heard her say all day.

I picked my panties up off the floor, sliding

back into them, the soaked cotton cold against my hot snatch. I pulled my skirt back down into position and did my buttons up, adjusting myself to look professional in the same mirror I just watched myself be fucked in. I pulled a tissue out of my pocket and wiped the cum off my inner thighs, but the smell of my sex still lingered, there was no getting rid of that.

I unfolded the piece of paper and looked down at the address written on it. Kendra and her pet had made me feel so good. Was I a lesbian now? I certainly couldn't say I wasn't interested in the offer without lying to myself. The thought of watching Taylor get fucked in the ass wasn't particularly appealing, but watching her submit herself completely to Kendra did something for me. There was a big part of me that wanted to go, mostly the part of me located in my tingling clit.

What are you going to do, Erin?

✦✦✦

I pulled out the piece of paper, triple checking to make sure I was at the right address before knocking on the door. My decision had been made for me by Kendra and Taylor in that change room, to tell myself anything else would have been a lie. I wanted this.

A few seconds later, the door swung open and revealed a woman about my own height with dyed, ruby red hair. She smiled at the sight of me.

"Hi! You must be Erin. Taylor said we should be expecting you. I'm Yasmin. Come in!" she announced.

'Yasmin,' I thought to myself as the pretty, fake redhead turned around and I followed her in. *'The one with the juicy butt.'* I looked down to confirm that she did indeed have a big, juicy looking ass filling out her tight shorts. The bottoms of her cheeks spilled out beneath the fabric, and I was mesmerized by the way they creased as she walked.

"Welcome to our home," she said as she led me through the entryway into the lounge room, where a couple of gorgeous blondes sat, cuddled up on the couch watching the TV. "This is Brooke and Amanda."

"Hi," they simultaneously offered me, peeling their eyes away from the TV to give me a once over. I gave a nervous wave in return before they looked back to their show, relatively uninterested in me.

"Through there is Allison, Dana and Laura," Yasmin gestured towards the kitchen off the lounge room. Again, all three girls were very beautiful, and all wearing the same amount of makeup as Taylor did earlier, as I did myself. I recognized a few of them from the store, having accompanied Kendra on her shopping trips. I of course now knew they weren't necessarily friends of Kendra but subservient to her. "The other girls are either out or up in their rooms," Yasmin continued.

"You all live here together?" I asked.

"It's a recent thing. This house belongs to Taylor's parents, but they are letting her 'friends' stay here since it's so close to campus."

"So it's like a sorority?"

Amanda snorted from the couch, earning a silencing pinch of her arm from Brooke. "I suppose kind of," Yasmin said. "We don't really advertise that we all live together having lesbian orgies under the submission of our mistress, Kendra, though."

There was a sentence I'd never heard before. "Yeah I suppose that's not something you'd normally lead with."

At that moment a cry of ecstasy resonated out from behind a closed door back near the entryway. My head spun to point towards the source of the pleasure scream.

Yasmin laughed, "Oh don't mind the noises coming from the master bedroom. Those are pretty common sounds around here."

"So uh… if you don't advertise, how do you find new members? I mean, there's a lot of girls here."

"Well," Yasmin said suggestively, "…you're here, aren't you?"

"Woah, sorry, I don't want to give you the wrong idea. I'm just here out of interest, I'm curious to see Taylor submit more to Kendra, and maybe see if I like getting my pussy eaten by a woman as much as I did the first time. I'm not moving in."

Another snort came from the couch next to us. Amanda again. This time Brooke jabbed her in the ribs, the two of them breaking out into a playfight before beginning to make out, not worried in the slightest by their audience.

Just then another beautiful woman made her way down the staircase, only she was completely naked, her tits bouncing with every step, her fit body on show for everyone, and like the two blondes making out on the couch, not bothered by the presence of others.

"Oh, hi Andrea," Yasmin said as the stunning girl reached the bottom of the stairs. She wore her hair in a pixie cut and her long, slender frame was absolute eye candy. "Who are you up there with?"

"Aubrey and I are having a bit of fun, I just came down to quench my thirst. Although I might not need it with this tall drink of water, who's this pretty young woman wandering into our midst?"

"This is Erin," Yasmin introduced me to the shamelessly nude Andrea. "She had a little encounter with Kendra and Taylor in a department store change room earlier today."

"Hi, nice to meet you," I said nervously, less at ease with Andrea's nakedness than she was. *Eyes up, Erin.*

"I knew I recognized you!" Andrea said. "I've been in your store with Kendra before and you helped her pick out a nice dress. I remember Kendra telling me that day that you were on her list of targets she wanted to seduce into our little club. It's nice to see that she got around to it."

She spoke so nonchalantly, as if the words coming out of her mouth were so normal. It felt strange to be referred to as a target, but on the other hand, I was completely flattered that Kendra had thought of me that way.

"Well, Erin was just telling me she's only here to watch Taylor get fucked and *maybe* have her pussy eaten," Yasmin said with an almost mocking tone. "She won't be moving in according to her."

"Well why would she?" Andrea replied sarcastically. "She would only have the most incredible and fulfilling sex life she could ever imagine if she did, who would want that? And by the way, you're going to have a lot more than your pussy eaten, as pretty as I'm sure it is."

Yasmin smiled at me, seemingly following what Andrea was saying. "Why don't you go and see Kendra and Taylor now. I have a feeling a couple of hours from now your mind will be changed," she said, gesturing towards the door off the entryway where I'd heard the scream emanate from moments earlier.

This was a whole new world for me. When I woke up that morning, the last thing I thought I'd be doing twelve hours later was entering a customer's house, her harem of sexually open lesbians all around the place, walking towards the door to her bedroom, on the other side of which was the potential to have my suddenly undeniable curiosities explored. Kendra had awoken something dormant within me, feelings I didn't even know were there. And now there I was, walking towards her door, not even feeling like I had control of my feet, merely following them and seeing where they led. *This is what you want. Tonight is going to be wild.*

The door swung open to reveal the erotic scene inside. On the bed, Taylor was on her knees, her rear end pointed at me, buttplug still being held by her asshole, the submissive sight mirroring the one she presented me with in the footwear aisle earlier, only now she was shackled to the head of the bed. Two pairs of handcuffs held each arm out and spread to the corners of the bed, securing them in place. Kendra sat upright on her knees next to her pet, wearing nothing but a lacy black bra and panties, her hand resting on the lower back of Taylor, her lips shiny with either lip gloss or Taylor's cum, I couldn't be sure.

"Erin!" the breathtaking temptress said without any hint of surprise. "I'm glad you're here. Did one of the girls show you around?"

"Yes, Yasmin introduced me to a few of your uh.."

"My good girls," she finished my sentence with a grin. "Did you see Yasmin's butt? Isn't it one of the most eatable asses you've ever seen?"

"Well I uh… have never thought about eating someone's ass," I admitted honestly.

"Well, you'll get to experience it soon enough." Before I could protest that I had no desire to be putting my mouth anywhere near someone's bottom, Kendra spoke again, "Did you shave like I told you to?"

"I did," I replied, acutely aware of the fabric of

my panties clinging to my hairless crotch. "Uh, hi Taylor," I said out of politeness to the bent over brunette next to Kendra.

"Hi Erin," she replied without being able to turn to face me. "You're going to be real glad you came."

"Isn't her ass just so pretty with the plug inside it, Erin?" Kendra asked.

"Um, I suppose," I said, still not in the business of admiring buttholes, whether plugged or not.

"Come here, watch as I take it out."

"Oh, that's all right, I'm good from here."

"No you're not. If you're going to come into *my* house and expect to be fucked by *my* good girls, you will do what I say. Do you understand?"

I wasn't so sure I was into this submitting thing just yet. I was more interested in getting eaten out and maybe trying eating pussy for myself, to see if I liked it. Still, Kendra had a point, if I was going to come into her house and expect sex, I was going to have to play by her rules for now. "Yes, Kendra," I replied after a beat, walking over to the pair and climbing up on the bed to the other side of the submissive brunette.

Kendra's other hand came up to Taylor's ass, gripping the heart shaped plug. "Breathe deep for me, my dear. This won't hurt a bit," she said to Taylor as she began tugging on it. Taylor's butt-hole pulled outwards a little, the thickest part of the plug pushing against her tight ring of muscle from inside of her. She exhaled deeply as Kendra pulled harder, her asshole stretching to unveil the plug behind it. The ring grew wider and wider until it was big enough for the circumference of the plug to pass through it.

Taylor's head arched back and she let out a grateful sigh as the thick end of the plug was released, the rest of the journey would be much easier on her anus as the plastic tapered down to its thin end, her ring contracting as it expelled the invader. Her whole body shivered as the plug popped out, her asshole returning to its natural, tight state.

"Good girl," Kendra said approvingly as she held the plug up. She got up from the bed and set the toy down on the nightstand, before opening a drawer and procuring another. I recognized this one, although I'd never seen one before in real life. Leather straps hung off the girthy pink dildo, unlike the plug it was uniform in thickness the whole way along. Kendra made her way back to the bed with the strap-on.

"That's going... in there?" I asked in disbelief that anyone could fit such a thing up their ass.

"It sure is," Kendra said with a wry smile.

"And you want that, Taylor?" I asked the cuffed sub.

"Fuck yes," she said back to me with a horny voice.

"Give me your hand," Kendra said.

"Why?"

"You don't question me, you just do what I say. Give me your hand."

Just do it, Erin. This is what you came here for.

Remembering my place, I held my hand out. Kendra grabbed it and placed it against Taylor's bare pussy between us. The first pussy I'd touched besides my own. My palm pressed against it, feeling its heat, causing Taylor to inhale sharply to my touch. Kendra's hand guided mine upwards, tracing my middle finger through the neat slit, Taylor's labia massaging either side of my finger as I felt her wetness coat it. With the tip of my finger, I could feel the little hood protecting her clit before Kendra pulled me further north over Taylor's vaginal opening. Kendra pressed a little harder on my finger at this point, causing it to dip inside the well of wetness, taking Taylor by surprise and causing her muscles to kegel and force me out. Kendra took my hand further north again, upwards over Taylor's taint and towards her anus. My hand resisted somewhat but Kendra pushed harder, willing it further up and over the tight pucker of Taylor's asshole, through the length of her crack, making the petite brunette shudder, the cuffs rattling against the metal bed frame.

I had to admit, I enjoyed the tour of Taylor's anatomy. Her neat little pussy was an inviting and well put together package. I also enjoyed the reactions it elicited from Taylor, watching her squirm brought a familiar warmth to my own crotch. I'd even enjoyed touching her backdoor, particularly as that got the biggest reaction from her, which was very curious to me.

"I think she likes you," Kendra said with a grin, as if I'd just been petting her cat or something.

"Mhmm," Taylor purred from the head of the bed.

Kendra let go of my hand and spread the labia of the submissive Taylor. I peered down at her blossomed pussy, examining all the parts of her I'd just felt. Kendra picked up the strap-on and placed the head of it at Taylor's vagina.

"Push it in for me, Erin," Kendra told me. As if hypnotized, I complied, pressing on the base plate that held the dildo and sliding it into Taylor's hole.

"*Ohhhh*," Taylor moaned as she accepted the full length of the fake cock. Its end hung out of her, leather straps dangling below and lightly flapping against her clit and backs of her thighs.

"Good girls," Kendra praised us as she let go of her pet's lower lips. "Erin, I want you to take all your clothes off and watch me fuck Taylor from that chair over there," she gestured to a chair at the side of the room that would offer me a good vantage point of Taylor's rear.

I complied again, leaning into my temporary submission to the confident Kendra. I stepped off the bed and began stripping while Kendra positioned herself behind Taylor and began strapping. The last leather strap fastened into place around Kendra's thigh and she turned to inspect my nakedness.

"Excellent," she said, noting my hairless crotch. "You look absolutely delectable, Erin. I'm going to eat you up a little later though, for now just sit and enjoy the show."

"Can I play with myself while I watch?" I asked, not wanting to take the initiative myself and upset my mistress.

"Oh, my dear. You saw how many gorgeous women there are out there. They hang off my every word. Tell me the name of one that caught your eye and I'll bring them in to eat you out while you watch."

"Wow," I said at the unexpected proposition,

perching myself on the chair as instructed while I thought about it. Kendra seemed to really have these girls under her thumb. "Well I suppose... Andrea was really pretty," I said, the pixie cut slut popping into my mind because of the impression she made with her nakedness more than anything else.

"Good choice," Kendra said before calling out, "Andrea! Come in here! You're needed!"

Outside the door, I heard the thumping of feet down stairs before the bedroom door swung open, the naked Andrea bursting through it.

"Yes, Kendra?" she asked, wanting to know how she could serve, seemingly not registering the fact that I was naked on the chair to the side.

"Erin here wants you to eat her pussy while I lubricate this dildo in Taylor's. Be a doll and make her cum for me, would you?"

"Yes, Kendra, I'd be happy to," the lesbian's hungry eyes now trained on me.

"Don't neglect any part of her," Kendra added.

"I wouldn't dream of it," Andrea responded as her slender figure stalked its way over to me.

Taylor began moaning as Kendra starting rhythmically fucking her tight pussy with the strap-on. Andrea pushed apart my thighs and dropped to her knees between them.

"You'll have to scoot further forward, Erin," she said, looking up at me with her pretty eyes and a devilish grin. I did so, slouching down so that my pussy hung over the edge of the chair and afforded her greater access. It glistened with wetness and begged to be licked. I still couldn't quite believe I was having this experience.

Andrea's tongue licked up the length of my slit, my tits heaving as she did so. I was having my pussy eaten by another woman for the second time not only of that day, but my whole life. My brow creased in pleasure as she dove back in, her obedient mouth devouring my freshly shaved cunt.

I alternated my focus between the pixie cut bobbing between my legs and Kendra plowing into the cuffed Taylor on the bed, unsure of which sight was hotter. Taylor moaned with every thrust that Kendra pushed into her, the dominant mistress holding onto her hips and pulling back on the petite lesbian as she did so. Taylor's pretty pussy coated the dildo in her juices, lubricating it in preparation for where it was heading next, an act I still couldn't quite get my head around.

Andrea's relentless tongue licked up and down my slit over and over with increasing pace, a whirlpool of sexual tension swirling around inside me, causing me to writhe in the chair and make involuntary faces that could be mistaken for disgust, but were really lust. My slickness coated her pretty mouth and tongue as I felt my juices flowing freely out of me, overwhelmed with how sexy it was to have this submissive smokeshow eating me out while another got fucked in front of me.

Kendra pushed a thumb inside Taylor's ass, her anus easily accepting the digit after wearing the buttplug around all day. The move earned an extra loud groan from the cuffed sub, as Kendra pushed on her ring in some last minute preparations for the dildo.

Her pumping stopped abruptly. "I think it's time, my dear," she said to Taylor. "The dildo is plenty wet now and your ass is as ready as it's going to get."

"I'm ready, Kendra. Please, fuck my ass. I need it," the cuffed Taylor said desperately, apparently eager for her anal training to be put to the test.

The pink plastic cock slid out of her cunt, along with a copious amount of her sex juices which formed a string between her pussy and the head of the dildo before breaking under its own weight. Kendra placed the lubricated dick at her tightest opening, pulling her thumb out and replacing it with the head of the dildo before the tiny hole had time to close shut.

"*Mmmm*," Taylor moaned, her back arched, excited for the test her ass was about to receive.

Eavesdropping on what was happening behind her, Andrea decided it was time to shift her attention ass-ways as well. Her hands reached up to spread apart my cheeks and her head dove south, her hot mouth forming a seal over my asshole and the tip of her tongue flickering against it.

The move earned an "*Oh*," from me as I instinctively tried to retreat from the slippery surprise, Andrea's head following me as my hips raised off the chair. But I quickly remembered my place and what I came here for. I wanted to try eating pussy myself and wasn't going to be kicked out of the harem house for being averse to having my ass eaten. Besides, it wasn't like I was the one chowing down on someone's back door, I didn't even mind the feeling of Andrea licking down there. *Just let it happen, Erin.*

I added the rimjob to the growing list of sexual firsts I was having, and told myself to lean into it. I concentrated on the pleasure Andrea somehow elicited from my asshole, somewhere I'd never thought I could experience such sensations.

On the bed, Taylor seemed to be employing the same tactic, as she pushed back on the pink dildo, frustrated with only having the tip dipped into her.

"No, wait," Kendra told her firmly. "I have to do this gently to make sure you enjoy it. Stay still." The domme pushed her hips forward slightly, pushing an inch of the dildo into the resistant butthole. The chains of the handcuffs pulled tight as Taylor held her breath and tensed her arms rather than her hole, her face squeezing as the pretend penis pushed into her. She made no sounds of protest.

Kendra pushed in another inch, Taylor's ring of muscle stretching to accommodate the girth of the dildo. Taylor's lungful of air burst out of her as she breathed hard through the pain.

"Control your breathing, my sweet Taylor. The pain won't last," Kendra reassured her.

I was so rapt in the ultimate act of submission happening on the bed that I almost forgot about the pixie cut lesbian eating my asshole. My pussy leaked cum down past my taint onto Andrea's waiting tongue, where she spread the sticky substance around my tight pucker. My asshole clamped completely shut as I sympathetically felt what Taylor was enduring.

Kendra pushed in the dildo halfway, Taylor letting out a cry as her overpowered clench tried to get used to the thickness.

"We can stop if you need, my dear," Kendra

said, showing the slightest bit of concern for the first time.

"No... Kendra, please. I want this," Taylor insisted. "Amanda said the pain is short lived and is worth it for how good it feels after."

"I assure you it is," her mistress replied. "Your submission won't go unrewarded."

My mind cast to the pretty blonde I met cuddling up on the couch, Amanda. She'd taken it up the ass for Kendra as well? The girls living here sure were kinky.

Taylor's cute bum accepted the rest of the length of the dildo at the same time that Andrea's probing tongue pushed inside mine. The cuffed brunette breathed slowly and deeply on the bed, the submissive pixie cut knocked forcefully on my backdoor.

"You have to relax your ass, bear down on it," Andrea coached from below my pussy.

"Sorry, I'm not used to having a tongue down there. And watching Taylor's get fucked in the ass isn't making it easier," I responded.

"I get it, it's kind of weird," her head raised between my legs to look me in the eye. "But I promise you, if you do what we say, you'll have the most ridiculous orgasms you've never imagined."

Perhaps it was the incredible levels of trust these girls seemed to have in Kendra, but there was something in Andrea's face that made me feel completely safe, and I tried my hardest to do what she said. I tensed my stomach and bore down on my back door, my anus unclenching and opening up for her. Andrea's face submerged again, and her tongue wriggled inside my naughtiest hole.

It was a weird feeling at first, like having a slippery worm writhing around inside me. But as she began moving her tongue in and out, licking my inner walls and causing a terrific dull burn in my ring, I began to enjoy the act.

My transition to pleasure was mirrored on the bed, as Kendra eased the dildo out of Taylor's rectum, the cuffed sub jerking and crying out in much less pained tones. As it neared being removed completely, Kendra shifted gears again and pushed it back into her, still slowly but more steadily this time, not stopping until her ass had swallowed the entire length.

"*Ohhhh*, that's better already," Taylor said, the cuff chains becoming slack again as she began to enjoy the ass fucking.

Kendra built up a rhythm as Andrea kept tongue fucking me. The head of the house looked over to me for the first time in a while, now comfortable with taking her attention away from Taylor's accepting asshole.

"Doesn't that feel nice, Erin?" she asked.

"Yes, Kendra," I replied, the requisite response for a good little sub girl. I watched her pump in and out of Taylor's little butt through half closed eyes, my cheeks flushed red and mouth open as I reveled in Andrea's rectal rimming.

"Do you like watching me fuck Taylor's tight ass?"

"Yes, Kendra," I said, surprising myself at how much I meant it. The thought of watching Kendra have her way with Taylor's behind really didn't spark any interest in me before. But watching it now, the way Taylor was willing to submit herself like that, the way she moaned in ecstasy at the pleasurable burn in her anus, my mind was changed. It was hot as fuck!

"I'm gonna play with her clit, do the same with yours. Soon you'll be as good a butt slut as Taylor is."

"Yes, Kendra," I responded, grateful I didn't have to think of anything else to say. I put two fingers on my clit and started masturbating myself while Andrea's stellar tongue worked my ass. Kendra reached underneath her strap-on to do the same to Taylor's sensitive nub as her dildo worked in and out of her at a proper fucking pace now.

Any sense of pain seemed to have completely diminished for Taylor as she screamed out in delight. Her head threw her short brown hair back and forth as she undulated her body against the pink dildo to Kendra's rhythm. The handcuffs rattled against the bed frame as her screams became louder and more wild. I'd never seen anyone writhe in so much pleasure before, she seemed as though she might explode.

I could empathize as my clitoral attention brought my orgasm to the brink. I rubbed furiously against the pink nub while Andrea kept tongue-fucking my virgin asshole between my cupped cheeks. The inevitable was coming and it was coming fast.

Taylor and I came at almost exactly the same moment. Her wild, high pitched screams turned to more guttural, bellows of pleasure as her head dropped and she pushed back hard onto the dildo, the cuff chains tightening again as she forced herself back. Kendra pushed inside her as deep as she could, all the way to the pelvic plate where the dildo connected.

My vagina and asshole pulsated in synchronization. The former seeped out my honey in larger volumes, where it was pushed inside my clenching butt by Andrea's tongue. My ass tightened and forced her out, before relaxing and sucking her back in like a hoover. It did it again and again, automating my anal. My whole body quivered in ecstasy, the feet of the chair shuddering against the floor with my movements. I let out a squeal of delight through gritted teeth as I was in complete disbelief of the intensity of the orgasm I was receiving.

Andrea withdrew her tongue from my ass and looked up at me with a wet grin on her face. My arms collapsed to my sides as I slouched in the chair, thankful it was there to hold me up. I looked at her in my dazed state, a mixture of cum and saliva dripping off her chin, satisfied with my reaction to her efforts. I shifted my attention to the bed, where the dildo made a lewd popping noise as it was taken out of Taylor's used butthole. From my vantage point I saw her gaped hole closing slowly shut, relieved of its abuser. She too, collapsed somewhat, the cuffs preventing her from laying down.

Kendra unstrapped herself and set the toy aside, before picking a key up off the nightstand and uncuffing her sexual pet. "Lay down for a moment, my dear. Collect yourself," she said to Taylor as she stroked her hair.

The sub rolled onto her back and looked up at her mistress, tits heaving as she sucked in air. "That was even better than what Amanda described," she said with a smile on her face.

Kendra returned the smile before climbing off the bed and walking over to the door. "Andrea, you're no longer needed, thank you."

"Yes, Kendra," the obedient lesbian below me replied before standing up and walking away. A pang of disappointment hit me, as I had my heart set on returning the favor to the pretty pixie cut, minus the ass eating. On her way out the door, Kendra pulled her arm and whispered something inaudible into her ear. Andrea looked back at me and smiled before leaving without another word, the door closing behind her.

My mistress for the night walked over to me, her stunning body on display in the sexy black lingerie. I wondered if instead it would be Kendra that I went down on, although I had to say the thought made me a bit nervous. I didn't want to displease the lesbian afficionado on my first time. Having caught my breath, I fixed my posture and sat upright in the chair. Kendra bent down and held my chin, pulling my head up as she gave me a kiss, her full lips taking me back to the change room at work earlier that day.

There was a knock at the door. "Come in," Kendra said, and the door swung open to unveil Yasmin, the fake redhead with the big ass that greeted me when I arrived.

"Andrea said you needed me, Kenda?" she

asked.

"Yes, Erin here needs someone to practice her pussy eating on. I want you to be my teaching aid."

"Of course, Kendra. I'd be happy to."

"Good, come over here," Kendra instructed and the redhead obliged, positioning herself a couple of feet away and directly in front of me. Kendra left my side and made her way behind her. She reached down and pulled at the bottom of Yasmin's tank top, the submissive pet raising her arms to allow her mistress to pull it over her head and toss it aside, revealing the lack of bra underneath. Yasmin looked down at me through her smokey eye shadow, watching me watch her as I took in her pale skin and small but pretty tits.

Kendra grabbed her hips and spun the obedient girl around, before pushing down on the waistband of her short shorts. On a lot of women the shorts would have fallen to the ground with the force of a push, but Kendra had to kneel down to assist the elastic over Yasmin's plump rear end. I'm not sure why Kendra had been shopping for underwear for her because Yasmin seemed to prefer none, the pretty pet going commando beneath her shorts. Her juicy, pale, round ass was one I was truly envious of, two dimples on her lower back completing the perfect package.

The sexy domme pushed the shorts down to Yasmin's ankles, placing her head on the side of her thigh and watching my face as she reached around and squeezed her pet's big ass cheeks. Her fingers dug into the fleshy rump and pulled them apart to reveal the tiny hole they concealed between them. I felt my eyes inadvertently widen at the lewd display, and Kendra's lips curled into a smile at my reaction.

She stood back up and told the now naked Yasmin to sit on the edge of the bed where Taylor was still recovering. With the required response, the loyal redhead walked over, her otherworldly ass bouncing with each step before she spun and perched herself on the edge of the bed. She leaned back on her hands and spread her legs, her neat, pretty slit peeling open to reveal her snatch inside, her juicy butt making the perfect seat for it to adorn. My heart raced as I stared at the hairless pussy, the first one I would eat, the one that would determine whether there was ever going to be a second. I bit my lip, aroused by the thought of going down on the gorgeous girl.

"I know you're hungry for her," Kendra correctly assumed, my need to explore these lesbian inclinations consuming me. "You may crawl over to her and eat her pussy."

"Yes, Kendra," I said, my eyes not moving off of the hairless snatch for a moment, completely transfixed with its beauty. Now that Kendra had given me permission, I slid off the chair onto all fours and began crawling over to the waiting Yasmin. I scurried quickly although it felt like slow motion, my knees burning with friction on the carpeted floor.

I arrived at my destination, my face mere inches away from the neat pussy. My eyes were wide and my heart pounding in my chest as I leaned forward with an outstretched tongue, exhilarated by the notion that this would be a defining point in my life. My tongue connected with the base of Yasmin's slit, her vagina already moist with arousal. I dragged my organ upwards as her flavor assaulted my tastebuds. She tasted like nothing else I'd ever had before. Her nectar was sticky and sweet mixed with something vaguely flowery. It tasted like the essence of a woman. I fucking loved it!

My tongue divided the walls of her labia as I continued north over her clit. The tiny gland flicked against the tip of my tongue as I pushed up underneath her hood. I pulled my head back to look at the licked pussy, a string of saliva connecting my lips to her clit. The gorgeous taco glistened with lubrication as I breathed out, totally taken aback by how much I'd enjoyed the singular lick.

"Oh my god..." I breathed.

"I think she likes your pussy, Yas," Taylor said from the pillows, partially recovered from her ass fucking and enjoying the show.

What are you waiting for? Lick her again!

I dove back in, now more sure of myself after the reconnaissance mission. I devoured Yasmin's delicious cunt. My enthusiastic mouth messily moved around the slick slit, spreading her love juices all over her vulva and my chin. The two of us moaned together, Yasmin sighing upwards into the air as her muscles periodically spasmed to my touch, me at the enjoyment of performing the act and the reactions it evoked from her.

My tongue lashed left and right between her labia as my mouth moved up and down the lovely snatch. I felt completely high on endorphins from the experience, absolutely loving every second of the minge munching.

"Make her cum, Erin," Kendra said from above me, her watchful gaze appreciating my newfound love of all things lesbian.

"Yes, Kendra," my reply came, muffled by a mouthful of cunt. I focused my efforts on Yasmin's clit, reaching up with a hand to lightly pinch at the sides of her hood, exposing the sensitive protrusion it protected. My tongue flicked at the little pink bean, with each tweak eliciting a jerk from Yasmin's gorgeous body. Her moans became louder with the clitoral attention, her breathing changing so that she inhaled sharply and exhaled slowly.

"Yasmin likes it in circles," Kendra suggested. I took her advice and started circling the tip of my tongue around the pretty pearl, occasionally pushing down hard on it to make Yasmin twitch. I was just doing the things I knew I liked but so rarely got to have done to me. I had a feeling that in this house, there was nothing rare about what I was doing then.

Yasmin grabbed a fistful of my hair and came all over my face. Her thighs tightened around my head and held it in place against her cunt as her sticky cum spilled out all over me, covering me from nose to chin with the flowery nectar. Her grip on my hair tightened as the orgasm hit her, which hurt a bit, but it only made the whole experience all the hotter. Her stomach tensed and she rolled from side to side on the bed, unable to keep herself still.

My eyes never even blinked, I had to see everything I did to her. I watched the pretty redhead contort to the orgasm I'd made her achieve, lapping up as much of her tasty honey as I could. Out of my peripheral vision I could just see Taylor and Kendra's eyes watching over me as I became a fully fledged lesbian. It was perhaps the greatest moment of my life.

Yasmin's climax eventually died down, the spent woman releasing my hair from her grip and collapsing onto the bed, basking in the afterglow of it all. My hair didn't feel much of a reprieve before Kendra grabbed hold of it, pulling my face out of the pretty snatch and making me sit on my heels to look up at her, cum dripping down my chin and neck. I felt very submissive looking up at the intimidating woman in this position, and I suppose that was the point. It felt good though, I liked serving Kendra even more in the bedroom than I did at work. She didn't kiss me or even speak to me, she just wanted to look at my cum covered face, well on my way to being her newest good girl.

At Kendra's instruction, the submissive redhead rolled over on the bed and presented herself to me, on her knees, thighs together. I stared at the upside down pussy and juicy rear end that sat atop it.

Kendra undid both sets of handcuffs from the bedframe and brought them over to us. I complied when I was told to reach my arms forward, and she attached a ring of each set to them. Yasmin reached back and the remaining rings were clasped around her wrists. The two of us were now locked together with me at her rear end. There was no escaping the generous booty right in front of me, Kendra had seen to that.

"You ate her pussy so well, Erin," she said. "Now it's time to eat your first ass."

I began to protest before being cut off, "Oh, Kendra, I don't thi-"

"You're in my house, and in my house we eat ass," Kendra said firmly. I looked up at her, wanting to please her but unsure of what to do.

"Y-yes, Kendra," I stammered, letting myself submit further to her. I'd come this far and loved everything I wasn't sure I would, so I had to trust her. *Looks like you're licking butt after all, you perverted slut.*

The head of the house climbed on top of Yasmin's back, her crotch pushing into the back of the redhead's neck. She leaned down, her big breasts still housed in her bra brushing against Yasmin's lower back. She reached down and grabbed a plentiful ass cheek in each hand, spreading the amazing rump and revealing what lay inside.

I stared at the little asshole looking back at me, feeling like I was unable to escape the inevitable with the cuffs tethering me to my meal. It was a tiny pink hole against the backdrop of Yasmin's pale crevice, already moist with excess Yasmin juice that spilled down during the cunnilingus. I suppose it didn't look entirely uninviting, but I couldn't hide the uncertainty from my face. I looked up at Kendra who returned my gaze with anticipation.

She didn't have to say anything that I didn't already know, the look on her face communicated everything. If I didn't eat Yasmin's butt, I'd have to leave, my chances of going down on any of the other beautiful women in this house, Kendra included, would go to zero. As would my chances of ever having them go down on me. After the night's events and revelations, those were things I certainly wanted more of. I was going to have to suck it up and eat this ass to please my mistress.

I closed my eyes and pushed my face forward into the open valley, my extended tongue made contact with the off-limits hole. I circled it quickly, my tongue tickling Yasmin, who squealed in delight and jerked beneath Kendra's body. Her asshole had a more intense flavor, it was somewhat metallic, like licking a penny, her surplus cum helped offset the not unpleasant taste.

"Good girl," Kendra praised me softly from above the bountiful booty, causing my heart to flutter. It turns out I didn't mind eating ass, and I *loved* pleasing Kendra.

I opened my eyes now that things weren't as bad as I thought they'd be and returned my tongue to the tiny hole in front of me. I burrowed my face in between her crevice and flicked against the tight opening, making a lewd squelching sound as my tongue writhed around over her naughty knot. Yasmin's body tensed as her moans of approval emanated around the room again.

I bobbed my head up and down lightly through the deep crack. My tongue followed, alternating between the flat top on the upstroke and the pointy tip on the return down. Yasmin's moans became muffled as Taylor had spun around on the bed and was making out with the redhead while she had her ass eaten by a first timer.

"So pretty," Kendra said, transfixed by my anal licking efforts, allowing myself to be debased for her pleasure. "Push in the tip, feel her clench."

I did as I was told, at this point fully submitted to the woman who until that day I'd only served as a customer. I pressed the tip of my tongue into the tight pucker, maybe an eighth of an inch entering the naughty hole before it was blocked by Yasmin's impenetrable ring of muscle. I licked at the rim of it, feeling it react to my movements, opening slightly and sucking my tongue in a bit more. Yasmin was squirming uncontrollably by this point.

The growing intensity of Yasmin's movements and moans caused me to lose myself in the moment. Any thoughts of hesitation I had previously had now completely melted away as I began enjoying the act of eating ass. The taste of her butthole had now been acquired, the mental blocks gone, I found myself moaning into her ass as I rimmed it. The act felt even hotter than eating pussy, perhaps due to the forbiddenness of it, perhaps due to our cuffed wrists, or perhaps due to the total submission I'd given to Kendra. Either way, I was a convert, and I loved eating Yasmin's booty like they were groceries.

Yasmin's muffled moans became high pitched as her body convulsed between the bed and her mistress, the chains of the cuffs clinking with her movements. Kendra let go of her plump bum, and the cheeks clapped against either side of my face, smothering me as they vibrated with her second orgasm. Cum gushed out of her pussy once again and spilled down onto the backs of her pale thighs. Her body twisted as much as it could under the weight of Kendra, who intently watched my face be consumed by Yasmin's derriere.

As Yasmin's moans subsided, I pulled out of her ass, gasping for breath after being suffocated from cramming my face too hard in there. Kendra reached down and stroked my face lovingly.

"Such a good girl, Erin," her praise made my heart sing. "You eat ass so well for a first timer. How'd she do, Yas?"

"Holy fuck," Yasmin breathed her response from behind my mistress.

"I thought so," Kendra said with a smile. "Now you're a submissive little butt slut lesbian, Erin. Do you like the feeling?"

"Yes, Kendra," I said resoundingly and honestly. I knocked on the front door of the harem house unsure of what I would find on the other side, unsure of whether my lesbian curiosities were real or just fleeting. After allowing myself to be used by Kendra, I had my answer. These feelings were very real. I undoubtedly had a love of the female form and the pleasures that can be had with it, and I wanted to do more of it.

Kendra beamed down at me, her newest good girl. She undid the cuffs and allowed me to sit back and catch my breath, inhaling the scent of the ruby redhead that perfumed my chin and neck, savoring the taste of her butthole lingering on my tongue. *Christ, Kendra is right, you're a submissive little butt slut lesbian all right.*

What followed was a night of unimaginable ecstasy. Kendra introduced me to the rest of her harem. The two cuddling blondes, Brooke and Amanda came in and both kneeled below me, Brooke eating my snatch while Amanda tongue fucked my ass. Aubrey came next and let me finger her tight butthole while an animated Taylor regaled her with how she got the whole strap-on up her butt, and how reluctant I was to eat ass at first before discovering how much I loved it. Dana came in and I sixty-nined her on the bed, my face being painted with cum once again.

The night continued, having orgasm after orgasm, eating pussy after pussy, exploring ass after ass as I was initiated as one of the good girls. Finally, after I'd met each and every other member individually, Kendra undressed herself. Her body was as magnificent as I already knew it was. Her big tits with puffy pink nipples jutted out from her chest. Her gorgeous pussy having the only pubic hair in the room with a delta of trimmed bush on her mound. Her paradoxically round yet pert ass begging to have a good girl between it, not a tan line to be seen on her flawless olive skin.

I was the chosen one to have the pleasure of rimming my new mistress. She lay on her back, hanging off the bed from the waist down. I backed in beneath her, sitting on the floor and licking up at the perfect asshole of the woman I felt compelled to please. Taylor straddled me, grinding her pussy into my pelvis as she ate Kendra's pussy above me. The blondes paid careful attention to her tits while Dana kissed her, giving her the taste of my snatch.

The rest got to watch the erotic display and

finger each other as the five of us saw to Kendra. For the first time in a long time, I felt like I was exactly where I belonged, under Kendra. I'd proven myself as one of the group and was willing to follow whatever order my new mistress gave. I used my newly acquired analingus skills on the beauty as her sexual generosity was lovingly returned.

Kendra's climax was my favorite part of a night filled with favorites. She quivered on the bed, her every erogenous zone seen to. Her ass sucked my tongue up into it as her ring spasmed, her pussy gushed copious amounts of cum that added to the plentiful amount that already coated my chin and neck; her wonderful, fragrant cum spilling all the way down to my tits. Taylor's snatch covered my hairless mons in her nectar, the obedient pet grinding hard enough onto me that she came along with her mistress.

With our domme finally seen to, the night had gotten late, and Kendra told the rest of her harem to go to bed. Only her and I remained in the room, the beautiful woman looking down at me from the bed.

"My sweet Erin, you've done so well tonight. I want you to sleep in my bed with me."

"Yes, Kendra," I replied obediently, thrilled at the thought of snuggling up to the feminine beauty. "I might need to shower first though, I'm absolutely covered in I don't know how many women's cum."

"Nonsense, you look beautiful glistening with sex. I want to breathe in your submission. Come to bed."

With that, she turned off the light and we got underneath the covers. Kendra wrapped an arm around me, the two of us reeking of feminine sex. She placed a sweet kiss on my forehead before closing her eyes and drifting off to sleep.

How the fuck did you end up here? I couldn't stop my inner monologue despite my exhaustion. The whole day had been a hell of a ride. I'd started it completely bored at work and somehow ended up submitting myself to a woman, eating *a lot* of pussy and discovering a newfound fondness for assplay.

It was a bizarre day, but my final thought as sleep took hold of me was how much I wanted to live in the harem house.

THE END

LEAVING THE LESBIAN HAREM

Aubrey III

My alarm went off, signalling the start of a day I had been dreading for weeks. My best friend, Laura, lay next to me, stirring at the aggressive sound of my phone and wrapping her arm around me as I silenced it. Without opening her sleepy eyes, she gave me a kiss on my cheek as I sighed. She knew it was going to be a very hard day for me, full of mixed emotions.

I broke free from Laura's sheepish embrace and slinked out of the bed, letting her go back to sleep for a little while longer. I made my way downstairs and to the kitchen, where Erin and Andrea were already eating their cereal. While Erin was dressed in pyjamas similar to mine, Andrea slurped down her breakfast completely nude. Always the exhibitionist, it was rare to find her wearing clothes in the confines of the harem house.

Of course, this had been my life for the better part of a year. I'd lived there with an ever expanding roster of women, my best friend included among them. So far there were eleven of us, all submitted in sexual servitude to a twelfth, the head of the house and our Mistress, Kendra.

The last year had been a wild ride, I'd broadened my sexual horizons a whole lot wider than I ever thought possible. I'd gone from your everyday accounting student in college, living in an apartment just off campus while balancing study with parties and boys, to moving in to a house with a harem of women, having sultry, lesbian sex almost every night, exploring avenues of pleasure previously closed to me.

And today was the day it would all end.

Today, I was graduating.

"Has anyone seen Kendra? This is late for her," I asked the pair at the kitchen counter.

"Nup, I don't think she's come out of her room," Andrea said before slurping down her cereal's milk straight from the bowl, a few drops spilling down onto her naked tits.

"Are you excited for today?" Erin asked. The newest member of our lesbian sex cult, I'd had only a few short weeks of enjoying her body.

"Hmm," I pondered. "Yes and no. It's going to be a lot to process."

Erin offered me a half-smile and touched my arm.

"Is there any milk left or is it all over Andrea's tits?" I joked as I poured my own bowl of cereal, desperate to avoid any downer talk this early in the morning.

"I mean, you're welcome to lick it off me, but there should be more in the fridge," the pixie haired dyke replied, poking her chest out. I rolled my eyes at her in jest and got the carton out of the fridge.

I was midway through my first spoonful of cereal when an excited Allison wrapped her arms around me from behind. "Hey pretty lady, big day!" she announced redundantly.

"Sure is," I agreed with her, silently hoping the whole day wouldn't be like this.

"Hey, when you're done with breakfast, why don't you come upstairs and join me in the shower so I can give you a goodbye present," the pretty brunette said into my ear before releasing me.

Allison was one of the OG good girls, one of the first to be seduced by Kendra into the world of sapphic sex. She was essentially tied for the longest time living under Kendra's rule and she still had another year of college left before the end of her degree. Lucky bitch.

"Can you make your present a quick one," Andrea said, "I have a class I need to get to and I need to shower."

"You could try not spilling shit all over you, you know," Erin retorted as I munched on my cereal. "Or, another option, you could wear clothes while you eat."

"And deny you girls all this?" Andrea said as she pulled Erin's head into her chest, shaking her tits against her face as the new lesbian laughed and play fought her off. None of us minded seeing all of Andrea all the time, of course. She had probably the biggest sexual appetite of anyone in the house and her near permanent nakedness always led to exciting evenings.

"We'll be quick," Allison said as she let go of me and headed towards the stairs. "Well, maybe not that quick. You're always welcome to join us."

Andrea raised an eyebrow as Allison dashed up the stairs, trying to decide if she had enough time for a quickie before class. I finished my cereal in a hurry and didn't bother cleaning my dishes, I definitely had time for a fuck in the shower, and if I was gonna get goodbye sex from everyone in the house, I was definitely going to take it all and make the most of my last day.

I raced up the stairs and burst through the bathroom door, my pyjama top already unbuttoned. Allison was naked and wet in the shower already.

"Come in, it's nice and warm," she said to me, her supple young body more inviting to me than the steamy shower.

I didn't need to be told twice, and I stripped off and climbed into the shower with her. Of course, this was the sort of scene that happened on a daily basis in a house filled with a dozen horny lesbians, and it never, ever, got old.

The two of us embraced beneath the warm water, kissing each other deeply, our tits and hairless groins pressing up against one another. Having perfectly shaven cunts was one of the rules of being in Kendra's club, you wouldn't find a pube in the whole house save for Kendra's own delta of fur, a physical reminder of our subjugation to her.

My body warmed from both the water and the feelings that Allison stirred in me as she fondled my ass, cupping the cheeks and squeezing firmly as her mouth kissed along my neck. One of her hands made its way to my front and she ran a finger up the slit of my pussy, which was now wet in two senses of the word.

Allison's head went further south and she suckled at my nipples, biting them lightly so that they stiffened. Her expert fingers that knew me so intimately played with my clit, flicking it and pinching it, causing me to moan into the steam. Without warning, she grabbed me by the hips and spun me towards the glass wall of the shower, pressing me up against it.

She dropped to her knees behind me and burrowed her face between my butt cheeks, rimming me while my hands, tits and face were squashed against the glass. Eating ass was a staple around this house, the act being responsible for all of the girls having the most intense orgasms we'd ever experienced. All of us relished in the back door, and Allison was no exception, while I couldn't hear her moaning over the sounds of the shower, I *felt* them in my ass, her voice vibrating my ring brilliantly as her tongue licked it over and over.

Just then, Anita entered the bathroom. She had become a good girl just after me, when Kendra had helped her and her friend, Yasmin, settle a dispute. Now, they both lived in the harem house. The lesbian barely registered the sapphic scene happening in the shower as she sat down on a stool in front of the mirror and started applying her makeup. These kinds of encounters were commonplace in the house, and you regularly had to go about your business while two or more girls fucked each other's brains out a few feet away, if you wanted to get anything done. The shower, the kitchen, the fucking laundry, I'd seen girls eating each other out in every single room of this house. Hell, I'd once prepared dinner while Anita got her pussy eaten on the counter right next to the stove. It didn't phase anyone.

Allison slipped two fingers into my vagina, pumping upwards as she rimmed me hard. Her tongue worked overtime in my ass, flicking against my rosebud and making me stand on my toes as bliss shot up my spine. Anita finished applying her lipstick and walked over to the shower screen, pressing her lips against it and placing a big, red kiss on the other side of the glass to where my cheek was pressed.

She stood for a moment and admired me as I came, Allison's mouth and hand work proving too much for me, as always. My ass cheeks quivered against her face and she dipped the tip of her tongue into my butthole. Cum spilled out of my pussy for the first time that day, dripping around her fingers as she mercilessly fucked me with them.

"Happy last day, Aubrey!" Anita said from the dry side of the glass, her face gleeful after having just witnessed me climax. She went back to her stool and continued applying her makeup as Allison stood. I spun and kissed her once more, tasting the saltiness of my own butt on her.

"I've cleaned my ass in the shower plenty of times but that sure was a new way of doing it!" I exclaimed, causing the pair of us to burst into laughter as we hugged.

The always nude Andrea walked through the bathroom door. "C'mon girls, wrap it up, I'm in a bit of a hurry."

"But I'm not even clean yet, only my asshole is," I protested playfully.

"Well then you should have had Allison lick you all over," she retorted. "Allison, there's hardly enough room for the three of us in there!"

Allison pulled a face and gave me a final kiss. "Have a great day, sweetie. I'll see you at the ceremony," she said before unwrapping her arms from around my neck and stepping out of the shower.

Andrea retrieved her razor from a drawer and took Allison's place in the shower with me. "Hello, beautiful," said, stroking my arm lovingly. "You always look surprised after you cum, you know that?" With her wet razor, she ran the blade over her mons and carefully down her vulva, ensuring any stubble was immediately eliminated, doing her duty as a good girl.

The pixie cut lez put down her razor and pumped a few squirts of body wash into her hand, soaping up her body, running her hands all over her tits, taut stomach, long legs and of course, snatch. She looked spectacular, standing there covered in the white suds of the soap, which accentuated her every curve. How could I leave this?

"Come here, honey," she said, beckoning me over to her as she filled her hands up with body wash again. This time, she explored my body, spreading the cleansing goo all over my tits, tummy and back. Once we were both adequately coated, we came together for a kiss, our hands caressing each other's bodies.

She reached down my back and slid a soapy finger between my ass cheeks, filling my crack with suds. I collected some of the soap off of her body and mirrored her actions, playing with her firm butt with my slippery hand. I slipped a soapy finger into her butthole, causing her to bite my bottom lip at the feeling, and roll her eyes into the back of her head as she moaned. Her anus choked my index finger as it penetrated the tight muscle. I began working the digit in and out of her as she applied similar pressure to my ass, entering me.

Our legs parted to each other, and we each ground our pussies into the other's thigh, our hairless cunts spreading our slickness across the other like a snail. Our anal fingering continued as we pushed hard against one another, trying to get as much friction as possible with our soapy body parts. We got just enough as we came together, moaning into each other's mouths as our sphincters contracted and relaxed over and over, pushing out the other's finger before sucking it back in a rhythmic sort of automatic finger fucking of our back doors. Cum spilled out of me for a second time, only this time it was onto Andrea's leg, her own pussy responding in kind.

Two orgasms down and I hadn't even been awake for an hour. It was going to be a big day. Andrea took the showerhead off its holder and we took turns in washing the soap off each other's bodies. We then stepped out and wrapped towels around ourselves.

"That looked pretty hot," Allison declared nonchalantly from the counter, where she had joined Anita in applying her makeup, no doubt watching us in the mirror.

"It felt pretty hot," I replied as I toweled the water and cum off my body. Next item on the agenda: picking up my ceremonial robes before lunch.

✦✦✦

Erin and I walked with our arms linked into

the gymnasium, one side of which was filled with tables; volunteers sizing up the graduates and handing them their robes from big clothing racks. The other side was filled with mirrors so that the students could ensure they'd look good, come photo time.

I was glad to spend some time with Erin. As she was the most recent addition to the roster of good girls, we'd had the least time together, and I had a feeling she had a goodbye present of her own to give me. Even though the fiery little brunette had only been living in the house for a few weeks, she'd taken to lesbianism like a duck to water. Anytime you saw Erin having sex with someone, you just had to stop and watch.

"So, you haven't seen her either?" I asked the petite brunette.

"No, I don't think she had come out of her room at all before we left the house," she replied.

"That's not like her, usually Kendra would spend every waking minute with us. The only time she spends in her bedroom is when she's sleeping or fucking. If she was fucking we would have heard it and she's always an early riser."

"I think today is pretty hard for her. You're the first person to move out of the house, after all. It'll be the first time the number of girls living with her has gone down instead of up."

"Well, it's pretty hard for me too. I sure could use the support of my mistress on a day like today. Kendra and I have been living together for longer than the harem house has been in existence."

"Oh really, I didn't know that?"

"Yeah, we were friends before we were lovers. We lived together in an apartment just off-campus. Both mine and Laura's initiation took place there. Andrea's as well, I suppose."

"I thought Andrea was the only one who was already a lesbian before she met Kendra."

"Oh she was, she was trying to expose our little group actually, planning to write an article that would have helped kick start her journalism career. But Kendra convinced her to ditch the article and submit herself instead. She opened her eyes to the wonders of group sex, domination and of course, ass play. Andrea hasn't looked back since."

"Wow, that is... quite something," Erin exclaimed, her eyes widened hearing the tales of initiation. "Oh look, there's Dana."

Sure enough, our housemate and fellow good girl was sitting behind one of the tables, earning her extra credit as a volunteer.

"Having fun?" I asked the bored looking Dana, her head in her hand, her other fiddling with her trademark sandy blonde plait of hair.

"Aubrey! Erin!" she perked up at the sight of us. "I'm bored as shit! I'm so glad you're here. This crap is *not* worth the extra credit. All you do all day is measure people, hand them their robe, end of interaction."

"Well I'm afraid that's exactly why I'm here too."

"Oh I know, and I already know your measurements, with the amount of times I've seen you naked."

I laughed, "Well then we're already halfway there."

Dana stood up and retrieved a freshly laundered gown and new mortarboard cap. "Now you know, you keep the hat, so feel free to do whatever you want with it, but best to keep the robe in good condition for when you return it so there's no problems getting your deposit back."

"Of course, I'll just go and see how it looks in the mirror."

"Oh, we actually have a change room. It's kind of meant for people with a disability but..." she leaned over the table and spoke in a hushed voice, "There's only two handicapped people graduating this year, we have a list, and they've both been in already, so it's just going to go unused for the rest of the day."

"I mean, I can just throw the robe over the clothes I'm wearing, it's not a big deal," I feigned ignorance. I knew what she was hinting at of course, but I couldn't resist teasing the gullible blonde.

"What? No, Aubrey!" she said, her frustration hilarious to me. "I'm saying, I think the three of us should go to the private room where we won't be disturbed."

"Don't you have to work?" I teased her still.

Dana looked to both her sides at the other volunteers performing their menial duties. "Yeah, I think they've got it covered. Come on!"

She walked around the table and grabbed me by the hand, pulling me out of the main gymnasium and into a secluded corridor, Erin in tow behind me. The scheming lesbian took one more look around to make sure no one was watching before opening an unassuming door, leading in to a room complete with a floor to ceiling mirror and bench.

"This isn't going to be what you're wearing underneath your gown, is it?" Dana asked me as she snapped the lock shut behind her.

"No, I was thinking of just a dress, you know, something nice."

"Well, you're not going to get a very good idea of what it will look like wearing jeans and a T-shirt then! You'd get a better idea if you took them off," she said, fiddling with the button and zipper of my jeans.

"Well, you're the expert, I guess," I laughed, slipping out of my shoes and allowing her to undress me. "Erin and I were just talking about the first time we became good girls."

"Oh, well then, Erin, this situation must be bringing back pleasant memories for you. Weren't you initiated in a change room at your work?" she asked the brunette as I stepped out of my jeans and pulled my shirt over my head, standing in only my underwear and socks.

"Well, yeah, kinda," Erin replied. "Kendra made Taylor show me the gorgeous butt plug she had in right on the shop floor!" Dana and I giggled, knowing the story, but happy to hear it nonetheless. "Then they took me to a change room and Taylor ate me out while I watched in the mirror, which was incredible. But I'd probably consider my real initiation to have happened back at the house. That was my first time eating pussy, eating ass, and really *knowing* that I loved women."

"I remember that night," Dana said, as she held open the openings of the robe for me to slip my arms and head through. "You were so nervous when you arrived, and so adamant that you weren't going to move in. You just wanted to get your pussy eaten and that was it," she giggled. "An hour later, you and I were sixty-nining on Kendra's bed!"

"It sure was a helluva night," Erin said, staring into the middle distance as she played back memories in her mind. "How'd they seduce you, Dana?"

"I was just out on my usual jogging route when I won the freakin' lottery. Taylor and Allison were sitting in the park and checking out all the runners. Taylor was a little too loud when she proclaimed to Alli that she wanted to eat my ass."

"That sounds like Taylor," Erin laughed. "What did you do?"

"I confronted them, asked why they were talking about me like that in the park. I was kind of pissed off, but that wasn't why I confronted them. There was definitely a part of me that was flattered and curious, and that part wanted to see where a conversation with these two gorgeous girls would lead. Turned out, it led to me being presented as a gift to their mistress, who handcuffed Taylor and opened my eyes to what my life could be if I submitted myself to her. Which, of course, I did."

"Fucking hell," Erin exclaimed. "It's a wild life we have isn't it." Her words weren't meant to sting me, but they did. It was a great life submitted to Kendra, a life I was giving up.

I put the thought out of my mind and twirled my gown as the three of us assessed me in the mirror. "It's not the most flattering, is it?" I said.

"Not particularly, it's a crying shame to cover up all that sexiness underneath," Dana said, grabbing a handful of my ass, causing me to laugh. I turned to face her, giving her a tender kiss. "I'm really gonna miss you," she said softly before kissing me again.

She reached around and grabbed another handful of ass through the gown, only this time it wasn't as playful. Our kissing became deeper as we exchanged tongues, her true motives for taking me to the private room revealing themselves. Erin touched both my shoulders and placed sweet kisses on the back of my neck, causing my spine to tingle and my tiny hairs to stand on end.

The pair of them hiked up my robe so that they could reach underneath, pulling down my panties and letting them drop to the floor. The moment I was relinquished of my underwear, Dana dropped to her knees, Erin following her lead behind me. The pair of them each disappeared under my gown, a hand encouraging me to part my legs. I did so, and heard the distinctive wet sounds of the two of them kissing, their faces brushing against the inside of my thighs as they made out between my legs.

Their focus turned upward, as the pair explored my nethers with their tongues in the darkness beneath my robe. I threw my head back and sighed into the air as Dana's tongue made contact with my pussy, and Erin's with my asshole. The pair pleasured me in every way they knew I liked.

Dana's tongue had probably spent a cumulative twenty-four hours eating my snatch over the last several months, and she was making the most of saying goodbye to my shaved twat. She kissed my vulva and nibbled at my labia, suckling on my wet folds. Her tongue dipped into my honeypot, filling my velvety channel with herself, coating her organ with my juices before licking up through my lips to my clit, which she flicked and kissed with pursed lips.

Behind me, Erin was indulging her relatively new lust for ass. She grabbed an ass cheek in each hand, squeezing them and spreading them so that her mouth could work my rear. Her tongue assaulted my rough knot, buttering it with her saliva as she moved her head left and right in enthusiasm, blindly licking me in my most intimate place.

My chest heaved as I let out little whimpers with each exhale, my orgasm rapidly approaching thanks to the stellar work the two lesbians were doing to either side of me. In my peripheral vision, I caught my reflection in the mirror, my unattractive black gown covering me and then draped over two huddled masses that were the good girls. I decided I wanted to see it when I came, so I pulled the rob over my head and tossed it across the room with no regard for my deposit.

The view in the mirror was divine. I stood in only my bra, my legs parted and knees slightly bent to allow for the two gorgeous women kneeling in front and behind me, their faces buried in my sex, the tongues lashing at me enthusiastically. Being a good girl did wonders for your confidence, and I had no problem admiring my own beauty in the mirror, my own femininity as the two lustful lesbians pleasured me.

I reached down to either side and ran a hand through each of the girls' hair, pulling them harder into me as I came between them. My orgasm thundered through me as I bent my head back and let out an almighty moan of ecstasy. The two girls shared my cum between them, each one taking turns to lap up the molten sex dripping out of my vagina and spreading it up their respective crevices.

The pair stood up, placing sweet kisses up my back and front as they did so, before the three of us exchanged passionate tongues, their chins dripping with my sex. Climax number three of the day. I wondered what the afternoon would bring.

✦✦✦

Erin and I returned home from lunch, my attire for the ceremony in hand. I kissed her and thanked her for accompanying me to pick up my robes, and for the terrific orgasm her and Dana had given me in the change room. Then I climbed the stairs and returned to Laura in my bedroom.

The house may have been big, but there weren't enough bedrooms for the whole dozen dykes to each have their own room. There were a few natural pairs who shared a room together, and Laura and I were one of them. We'd been best friends since high school, and shortly after I had submitted myself to Kendra, I got to be involved in Laura's initiation into the gang. When best friends say they share everything together, that doesn't usually include a bed, or their submission to a sexual Goddess, but for us, it absolutely did.

I opened the door to find Laura on our bed, putting some finishing touches on her toenails.

This was the room the two of us would retreat back to after an orgy with the other girls, cuddling each other and tending to any sore areas we had. It was a bed that I had sex on regularly, but not exclusively, with Laura. There were a lot of sweet memories here. It was strange to think there were no more to be made.

"How'd you go?" Laura asked as I hung the gown on the doorknob of our closet.

"Good, we saw Dana, diligently earning her extra credit."

"Oh, did she end up taking you to the private change room for some *extra,* extra credit?" my best friend asked with a cheeky grin on her face, capping her nail polish and setting it aside.

"She sure did. How'd you know about that?" I asked as I crawled onto the bed between her legs, giving her a kiss and then nestling my face against her bosom.

"She may have mentioned it. These girls all want their own piece of you on your last day."

"Ugh, don't say 'last day' please. It's hard enough just thinking it."

"Oh, Aubrey," Laura said as her comforting arms wrapped around me, squeezing me tight. "It'll be okay, just because it's your last day living here, doesn't mean it will be your last day seeing us."

"I know. I know. It's just, what kind of sexless life will I be walking into once I start my job. I'm gonna be one of those people who has nothing to talk about besides work. And what am I meant to do, just settle down after nearly a year of the most terrific, mind-blowing sexual experiences imaginable."

Laura laughed a little at my confession, annoying me. "Aubrey, I'm quite sure whatever life you lead after this house will certainly not be sexless. You're just growing up. It's not like we can all stay in this house growing old together and working part time at coffee shops and department stores."

"I don't see why not," I said, depressed but playfully. "We could be the dirty dozen lesbians. We'd be legends around campus. A myth for horny boys and a life-changing experience for horny girls."

Laura laughed again, kissing me on the forehead. "It does sound pretty great, doesn't it?"

"It does. Anyway, what other surprises do the girls have in store for me today? I need to know how hydrated I have to stay."

"I'm not telling you! You'll just have to wait and find out. Although, Taylor did ask me to text her when you got home. She's got something I really think you're gonna be excited about. Are you okay if I text her now, or do you want to cuddle a bit longer?"

"No, text her please!" I said. Sex was the best distraction from my sadness and if anyone could come up with a wickedly sexy surprise for me it would be Taylor. That girl took her submission to the next level, her appetite for girls was insatiable, and her ass could take more abuse than any of the rest of us. I'd seen that girl tied up and assfucked more times than I cared to count.

Laura picked her phone up from the bedside table and tapped away at the screen, sending the requested message to the resident nymphomaniac. I immediately heard the thud of her footsteps racing down the hallway before the petite little buttslut burst through our bedroom door.

She looked the part of a perfect university student, wearing white stockings beneath her short, plaid skirt. A hot pink polo shirt hid her tits that were much bigger than her short, thin stature would suggest. Her straight, brown hair was pushed back by a headband. She looked like a model you'd find on a college poster. Of course, if anyone knew the things she got up to behind closed doors, they certainly wouldn't be putting her on a poster.

"Aubrey! You're home!" Taylor said, staying by

the door as I rolled over on top of Laura to face her.

"Hi Taylor. You're looking awfully straight today," I remarked at her choice of clothes.

"Urgh, I know, my parents are gonna be at the ceremony this afternoon. My brother is graduating this year, so I thought I better play the part of the innocent little college student, the good daughter they've entrusted their investment house to."

"Oh, you mean, you haven't told them their house is being used for the secret lesbian sex club which you yourself are part of?"

"Nope."

"Or that a dozen horny women are all living there and the leader; who you're submitted to and sleeps in the master bedroom; uses your snatch and asshole on a nightly basis for her own sexual gratification?"

"Nope."

"Or that those red rings around your wrists aren't from taping them too tightly for gymnastics, but are in fact ropeburn?"

"Nope."

"Fair enough," I said, giggling at her casualness as Taylor beamed at me with her trademark smile. "Laura says you have a *sexy* surprise for me. I've gotta warn you, I've had a few of those already today, so the bar is high."

"Oh, I dunno, I think I can top them," Taylor said as she twisted her hips side to side, causing her skirt to twirl and... a phallic shape to swing from side to side from beneath the fabric. "By having you top me," the nymph added as she noticed me noticing the object underneath her skirt.

I laughed at her move. "What do you have under there?"

"Oh, I think you know," she said as she pulled her skirt up, flashing the big, blue plastic strap-on she was wearing underneath. "Ah!" she exclaimed with a flare of showmanship as she proudly displayed her silicone cock.

"I've always wanted to use that thing on you," I confessed, having witnessed Kendra plowing it deep into Taylor's tight butt on many occasions with envy.

"Oh, doesn't everyone," Taylor rolled her eyes playfully before she undid her skirt and skipped over to the bed, her blue dick bouncing hilariously as she did so. She climbed onto the bed on her knees and gave me a kiss, the dildo poking awkwardly into my groin. "I'm gonna need your help to lube it up though before my ass can take it."

With a practiced hand, she unbuttoned my jeans with ease. Laura, my human pillow, reached around me and fondled my tits over my shirt, helping my pussy to get started on the lubrication that Taylor's back door required. Taylor peeled my skinny jeans down my legs along with my panties, tossing them aside.

The naughty nymph then pulled her own pink shirt over her head and unstrapped her bra, so that she knelt on the bed nude except for the white stockings, pink headband and strap-on dildo. Now this was an image I could more closely associate with Taylor. The sweet, innocent girl on the outside, naughty sex demon on the inside. She smiled at me as I gazed upon her lovely, round tits, unfairly big for a girl that small. Then she dropped her perfect little virtuous face down between my legs, and ate my pussy like the pro she was.

I rocked my hips in rhythm with her licks, biting my lips as I watched a master at work. My best friend continued to caress my tits, occasionally pinching my nipples and circling the hard little nubs with her fingers. It didn't take long for my cunt to become slick with wetness once again.

Once I was adequately wet, Taylor looked up from my snatch, her usual big smile now glistening with my own cum. She grabbed me by the hips and flipped me over, pulling me down a bit too with her small but powerful arms. I faced Laura now and my best friend pulled my shirt over my head before undoing my bra, leaving me laying naked and prone on the bed, my head at her groin.

Taylor's hands caressed my bare ass before she gave it a little smack, causing me to rock back slightly on my knees, lifting my butt up in the air just enough that she could see my slit. Immediately, her hands grabbed my hips so that I didn't lay back down and she straddled the backs of my thighs, the tip of the dildo she wore smacking clumsily against my cunt. The short-haired lesbian spat on her own hand, applying the saliva to the tip of her wearable dick, before she pushed the head of it into me, my vagina opening gratefully as it was filled with the spit covered plastic.

I moaned onto Laura's skirt as Taylor penetrated me, easing inch after inch of the strap-on into my slick channel, slow enough to not hurt me, but fast enough that I felt the pleasure of it. My body shuddered as she worked the final inch into me, her stomach pressing against my ass cheeks as she filled me up. She then slowly worked the dildo out and back into me, gaining speed with each successive pump, the silicone becoming painted with cum.

"I can see the remnants of your fun-filled day," Taylor remarked from behind me. "I see your own cum already dried on the backs of your thighs, but is that Dana or Erin's saliva in the crack of your ass?"

"Erin's," I giggled in response, thinking back to the horny shop assistant rimming me earlier.

"That girl just can't get enough."

"She'll be giving you a run for your money soon enough," I goaded the nympho into fucking me harder, her thrusts making my speech stutter.

"Bullshit," Taylor replied, taking the bait and sinking the dildo into me with greater speed.

Suddenly feeling the urge to eat some pussy myself, I reached under Laura's skirt and pulled her panties down her legs. Unable to remove them completely in our current pretzel of a position, I let the paltry thong be stretched to its limits between her knees, and positioned myself beneath it. I dove straight into Laura's cunt, which was already soaking wet from the show Taylor had been putting on. I lapped at her pussy like a dog drinking water, relishing her every drop of sweet nectar as I explored her folds and cave.

Taylor was now at full speed, pumping into

me now that she knew my pussy was accustomed to the dildo's size. She pushed hard and deep into me while I swam in my best friend's snatch. I could feel my ass ripple against Taylor's stomach with every swift push she did. Our skin slapped against each other, mixing with the sounds of my wet pussy being plundered and my moaning into Laura's twat, who in turn moaned from what my mouth was doing to her beneath her skirt.

I came yet again as the tip of the dildo rubbed against my G-spot, causing a monsoon of cum to fill up what little space was left in my vagina and spill out of me, running down the backs of my own thighs and adding another layer to the dried cum already on them. This triggered Laura as I gave her what must have been the thousandth orgasm on this bed. Her own liquid sex covering my chin and cheeks.

Taylor waited for our climaxes to die down before announcing, "That oughta do it!" She withdrew the thick strap-on cock from my pussy, my vagina closing up as it was emptied of the plastic. I heard the clicking of clasps as Taylor unstrapped herself. "Are you ready, Aubrey?"

I spun around again, the back of my neck now resting against Laura's mound as she played with my hair in her post-orgasm haze. "Are you sure you can take that with no warm up?" I asked with misplaced doubt in Taylor's asshole.

"Who said I haven't had any warm up?" she asked coyly as she hopped off the bed, turned around and bent over to reveal the heart shaped jewel that was the end of her favorite butt plug nestled between her cute little butt cheeks.

"I should have known," I said with widened eyes at the lovely sight before me. "Just like the old saying goes: Never trust Taylor with your house, but always trust her to be ready to get fucked in the ass."

Taylor laughed as she stood straight and turned again. "Ah yes, very famous saying. Well, spread your legs," she said as she positioned the base plate of the big blue strap-on against my mound, the dildo lubed up with copious amounts of cum.

I held the toy in place as Taylor secured the straps around my legs and lower back, giggling as I was dressed by the sub girl who's ass I was about to fuck. It felt amazing brandishing the strap-on, something I'd never had the pleasure of wearing myself. I felt strong and confident wearing the detachable pecker. I was going to properly fuck someone, instead of being fucked. She gave me a quick peck on the cheek before we traded places and she bent over on the bed, presenting herself to me, the heart shaped plug staring back at me as if to say, *'Well, we're waiting.'*

Laura watched on in glee from the head of the bed as I reached down and gave the jewel a little tug and twist. Taylor's butthole bulged a bit from the thick end of the plug resting just inside her.

"You'll have to pull a little harder than that at first," the incorrigible Taylor encouraged me. "Don't worry, it won't hurt. Just the opposite, in fact. Maybe give it a little lube first, though."

I bent over and spat into the top of Taylor's crack, my spittle dribbling down to her asshole and around the toy penetrating it. With a little more confidence, I pulled at the heart jewel again, twisting it back and forth, Taylor's tiny ring of muscle stretched around the bulbous end of the plug, once that was through, her anus simply pushed the rest of it out, contracting gorgeously so that her pretty little back door became a tiny, tight knot of wrinkled skin once again.

"Spit on it more," Taylor suggested from up front. I leant over and did so, my string of saliva sliding down the trail made by the previous until it reached her butthole, which she somehow expanded just enough to swallow the loogie before closing back up again, my spit lubricating her insides. "Mmm," she moaned as the saliva made its way down her rectum. "I'm ready," she announced.

This was fantastic. It always looked so hot

when Kendra fucked one of her good girls in the ass. So far I'd seen Taylor and one other, Amanda, have the pleasure, but a few of the other girls were in training for it. I always assumed since my tenure was so limited I'd never get to be one of them, and as a sub that I'd never get the honor of wearing the strap-on myself.

I pressed the head of the dildo against Taylor's rear, applying some light pressure to the opening. Sensing my hesitance to hurt her, the seasoned anal professional pushed back against the rigid plastic, her asshole swallowing the entire head of the fake cock in one move. Her back arched in delight as I entered her, being the good girl she was and taking it up the ass for my pleasure. While there might not have been any physical sensation for me from the phony dick, the visual was quite the erotic treat.

Taylor looked so fucking sexy as I pushed the thick dildo in her, her butthole gladly accommodating its girth. I felt powerful and dominating as I inched the plastic prick further into her. My head was flooded with hormones I usually felt when a girl was eating my pussy or ass, but the sight of this, the willingness with which Taylor accepted the dildo, it was sure to get me through any lonely nights that might be in my future.

I reached forward and held onto Taylor's hips, pulling her back against me as I began slowly pumping in and out of her tightest space. Her head dropped to her hands as she let out guttural groans of pleasure, loving the butt-fucking as much as I was. I sped up my rhythm, her anus gripping the sides of the blue plastic every time I withdrew and caving inwards with each push, working slightly deeper and deeper into her with each thrust until eventually, her ass took the whole thing.

I fucked her for as long as I could, relishing every second of the anal I didn't know if I would ever get to do again. Nothing gave Taylor more intense orgasms than being ass-fucked, and this time was no exception. She let out an almighty scream as her legs locked and quivered beneath her, her cute butt vibrated as she pushed back hard against the dick and squirmed her rear end left and right, swallowing it up and moving it around inside her butthole herself. My eyes went wide at the sight of her cumming against the dildo, I loved it, it was one of the hottest things I'd ever done.

"Oh my God," I breathed as I savored the sight of the quivering fuckdoll with my toy in her ass.

I pulled the head of the cock out of Taylor's ass with a wetly lewd popping sound, her legs giving way beneath her as she collapsed to the floor, recovering from the intense orgasm. Laura and I locked eyes, smiling uncontrollably at what I'd just done.

The sexy little nympho picked herself up off the floor, redressed in her innocent attire and composed herself. We kissed each other again before she took the strap-on from me and left the room. I wondered if her father would smell my pussy on his daughter's cheek later on.

It turned out there *was* another memory to be made in this room, after all.

I made my way downstairs, not bothering to redress myself after my session with Laura and Taylor in my room, walking through the house like Andrea usually did. There wasn't long to go before the ceremony began, and I still hadn't seen my mistress, Kendra, for the whole day. I thought this must have been the longest I'd gone without seeing her in a year.

I nakedly walked into the kitchen in desperate need of a tall glass of water after the marathon of sex I'd been having all day. I poured myself a glass, downing it all at once before refilling the cup. Alone with my thoughts in the kitchen, sadness began to creep back into my mind. I needed someone to distract me at least until it was time to leave for graduation.

"Aubrey, is that you?" a voice came from the living room.

Relief washed over me, thankful for someone to talk to. I poked my head around the wall and saw the voice belonged to Anita, who was talking from the couch. Her best friend and fellow psych major, Yasmin sat next to her, the pair joined by Amanda on another couch.

"Oh, hi girls. I was just getting a glass of water."

"Why don't you bring it over here?" Anita suggested, smiling. "We wanna talk to you."

I exited the kitchen, revealing my casual nakedness to them as I walked into the living room and found my perch next to Amanda on one of the couches. I was suddenly aware of how much I reeked of sex, my own dried cum all over my thighs, the aroma of Laura still on my breath.

"Having a fun day?" Anita asked, her face amused at my state of undress.

"Sure smells like it!" Amanda joked, sitting next to me and exaggerating her breathing in the scents I was wearing.

"It's been… a pretty wild time," I admitted.

"Amanda was just discussing with us how cleansing she found her punishment after she nearly exposed us," Yasmin said, catching me by surprise.

"Really? Why?" I thought that was all ancient history. It took Amanda a little longer than the rest of us to accept her lesbianism, and in a drunken mistake, she spilled her guts to a random guy at a party one night about our sexy club, putting Andrea onto our scent and nearly exposing us to the entire college. Fortunately, Andrea was able to be convinced to join us instead of ruining us. Still, Amanda's indiscretion earned her a humiliating punishment in this very room, where she was chained to the ceiling and embarrassed by Kendra and the rest of us.

"Well, we heard you were having a bit of a tough time," Anita said, reaching across and placing a hand on my naked thigh. "We were just wondering if there was anything from Amanda's experience that might benefit you."

"Wow, you're leaning into the psych major cliche a little, aren't you?" I quipped at the overzealous second year students. They both laughed in acknowledgement at how they were coming off.

"I know, I know," Yasmin said. "But seriously, we think we might be able to make you feel a bit better."

"The other girls have been making me feel a bit better all day!" I remarked, moving my hands up and down my body to redundantly point out my nakedness.

"Oh I have no doubt that Laura and everyone else has been making you feel fantastic physically," Anita said. "But there's an interesting psychotherapeutic method that could make you feel good within yourself. It's called flooding."

"It's kind of like... exposure therapy," Yasmin interjected. "We think by putting you in a familiar, comfortable situation and then exposing you to the thing you're afraid of, you'll be cleansed of that fear."

"That's how I felt after I took my punishment," Amanda said. "It's like the worst had been done to me, and anything after that would just be... not as painful. I felt kind of invincible."

"So how do you plan to expose me to my fears?" I enquired.

"Well, we thought we'd do it similar to how we did to Amanda," Anita suggested. "We'd handcuff you to the ceiling, and break you down, then we'd let you down and make sure you knew everything was okay. Whaddaya say? Shall we give it a go?"

I thought about it, unsure if being 'broken down' was really what I needed right now. But I figured if anything it would at least give me a distraction until it was time for the ceremony.

"Alright, let's do it," I decided finally, much to

the delight of the three girls around me, particularly the psychology students. "How should we do this?"

"Well, you're naked, so we're halfway there already," Yasmin giggled as she reached behind a pillow and produced a pair of handcuffs often used in the harem house. Anita and Amanda pushed the coffee table out of the way, giving us some space in the middle of the room. "Stand up, you know where," the dyed red head said.

I did know where. I'd seen girls standing there plenty of times, including myself once or twice. I stood up from the couch and took a step forward, positioning myself beneath the hook in the ceiling. I held my hands out and allowed Yasmin to cuff my wrists, the metal teeth of the restrictive tool zipping shut tightly. I voluntarily held my hands above my head, Yasmin jumping off the floor to throw the chain around the hook. I was tethered to the ceiling, hands over my head, exposed and vulnerable.

Anita reached behind another pillow and pulled out a blindfold. "You guys got anything else back there?" I joked, finding the psych students' ploy quite amusing. "Maybe a coke? Or some deodorant?"

"You shut the fuck up," the usually chirpy Yasmin said to my face, a look of disgust on hers. "You don't get to talk to us like that when you're leaving us!"

"What...?" I asked, my voice breaking at the horrible, stinging remark. Just then, the blindfold was placed around me, blocking Yasmin's outraged face, although the image was burned into my retinas. Darkness overcame me as my sense of sight was taken away, feeling more vulnerable again.

"Explain yourself," Yasmin continued, sounding upset. "How could you leave us, Aubrey?"

"I... Yas," I started, before a plastic ball was stuffed into my mouth, the leather strap of the gag securing in place behind me, robbing me of my chance to explain.

"You want to leave all this?" Anita said from behind me, before I felt a flash of white hot pain on my ass as she spanked me. I raised my legs momentarily off the floor as I recoiled, the hook holding my full weight. "What, you think there's something better for you out there?" she said before spanking me again in the same place, any effort to avoid the attack pointless.

"Don't you love us?" Amanda asked, before spitting on my bare chest, just as I and everyone else had done to her months prior. I'm sure she was enjoying being on the other side of that one. "Don't you love Kendra? Don't you love Laura? Why would you do this to them?" I pointlessly tried to talk against the ball gag, my words a mumbled mess, uninterpretable to anyone with ears.

Yasmin pinched both my nipples, hard, causing me to whimper in pain and raise my legs off the ground again, bringing my knees to my chest. "You think your life after today will be better, but it won't, it will be sexless, stressful and boring," she said calmly, her words hurting me far more than any nipple torture could.

A tear escaped my eye and rolled down my cheek, not going unnoticed by my taunters. "Oh, she's crying, maybe because deep down she knows nothing will ever be as good as living here. She'll never find anyone who loves her the way we do," Anita spat with venomous words. I sobbed into the blindfold, saliva spilling out the side of my mouth.

There was silence from the three girls, they just let me hang there, crying in despair at the thought of leaving the house. Maybe I didn't have to do it, maybe I could tell my employer I wasn't interested anymore and I could stay in the house, get some more hours at the college cafe. My degree would be wasted, and my personal growth stunted, but at least I could stay here. At least I could stay with my girls.

Suddenly aware of the quiet in the room, my sobbing stopped, as I peeled my ears for some hint of what was going on around me. With a quick move, I felt a hand unstrap the ball gag, and I spat it out, breathing in deeply, drool hanging down from my mouth. Next was the sound of a key in the lock of the handcuffs, one by one, my hands were released from their metal restraints. I fell to my knees as I tried to compose myself, emotionally spent from the mental anguish inflicted on me by three women I loved and admired.

I took the blindfold off myself as I sucked air into my lungs. When I looked up from the floor I saw Anita, Yasmin and Amanda all sitting on the couch in front of me, all three of them as nude as I was.

"Oh, Aubrey," Yasmin said as she slid off the couch and onto her knees in front of me, she held me by my chin and pulled my head up. "Those may have been the things you were afraid of, but none of it is true, honey. None of us think any of those things. So chin up, everything's going to be okay."

With that, she kissed me. A sloppy kiss at that, with my ability to swallow having been restrained for the last several minutes. She broke the kiss and sat back down on the couch, the ruby redhead taking her place between her brunette best friend and the blonde inspiration for the experiment. The three of them smiled lovingly at me, a crumpled mess on the floor.

"We still love you all the same, you're our Aubrey," Anita said. Now I felt like crying for a different reason. My heart felt full and my mental state fragile from the emotional whiplash. "Come here."

I crawled over to the couch and the trio made room for me between Yasmin and Amanda. I sat between them, looking down at the floor, tears still occasionally falling from my face. Yasmin and Amanda embraced me and kissed at my running mascara. Anita stepped off the couch and got to her knees in front of me, pushing my legs apart with her hands and placing sweet kisses all down my thighs and stomach.

It was then that I became aware of how wet I was again. The distress of being scolded by loved ones had overshadowed the eroticism of being chained up, spanked and spat on at the time, but those were all acts that turned me on under normal circumstances. Perhaps the humiliation and pain had added to that too, because I suddenly felt the desire for Anita to ram her face between my legs.

Turns out, I didn't have to wait long before I got my wish. Anita's loving little kisses made their way inward, until she was kissing my pussy all over. She worked her way around my vulva, placing her lips slowly, deliberately on every spot, lingering as she found the sensitive areas of the erogenous zone. Then she nibbled at my labia, my vagina and finally, my clit. She pursed her lips and sucked in the sensitive nub, hood and all, through the tiny opening into her mouth, causing my abs to flex as she rolled my clitoris around with her tongue.

My fragile whimpers slowly began to be replaced with the sharp inhales from sexual stimulation, my facial expression relaxing from the creased look of distress, to the serene look of pleasure. Yasmin and Amanda made their way further south, each one taking one of my boobs in their hand as they nibbled and licked at my nipples. The neon red hair of Yasmin and the natural blonde hair of Amanda dangled down, the ends tickling my taut stomach as they worked their magic on my breasts.

I squirmed between the triangle of pleasure points. My tears stopped, my despair gone, now I felt only love and bliss that these three beautiful women gave me. I felt cleansed, just as the budding psychologists had thought, the flooding had worked. My fears about leaving the harem house had been addressed, and I felt like everything was going to be alright after all.

Overwhelmed with love, I came for the fifth time in less than twenty four hours. Thankfully, months spent living the way I had required your sexual stamina match the other eleven raging libidos in the house. Multiple orgasms in a day or even just a night was standard practice around here. Anita gratefully swallowed my cum as she penetrated my vagina with her tongue, creating a sort of slippery slide for my nectar to run down the back of her throat. Yasmin and Amanda sucked hard on my nipples while I came, elevating my pleasure.

As my climax settled, the pair began making out over the top of my chest, little hickeys forming on my tits from their rough nipple-play. I watched the sexy pair kissing each other passionately as Anita moved her head away from my snatch, sitting back on her feet as she relished my flavor.

I slid out from underneath the pair of kissing lesbians, wanting to embrace Anita, wanting to thank her and the others for the gift they'd given me. Not just for a terrific orgasm, but how they relieved me of a lot of my stresses. I landed on my knees in front of her and we embraced, kissing each other as the other two did on the couch, tasting the full flavor of my own pussy as our tongues entwined.

"Look at them," Anita said with a smile as she broke our kiss, prompting me to look over my shoulder at the pair on the couch. Yasmin had climbed on top of Amanda, straddling the blonde and grinding her pussy into hers as they made out. "This day is meant to be about you and they just can't help themselves," she added, shaking her head in sarcastic disappointment.

I was going to miss Yasmin's ass. It was the stuff of legend around this house. The petite, dyed red head had a small frame, with small-ish boobs, but she more than made up for it in the ass department. The thing was giant for someone who never did a squat in her life. It was round, natural and perfect, and I watched it tense and release as she tribbed Amanda on the couch.

"I'm sure not complaining," I said, entranced by the movements of her juicy butt for the ump-teenth time. I decided I couldn't leave before burying my face in it one more time.

I spun around on my knees and grabbed Yasmin's booty with both hands, pushing her hard against Amanda before spreading her lovely cheeks. I then bent over and poked my tongue out, licking up from the bottom of Amanda's snatch, all the way through it, then through the folds of Yasmin's cooter, and finally through the substantial crevice that was her ass. The two girls squirmed as my tongue made its jour-ney over their respective private parts, collecting every bit of flavor it could along the way and making a fantastic lesbian cocktail in my mouth.

Yasmin's undulating against Amanda's snatch resumed as I stayed nestled in the crack of her ass. Anita walked around behind the couch and perched herself on top of the backrest, allowing her best friend to eat her snatch from above while Amanda tilted her head back and tongued her asshole. It was a glorious pretzel of rimming and fucking we'd arranged ourselves in, and it wasn't long before the three girls collective moaning started to get louder.

My tongue lashed Yasmin's cute little butthole unrelentingly as her cheeks rhythmically tensed, squashing my face and smothering me fantastically. My head moved with her hips as she ground her smooth pussy hard against Amanda's equally hairless one. Up on the couch, Anita pinched her own nipples as her nethers were seen to by the tribbing couple.

It all seemed to happen at once. I think it was Anita who started to cum first, powerless against her best friend's mouth on her snatch while Amanda rimmed her from below. Because of how far Amanda's head was tilted back, Anita's goo spilled down the bottom of the blonde's chin and all over her neck. This triggered a simultaneous orgasm in both Yasmin and Amanda. Yasmin's ass clenched around my face as her cum spilled down into Amanda's open pussy and onto the couch cushion. The three of them all moaned and quivered together as they rode out their respective orgasms.

Needing to breathe, I pulled my face out of Yasmin's generous ass and enjoyed the sight of the three of them all swapping cum as they climaxed together. It was then that my eye caught sight of a fourth girl cumming at the same time! Laura must have heard the commotion and was sitting on the stairs, watching the scene with her hand shoved in her panties. Her face was one that I would recognize anywhere as we locked eyes while she came.

The three girls on the couch all started making out with each other as they came down from their collective orgasm. Laura too, seemed to finish up as she took her hands out of her panties, adjusted her clothes and stood up.

"We're going to have to get going soon, Aubrey," she said, reminding me of the impending ceremony. "You're probably gonna need another shower after the day you've been having."

She was right of course, another shower was in order. I was covered in cum; both my own and others; as well as ass. Not to mention I'd worked up quite the sweat from the day's workouts.

I walked up the stairs and jumped into the shower, all my anxieties having been washed away. All that is, except one. Was I going to see

Kendra before I left?

✦✦✦

The ceremony was long and boring and hardly worth remembering. It made me question why I even attended in the first place. Three hours of self-important speeches from the faculty and president of the student union as I struggled not to fall asleep, exhausted from all the sex I'd been having.

I looked out over the crowd as I walked across the stage to accept my piece of paper and saw the row of ten stupidly hot women all whooping and cheering me on. As good as it felt to finally get my degree and be supported by the girls I loved so much, it still stung that Kendra was not amongst them. The olive skinned Aphrodite and my mistress had chosen to remain a recluse all day, and her absence was sorely felt.

After the ceremony, we all stood in a group amongst the crowd outside and watched the act Taylor was putting on for her parents from afar. The sweet little daughter in her plaid skirt and polo shirt, looking incapable of disappointing her wealthy father. I wondered what he'd think of the thing she got up to in the harem house.

"Do you think any part of them suspects that their daughter takes it up the ass on a regular basis?" Brooke said, prompting the rest of us to howl with laughter at just how thick the wool was that Taylor pulled over her parents' eyes.

Brooke was the only other good girl I hadn't seen all day. The fit blonde was close friends with Allison and Taylor from high school, and was the first to be seduced by Kendra. As such, she was sort of Kendra's unofficial right hand woman. If anyone was to know what was up with her, it would be Brooke.

Taylor shot us a look from across the quad as she heard our laughter. "What happens if he wants to come over and see how his investment property is doing?" Dana asked.

"There's no way," Allison reassured her. "Taylor has played the part of the innocent youngest daughter for a lot longer than the harem house has existed. If he brings it up she'll come up with some reason to prevent it from happening."

"Brooke, have you seen Kendra today?" I asked, unable to help myself. A sort of hush fell over the group, as our joviality gave way to more serious matters.

"Oh, she wanted to be here, Aubrey," Brooke said, touching my arm sympathetically. "I'm sorry she's not, she's just having a really tough time with the thought of you leaving."

"Yeah…" I said, unsatisfied with the response.

"C'mon, let's go home," Laura suggested. "Taylor has to have dinner with her parents and brother, so there's no point waiting around for her."

"Okay," I agreed before making eye contact with the tiny butt slut across the grass. She blew me a kiss as she saw us leaving, earning a little half smile from me.

As the ten of us entered the house, most came and sat with me on the living room couches, which still reeked of the sex that occured there a few hours prior. Amanda helped me out of my robe while Brooke peeled off from the group, walking through the door to Kendra's room.

I adjusted my dress now that the baggy gown was off me and sat down, Erin bringing us all a round of drinks. We sipped our beverages and chatted amongst ourselves about my new job, where I was going to live, how much Taylor would be hating dinner right now. It was a great evening, and I realized that I would miss this just as much as I would miss the rampant sex. Well, at least almost as much.

Our happy conversation was suddenly interrupted as we heard yelling from behind the door to Kendra's room. We all immediately fell silent, the anger piercing all of our ears. It was an emotion none of us had heard between these walls, and we all stared at the master bedroom's door in doubt of what we just heard.

It happened again! More yelling, too muffled to hear what was being said but it sounded like... Brooke's voice.

"Is that Brooke?" Dana asked, unsure whether she believed her own ears.

"No, it can't be," Andrea said in shock.

"Oh, that's Brooke all right," Allison confirmed. "I haven't heard that tone since her Mom tried to tell her she wasn't going to prom because she didn't get an A on a math test."

"But the only other person in there is... Kendra," Laura pointed out.

Laura's point was an obvious one. There was simply *no way* any of us would yell at Kendra, especially not Brooke. Brooke was Kendra's loyal lieutenant in the quest for lesbian domination, the very first good girl, the ultimate submissive. For her to go against Kendra would be like... the Pope announcing he's Jewish.

Just then, the door swung open and Brooke stormed out of it, her brow creased with fury. She walked over to the couch where I was sitting, took a second to compose herself, and then spoke with a calm tone. "Aubrey, Kendra would like to see you in her room."

I was stunned. I didn't know what to say. So I simply did as I always did when Kendra requested something of me, I obeyed. I set my drink down and followed Brooke to Kendra's door, seemingly in slow motion. The blonde followed me in and closed the door behind me.

Kendra was sitting cross legged at the head of her king size bed. Her face looked up at me with a look I'd never seen from her before: shame. Her big brown, Disney princess eyes were welled up with tears and her hands fidgeted in her lap. I'd only ever seen my Mistress completely confident in herself, assertive and commanding of every situation. Her long brown hair, large bust, feminine curves and toned ass and legs, the picture of what every woman wished they could be. To see her vulnerable like this was confronting. My mouth hung open in search of words but found none.

"Kendra has something she'd like to say," Brooke said.

"Yes, I do," Kendra spoke. "Come, Audrey, sit with me," her tone was less demanding than her usual instructions, but I complied nonetheless, leaving Brooke standing by the door as I joined my mistress on the bed. She took my hands in hers.

"Aubrey, I'm so sorry I wasn't at your graduation. I know it's no excuse but I've been having a really hard time with the thought of you leaving. I've just stayed in bed all day, crying and trying to come to terms with it all. But I know, as your mistress, someone you've given everything of yourself over to, you deserve the same of me, and I've let you down. So for that, I'm sorry."

"Oh, Kendra," I said in a daze, trying to process her words. Of all the new experiences I'd had under her sexual tutelage, I didn't expect this to be one. "I'm one of yours, you don't have to apologize to me. You can do whatever you want to me," I stammered, still her submissive after all.

Kendra shook her head as a tear rolled down her cheek. "No, Aubrey. Everything I do for you girls I do for your own good, your own pleasure, your own sexual gratification as well as mine. What I did today was not for you, it was for me and me alone, too scared to face the fact that you all have futures outside of this house, outside of me."

"Kendra!" I exclaimed, my own eyes welling up as I hugged her tightly. "I've been so miserable all day at the thought of leaving you," I confessed. "Nothing will ever be as good as my time here. I've had the best sex of my life, had so many new experiences, felt so much love. We're all always going to love you and come back to you."

We kept hugging, kissing each other's shoulders and sniffling as we made peace with what was to come. I hated seeing Kendra like this, but admittedly, it was kind of nice to connect with her on equal footing for the first time since she turned me.

"You and I have lived together for the longest, you know?" Kendra pointed out as we eventually broke away from the hug. "It was originally just the two of us in our apartment together."

"Oh, I remember," I said, smiling as I thought back to the times we had in that apartment. "Thank god I answered that ad looking for a roommate! Of course, Brooke was the first good girl," I cocked my head towards the silent blonde standing by the door.

"Yeah but I'd wanted to fuck you for longer," Kendra admitted. "From the day you moved in I wanted to have you. That was before I even met Brooke at the gym."

My heart fluttered at the confession. "I never knew that. Well, now you have me."

"Do you remember the first time we had sex? Brooke was there too."

I laughed as I thought back to how naive I was of my own sexuality back then. "How could I forget, Laura gave me the idea. We were trying to decide if you were gay, so I hid in your closet to see if I could catch you and Brooke in the act."

"Instead we caught you in the act!" Kendra laughed as her tears dried up. "You had your hands down your pants while you watched Brooke rim me, and you still had the gall to deny you were a lesbian when we opened the door."

I laughed as I remembered back to how petrified I had felt in that moment. Of course, I needn't feel ashamed of it anymore, there was total acceptance in this house. I'd even snuck into a few closets from time to time and watched the girls fuck each other, recreating my first night. No one minded.

"I wasn't a lesbian!" I protested. "You made me one with your ridiculous ass and phenomenal head game," I smiled as I leaned in, kissing my awakener and Mistress. I'd given every part of myself to this woman over the last year or so, but I still owed her so much.

"Are you still my good girl?" Kendra asked me, her hand holding my head.

"Always," I replied, smiling, still completely submitted to this Goddess of a woman.

"Then I want you to do something for me."

"Anything."

"I want you to fuck Brooke like you did that night in our apartment."

Giddy with excitement, I felt the familiar horniness well up in my groin. Brooke made her way over to the bed, re-assuming her role as the loyal lesbian to Kendra. I hopped off the bed and the two of us undressed each other. I admired Brooke's body the same way I did every time I saw it, sculpted by hundreds of hours at the gym, the outline of her abdominals visible below her perky B-cups. Her round ass formed by countless squats, her shoulder length naturally blonde hair swaying with her movements. She was muscular but still feminine, and she was absolutely gorgeous.

Kendra got off the bed too, making her way over to a chair in the corner of the room, just as she did the night she seduced me into submission. "Well, don't you remember?" she coaxed us into getting on with it.

I smiled at my mistress, before taking Brooke's hand and leading her onto the bed. She sat herself on top of the frame at the head of the bed, spreading her legs wide so that her lovely, shaved cunt flowered open for me to enjoy. Her butt was spread apart too, with her delectable little pink asshole on display. I wanted to eat that too, but I put myself back into the mindset of that night, when the idea of eating ass was an alien one.

I licked up her slit in one long, slow motion, savoring the flavors of her pussy as each drop of her cum hit my taste buds. She exhaled heavily with the motion and I ran my tongue over her clit. I ate her out in every way I remembered from that night, eager to recreate the scene for Kendra. While I was an eager amateur pussy eater back then, my tongue was that of a practiced professional now, as I devoured Brooke's snatch with not only enthusiasm, but precision too.

I licked the walls of her labia and inserted my tongue into her channel while my nose tickled her clitoris. Her juices covered my face and chin and dripped down below, over her taint and collecting around her butthole. The bed frame shuddered against the wall as Brooke moaned and shook in pleasure. Just as I was back then, I was in heaven watching the effect my tongue had on another woman.

"Look at how her wetness has slid down and moistened her adorable little asshole. Do you think it looks tasty?" Kendra asked from the chair, enjoying the side-view of what she was orchestrating.

"I do," I said, as honest as I had been back then, but a lot more willing to eat it.

"Be a good girl and lick her asshole for me, then," Kendra instructed.

I pressed my tongue against Brooke's waiting entrance, feeling it contract against the flat of my tongue as Brooke let out a higher pitched squeal, the same way she always did when someone started rimming her. I licked up and down, then around circles around the tiny, wet crater of Brooke's ring. Kendra stood from the chair and made her way over to us, still fully dressed. She climbed onto the bed and began attacking Brooke's clit with her tongue, just as she had done that night. Brooke began moaning harder, her orgasm rapidly approaching.

"Aren't you gonna stop?" the fit blonde said from above us.

"What do you mean?" I asked as quickly as I could, minimizing my time away from her asshole.

"You didn't let me cum yet the first night," Brooke reminded us.

Kendra stopped her assault on Brooke's clit, and pulled my head away from her ass. "She's right," the sexy domme said. "We're forgetting, Brooke cums best when she has a finger in her ass."

With that, Kendra took my hand and slid my forefinger between Brooke's soaking wet labia, coating it in the blonde's honey. She then lowered my hand below the perched lesbian, and placed the tip of my finger to the entrance of Brooke's tightest, naughtiest hole.

Brooke exhaled slowly, relaxing the muscles of her ass, begging me to come in. I did so, inserting my finger up to the first knuckle. Brooke's ass contracted, sucking my finger in even further, up to my second knuckle. Her leg twitched involuntarily at the invasive feeling. I forced my finger deeper still, pushing it further into Brooke's warm, impossibly tight space. As always when I fingered Brooke's ass, I could feel her pulse from a nearby blood vessel, her heart beating fast with excitement. With one last contraction of her ring, Brooke beckoned my finger further in, until she'd swallowed the full length of the digit.

I admired the sight before me, one that I would surely miss once I left. Brooke's cunt glistened with arousal, oozing sweet nectar down below, lubricating her asshole for my finger as I wore her like a piece of jewellery. Just as I remembered what happened next on the first night, Kendra reminded me, the beauty had silently moved behind me and buried her face in my ass, licking my asshole, her warm tongue welcomed between my cheeks.

I dropped my head and sighed at the feeling, before Brooke grabbed me by the hair and thrust my face back into her pussy. I multi-tasked, devouring the blonde's snatch while my finger worked in and out of her anus.

"Fuck, that feels so good," Brooke encouraged,

her eyes fixated on our mistress eating my rear enthusiastically. "Fuck my asshole faster!"

I obliged, her hole fully accepting my finger as I pumped it in and out of her with greater speed. I felt a familiar swirling in my ass, as Kendra did things to me in a way only she could. I circled my tongue around Brooke's clit, applying pressure to the bundle of nerves while her lubed asshole made wet sounds as I finger fucked it.

Behind me, Kendra's slippery tongue wormed its way inside of me, sliding it in and out, her powerful organ overwhelming my anal defences with ease. I came hard, my scream muffled by Brooke's cunt. This set off a chain reaction in her, cumming hard against my face, her clenched asshole sucking my finger in so tight I thought she might suck up my whole hand. Her legs quivered as she tried desperately not to slide off the bed head, which rattled along with her. Just as I thought her orgasm was winding down, her ring relaxing, I withdrew my finger, which just seemed to set her off again. She took my head in her hands and hunched over to kiss me while I rode out the fantastic anal orgasm Kendra was giving me.

My ass belonged to the woman eating it, as did the rest of me. My servitude to Kendra wouldn't end after tonight, it just made every action, every orgasm, so much more intense. Eventually, Kendra removed her tongue from my ass, allowing me to collapse onto the bed. Brooke stroked my hair as I lay there, twitching with aftershocks. A loogie of cum dripped down from her pussy and onto the pillow next to me. I breathed it in gratefully, basking in her scent as my ass thrummed with delight.

"I think it was at this point you left us," Kendra said in between planting gentle kisses all over my rump and back. "But I don't want you to go anywhere tonight. I want you to stay and make your mistress orgasm, and willingly accept her cum, because you are her submissive."

My body felt suddenly electrified in its postorgasm state. Kendra's words made my every nerve light up. I was her sub, her slave, her obedient, unyielding sexual servant. I would do whatever she told me, no matter how depraved the act, how humiliating it was for myself, it was worth it to please her.

"Yes, Kendra," I said, my loins once again alight with passion, my heart full of desire to obey her.

Kendra leaned over my body and whispered in my ear, "*Good girl.*" It sent shivers up my spine. She pulled me off the bed, allowing Brooke to fall off her perch and sit on the pillows. She kissed her way all around my body, every inch of it hers. She instructed me to take off her dress, which I did, the Goddess now standing before me in only a black lace bra and panties that accentuated her every feminine curve.

Kendra pulled me down into her ample cleavage. I breathed in the aroma of the thin sheen of sweat on them and licked at the inside of her tits. She unclasped her bra, letting it fall away and freeing her otherworldly breasts from their lacy confines. I spread my saliva all over her chest as I fanatically kissed and licked her tits. The large breasts more than filled my hand when I grabbed one, I brought her puffy nipples to attention by lightly biting them, my mistress pushing her chest out as she enjoyed her obedient pet.

Her tits adequately seen to, Kendra pushed down on my head, forcing me to my knees in front of her and telling me to take off her panties. I didn't need to be told twice, I hooked my fingers around the lacy string and pulled down, peeling the fabric out of her gratuitous ass and making Kendra as naked as I was. Getting to see Kendra in all her glory was usually the act saved for the end of the night, once all her good girls had done her sexual bidding with each other, they were rewarded with the body of their Mistress. And what a body it was. Kendra's amazing genes had been honed to perfection in the gym with Brooke. Her womanly figure with wide hips and lovely, round ass was the envy of every woman in this house, and every woman outside it too.

I was eye level with Kendra's neatly trimmed delta of pubes that adorned her otherwise clean shaven pussy. It was the only hair you would find lower than the eyebrows in this house, one of the requisites of remaining one of Kendra's good girls. It was a physical reminder of this woman's domination over us, that she was the only one woman enough to deserve it, which of course, she was.

Kendra pulled my head into her crotch once she'd had enough of me admiring it. My tongue went to work straight away, eating her cunt like a hungry animal, inhaling the fragrant sex that was trapped in her pubic hair. Nothing made a good girl happier than having the pleasure of eating out Kendra. I looked up at her face between her heavy breasts, rapt in the facial expressions she made as I tried my best to please her.

Kendra rocked her hips forward to allow me better access to her sweet pussy, as she held my hair and drove my face hard into her. All of a sudden, she pulled me back, my tongue still hanging out of my open mouth like a panting dog, and she spat directly onto it, her saliva rolling down my tongue to the back of my throat. I gratefully accepted the spittle, subservient to her and happy to be humiliated. She rammed my open mouth back against her pussy, holding my head still as she used her hips to fuck my face.

"Oh, that's it. Such a good girl," she encouraged, the two of us making direct eye contact while she used my mouth like a fucktoy. "Swallow my cum," she said, before throwing her head back, her hand pulling my hair hard as she came.

My scalp hurt but I didn't care. I slurped every last drop of cum I could out of my mistress' snatch. The liquid gold was what I lived for, and I wanted as much for myself as I could. Still, Kendra's undulating hips made it difficult while she was holding my head still, and I had no choice but to let her coat the entire bottom half of my face in her love juice.

When she was finally spent, Kendra pulled my head out of her groin and released me, my face shimmering with her cum. "I'm going to lay down now, and I want you to give my ass the attention it deserves," she instructed.

"Yes, Kendra," the required response came from me, as her cum cooled quickly against my face in the night air.

She climbed over me and onto the bed, laying across the king size mattress prone. I picked myself up off the floor and joined her, straddling her calves, my pussy lips gripping her toned, muscular legs with its wetness. I massaged her copious ass cheeks as Kendra beckoned her number two over to her, Brooke slinking over from the pillows

490

and laying on her stomach so the pair could kiss passionately.

"I'm sorry you had to yell," Kendra said to the obedient blonde. "But that doesn't mean you're not still my good girl."

"Yes, Kendra," Brooke replied, smiling in relief. The two of them made out heavily.

Unable to access her most private of places as she lay in her prone position, I spread Kendra's bountiful booty with my hands and leant over, pursing my lips against her sacred butthole and spitting into it, causing Kendra to shiver and moan in delight at the sensation.

"That feels so good," she confirmed. "Now lick it."

Obligated to obey, I stuck my tongue out and licked over the pretty little knot, which tightened in response. The wet sounds of Kendra and Brooke making out mixed with the wet sounds of me salivating against her pucker. I pushed the flat of my tongue to it and licked up roughly, and then circled the crinkled ridges with the tip. Kendra moaned into Brooke's mouth in appreciation.

I made my tongue stiff and dipped the tip into her back door, unable to get further than her clench. On my second trip though, Kendra relaxed herself and I was able to push most of my tongue inside her, before I pulled it out. I pushed back in, and pulled out. Kendra gyrated slowly beneath in response, enjoying the anal tongue fucking I was giving her.

I pushed my tongue into her as far as I could, swirling it around inside by moving my head. This caused Kendra to break from her kiss and bite the bed cover in ecstasy. I did it over and over, pressing into her, her ring choking my tongue but my tongue persisting, and then swirling it around, filling her to the walls with my organ. I made my mistress cum again.

Her juices bubbled between her thighs as her butthole quivered around my tongue, spasming and sucking me deeper into her. I moaned in delight, my saliva spilling down my tongue and into her fluttering asshole, my top two teeth biting into her tailbone as I was consumed by her delicious hole.

Her climax looked like the best I'd ever given her, and I was filled with glee that I could do that for her. Once she'd finished riding the waves of her orgasm, she rolled over beneath me, her ass being taken away from my tongue, and she pulled me up to her, kissing me deeply and lovingly as our naked bodies pressed into each other on the bed.

The two of us rolled so that I could lay next to her while Brooke stroked my hair from above. "I'll come with you to the airport in the morning," Kendra said before giving me a peck on the lips.

"That would be nice," I responded.

"You're going to have to come visit."

"Oh, you know I will. Hell, I might even come back and do my masters degree," I said, earning a smile from my Mistress.

"Or perhaps a PhD," she suggested. "That would take longer."

We laughed. "Oh yeah, I'll be the professor of accounting, Doctor Aubrey."

"It has a nice ring to it."

"You know you're overlooking a crucial part of me leaving?"

"What's that?" Kendra's brow furrowed as she tried to think what I could be referring to.

"You get to find my replacement!" I exclaimed, causing Kendra's eyes to go wide at the thought of seducing another girl into her arms, or perhaps more likely, her ass.

The three of us giggled and talked, before one by one, all the other girls filed in. Clothes were shed immediately, and an orgy for the ages broke out in Kendra's room. Taylor came home from dinner with her parents, horny as hell from the repression of her true self and the sight of the rest of us fucking and sucking one another. She quickly ditched the schoolgirl apparel and let us enjoy all her holes, her ass taking in just about every one of us at some point in the night.

Laura and Andrea sixty-nined each other while Yasmin's big butt was passed around from mouth to mouth. Erin's arms were handcuffed around Dana's thighs, her face unable to escape from her cunt as she got fucked by Allison wearing the strap-on.

I was surrounded by eleven women I loved so very much. We had conversations in between orgasms, or watched two others go at it while we drank or ate a snack. And of course, we all did whatever Kendra told us to, arranging ourselves in whatever position her mind could concoct.

Eventually, once we were all fucked out of our minds, we fell asleep together. The bed accommodated half of us, with some of the girls bringing in blankets and couch cushions so they could sleep on the floor.

The next day I would wake up and start my journey into a new life.

But tonight... tonight was the best night I would ever have.

THE END

Message From The Author

Thank you for buying this book! I really hoped you enjoyed reading it. Trust me when I say I love writing them even more than you love reading them.

My Dormant Desires was the first complete series I ever finished and *Submitting to Kendra* was the first book I ever published. I am very proud of the series and am glad it continues to live on years after I started writing it.

If you enjoy stories of lesbian sex, age gaps and back door fun, then check out my Amazon author page or my website for plenty more hot stories.

'til next time,

A.S.
xx

Printed in Great Britain
by Amazon

16550624R00283